FRACTURED SHADOWS

A MOSES AND ROCK NOVEL

A. D. DAVIES

www.addavies.com

NOVELS BY A. D. DAVIES

Moses and Rock Novels:

Fractured Shadows

No New Purpose

Persecution of Lunacy

Adam Park Thrillers:

The Dead and the Missing

A Desperate Paradise

The Shadows of Empty men

Night at the George Washington Diner

Master the Flame

Under the Long White Cloud

Alicia Friend Investigations:

His First His Second

In Black In White

With Courage With Fear

A Friend in Spirit

To Hide To Seek

A Flood of Bones

To Begin The End

Standalone:

Three Years Dead

Rite to Justice

The Sublime Freedom

Shattered: Fear in the Mind

Co-Authored:

Project Return Fire – with Joe Dinicola

Lost Origins Novels (as Antony Davies):

Tomb of the First Priest

The Reaper Seal

The Eagle Plague

Gwna dda dros ddrwg, uffern ni'th ddwg

an old Welsh proverb

Repay evil with good, and hell will not claim you

PROLOGUE

Under the harsh lights of interview room number four, Moses Glynn didn't just look tired; he looked broken.

In the shapeless, papery overalls issued upon his arrest, he hunched over, elbows resting on his knees, the position failing to hide the bulk of the man—like a bear crossbred with a bull. Battling clear exhaustion, his eyes never dropped from the camera, boring straight into the lens which filmed from ten feet away, shooting him at shoulder height. His deep brown irises radiated through the HD screen, the white cracked with red.

Observing the image three floors above on a feed no one in this building knew she could access, DCI Morgana Wearne glanced at Zachary Shepherd, the handsome salt-and-pepper-haired man to her right, then thumbed the mic at her fingertips. "We're ready."

The pair watched as a man entered the room with a thick-sheaved clipboard under his left arm. *One* man. Caucasian, unshaven, a loose tie, as if he'd been roused from a drunken doze and dragged here unwilling and under-prepared.

"Good morning, DI Glynn," the newcomer said, crisp and clear through the omnidirectional mic in the ceiling. "Or is it DI Moses? I hear you prefer Moses."

Moses Glynn wafted a hand in reply—*doesn't matter.*

"I'm DCI Blake. I understand you and my men have had quite the night."

The detective inspector eased himself upright, arms folded, legs spread. "*Your* men. So, you're responsible."

Blake seated himself opposite and half-reclined, almost mirroring Moses, but added an amused twitch. "Do you mind me saying it's so weird hearing a Welsh accent on a black man?"

"Do you mind if we skip the bonding phase and jump straight to you telling me I'm free to get going?" The hulking detective pressed his palms on the table to rise.

Blake said, "Nope. Not yet."

Moses Glynn slid back into place, resuming his spread-leg, folded-arm manner.

"You've seen his record," DCI Wearne said to

Zachary Shepherd. "He knows what that body language is conveying."

"He looks like a criminal, Morgana," Zachary said, still bright despite the three a.m. wake-up call. "He's baiting the senior officer. Are you sure he's the right man for this?"

On screen, DCI Blake sighed, took out a pen, and poised it over the pad on his clipboard. "Once more. To be sure we get all the details this time."

It was the tenth night of Moses's operation. The National Crime Agency had needed an officer who'd never been to Plymouth, who could pass for an out of town big hitter. Someone who'd succeeded despite life's many challenges. An unusual accent helped and the ability to speak "foreign" was desirable, although Moses didn't see his Welsh language as foreign; it was as much a part of Britain as English, and to hell with anyone who said otherwise.

Cenedl heb iaith yw cenedl heb gallon, as the tattoo on his first Welsh tutor's arm proclaimed. *A nation without a language is a nation without a heart.*

The DCI from Moses's vice squad had approached him about the joint CID-NCA operation, and since Moses had experience in UC ops, he fit the profile. It didn't take long for him to accept.

His tenth night.

The eighth night since he first made contact with Mohammad Ishtar, an Egyptian man who aided the transfer of people into the UK for whom passports and visas were an inconvenience too far. People who would be forced into menial jobs for little or no money, sometimes just for the pleasure of sharing a two-bedroom flat with three other families. A trade in human beings, holding power over their charges, *owning* them.

Like slaves.

But that wasn't the point. The point was the preservation of life.

Men, women, children—smuggled in hidden compartments in vans, lorries, shipping containers. Most survived. Others did not. Statements from surviving relatives, arrested on unrelated charges over the past year, led to deals being cut, as victims spoke of how they arrived, of the dread that Mohammad Ishtar would never allow an "expired import" to be buried in a conventional manner. More commonly he'd order the corpse interred in the boot of a stolen car on the edge of a disused railway line or some back alley, before local men in thick rubber gloves poured chemicals inside, dissolving flesh and bone then setting the car alight. Nothing ever remained.

Moses Glynn's pitch to the National Crime Agency was that he'd pose as a county lines drug dealer in search of "talent."

"You need *people*?" Ishtar had said, sat across from Moses in a motorway service station KFC.

"That's right." Moses sensed eyes upon him, his

sharp suit and fine personal grooming more suited to a footballer heading for the city's hottest night-club than chatting with a tracksuit-clad fast food aficionado.

"In Cardiff." Although fluent in English after fifteen years here, Ishtar retained an accent, rolling the R in *Cardiff*, which made him sound exotic. And he'd be unlikely to differentiate the subtleties in the Welsh accent, between the nation's capital city and Moses's home in the Valleys.

"Not in Cardiff," Moses had told him. "We don't operate in the city. That's why I'm out here. We recruit in smaller towns. Tiny operations, but lots of them. They add up."

Ishtar nodded slowly, constantly, as Moses spoke.

"Usually, it's local kids who think their cut is big money. But we cream off the bulk and reinvest. Thing is, when some local busy copper gets wind of it, they go after our guys and make a ton of noise. Puts off others. Makes recruitment hard."

"And you wish for a better supply of salesmen."

"One gets arrested, we import another."

Although he walked the entrapment tightrope in a grey zone that he'd deny should the Crown Prosecution Service question his actions, it had been a simple start, inviting Ishtar, a successful asylum seeker but failed businessman, into a big operation. A secretive one. If Ishtar dug too deep, other county lines gangs would advise him, quite robustly, to stop asking questions about dealers from Cardiff.

To build trust and monitor Ishtar, Moses swanned about Portsmouth, buying their target some neat threads as a thank you, getting him into the best clubs, floating through the bright lights in the city. Music, pornographic dancers, VIP lounges awash with champagne; living like newly minted reality TV stars whose celebrity lifestyles were about to burst, compelled to make the most of their five minutes. It was a life Moses had to remind himself was just borrowed.

Bend the rules. Push the limits. Don't ever step back over that line.

As his wife had reminded him before departing for this operation, "If you go back there, be that guy again… you might never come home to me."

"I will," he'd said. "I'll always come back. No matter what I do. You know I hate this."

"You don't hate it, though," Frankie told him. "You don't hate it nearly as much as you think you do."

Through loose lips and trusting comrades, Moses embraced his new world. Hating-it-not-hating-it, he soon learned Ishtar's money from his "import business" swept up a chain to the actual bosses. Ishtar served as a minor cog in a labyrinthine mechanism, something Moses had suspected weeks earlier when he spoke to one sobbing man whose suffocated wife had been turned to vapour and then burned.

The ploy worked better than hoped. And *not-hating* the job morphed into something more, something without words yet made Moses's heart race and his fear of discovery drop into a hole of his own making. He was going to win.

Playing to Ishtar's sense of failure as a business-man, he persuaded the Egyptian to continue im-porting the migrants as his bosses commanded, take his fee, then introduce the desperate people to Moses. Sure, those higher up would demand the re-cent arrivals perform their slave jobs, but they'd be filtered out over time, disappearing into the anony-mous world of cash-only transactions.

Despite the questionable tactics, he was certain the op would reveal the true slave masters who ran a dozen men like Ishtar, scattered along Britain's coastline.

Ishtar, though, wanted to move too quickly.

Like an excitable university graduate clamouring to launch a start-up before it was market-ready, he bulldozed onward, upping the quotas of people he was due to bring in. He favoured younger men who'd be more willing to push the boundaries, more susceptible to the siren call of ready cash.

After one week of schmoozing, Moses met Ishtar's ground crew, a trio of bald local men who'd fallen afoul of an ailing fishing industry, but who knew the waters, knew the shipping routes, the customs and local constabulary. *Mick, Jimmy, and Spike.* Names Moses might have picked for cockney wide-boy satire, but who were deadly serious. The pubs in which they drank were far too grotty for Moses's quality threads, like those on the estate where he grew up, close enough to Swansea to class them as city pubs, but far enough out for low-income folk who encountered a black man rarely enough to treat him some way between a curiosity and a mortal threat. Much like the men working for Mohammad Ishtar.

The first night he dared commit to a recording device, Moses listened—over pints in one such pub—as the men expressed hatred for the migrants they helped bring in, hinting at their desperation to accept money for doing so.

The night Moses's world collapsed was days later. Long past last orders. Spike's birthday.

Moses's tenth night.

The card game venue used to be a bowling alley, positioned on the boundary of a shipping container yard along with a bunch of warehouses converted to climbing walls, a gym, several chain restaurants and fast-food outlets, with a cinema commissioned but never built. All that had ended years earlier. Only the shells remained, occupied by rows of camping beds and well-used sleeping bags—perfect for ushering human cargo off their transports; to assess them, to treat any ailments, arrange for body disposal, or to euthanize any who were unlikely to benefit their masters.

Tonight, Ishtar expected ten people and Moses had asked to be there. On Spike's birthday. Red Bull and Monster drinks only; no alcohol. Not until later, once the cargo was secure—a cargo for which Moses felt responsible, having made his demands.

A card game to pass the time. Pizza. Which Moses declined, lying about a dairy intolerance instead of the truth.

"This really is an odd choice of career," Moses said over a lousy hand which he was bluffing as a winner.

"They want open borders," Spike said, who was also bluffing but doing a crappy job of it, "we'll give 'em open borders. Their choice, not ours."

"Worst part," Jimmy added, his teeth a random hotchpotch of yellow shapes, "is when they die. Such a mess, and I'm always late getting back home."

The table was green felt, like a casino, but the former bowling alley was a dusty wreck that smelled damp. Sweaty too, with a hint of weed. The four men occupied a spotlight of halogen lamps and three fan heaters, Ishtar the only one absent. He remained under constant observation by NCA teams in the hope Moses's plan would unveil the top men.

"Ishtar's a good guy," Moses said, upping the pot. They were playing pennies, the men earning just over minimum wage, topped up by unemployment benefits and Mick's fake disability—a disc in his back which no treatment appeared to appease. "He'll cut you in."

"He better." Mick folded.

Moses couldn't push it. His newcomer status had kept them suspicious of him, regardless of Ishtar's endorsement. The listening device hidden in his phone—lying out on the table like the other men's—was recording, not transmitting, so his handlers only had visuals on him. Well, visuals of him entering the building. "If he cuts you off?"

Moses cast a glance at his phone and instantly regretted it.

Amateur mistake.

"Why?" Spike clocked the phone too.

Then Jimmy drew his eyes to it. "If he cuts us off? I dunno. What do you think?"

It was a mistake to think they were stupid. Moses had realised that during their first get-together. They understood economics, politics, whittled their way through life, surviving where others would cave.

Moses shrugged, eyes on his cards. "Don't get me wrong, lads, I'm just sayin'. I seen it happen, that's all. Guy in charge makes it big, cuts loose the folk around him. I don't think Mohammad'll do that, though," he added with a forced a smile. "Spike, you playing?"

Spike stared at Moses as he sipped the green

Monster drink. Lowered it. Reached for Moses's iPhone. "That's nice. Latest model?"

"Of course." Moses nudged the handset toward Spike. "Check it out."

Spike laid his cards face down and lifted the device, the screen activating. His thumb tapped the glass. He looked confused.

"Facial rec." Moses took the phone from him and showed his face to the lens, then handed it back unlocked.

It was a casual act on the surface, but the three bald white men had fallen still. Cards forgotten. Moses sneaked a peek at Jimmy's hand while the man was distracted. It was better than his own.

Spike turned the handset over twice, thumbnail picking for any seams. There wouldn't be one. Moses's NCA handlers had secured the bug deep inside the sim case. Spike gave a grunt and placed the phone on the felt surface and slid it back to Moses. Stared a beat, then said, "I fold."

"Me too." Jimmy slapped the cards down.

Moses swept the £4.35 in silver and copper into his pile, as gleeful as if he'd broken bank at Monte Carlo.

Jimmy gathered the cards and shuffled. "I'm gonna win that back."

"Only if ya cheat," Spike said, and Mick laughed.

"We'll see." Jimmy paused the shuffle to rummage in a pocket of his cargo trousers, then produced a snub-nosed revolver and placed it flat on the table. As they all stared at it, Jimmy recommenced shuffling, his yellow Tic-Tac smile more gum than tooth. "Precaution." He levelled his eyes at Moses.

"We got a problem here?" Moses asked.

"Nope." Jimmy dealt. One at a time. Stroked the .22 as he received his own card, then threw out the next round.

Moses picked up the two cards dealt so far, slouched in a way that enhanced the broadness of his shoulders. "Because if we do, I can move on to the next poor-ass bunch of traffickers who'd be more than happy to take the money I'm offering."

"Peace, brothers!" came Mohammad Ishtar's voice through the gloom.

The four men stood. Jimmy snatched up the gun.

Ishtar led a group of ragged individuals from the back of the alley, up a lane that once ran heavy balls toward a stack of pins. The wood was frayed and bowed, the metal in the gullies stripped. Ishtar held out his arms, a saviour leading his people to paradise. Moses counted nine in total. Seven men, all around twenty years old, but could have been younger, given the harsh lives they'd lived to get this far. Two women, both exhausted, clung to the arms of men.

"Hello." One shaggy-haired young fella—perhaps twenty, but again maybe younger—raised a hand in greeting toward Moses, his English strained but polite. "Thank you for—"

"What did we discuss, Shak?" Ishtar said.

Clearly, that Moses was the one who brought them in, hence that kid's expression of gratitude.

"Sorry." The youthful man—Shak—lowered his wave and looked at the floor. "I speak when asked."

"Right." Ishtar clipped him round the back of the head before approaching the card game.

Moses beamed, a hollow gnawing within his gut as he and Ishtar clapped one another's shoulders. These people, all of them, not just the lad, had been promised the world, when all they'd be getting was an economy class ticket back to their homeland or, at best, a safe country that *might* take them in.

If they were lucky.

"That's a beautiful sight, my friend," Moses said. "I cannot wait to get started."

Thunderous booms crashed across the open space. Dust in the air and on various surfaces shifted with the physical report of the explosions. Only, not explosions. Shotguns blowing the hinges off the entrance. Muffled blasts out back brought down the rear. Men decked out in full tactical gear bearing the word POLICE, shouting, announcing their status as "Armed police," and instructions to "not move."

The migrants clumped together in a group, a herd forming strength in numbers. Hands up. Eyes wide. They knew not to flee, not to fight. Shak's head jerked back and forth, his boggle-eyed gaze meeting Moses's.

"Hold still," Moses told everyone. "Do as they say. Keep calm."

Jimmy, though, made a poor choice. He whipped up his gun toward the four officers storming the front. Moses threw himself to the floor, knowing what would happen next—what always happens.

A deafening clatter of MP5A submachine guns split his eardrums. Jimmy's chest, neck, and thighs popped and spurted in a red mist before he flopped to the ground.

Spike doubled over as a stray bullet raked his gut, and Ishtar threw himself to his knees, hands on his head.

Mick made a run for the rear, but six more shock troops had that covered; they breached and aimed firearms, forcing Mick to the ground and securing him with zip ties.

Moses kept his head down.

This wasn't the plan. This couldn't be the NCA op. They were supposed to track the people Moses rejected to the source, people on whom Moses would place a tracker. He'd already picked one, the skinny kid with big hair, Shak. The same skinny kid now peeling away from his group, venturing to one side.

Still pinned to the filthy floor, Moses yelled at him, "Stay there!"

Shak glanced at him once. His face morphed from shock to disappointment, to abject misery. It was as if hope were physically draining from him, water pouring from a punctured sack.

"No…" But Moses's plea would not reach him.

Shak turned toward the phalanx of armed police winding through the smoke and dust at the rear, dropped his hands, and took flight, evidently aiming to dodge through them. Perhaps he was confident they wouldn't shoot an unarmed man. Maybe he didn't care. Whatever was going through Shak's mind, whatever the logic, one officer was already raising his gun. Already drawing a bead.

Moses turned over, sat up. "Wait! He's unarmed. No threat!"

It was no use. A burst of three from the black-clad officer cut the kid down as he ran. His back arched, knees buckled, and his face contorted in wide-eyed in shock as he toppled and half-rolled on the filthy floor. The team pushed on alongside the shooter.

"Looked like he had a weapon," the armed officer said, still aiming at the corpse.

Another came alongside. This cop said, "Could've been anything."

"Hey!" Moses called. "I'm with the West Midlands—"

Before he could identify himself, something slammed into the side of his head. A flash of white. Then he leaned over without falling.

"Down," came the instruction.

Pressure on his back, which Moses could have resisted, but he allowed his hands to be pulled behind him. The guy zip-tying Moses called to his colleagues, "Anyone else hear an 'Allahu-Akbar' when the bad guy ran?"

Moses couldn't see much from the floor, but what he did see involved nods.

Someone said, "Yeah, could've been a suicide bomber."

Another said, "I thought I saw a weapon too."

Moses ground his teeth, gritted them as the copper yanked his shoulders back.

Now, Moses resisted. "Get *off* me."

"I'm sorry, my boy." The cop showed Moses the barrel of the MP5A. "Oh, you don't like the term 'boy'?"

"Suits a hillbilly sheriff more than an AFO who stumbled into the wrong operation."

"Huh. That sounds like a threat. You threatening me, fella?" The armed officer pressed the barrel into Moses's cheek, an action going completely against regs. He whispered, "A local nigger helping camel-fuckers sneak into our country? That's not gonna end well for you."

Moses took a deep breath through his mouth and as the officer kneeling on his back chuckled, he let the air out through his nose. Throughout the exhale, his hands tingled, the muscles in his arms tightened, and the migrants' cries of fear and despair echoed around the place.

His lungs empty, Moses took a regular breath and said, "I'm DI Moses Glynn. Undercover officer with the West Midlands Police and National Crime Agency joint task force." The pressure eased minutely. "Now get the *fuck* off me and show me to whoever's in charge!"

DCI Morgana Wearne observed Moses Glynn's recital. His use of the N-word in the third person calm, almost deadened. It was either a good thing or very troubling.

"Here's the thing," DCI Blake said, laying his pen down. He had written nothing since Moses commenced talking. "The NCA only informed the Assistant Chief Constable, and her office only cascaded the instruction to the immigration divisions and Customs and Excise. Not us. It's a balls-up all right, but it's not a narcotics balls-up. We went in expecting packs of heroin. Apparently, a county lines drugs kingpin came to town a week or so back. Been living it up, flashing his cash. And we ID'd Mohammad Ishtar's gang as helping him. Figured they'd stepped up from human cargo."

Moses sighed, eyebrows raised. Other than that, he remained motionless.

"And another thing," Blake went on. "Even though there were no drugs, it was a good take down. One illegal who attempted to assault our officers with what appeared to be a firearm—"

"There was no gun."

"No, but the metal pipe he was holding looked like one. And his threatening language—"

"There wasn't a weapon, a pipe, or anything else. And he didn't say a damn thing."

Blake tutted, a rueful *tsk*. "That's not how it went down."

"I got a bunch of it recorded. You *got* the recording. No denying that."

Blake clicked his pen closed. "Unfortunately, Mr Ishtar's jamming equipment disrupted our AFOs' transmitters. And those small SD recording devices are so delicate. It damaged the one you provided from your phone."

"It doesn't get damaged, it's designed to—"

"It's *irreparable*. Which leaves this as your word against a team of highly decorated AFOs. A situation that might cause more problems than it solves. But it doesn't have to." He pointed at the camera, which was live but hadn't recorded Moses's third statement of the night. "I can tape over your other statements… the ones you failed to recall properly… with the correct version of events. It'll make things easier for us all. You get me?"

Moses barked a single laugh. "*Get you*? You talkin' street to the Valleys boy?"

Wearne stifled her own laugh at Blake's obvious

discomfort. Watching the screen. Sensing Zachary Shepherd's doubts.

"You got the power here," Moses said. "Oh, I know you'll get away with it. Your type always does. But that don't mean I'm gonna make it easy for you. No. Fuck you. *And* the racist, trigger-happy bastards you're covering for."

Blake stood and pulled his jacket straight. Tucked the clipboard back under his arm. "That's disappointing." Then DCI Blake exited.

Moses resumed staring with his bloodshot eyes at the camera.

"Yes," DCI Wearne said. "I'm positive he'll fit right in."

WEDNESDAY

1

Juliette Rock flicked off the hairdryer, her thick red hair cut into a short bob for the first time since leaving the Army. She fluffed it out and headed downstairs to her kitchen-diner, which she expected would be flooded with early summer sun through the skylights.

Still in her bathrobe after the long, steamy shower, she planned on whipping up a fresh croissant from the freezer and brewing a large espresso to enjoy on her patio—assuming she could get the damn doors to open without grating or outright sticking. It had been a recurrent source of annoyance since she moved into the new-build house and was a common complaint in such properties. The construction company wouldn't do anything for a while, claiming the house was "settling" and any fix would be short term. They'd sort it soon enough, so they said, although Rock wasn't confident she believed them.

One thing she'd learned about civilian life was that, where spending money was concerned, if people could get away with breaking a promise, their word was far from their bond. Still, she remained hopeful of a brief but luxurious half-hour of solitude before what promised to be a trying day.

Only there was cooking in the air.

"Sam." She stopped in the kitchen doorway, finding her boyfriend at the counter, spooning out poached eggs onto two plates brimming with sausage, bacon, mushrooms, baked beans, and black pudding.

Sam returned the pan to Rock's range cooker top and turned off the gas. Smiled proudly. "Figured you could use a decent feed. Big day."

Rock tried to ignore the random stack of other pans gathering in the sink, or to its side, forced herself to return the smile, and advanced on the centre island where she'd positioned a rack with half a dozen cookbooks. She climbed onto a breakfast bar stool and pulled one plate toward her. "That was nice of you, Sam, but you really didn't have to."

"I wanted to." He sat opposite and offered brown sauce.

She accepted the bottle and squirted a trail over the meal. "I thought you were leaving when I got in the shower."

"I was. But then I figured… breakfast." He

popped a chunk of ketchup-dipped sausage in his mouth. "Good?"

Rock sampled a mixed forkful of black pudding, mushroom, and bacon with the requisite brown sauce. *Always* brown sauce with a full English fry-up. Never ketchup.

She swallowed. "It's great. Thanks, Sam."

Her knife and fork worked at the meat, a slash opening the egg yolk. Dunk. Chomp. Yum. There were worse ways to tolerate an uninvited chef.

"You never finished telling me about this 'unique' division," Sam said.

"I don't know much. Sounded interesting. A challenge. Less bullshit than regular policing. Maybe something that genuinely makes a difference. They were a bit cagey."

"But you went for it, anyway."

She eyed the mountain of dirty pans. Another issue with modern, new-build houses was the lack of space, which made them hard to keep tidy, although it was a burden she sometimes welcomed. When it was *her* mess. "Yes, I went for it."

"Right…"

More eating. A slurp of tea apiece.

"What time do you reckon you'll be home?" Sam asked.

"Not sure." Rock was halfway done; no espresso on the patio today.

"There's a comedy night on at the Mac." Sam

had stopped moving. "Doors at seven. Show's at eight."

Rock continued to eat. "I doubt I'll be up for it. Think I'd rather crash. Put on one of those Netflix shows you hate. Open some wine."

Sam stuck his fork into a sausage. "Just Netflix, no chill?"

Rock looked up at him. "You don't mind, do you?"

"Of course not." He sliced the sausage but paused with it halfway to his mouth. "Is everything okay?"

"Sure." Rock sipped her tea.

"Really? You seem… off."

"No, it's… first-day nerves."

"You never get nervous."

She *did* get nervous, but it rarely showed. Although Sam was an accountant—the world's go-to profession to highlight boredom—he wasn't some balding beach ball of a saddo. Rock had met Sam halfway up a climbing wall, as impressed with his physique as he plainly was with hers. Unfortunately, despite a mutual appreciation of heights, running, and athletic sexual marathons, once the initial rush wore off, he became thuddingly reliable. Not *boring* as such, just… reliable. Nice. Safe.

But, oh, the sex…

"I'm not entirely sure this is going to work long-term," Rock said.

Sam laid his knife and fork down. "You mean us?"

"Us." Rock allowed her eye to rove the contours of Sam's shoulders: defined but not huge, even under the formal blue shirt. She pictured the cable-like biceps lower down, the steady swell of his chest, his cobblestone abs. "It's great. Mostly."

"So, what's the problem?"

"Sam, don't take it personally—"

"You're dumping me, Juliette. How can I not?"

"I'm not dumping you." She scraped the remaining food to the side, no longer hungry. "I'm suggesting a…" She struggled for the word.

"Break?"

She was about to say yes, but it'd be a lie. "It's run its course, is all."

"Fine." Sam pushed his plate aside and stood. "Do I have time grab my things?"

"You did nothing wrong. I did nothing wrong. You're the most decent man I've met since my husband."

Without raising his eyes, Sam made his way around the counter, heading for the door.

"*Better* than him," Rock added.

He paused.

"Best ever," she went on, stroking his ego but not lying. "It's been the best three months of my life. In *that* respect."

He still didn't face her. "The sex, you mean?"

"And the fun. The adventurous days and weekends. It distracted from the divorce, and now I'm *strong* I made the right decision. It was a great time. Not *only* the sex, I promise. It's…" She didn't want to lie, but likewise didn't think it fair to be brutally honest regarding his *reliability*. "I don't need any distractions at the moment. I can make a real difference in this unit and I want to give it everything."

Sam faced her. A trace of anger bloomed, a tinge of red to his cheeks—a reaction Rock had never witnessed in him before.

She pretended not to notice and slipped off the stool with a sympathetic head-tilt. She planted her feet, ready—if she'd misjudged the guy with whom she'd shared so many nights—to pivot and swing a fork into his eye.

"Have you decided you like girls again?" he said, that twinkle of anger leeching into his voice.

"Don't play that shit with me," Rock replied. "If I were dumping you for a man or a woman, I'd have the guts to say so."

"It's all about this awesome job, then?" He sighed through his nose. "Fresh start?"

Rock assessed his position. Seeing no immediate threat, she considered her motives. "Maybe there's a certain symbolism to it."

"'Make a real difference', eh?" Sam shook his head. "You think you're such hot shit, don't you?"

"Excuse me?" The hairs on the back of Rock's neck stood on end.

"They'll never accept you. Coppers hate fast

track wunderkids. No matter how perfect your old career was."

"You know what?" She strode forward, shouldering past him with a thump to his chest. "Actually, you *don't* have time to get your stuff. Leave now. Come back when I'm not here, then drop off the key."

"Fine." Sam turned away to grab his jacket.

Halfway out to the hall, Rock turned to him. "Sam, wait."

He remained in place, shrugging on his coat, moving from a hurried motion to smooth. "Right. Sorry, Juliette. I… I thought we had something. If you're willing to put this on pause—"

"No. Not a pause." She set herself and used the authoritarian voice she'd learned in the Army, the one that commanded over a hundred men and women on both allied ground and in theatres of war, which she believed gave her the gravitas that'd help fast track her career to a command position with the police. "*You* made this mess. Wash it all up before you leave. I'll be getting dressed."

2

Sergeant Gavin Grosse was happy in uniform. He knew many of the younger unis saw stripping off the dark blue, venturing up a floor to CID and donning civilian attire as a "promotion," but Grosse had weathered the streets for fifteen years, learned their moods, their intricacies, their subtleties and depravities. His was the first name on the list when experience was required, the first to be called when a newbie constable with a good attitude but suboptimal skills needed mentoring, and he was first on scene this morning when a girl reported missing three days earlier had been found face down in a small park's manmade lake—two hundred square yards of stagnant water with an island in the middle. The island used to be covered in flowering bushes but had become home to more duck and goose droppings than the elderly groundskeeper could cope with.

Grosse had been a lowly constable when the park first reopened following a major investment across the public sector, the mindset being that giving the poor of these communities a nice open space, non-judgemental attention to expectant parents in things like Sure Start centres, and increasing health education, might just improve their lives. And it did, if Grosse was perfectly honest. People were less fractious than they were today, less likely to blow up an argument into a fistfight. Added policing helped, too, and educating the police—not only the communities—gave Grosse new insights that aided in his duty. People tutted and rolled their eyes at terms like "community policing" but, in his experience, it was this that wrought more trust and less crime than storming around with Glocks and full-face helmets, which was where most investment landed these days.

Grosse wasn't "liberal" or "left wing", either. He'd voted for Brexit and for the Brexit Party (although never UKIP), largely because mainstream politicians seemed interested in nothing more than their own careers. Even when they did the right thing it was out of self-interest. And—bottom line—it was a cast iron solid *fact* that when you have more police on the streets who understand they serve the public, *with the public's consent*, there was far less need for firearms, tougher sentences, or chest-thumping socialism.

Sergeant Grosse had plenty of time to think about this as the crime scene techs ploughed into their work. Crowds had gathered as people awoke. The school run, commuters, residents who hung around the park on dry days for their own reasons, all questioning why the hell they couldn't go through *their* park. It was almost impossible to cordon off a sensible area, so Grosse had closed the iron gates at all three ways in and out. As almost every person he spoke to worked a phone, he had requested additional bodies to help sweep out and interview the handful of rough sleepers, then shore up the perimeter.

Within half an hour, the crowd from the estate numbered over one hundred, all miffed at the lack of information, raised voices declaring they had "a right to know" what was going on. Word got around that it was a body, and more than one person screeched at Grosse that they *needed* to learn who.

Every time someone gave off that whiff of self-centred entitlement, Grosse wondered what things would have been like if funding for places like this park hadn't been torn from under them. But treat people like animals, they become animals; always on edge, always angry, always ready to boil over at the slightest inconvenience. If funding returned, might this auto-anger fizzle out, or at least tone down, in another generation or two?

"It's Gabriella," one woman said in a half-snarl. "And I know who killed her."

The crowd parted. Grosse zeroed in on her. She was in her twenties with the lines of a forty-year-old gracing her face, hair mussed and dressed like she'd returned from a nightclub in the seedier part of town. She tottered as she walked toward Grosse on six-inch blocky heels, but her hips swayed, and her finger pointed.

"Tell us the truth," she said, stale alcohol and cigarettes carrying on her breath even from a couple of feet away. "It's her, isn't it? He killed her."

Grosse knew of Gabriella Childs, had encountered her in the past. Just shy of a full-on junkie, she'd experienced and occasionally initiated violent confrontations before, from screaming rows with various boyfriends to assault with a bedside lamp. Grosse's only curiosity had been whether it would be the booze or the drugs or the violence that put her in the hospital, prison, or an early grave. In the end, he'd felt almost nothing when he responded to the groundkeeper's 999 call.

Someone had beaten the body purple, causing a massive contusion to the head, so severe it had misshapen her skull. In years past, the waste of life would have gutted him; the impact on the family, the community. But today he pushed it down into a box marked *inevitable*. Perhaps Grosse, too, had fallen afoul of an orchestrated propaganda machine designed to dehumanise the poor, the uneducated, the left-behinds.

He saw Gabriella's friend, Veronica Meda—the girl with the face scrunched up in petulant anger—as being equally flawed, equally doomed to this same fate. Affray, assault occasioning actual bodily harm, a complainant in several cases of domestic violence… It could easily have been Veronica face down in that water.

"I'm sorry, ma'am," he said. "We cannot say anything until the family has been informed."

"That witch won't care." Veronica threw her hands up. She was right, though. If Gabriella's mother, Astrid, was awake, she'd be drunk already. "And I know you lot don't care either."

"We'll do everything we can to catch whoever did this." Grosse chided himself at the non-comment, wishing he could offer more. Perhaps he could. "If you have information that may be of use, let me take your details and we'll get a detective up here." He then lowered his voice and dipped it an octave, sounding almost conspiratorial. "If—and I'm not saying it is—but *if* it's Gabriella down there, I'm sure they'll want to speak with you."

Veronica's bottom lip quivered. She snapped her head to the park, then back to the group of locals, who'd fallen silent. Her hand clapped over her mouth and a tear rolled down one cheek. "Oh my God. He did it, didn't he? He really did it."

A woman the size of a compact car with a pushchair containing a fat two-year-old guzzling a chocolate bar reached for Veronica and touched her arm. "Don't, bab. It's not worth the risk."

Veronica sniffed. "No, it *is* worth it. It has to be. Someone has to *do* something."

Grosse thumbed the radio clipped on his lapel. "Sergeant Grosse to SIO. I need someone at the north gate. Possible witness."

"Acknowledged," came the reply.

"Don't," the fat woman said. "Don't grass him."

"*Joshua Sevan*," Veronica said. "And I don't care who knows I grassed on him. It was Joshua Sevan, that steroid-freak coke-head prick. I don't care who knows, and I don't care who his father is. He's got to go down for what he did."

Joshua Sevan. Sergeant Grosse dipped his head before perking back up.

"Useless," Veronica said, with that same despairing flip of the arms she used to punctuate her mention of Astrid Childs. "All of you. You're gonna do nothing, aren't you?"

The number of times the Sevan family had slipped through the legal net, Grosse feared she might be right. Still, with his most reassuring tone, he said, "We'll do everything we can."

3

Moses looked fine. Not fine as in "okay", but *fine*. His three-piece charcoal pinstripe was understated enough to pass as a copper, although his white shirt was pure cotton, bringing out the tone of his silk dark purple tie. After the Plymouth job had gone sour, he'd spent most of his time either reading or gardening. He even paid little attention to his facial hair, allowing it to grow untamed. Frankie had put it down to his acceptance of never being a copper again, something he slid into with quiet resignation. He told his wife it was a relief, happy to spend quality time with her and their daughter, Eko. Told himself that too.

But yesterday, having received orders to either report to Division 43 or to make his suspension permanent in writing, he'd been surprised how quickly he chose to delve back in—albeit into this "special" department he'd never heard of before. Frankie wasn't surprised, though; she said he was like a domestic abuse victim returning to the same partner, insisting it would be different this time. Moses promised he'd learned from Plymouth, from the other times he'd been bitten, and this unit really felt different. If it wasn't, he was gone. Forever this time.

Frankie said, "Hmm," and traced the line of his scruffy stubble.

Unsure of how much he believed his own words, Moses hit the barbershop on Townhill Street and had the side of his scalp shaved to a dusting of black, blending into the top, a smooth quarter-inch of tight hair. He also paid for the clippers to shape his beard into a pencil thin line from his ears, along his jawbone, into a close-cropped sweeping oval around his mouth.

On his way out to his first day back on The Job, his wife, Frankie, had patted him on the backside and said, "Welcome back, hot stuff."

"Good to be back," he'd said, before kissing her on the lips, pecking his daughter's forehead as she ate breakfast whilst engrossed in a Diary of a Wimpy Kid novel, and heading out into the unknown.

Division 43 was housed in a former fire station midway between two Staffordshire towns—Rugeley and Stoke. *Former*, because three stations had been "rationalised" into one, enabling crews to access motorways and the nearby A50 more readily, relegating residential fires to secondary concerns. Moses's research showed there were still part-time stations around the region, but places like this one—only ten years old—had been scaled back. Then there was the location which vexed Moses.

Not so much the distance from his home in Sutton Coldfield, as the time to reach here was actually five minutes faster than driving to his old CID post in Birmingham Central; what made him uneasy here was the remoteness. The station's position facilitated easy access to nearby Cannock Chase—a massive forest prone to fires in the summer months—and the many rural locations often underserved by such services. A police division had no business being here.

The hedges along the main road were tall, too, verging on overgrown, hiding the building from passing motorists. No signage signalled its presence, and other than a right-turn channel in the chevrons, there was little indication of anything to access at all.

As he parked his two-year-old Lexus F-Sport amid eight other cars in one of the twenty spaces around the back, he saw none of the usual police crests, either. Just a small plaque with chequered branding associated with the service as he'd passed the front door. All the windows appeared sealed. The doors closed with RFID pads and numerical input backup, and the entire grounds looked to be in need of a bloody good clean.

The main entrance, he'd been told, was via the back, which looked as anonymous as the front. He approached the only viable option—a pair of double steel doors. Pausing, he read another sign, white writing on a dark blue rectangle plaque speckled with the same white-and-blue checkered bands as out front:

West Midlands Police
Intelligence Gathering Section
Division 43

Odd, since they were physically located in Staffordshire, a different police district.

More hoping for a good outcome this morning than expecting one, Moses tried his Birmingham ID on the scanner and to his surprise, the magnetic locks disengaged.

"Tidy." He pulled the heavy door and entered.

After a small passage of clean white tiles, he found himself in what at first resembled any number of CID squad rooms: A dozen desks positioned in squares of two, one pair of men and a pair women in standard clothing—ostensibly formal, yet inexpensive and hard wearing—and a glass office cubicle in one corner with the blinds open. In there, a woman with long dark hair manned a desk and another woman with bright copper hair in a bob and wearing a functional pantsuit was seated before her. The four detectives—Moses assumed they were detectives—stopped what they were doing and stared at him.

"Hey," he said. "I'm—"

"DI Moses Glynn, we know," said a square-headed white guy in his early thirties—loose tie and striped polyester shirt, good hair. "You're to go straight in."

The detectives returned to their work, in male-male and female-female pairs, one of the women working a computer with a degree of concentration that suggested she was trying to bore a hole through the screen with her eyes.

As Moses sidled through the setup toward the glass office, he noted the TVs around the walls running various news channels, police incident feeds from West Midlands, Staffordshire, Derbyshire, North Wales, and East Midlands; the desktop screens appeared to be high-end models; one door led to a room he marked as a kitchen with a decent-sized espresso machine and a coffee maker that used pods, along with a teapot and a huge refrigerator. Other doors at the far end had no signage, but were lit up, suggesting more activity beyond.

Moses lifted his knuckles to knock on the door bearing the decal *Detective Chief Inspector Morgana Wearne*, but a firm, "Come in," from the long-haired woman pre-empted his knock. He obeyed and joined the pair.

The woman behind the desk stood and offered a hand. "DCI Wearne."

Moses shook the hand, his palm engulfing the woman's bony fingers. He applied enough pressure to say, *I'm tough,* but not enough to say, *I'm overcompensating*. "A fellow Welsh immigrant. *Braf cwrdd â chi.*"

"Nice to meet you too, Inspector, but I only speak English on duty. Manners." Wearne took back her hand and gestured to the red-haired woman, who stood and repeated the handshaking. "This is Detective Constable Juliette Rock. DC Rock, meet DI Glynn Moses."

The woman with the striking red hair was nearly as tall as Moses. Unlike most women approaching six feet, she didn't strike him as skinny. Her firm grip accentuated a hint of muscle around her neck, and he expected she was proficient in at least one contact sport—boxing, MMA, something like that.

"Rock," Moses said. "Cool name. And it's just Moses."

"Glynn Moses, Moses Glynn," Rock said. "Make up your mind."

"It's Moses Glynn." He indicated his warrant card, which read *Glynn Moses*. "Mix up at the printers."

Wearne was watching them. "Okay, if we've finished playing word games, let's get to work. DI… *Moses*, I'd normally place two new starters with people who've been around the division a while, but everyone is engaged in business we need for court. DI Xian and DS Ellingham are on an OCG case, with

DI Archer and DS Tahana tied up on a child protection take down—a charity if you can believe that. And Banner and Clarke are in the field. Means I'm pairing you two off temporarily. Breaking you in."

Wearne tapped her fingers on the desk and looked up at one of the two walls not made of glass, where a 60-inch screen showed a scanned missing person's report. Back on her desk, Moses saw it contained a touchscreen keyboard.

"Gabriella Childs," Wearne said. "Reported missing three days ago, landed with us this morning as a—"

"Wait, wait, wait a minute." Moses's head was spinning. He swiped at the air as if breaking up a barroom brawl. "Where the hell have I landed?"

Wearne's eyes drooped to the touchscreen desk, then she pushed to her feet. "Where the hell have I landed, *ma'am?*"

"Sorry, ma'am." Moses stood a little straighter. "I was told to report to Division 43 and given this address. I'm eager to get back to work, ma'am, but… I don't even know what my DI duties will be. Am I supervising a team like most DIs? Am I out in the field? SIO? I assume you want me in the field with the detective constable here, but—"

"Yes, we view rank in this team as experience, Inspector," Wearne said, seeming to tire of his ramble. "Use your *skills*. Pass on your experience."

Moses nodded his thanks at the clarification.

"But more importantly, my biggest concern here… I'm just sayin', ma'am, I need to know what this place is."

"You didn't research Division 43?"

"There wasn't much out there. Specialist unit dealing with advanced intelligence."

"That's the official briefing," Rock put in.

Moses found the detective constable had squared her shoulders and was staring hard at him. A faint frown. Probably would be more perplexed if he didn't rank above her. He was about to call her on it, when the woman who outranked him delivered her own query.

"You had a little over twenty-four hours' notice to check into us," Wearne said. "You didn't even ask around about the rumours?"

"No, I—" He stopped talking, facing the DCI. The correct answer here was not, *I spent three hours picking out a new suit and two hours getting my hair cut.* "I got burned by the Plymouth guys, disowned by the NCA, and my old friends in Birmingham are treating me like some snitch."

"Hence the formal complaint you made."

"Which was building to constructive dismissal until you folks called. I *assumed* there would be an induction."

Wearne and Rock shared a smile.

"They dig deep," Rock said, the hint of condescension hidden beneath a formal tone. "Deeper than our colleagues in CID are able. Big-time anti-corruption."

Moses shook his head. "Internal affairs?"

"Not quite." Wearne tapped her fingernails—not using the touchscreen this time. "The full functionality of D43 is confidential until you sign with us permanently. It's need-to-know. But—"

"I won't beg," Moses said. "When I refused to change my story about Plymouth, no other division wanted me. But I'm not a grass."

"You didn't think it'd end this way?"

"You say I'm a good fit but won't explain it in full."

Wearne's face pinched. Almost seemed thinner than it already was. "You were both recruited because of your physical and mental skill sets. People who can handle themselves. Sharp, authoritative, and strong willed. Coppers who won't quit because something's hard and who won't be intimidated by threats."

Moses glanced at Rock, not sure what he was looking for in her firm gaze, but he disagreed with Wearne's assessment of him. "Knowing when I'm beat is how I've kept my job this long. How I made inspector."

"No." Wearne stiffened, either annoyance or pulling rank, it was hard to tell. "Another reason you were both picked up, DI Moses, is what kept you going throughout an… inconsistent career. You can both improvise. We need that."

Moses couldn't argue there. Pivoting, laying down in some situations, hitting back harder than he got hit in others. "Says more about us than you. I still don't have the full brief."

"Like Detective Constable Rock said, we go deep. Deep corruption. D and C. Four and three. The letters of the alphabet, hence Division 43. Cute in-joke by Zachary Shepherd."

"The new Police and Crime Commissioner?" Rock said.

"The same. He obtained money from the Home Office to establish a unit that could go where regular CID couldn't. We have more tech, more funding, more power to commandeer local facilities when needed. I have the authority of a judge, granted under emergency powers by the Home Office, to issue warrants, extend detention, and instigate surveillance—"

"Sounds a bit Big Brother-ish," Moses commented.

"But *only*," Wearne said, "within the confines of existing laws. The kinds of police powers that get extended for large-scale demonstrations or in the wake of terror attacks, we have this as a default. Because the cases we handle require those powers. They're not to be abused on petty criminals or everyday crimes. Understood?"

Moses wasn't sure he did, but said, "Understood ma'am."

"I'll give you that much for free, which is more

than I have to. The rest is confidential. Need to know."

Moses glanced between the two women, the buzz of activity in the office behind him, the breath of air conditioning all around. "Maybe I should have quit over the Ishtar thing. Even with your warrants and surveillance, doesn't matter if it's a senior copper with a flea in his ear from an MP, or a back hander from a drug dealer, that kind of corruption is inevitable."

"And you accept that?" Rock said. "Because I don't."

"This place still smells like Internal Affairs, or Professional Standards, or Anti-Corruption, whatever it's called this week. I'm not taking down other coppers."

"Even racist, trigger happy thugs?" Wearne said.

"I wasn't hunting them down. *They* picked *me* out."

"And what did they get?"

Moses's gut spiked, but he didn't rise to the bait. "Ma'am, the man who shot the kid got a commendation. The one who dropped the N-bomb on me had to attend sensitivity training—a compromise, they said."

"Hmm, yes. He-said, she-said situations are tough. A no-fault settlement hardly seems fair."

"The gaffer destroyed evidence to protect his men, ma'am. Like I said, I won't go hunting for colleagues. But refusing to protect them doesn't make me a grass."

"Good enough." Wearne nodded to the screen with the missing person's report. "I promise you this: We're not internal affairs. You'll understand soon enough."

"How?" Moses read the profile headlines of the twenty-two-year-old woman, Gabriella Childs, reported missing by a friend three days ago, then again by her mother two days ago. "Since when is a misper deep corruption?"

Wearne swiped her desk and the MisPer report became a photograph of a corpse. Same girl.

Moses took in the soaked hair, the disfigured face and head. "Murder, then. Question stands." When DCI Wearne didn't respond, he asked, "DC Rock, do you have more information?"

Rock turned from the screen, still seated. "Not much—"

"You wanted an induction..." Wearne turned her back and opened a drawer from a wall that looked like a solid mass of tiles. She took out a pad of paper, wrote something Moses didn't see, and folded the paper into an envelope. She licked the seal and pressed it closed, then signed her name over the join. Handed him the envelope. "Gabriella Childs was murdered by Joshua Sevan, the son of one Kaspar Sevan."

"The Armenian crime family," Rock said.

"The same."

Moses turned the envelope, switching it between the fingers of one hand the way a magician might play with a card. “Sounds more OC.”

“Our Organised Crime Units have had ten years to figure the Sevans out.” Wearne jabbed an open hand to the screen. “This has all been sent to your PALs. The case will be your induction.”

“No tour?” Moses said.

“You’ll learn as you go. And you get to tutor an ambitious detective constable along the way.”

Rock nodded once.

Wearne waved a hand between them. “While I wouldn’t typically pair two newbies together, with your experience I’m sure you can handle an open-and-shut murder. Wherever it leads.”

“And this?” He nipped the envelope between a thumb and forefinger.

“It’s the clincher. I know this is an unusual approach, but if you refrain from asking more questions, and go with me here, open it when I say, you’ll be sold. I assure you. You’ll realise you are needed here.”

“We’ll see,” Moses said.

Wearne dismissed the pair, and Moses figured he’d give it his best shot before telling them to stick it.

4

Kaspar Sevan liked women. Naked women, skimpily clad women, hot businesswomen. He liked them. No, he *loved* them. He didn't care that sitting two nineteen-year-old Russian girls on his knees, his hands snaked around their lingerie-draped forms, constituted a sleazy Eastern-European gangster cliché. If anything, he leaned into it. Image-wise, anyway. In life, he veered toward the unexpected. Whereby the cliché demanded a potbelly and a mass of sweaty folds around his neck and triple chin, he was fifty-four with the body and constitution of a thirty-year-old. He stuck with the loud shirt, though, unbuttoned to his naval, which required gold chains around his neck complete with religious iconography, and he wouldn't be seen dead without his bulky Rolex.

That he currently occupied an office above a

twenty-four-hour gentlemen's lounge—or *strip club*, as they used to be known—might also lend itself to cliché-town. In fact, three minutes earlier, he'd been unbuttoning his trousers in preparation for the pair of girls to deliver his morning pick-me-up when Carl and Travis knocked at the door at the bottom of the staircase leading up here. Kaspar yelled at them to go away but Carl's reply came back firm and somewhat urgently, "It's Joshua."

Kaspar had made himself decent and called the pair to enter, although he shifted the girls on his lap so they knew they weren't dismissed yet. Carl, as usual, shambled in directly, while Travis always seemed in awe of the office, decorated in movie posters from both the olden days and the modern age. His newest one was a French sheet for the movie *Inglorious Basterds*, which he'd picked up at auction in Paris two weeks earlier.

"What about Joshua?" Kasper said.

They explained about Gabriella Childs being found in some sort of pond near her neighbourhood.

Kasper bit the inside of his cheek, then poked his tongue at the same spot, sighing. "The girl he's been showing off all around town?"

"Yes," Carl said.

"And we cannot find Joshua," Travis added.

The two men were twins, non-identical but close to it, who served as bodyguards to Kasper and bouncers for the clubs and whatever else required strong men to exercise their strength. They had arrived in the UK from the homeland ten years ago, possibly more, their accents just shadows over their English, same as Kasper. But Joshua was born here and embraced the life. Unfortunately, he broke several of the self-imposed rules that had kept Kasper safe and prosperous, the key one being not to sample one's own product. It had made Joshua sloppy.

"The only things dumber than my son don't have a heartbeat," Kasper said. "How bad is it?"

"We are tracking his movements," Travis replied, his gaze catching a Spider-Man poster signed by Stan Lee, before snapping back to his boss. "We will wipe the CCTV in any club he has entered with her."

"Even if it isn't ours," Carl said.

"No witnesses are talking except one. But she is holed up with the cops at the moment."

"How strong is she?" Kasper asked. "Credible?"

"I do not know." Travis hadn't blinked in a while, as if it was an effort to peel himself away from the posters.

Kasper suspected the enforcer fancied taking up such a hobby, were he able to afford the original prints. If only he knew the true purpose of them, and the real owner.

"Mr Sevan," Travis said, "it is only a statement at this point, but we hear… We hear…"

Kasper shoved one of the girls off his thigh and slapped the table. "*Speak, damn it.*"

"Mobile phone footage," Carl answered without flinching the way Travis had.

The girl Kaspar shoved didn't flinch either. She sashayed to the windowsill and draped herself there.

"It shows Joshua yelling at the girl," Carl said. "A fight in the street outside a club. Grabbing her, but not striking her."

"Nothing." Kasper calmed. "No one will convict on that."

"He said he shall kill her," Travis said. "On phone. He said he will kill her. Leave her in the lake for slag friends to find. Make example—"

Kasper leaned forward, head in his hands, the other girl forced to slide off him and take to her feet. "Dumb kid will be the death of me. He could ruin everything."

He brought his head up and signalled the two girls to leave, telling them in Russian that he wanted them back here in an hour. When they were gone, he sat back in the chair, debating his next action.

"Get me Silas," Kasper said.

The two men tensed.

"You are sure?" Travis said.

Kasper leaned in to another gangster cliché, one he was sure extended far beyond the realms of prostitution, narcotics, and Rolex watches. With his fingers laced over his firm stomach, he said, "I don't take chances with family."

5

Moses had expected Wearne to at least introduce him and DC Rock to the rest of the squad, but he was a big boy. He could handle some on-the-job initiative. As Juliette Rock closed Wearne's door behind them and the blinds to the DCI's glass office whirred closed, he approached the open plan workspace and stood until someone noticed him. Rock halted alongside, chin up and shoulders square.

"Military?" he side-mouthed.

"Army," she replied in the same manner. "Am I that obvious?"

"I'm good at reading emotional responses. You're a ball of frustration. Like most ex-military joining the service. Itching to branch out from civilian protocols, but tied to your discipline, so you'll never be insubordinate. This Division with its slack approach to police regs must have been a dream come true."

"Is that a good thing, or not?" She seemed genuinely curious. Pleasant manner without sucking up.

Moses asked, "Been a copper long?"

"Two years."

"Detective already?"

"I'm tenacious."

Moses smiled. "I bet you are." He snagged the eye of the square-headed white dude in a blue shirt and yellow tie—late thirties, broad and lean. Judging by the cauliflower ear and the two kinks in his nose, Moses guessed some rugby featured in the man's past. "Morning. I'm DI Moses Glynn, this is Detective Constable Rock. Wanna show us to our desks?"

All paused what they were doing except the mousy woman typing furiously on a slim keyboard with no wires.

"Reuben Ellingham, detective sergeant," the kink-nosed detective said, leaning back in his chair. "DI Bobby Xian is the gaffer when Wearne isn't around." He pointed a pen at his colleague, a mixed-race chap who Moses guessed at Caucasian-Chinese—thinner than Ellingham and looking only a little older, but the eyes and gait suggested early fifties.

"Noobs want some intros," Xian said, standing.

Not unfriendly, just a busy guy. "Raise your hands when I call your name. DI Brienne Archer."

The stocky, jet-black-haired woman in jeans and a black POLICE t-shirt was leaning over the desk of her colleague who continued typing. Both women wore shoulder harnesses with gun holsters but no weapons.

DI Archer flicked an irritated salute. "Prepping for court. Nice to meet you." She lifted her typing partner's hand, the woman's almond-shaped eyes remaining on the screen. "This is Kyla Tahana, recently promoted DS." She let the hand drop, and the fingers resumed their clattering dance. Brienne Archer said, "Don't believe all you hear about friendly Kiwis."

"Not unfriendly," Tahana said, waving at Moses and Rock. "Documenting some fresh death threats now the court date's looming." Since Kiwi meant New Zealand, Moses assumed her features made her at least part-Maori.

"DS Banner and DC Clarke are out. Working." Xian held a stern expression, hard to read. "Happy now?"

"I'll never remember all those names," Moses said. "But thanks. Just need a desk. And for some kind soul to tell me what the hell a 'pal' is."

The four chuckled.

"She's throwing you right in at the deep end," Xian said.

Ellingham's meaty eyebrows bobbed. "It's the mystery that hooks you in."

"But you stay for the sweet, sweet justice," Archer added.

Xian faced Rock. "You know what a PAL is?"

"P. A. L.," Rock said, angling on Moses. "You really didn't have time to read the briefing notes?"

Moses wandered toward an empty desk, one with another workstation between Xian and Ellingham. "I'm a people person. Figured there'd be a more… personal welcome. But it's all good. I'll pick up this Joshua Sevan prick and smack ten bells of shit out of anyone covering up for him. Sound anti-corruption enough to you guys?"

Rock twisted her head as if stretching her neck. "Shall we get to work?"

"Good idea." Xian sat back down. "You can use your previous log-ins once but change them to something more secure straight away. Other than that, let me know if you need *anything*." The *anything* did not sound sincere.

Busy man.

If Moses had expected to remain a police officer much longer, he'd have been seriously annoyed at the greeting, but this was clearly a proactive squad expected to take the initiative. Not a problem.

He logged in on a terminal the size of a small briefcase hung beneath the desk, the soft keyboard and 17-inch monitor the only items on the surface. Rock did the same on the workstation opposite, so they faced one another. Moses's password for his old position was the names of his wife and daughter with every letter A converted to an @ symbol and every O and E converted to zero and the digit 3, respectively. When prompted, he altered the password to the identical words, but switched around. It was denied as being too similar to the previous password. He tried *5ecret5quirr3l,* which was also rejected as not strong enough. For the third attempt, he wrote *IH@t3Th1sPl@c3*.

Success. A pass*phrase* rather than a pass*word.*

Rock was already reading her screen, clicking twice as she navigated her new profile.

"PAL is a project organiser," Rock said. "Like Slack or Asana."

Moses had never used either, but was distantly familiar with them. He checked his desktop and there was a new icon which he hadn't installed, a little red circle on the corner with a number 2 in the middle, like he was used to seeing on apps for his phone.

He clicked and messages popped up. "Great, another over-complicated email client."

First: *welcome to your Personal Assignment Log.*

PAL. Personal Assignment Log.

Second: *Gabriella Childs.*

He clicked the Gabriella Childs entry and a new screen opened with what looked like a task, some notes featuring the highlights of what Wearne had said: a simple case to break Moses and Rock in, a note she'd reassigned them to more experienced Division 43 officers in time, and to not take any crap from the locals; if they chose to have jurisdiction, much like anti-terror squads around the country, Division 43 could snag jurisdiction.

There were three attachments.

The first he clicked was the West Midlands Police file, which popped up as a lengthy PDF. Going by Rock's manner, she was reading too.

Murder victim. Beaten to death by the looks of it, although an autopsy was pending. Found in a park's water feature on the edge of the Hampton Estate, one of the few predominantly white estates with a Birmingham postcode. Hampton had been notorious even with neighbouring forces, the enterprises based there having extended tentacles to almost every urban environment not already ruled by an organised gang. Moses and his colleagues had often joked about Hampton being the region's capital of *dis*-organised crime.

"Joshua Sevan," Rock said. "OCG, I guess he's protected by more than violence."

Moses hadn't got that far yet, but since Wearne already name-dropped the Sevans' organised crime gang, he figured there was good reason to make Sevan Junior the prime suspect. "Must have some coppers taking back-handers to look the other way."

"Has to be more to it than that."

Moses could almost feel the weight of the envelope in his inside pocket. Why not *tell* him outright? Why go through the charade? He had to admit, Wearne had piqued his interest with the note.

It's the mystery that hooks you in…

"He's still not much more than a low-level dealer," Moses said. "His dad runs a dozen legit businesses and two dozen illegal ones."

"Launders the money through his real interests," Rock said.

"You've been into these guys?"

"Not personally. But I'd happily burn their buildings, shoot everyone, and call it a day. Apparently, we still need evidence." She offered a grin.

Moses read it as an attempt to bond. He pushed his keyboard back a couple of inches. "That might work in the mountains of Afghanistan or the Iraqi desert, but we're not some paramilitary offshoot of regular bobbies. We have rules to follow. Evidence to gather. Trouble is, the bad guys know the rules too, and there's a hell of a lot of money guiding bad guys around those rules."

"Sounds like you find the rules as frustrating as me."

Finding common ground. More bonding one-on-one.

"Problem is," Moses said, "those rules also protect me, my wife, and my daughter. If this place oversteps the rights of people like me, we'll have a problem. I won't think twice in exposing it."

Rock's lips pressed together into a line. Bonding failed.

"Relax." Moses didn't want to go too far with the bonding-deflection; they had to work together at least one day. "I'm not on some crusade. But we gotta make those rules work. Even when they don't."

"We have more leeway here." Rock looked around the office space, the others still engrossed in their own things. "Warrants, surveillance, armoury… We can go to these meetings armed."

Moses recalled his last firearms course, his exemplary score, and how he hoped he'd never have to use a gun again. "I don't think we're at the threshold where firearms are needed, corporal. Let's—"

"It's *captain*, actually." She displayed a mix of pride and defiance, as if challenging him to doubt her. "Dozens of live enemy engagements, including two years as a sniper. I'm proficient with a wide range of weapons, and I understand the dangers. And besides, isn't it my choice?"

"If you're riding with me, no. It's mine. Folks in these neighbourhoods see a gun, they see a threat. They either try to take it off you or they break out their own. Right now, all we're doing is asking questions."

"But—"

"If intel says we need shooters, I won't pussy out. But we're on a murder case. Not a raid. We work the forensics, the witnesses."

"We already have the statements." Rock pointed

to her screen. "And camera footage of Joshua abusing the victim hours before her death. Not to mention crime scene techs have pulled out bucket-loads of DNA."

"Okay, that sounded gross. Thanks." Moses clicked one of the other attachments and a silent video launched in VLC Player. It had auto muted and he didn't turn it off. He'd heard of Joshua Sevan, seen his face in reports, but had never paid much attention. It wasn't his patch. Yet, there he was, yanking a girl around, the living, digital version of the corpse found floating earlier today; this rangy guy—mid-twenties, short-sleeved shirt and fashionably ripped jeans, tats on his hands and forearms extending up his neck—bang to rights on this, several witnesses to him threatening her, whose whereabouts were unknown. Few cases were this slam-dunk.

But you stay for the sweet, sweet, justice…

Moses slipped the envelope from his jacket and laid it on the desk.

"Are you going to open that?" Rock asked.

"No, Captain." Moses stood. "I'm going to go over the evidence myself. Then—and only then—will I use the snazzy Home Office powers of Division 43 to track down Joshua Sevan. *If* I agree with what's in this file."

He made for the door.

Rock came up alongside. "You don't trust the locals?"

"When I've been told almost nothing about the job I'm meant to be doing? When something looks this simple? I wouldn't be a very good copper if I trusted anything that's happened so far today. I can do it on my own if you prefer."

"I'm in. Are you bringing the envelope?"

Moses glanced back only once, catching Xian's eye and exchanging a nod before scanning the door to unlock it. "No, it can wait. If by the end of the day I plan on sticking around, maybe then I'll take a look. At the moment, I don't want it confusing matters. And by the way, you're driving."

6

DI Barney Gray had worked Missing Persons for five years. He was the de facto chief in all but official title and salary, and he liked it that way. Without the title, he could stay out of politics, and the way he lived his life didn't require much remuneration from the police. In fact, as he thanked Sergeant Grosse for his quick thinking in taking Veronica Meda's statement before the woman tutted, dropped her head, and shambled away, he felt little in terms of sadness at Gabriella Childs' passing.

He trudged back down to the white tent still housing the corpse on the edge of the lake, the path winding back on itself in a series of hairpins, designed so the flabby and lazy residents of this area had to exert only minimal energy. It reminded him of the roads he'd seen in movies set in the Los Angeles Hills and, he vaguely recalled, somewhere European—he wanted to say Italy; a Bond movie, perhaps, or that ancient one with the Minis starring Michael Caine.

Several metres outside the forensics tent, two members of Barney Gray's team waited, decked out in the white overalls reserved for detectives on homicide duty, although they'd removed their face masks and hoods now they were no longer in danger of transferring their DNA to the Childs girl.

DS Rudolph Kortenberg, a black South African who'd grown up on the British south coast, carried a languid gait that concealed his geek-chic personality and habits, meeting the inspector with an iPad showing the most recent snapshot of the dead woman: white, bloated, with faint pink lips and damp hair. "Boss, we need this one." His South African accent was faint but detectable, and Gray loved hearing the man talk. It was like a lullaby. "She was strangled too, by the looks of it."

"But that wasn't what killed her." By contrast, DS Clara Burns' tone cut like razor blades on a winter's morning. She was heavyset, but Gray knew that didn't mean *fat*; hours at the gym, cycling, various fighting arts. But she radiated a gentle demeanour, especially when she needed something from a family or a witness. "Looks improvised to me. The strangulation was impulsive, typical of a piece of shit like

Joshy-boy, but someone pulled him back from the brink. So there's marks. I'd say he either did it this way to torture her, or he pulled up short of killing her, but finished the job later with the beating."

"SOCOs have pulled skin and blood from under her nails," Kortenberg said. "Already on the way to the lab."

Gray gazed out on the lake. If it could be called a lake. But he could see how it benefited families for a short time. *Let's go and see the ducks.* Kids would throw bread—which was terrible for ducks and geese, by the way—while the parents smoked, maybe drank too, and always buried their heads in their phones while their offspring delighted in poisoning the wildfowl. Still, it was pretty on the surface.

He said, "Domestic violence cycle completed in one night."

Kortenberg let the iPad fall by his side. "Boss?"

"The temper, the violence, the apology, then escalation, ending with death. How many times have we seen this?"

"Too many to count," Burns said, flatly. "Do we get this one? Continuation?"

Gray nodded. "We started with the misper, we have relationships with the relatives. Might have to report in to a different DCI, but..." He let the words peter out, knowing the awkwardness that scenario would bring to his tight-knit team. He gathered himself for a beat, then called their Detective Chief Superintendent.

"DCS Cleland," came the man's clipped tone.

"Gaffer, I'm at the Hampton Park crime scene. It's definitely her."

"Okay, you can hand over to—"

"Sorry to interrupt, sir, but we can handle this."

"She's no longer missing."

"No, but there is precedent. We have relationships established, solid witness, video evidence, and—"

"My turn to be sorry for the interruption, Barney. And I really *am* sorry. But we have already turned it over. DCI and DI both assigned."

"Who is it? Jerry Manford? Denise?"

Cleland was both erudite and a man of few words, the kind of straight down the line, no-nonsense manager that coppers up and down the country yearned for. Which was why the pause that followed Gray's fishing for names hung ominously over the phone. Gray also knew not to interrupt again.

Finally, the DCS said, "Unknown. Confidential."

Gray felt his face contort into an exaggerated soap opera actor's impression of "incredulous." He reset himself, but Kortenberg and Burns already appeared concerned. He tried to keep his tone even and calm. "Confidential? What does that mean?"

"It means a new intelligence unit has decided

they want the case. Division 43. I assume it's to do with the Sevan family."

"That's OC," Gray said. "Aren't intelligence all up in the arses of Islamic extremists and Nazi-wannabes?"

Cleland's nasal sigh was loud enough to convey a verbal shrug too. "Sorry, Barney. They want it, they've got it. You have an hour to mark it unsolved and send it up the pipe. Earmarked for Davina Mishkin up in Stoke."

Stoke-on-Trent was a town in Staffordshire, therefore a separate police body to Gray's West Midlands territory. "They're sending the body to a different *county*?"

"From what I hear, Barney, Mishkin's a good pathologist. Works with NCA as well as the locals. With her involved, and this intelligence division, you can rest easy. They'll get the result."

Gray was sure to hang up with courtesy and lots of *sir*s and even a *thank you*. Having cultivated a ton of leeway with the man and earned his respect, it was important to maintain their position. There were DCIs with less access to the superintendent than DI Gray.

After disconnecting, he formed a fist but released it without punching anything. "That man is a moron."

"Boss?" Burns said.

Gray's phone was in danger of shattering if his grip didn't ease. He put it in his pocket.

"We've lost it?" Kortenberg asked.

Gray paced away from the forensics tent, working the tension from his jaw until he and his detectives were out of earshot of any others. "Division 43. 'Intelligence', whatever that means."

"Never heard of them," Burns said.

Gray filled his former smoker's lungs to capacity, longing for a nicotine hit. He'd given up before vaping became a thing and never intended to embark down *that* road. Birds sang. A goose landed on the water with a splatter rather than a splash. Too much bread in its gut, probably. The sun filtered through thin cloud cover. And Gray's anger seeped from him, a necessary step for a clear head. Unfortunately, what replaced it wasn't much better.

Gray faced the pair. "If they uncover too much, it might mean trouble."

Burns held his eye.

Kortenberg nodded. "There's nothing to connect us, is there?"

"No." Gray meant it. "We hold all the cards on this one. But just to be sure…" He considered whether to push it, whether it'd be easier to let Division 43 go about their business and roll with whatever scraps they might find. Not that they should find any. "Clara, go grab that sarge before he learns we've passed on the case. Get the witness's address. We can visit as a friend of the family, not detectives."

Clara Burns left without a word.

"And me, gaffer?" Kortenberg asked, his velvety voice higher pitched than usual.

Gray touched the detective's firm shoulder. "I'm not worried, but you never know. Find out all you can."

7

Joshua Sevan awoke in a place he didn't recognise. It smelled like the kind of men's room that infested the cheapest, nastiest pubs on his dad's books. Thankfully, whatever he was lying on was soft, conclusive evidence he hadn't passed out on the floor of some urine-soaked bathroom again. There had definitely been alcohol involved, though, his body attesting to that via the medium of excruciating pain. His brain had been hooked through the frontal lobe, held in place by twine and reeled in by an unseen hand as he shifted.

He opened his eyes.

Light coursed through him, bolting into his gut, swirling there rather than stabbing more pain through his skull. Or maybe it was doing both. But his bigger concern was the prospect of throwing up.

Embarrassment—the only thing Joshua deemed unacceptable.

If he'd found a quiet spot in one of his dad's swankier clubs, he'd be in for a minor beating by the old man, one he'd no doubt indulge himself in front of people Joshua knew. Men, women, employees; muscle, strippers, hookers, whatever. Kaspar Sevan liked to show Joshua up in the presence of known associates, as if embarrassment was a proven motivational tool.

Cutting him off financially never worked, because Joshua was clever, knew how to get cash, and even had his own side-businesses that didn't fall under his dad's umbrella. Oh yeah, he'd snuck those businesses into place without triggering his dad's radar, new businesses all of his own. Not that they were the kinds of places Joshua like to hang out; dirty and cheap, they attracted junkies unconcerned with the quality of the product, and horny men led more by low prices than the smoothness of the flesh they were defiling. No, Josh wouldn't touch either the drugs or the women in those establishments.

Still, they brought in money independent of his father—a man for whom things like tradition, discipline, and control overrode notions of progress and ambition. Notions Joshua expected would propel him to the head of the family in shorter measure than his dear old daddy expected.

If only he could learn moderation.

It was his one weakness. When Joshua indulged,

he waded in up to his neck, and often—as it seemed he did last night—ducked right under and stayed there until his lungs burst. Or his gut.

A grumbling surged, at first swirling like water from a sink, then mouthward. Joshua snapped upright and blinked back the pain inflicted by the sadistic fisherman on the end of the rod manipulating his frontal lobe, willed his legs into motion, and bounded for a door that he somehow knew led to a bathroom. A pint of something pungent and lumpy flowed up this throat and into the toilet bowl, already stained brown. Out of breath, he wretched a couple more times, taking in his surroundings.

Not the worst loo he'd ever thrown up in. Dingy, but at least there was no mould climbing the tiles. A thick, brown-yellow air, dominated by an acidic stench, although he'd contributed a lot to that himself.

Once empty, he resisted using the faucet and ventured back out into a flat which he recognised as belonging to Ashley Mars, a guy who wanted in on the ground floor of Joshua's ventures. He trusted Ash, too, allowing him to run two of the brothels. Solid bloke, decent banter, could handle himself when called upon. Yeah, Ash was a good guy.

"Ash?" It was more of a croak. He found a pack of sealed water bottles on the side of the tiny kitchenette and ripped one free, popped the top, and drank. The motion hurt his left arm.

He rolled up his sleeve to find a partially scabbed cut about the size of a table tennis ball. No —a series of cuts, little gashes. Had someone *bitten* him?

Thirst pawed harder than the mystery of a bite mark, so he left the injury for the time being and put the bottle to his lips. From experience, he knew not to gulp, no matter the temptation. This time, he shouted Ash's name. Closer to the guy's bedroom. He shouted again, growing angry at being ignored.

"Yeah," came a groggy reply.

A flash of memory blistered into Joshua's consciousness.

"*Yeah, yeah, yeah, that's what you always say.*"

What was that about? Sounded like a female to Josh.

"How'd I get here?" he called.

"One sec, man. Be with you."

Having to wait wasn't fun, but Joshua bit back the irritation and took the opportunity to sip more water and make his way back toward the sofa on which he'd woken. His right eye felt crusty, probably an accumulation of sleep, but he could see okay.

The room was in disarray, with an empty vodka bottle, two polystyrene takeaway containers with the remnants of donner kebabs spilled around, some Pepsi Max cans, and a pooled stain on the floor close to where Joshua's head had been. Clearly, this morning wasn't his first time vomiting.

Ash had a nasty clean-up waiting on him.

Another memory flash, another spike of white light: *"You're saying that here? In front of my friends?"*

Then him, yelling. He replayed it and a vision accompanied this one, from his point of view, his finger jabbing at that scrubby lass, Gabby. Scrubby but a fab body when she took those cheap slut-clothes off, and banging her… that was—

His hands around her throat. Squeezing, squeezing. Gabby's teeth red with blood. Her eyes, blazing with sheer anger, not fear. Slapping at his hands. Scratching his arms. Him, calling her a bitch, telling her to die, just die!

"Whoops," he said.

He plopped himself on the couch, the opposite end to the vomit stain, but he could still smell it, which threatened a repeat of his chunder-run to the bathroom.

"Hey." Bleary, staggering a little, Ash wandered past in his boxer shorts and vest, and went into his bathroom. "Be right out, man."

Joshua then flashed on more of last night.

A friend of Gabby's—Vicky, maybe? Veronica? Didn't matter, he'd find out soon enough—hitting him in the face with a bottle, him slapping the bitch, and Ash pulling him away, telling him not to, not here, leave it for now.

And he had. The crusted sleep around his eye was dried blood. *His* blood.

But then there was more. *Somewhere darker. No*

streetlamps. Fists flying. A face plunged into grass. A field. No, a football pitch. His boots digging in. Running up to the prone form of Gabby Childs. "And it's Sevan with the penalty that wins England the World Cup. Miss it, and it's heartbreak all over again…" Ash, telling him she'd had enough, to please think *about it… And then he's running, sprinting, drawing back his leg, and—*

Joshua looked down at his boots—£300 designer slip-ons. He was still wearing them. Must have been properly mullered to not remove his shoes.

He pulled his right foot onto his knee and checked the toe. Yep, there was blood on it. Some mud, too. A streak up his trouser leg.

"Hey Ash, I need to set fire to some shit."

From the bathroom, over the tinkling of a very long pee, Ash called back, "Yeah, I told you to do it last night right after we dropped her off. You wanted a kebab."

"We dropped who off? Gabby?"

"Yeah." The peeing stopped.

"We took her home?"

Several aborted flushes sounded before Ash emerged. "You ready to be sensible, mate?"

Joshua didn't like his tone but conceded it might be the hangover. Besides, Ash had never let him down. Even now, tossing Joshua a pack of fags and a lighter, Ash headed to the kitchen, returning with a black bin liner.

"Clothes in here," Ash said. "Sorry, but you're gonna have to wear some of mine, then burn these."

"Sure." Joshua thought Ash had the fashion sense of a blind art teacher from the 1980s, but it wasn't a crime to dress like that.

"Steam shower at the gym, not here. And defo not at your place, or your pop's, okay?"

Joshua nodded and lit a cigarette. Looked around again at the chaos and mess. "Thanks. Appreciate the help. Bonus packet for you this month."

"We should do it quick. Before the cops start looking for you."

"Don't worry." With the cig in his mouth, smoke stinging his eyes, Joshua began unbuttoning his shirt. "It'll be a couple of hours before they cotton on."

Joshua stripped to his underwear, stuffed the clothes in the bin liner, and Ash announced he'd grab replacements.

"Nothing with flowers," Joshua said.

"No worries. One hour, you're in the clear."

Good man, that Ash.

But then a tremendous *crack* filled the small flat. The door down the hall crashed inward. Thundering feet. Ash stumbled back into the lounge. A deep call of, "*Police!*"

Ash abandoned the bag, rolled, reached under the couch and came up with a cricket bat, leaping to his feet. He swung it at the first person around the corner—a huge black man in a nice three-piece suit.

The copper dodged inside the swing, slapped the bat from Ash's grip and elbowed him so hard he flew four feet, landing on the pool of dried sick.

Joshua grinned, hands on his head.

A female redhead joined the giant black guy, backed up by two uniformed coppers, who flinched at the state of the place.

"Morning," Joshua said. "Can I help you?"

"Joshua Sevan?" The well-dressed man held out a warrant card. "DI Moses. Morning. You're nicked."

8

Before bringing in Joshua Sevan, Moses discovered another aspect of Division 43 that he hadn't considered—they didn't have formal interview rooms. Or holding cells. Suspects could not be taken there, such was the degree of confidentiality—which Moses was beginning to read as paranoia—meaning any arrests made had to be processed through a nearby police station. Juliette Rock, conducting her own inquiries, also learned they could commandeer National Crime Agency facilities, MI5 safe houses, and stash suspects at remand centres, using existing British laws on detention while circumventing certain aspects commonly known as "red tape."

Frankly, if they kept barging into local stations and stomping all over them with their Home Office mandate brandished aloft, Moses couldn't see how

Division 43 could remain a *secret* intelligence branch for long. Coppers talked. A lot. And when something violated a police officer's territory—through secretive means or not—rumours spread faster than a tsunami.

To deal with this morning's collar, they'd picked the relatively new facility at Lichfield, a station outside the Sevan family's known concerns, but geographically nearby. Moses guessed he'd handled that part okay. Asking rather than demanding. He apologised for the short notice and explained to the custody officer about a covert operation connected to organised crime in the region, lying that someone up the chain had screwed up. Like custody officers up and down the country, this chap had more than likely seen his fair share of administrative blunders that coldcocked personnel on the ground. He found room for Joshua without being strong-armed.

"Told you you'd figure it out," Wearne said when he called in as they waited on Joshua Sevan's legal rep. "How's Rock?"

"She hasn't shot anyone yet," Moses replied. "You need anything else?"

"Update your PAL when you're finished. I'll know what you know. Be seeing you."

She hung up without a goodbye and Moses thought again about the brusque manner, how she refused to guide him in any way. Him or Rock. It felt like a power play or dishonest pantomime. Still, he'd keep his word and assume all would become clear in time—both what Division 43 was hiding and the reasons for Wearne's reticence.

Moses and Rock discovered the PAL app had been added to their police-issue mobiles along with secure apps for conducting interviews in the field, plus a couple with functionality yet to present themselves. Rock was more impressed than Moses.

"It's bloody great," she said, complying with the order to update the PAL, typing as she spoke. "Instant notifications of updates, the boss can check in anytime. You can even leave a quick voice memo while you're driving. Personal observations that aren't shared with others on the network, except the boss."

"Personal observations?" Moses said. "I can leave notes assessing your performance to review later?"

Rock responded with a cheeky smile. "And I can state whether you're an effective manager or chaos walking."

Moses didn't see the humour. This might be the final phase of his police career, and he had no clue what he'd do next. If this didn't work out—and it looked very much like paramilitary overreach, of which he could never be a part—he saw little chance of a new posting in which he'd be accepted. He was thinking of a uniformed inspector posting in a quiet village, a seaside town or back in the Valleys perhaps, but hadn't yet discussed that with his wife. If that wasn't an option, he'd resume his exile, hasten his unfair dismissal claim, and get to taking the bastards to court.

Back to the matter at hand, he deadpanned his partner. "And you think this'll make a difference to how effective we are?"

Rock finished the PAL admin without further gushing and Moses's phone bonged to notify him of an update. She said, "Not by itself. But it's better than what I've been facing."

"We still have to pass the same thresholds for convictions. Can't just dump suspects in POW camps and waterboard confessions out of them."

Rock held her phone in both hands, her mouth a pink line in her pale, freckled face. She lowered the handset without relinquishing it. "Do you have a problem with my Army record?"

"Haven't seen your record."

"Soldiers in general, then."

"No, Cap'n. I have a concern that you wanted to break out a gun this morning when there was no sign of firearms in play."

"It's organised crime. There's always the possibility of firearms."

"Not careful guys. Not like the Sevans."

"He beat a woman to death after letting himself get filmed threatening her. Left her where she'd be found easily. There's more DNA than we could hope for. This isn't a careful guy. It's a lunatic."

"Even lunatics want to stay out of prison." Moses's phone pinged rather than bonged, which he looked at this time. "Text from the front desk. Solicitor's ready."

Being a new station, the interview suite boasted the latest recording facilities and security features, and the patched-up Joshua Sevan appeared calm and relaxed in a papery onesie similar to the garment Moses had been issued after the raid in Plymouth. The twenty-four-year-old's legal rep demanded his client's release, citing lack of evidence, at which Rock smirked and sat opposite the pair without a word. She set up a tablet computer, issued to her before Moses had arrived that morning, its 5G connection linking it to their PALs.

Chairs in these places were normally a tad small for Moses, and this was no exception. It was sometimes an advantage, though, an added layer of intimidation, as the effect often made him look like a giant.

After the formalities for the digital recording, Moses took the lead. "Take me through last night."

"Oh, man." Joshua played with his fingers, a bemused shake of the head. "I was smashed. Sorry."

"Too smashed to recall your movements?"

"Yeah, man."

"*Any* movements?"

Big smile, teeth showing. Very pleased with himself. "Took a dump around six."

Moses didn't move. Didn't even blink.

"Fine, I left the house at eight." Joshua paused, leaned in. "That's it. Woke up to you and my mate fighting. Then I'm brought here."

"Let's try it a little differently." Moses activated the computer tablet's screen. Constables had already recovered CCTV from Joshua's known haunts. "This is you at ten-twelve p.m." Moses showed footage of Joshua, Gabriella, and an as-yet unidentified couple entering a vodka bar, arm in arm, Gabriella exhibiting an unsteady gait already. "Where were you before this?"

"Oh…" Joshua tapped his head in exaggerated concentration. "The White Horse? Maybe King's Gin Bar." It wasn't clear if he was dicking with them.

"There was a takeaway bag from AbraKebabra in Ashley Mars' flat. Where were you before there?"

Joshua shook his head. "I'm too fucked up, man." He appealed to his solicitor. "Do I have to do this now?"

The older man whispered in Joshua's ear.

Joshua returned to Moses. "I don't remember."

"Your clothes?" Moses said. "Why were they in a bin liner in the flat?"

"I don't see how you can prove they were mine."

The solicitor leaned into Joshua's ear, whispered something inaudible. Joshua nodded, again exuding that cocky grin.

"They'll have your DNA on them," Moses said. "Along with mud from the park where Gabriella

Childs' body was found. Plus Gabriella's blood. How do you account for that?"

The solicitor interjected. "The clothes were taken only ninety minutes ago, Inspector. I do not believe even a priority test can return such clear results so swiftly."

"Not that quickly, no," Moses said. He lowered himself to Joshua's eye level. "But we all know what it's going to show."

"She had a hell of a temper." Joshua waved the solicitor away as he leaned in again. "If there's blood on clothes that you can prove are mine, I was defending myself from a psycho bitch who didn't like a real man expressing his opinion."

"Did she often get violent?"

This time the solicitor darted in, mouthing the words without having time to cup his lips. Moses picked up the advice: *no comment.*

Joshua's eyes flicked to Rock and stayed there. "Hey."

"Hey." Rock's expression was as barren as Moses's.

"You like a strong man?" A head-bob toward Moses. "Like him?"

"I don't know. I only met him this morning."

"It's enough to know whether you'd like to bang him, though."

Rock remained a blank slate.

Moses asked, "Did Gabriella Childs often get violent?"

Joshua flashed that grin at Moses again, brow low, fighting a hangover that no one could fake. "She wants to bang you."

"Did Gabriella Childs often get violent?"

Joshua leaned back, head lolling. He turned to the solicitor, then sat upright. "Okay, I'm bored. No comment."

Moses had expected this. What had been *un*expected was how long it took to reach the no-comment phase. "Where were you between one a.m. and three a.m.?"

"No comment."

Moses gave Rock a signal, a nod to the tablet, and Rock activated it. "What were you arguing about here?"

Joshua perused the screen with the phone footage retrieved from Veronica Meda, filmed by her, as Joshua's hands wrapped around Gabriella's neck. A man identified as Ashley Mars pulled at Joshua's arm, blurting the usual stuff supposed to calm an out-of-control arsehole—"she's not worth it" and "let the bitch go, she's baiting you on purpose"—and a few unintelligible murmurings. Veronica's voice could be heard, too, calling Joshua various names, and a telling phrase, "You won't get away with it again!"

Moses paused the footage with a tap. "*Again*, Joshua? What does that mean?"

Joshua shrugged. "I was holding her off. Looks like I'm hurting her, but that's my blood on her teeth. *She* bit *me*." He pulled up his sleeve to where the nurse at the minor injuries unit had cleaned up the broken skin on his forearm, along with the cut to his forehead, and applied a padded gauze. "See? Violent."

"You won't get away with it again," Moses repeated. "Sounds like you've done this before."

"You won't get away with it again." Joshua rolled down his sleeve, flexing his finger to demonstrate how so-in-pain he was. "Sounds more like that bitch who hit me with a bottle was talking to her psycho friend. She bit a decent, upstanding bloke. She shouldn't get away with it… *again.*"

"Yet here you are strangling her."

Joshua again seemed bored. "No comment."

"Listen…"

The footage started again, on which Joshua shouted, "You're gonna *die* this time." Rock dabbed the screen, skipping the footage back ten seconds, then let it repeat. "You're gonna *die* this time."

"No comment."

Moses gave Rock another signal to the pad, and she complied, closing the video and pulling up a pic of the clothing, bagged on a white background. He said, "You can't remember what you did, but we have your clothes. Samples consistent with the area in which they found Gabriella, blood consistent with kicking a person, and a body that has been bludgeoned to death. Are you honestly trying to deny killing her?"

"No. Comment."

"Witnesses say you took her away following this altercation. Where did you go afterward?"

"Can't remember."

"Veronica insisted Gabriella come home with her, but you slapped Gabriella then dragged her into a taxi along with your mate Ashley."

"No comment."

"That was the last anyone saw of her alive. That we can find."

"No comment."

"When we locate the taxi, where will it have dropped you?"

"No comment."

"The fields behind Hampton Park?"

"No comment."

The solicitor stepped in. "My client has already stated that because of his excessive inebriation he cannot recall his movements. Perhaps after a short rest period he may recover these memories."

Moses locked eyes with Joshua, who reinstated his grin.

"This is dumb, you know," the thug said. "Wasting your time and mine. Everything you got? Circumstantial."

Moses lowered his voice to a growl, readying to stand. "All evidence is circumstantial. Even the blood on your boots. The question is reasonable doubt. You really believe with all the footage, the witnesses, and the DNA, that you're not going down for this?"

"Oh yeah, I do."

Moses stood fully, pulled his jacket straight, recalling how Division 43 was supposedly more effective, less bound by red tape. He'd promised to give the job a fair shot, so went with it, exuding a confidence he didn't completely feel. "Because we're not normal plod, Josh. We're here to handle cases where arseholes like you can't worm out of things by having big bad daddy intimidate witnesses or bribe bent coppers into looking the other way."

There was a twinkle to Joshua's cocky demeanour, and it didn't fade one iota. "Good luck with that, DI Moses."

Outside the room, Moses and Rock took to the office that had been provided for them—not a courtesy he'd expected, but accepted anyway.

"You don't like it?" Rock said.

"Something's off." Moses ran a hand over his recently shorn head, still loving the fresh cut feel. "Could he have more than a bite mark up his sleeve?"

Rock leaned on the desk, considering it. "I don't see how. The physical evidence is with Division 43, the body on its way to a pathologist called Davina Mishkin—she's NCA-vetted. His dad can't touch any of that. The blood spatter on his trousers will nail him. The killing blow."

Moses shook his head. "It's not that simple. Never is. And they can still get to witnesses."

"Not with us running it."

"And that's the other thing. If Division 43 is such a hot department, and this is as straightforward as murder cases get… why are we even needed?"

Rock seemed about to reply but stopped herself short. "So, what do we do?"

The cues from Joshua were clear. The questions Moses posed designed to elicit one response or the other. And Moses was now certain of the suspect's personality type, of the buttons they needed to press. He said, "We get him to confess, Cap. Which means you need to lead."

9

DI Barney Gray slammed through the double doors to the shared CID room, letting them flap back into the waiting palms of DS Kortenberg who had accompanied him back to base. Although areas were delineated by glass panels occupied by various CID squads, it was essentially a massive gopher farm like the call centres he'd worked in during his student days a couple of decades ago. He marched toward the area reserved for MisPer, his heavy glare a signal for those rubbernecking at his entrance to leave him alone.

Gray's reputation as a Pitbull was not because he resembled a squat, muscular dog, nor because he was reputedly bad tempered; he simply never let go unless you pried his jaws off that bone, stick, or shinbone with a pneumatic jack. It was one reason he got such stellar results in missing persons. Frequently, a missing girl—over the age of sixteen—would be located in some guy's place and she'd refuse to leave because she was there by choice. Okay, it was *usually* girls, but not always. Said girls were rarely aware of the abusive nature of the relationship, even if their new beau cheated on them, beat them, or controlled every aspect of their lives. A burgeoning sexual prowess delivered more pleasure than studying algebra and English Literature, along with ready access to booze, drugs, and whatever other small pleasures fogged the victim's mentality. While Gray's predecessor wiped his hands and forwarded those cases to a social services inbox to be ignored for all time, Gray and his team always came up with ways—sometimes inventive and even sly—to persuade the runaway to return home. Those who didn't end up dead, or held against their will.

Sending the abuser down for a stretch unrelated to the abuse was a favoured tactic, often thanks to drugs, guns, or other illegal paraphernalia around the property. With nowhere else to go, the girl could be deprogrammed in the care of parents and social workers. Temporarily, anyway. It'd just be a matter of time before a sixteen-year-old victim grew into a twenty-year-old slapper—probably with a substance abuse issue and a handful of kids in tow. Not something they could help prevent, but Gray had to try everything he could.

He bustled into his team's allocated zone and sat, feet on his desk, pinching his bottom lip.

"Boss?" Kortenberg said, arriving beside him.

Gray said nothing.

Gabby Childs had managed to avoid birthing any kids, although rumours about abortions had surfaced during their brief inquiries. She didn't deserve what happened to her, and her family needed closure. Justice. Whatever form that took.

"It was *our* case," Kortenberg pressed. "You've taken murders off other detectives before. We can fight for it back."

"Gabby's family should see a factual reckoning," Gray said. "Not some intel department using her death for the glory of the 'bigger picture' or however they're justifying it."

"Boss?"

Impatience brewing within himself, Gray needed to act, to move, to *do* something. "I don't think that line will wash with the brass. If the detectives have the authority they seem to."

"What kind of unit can do that?"

Gray scanned the five other desks, littered with smart piles of files. All in order. A professional, committed bunch.

"The only time I've seen this type of thing was when our vic was suspected of running off to join ISIS. And this isn't MI5 or National Crime Agency. It's something else."

"The Facilitator has been in touch. He found the taxi driver. Do we start with the usual?"

Gray pinched his lip again; an annoying habit

he'd developed. Or one he'd only noticed recently. "No. We'll have to go the other route."

"You want me to take care of it?"

"I need you here, K. Send Cole instead. You look more into this Division 43. I want to know everything before I stomp them right off our patch."

10

Moses's comment about why Division 43 was even needed in the Gabriella Childs case nagged at the back of Rock's mind until Joshua's solicitor confirmed the glass of water and two coffees had rejuvenated his client enough to resume the interview. Although she was as frustrated as Moses about Wearne's lack of clarity, she trusted all would soon become clear.

Lowering herself opposite Joshua Sevan, his cocky sneer shifting up and down her body, Rock resisted the urge to tug at her blouse to make sure no buttons were gaping wide enough to see even a glimpse of bra. She formally resumed the interview and reconfirmed who was in attendance, this time with Moses manning the computer tablet.

Despite neither being trained in psychiatry, she

and Moses had agreed Joshua was both a misogynist and a classic narcissist; a hatred of women that he couldn't see because he enjoyed sex with so many of them, combined with an inability to understand he'd done anything wrong—ever. Even if he experienced sadness about Gabriella's passing, one thing a man like this would never feel was *guilt*. Raised by a father who likely indulged his every whim, surrounded by people paid to keep him happy and to never, ever allow any consequences to befall precious Joshy... how could he have turned out any other way?

She ran through the same questions as Moses had, receiving a "no comment" in reply each time. While the words were identical, the leering at Rock grew more pronounced. She was used to it, though, so it didn't faze her. Okay, she wasn't really *used* to it. But she'd grown to *endure* it. And it didn't matter that she saw herself as gawky and clumsy, having only bulked up to meet the physical demands of the front line and the constant training.

"Joshua, let me ask you something not directly related to the case," Rock said after the thousandth *no comment* slimed from between the man's lips.

The solicitor shook his head. "That's not acceptable."

"Nah, it's fine." Joshua folded his arms and spread his legs. "Ask away, Detective Constable Rock."

"Why are we here?" she said. "Myself and DI Moses. Why does a guy as dumb as you require our attention?"

On the word *dumb*, Joshua's legs eased closed and he sat upright. "Yeah, maybe I don't wanna get into this."

"I used to be in the Army. I saw combat. Killed through a sniper scope and later blew up outposts while commanding a tank division. We backed up law enforcement in countries where the concepts of 'policing by consent' or 'protect and serve' are as alien as torturing you with bamboo under the fingernails is to my colleague here."

Joshua checked his fingers but did not reply.

"Toward the end of the war in Afghanistan, there was this poppy farmer, a known supplier of heroin to the Taliban, who we needed to question. Farmer had barricaded himself on his property and we'd rolled up with this Warrior. That's a tank, by the way. I was a corporal back then, responsible for a tank and a bunch of soldiers, all of us up for this arsehole to spill what he knew. But we were under orders not to open fire unless fired upon. It wasn't like I could simply blow a wall out. We consulted what passed for the local cops, but they were more concerned with keeping the town's elders happy and not drawing fire from any Taliban stragglers. Then we get intelligence that the reason the farmer is locked in is that one of the senior logistics guys for the Taliban is right in there with him. So it's even more imperative we don't blow the place up… even *if* they open fire."

Joshua was paying attention, but he seemed to be watching her mouth. Rock paused, her tongue on her bottom lip, and Joshua shifted minutely in the chair, his own tongue poking its tip through.

Rock went on. "But I got around that. I briefed my men, and I had them drive that Warrior through the wall of the farmhouse. Took the corner off. Surprised the people inside. Then we stormed through. Got the bastard. Turned him and smashed a ton of routes leading right back home."

"Is there a point to this, Detective Constable?" the solicitor asked. "Or can my client be excused? I'm sure you will happily arrange transport—"

"That's how I do things, Josh," Rock said. "That's how I do *everything*. One way or another, I bludgeon, smash, crash and blast my way into the lives of people who don't want me there." She let that sink in. "I'm going to raid every club, every bar, every hovel and drug den that you're even remotely connected with. *Me*. Tearing down your pathetic imitation of daddy's empire."

Joshua lurched forward but remained seated. "It's not pathetic."

Rock extended her little finger. "I've seen it, Josh. It's tiny compared to your dad's." She poked the finger close to her mouth and, seeing Joshua's face redden, pushed it further. "And a big bad girl like me is going to enjoy it. You're going to have to go running back to daddy to ask for help. Hiding from the lady taking all you've built."

"No…" His voice broke, jaw tense. He squinted. Pure anger. "You can't. I'll finish you." To Moses, "Both of you."

Moses shrugged. "Hey, it's her play. Don't bring me into it."

Rock liked that. "Taking out the Taliban farmhouse got me a black mark but a big tick. More good than bad."

"So what?" Joshua's tone resembled a petulant bully, caught in the act.

"*So…* you can avoid that. You tell me exactly what happened last night, do a couple of years if your lawyer here beats it down to manslaughter, and it's all waiting for you."

The solicitor addressed Moses, not Rock. "Detective, this is not how things are done. Please end this."

Moses dead-eyed the man.

"Gabby was disrespectful," Rock said. "Laughed at you. Gave you grief over something she had no right to."

Joshua glanced at the tablet, now silently replaying the scuffle as he had his hands around Gabriella's throat.

Rock's softened her voice. "We're just talking

about why you ended up doing that, not the killing. What did she say? What did she do?"

"Thought I was cheating…"

"Were you?"

"No, not really."

"Not really?"

"Prossies aren't cheating."

The solicitor leaned in, whispered.

"No comment," Joshua said.

"Too late," Moses said.

"Fuck you!"

"Thanks."

"She laughed at you for using prostitutes," Rock said, voice still soft, relaxed. "That you have to pay for it."

"Never paid for it with Gabby." Joshua grabbed his crotch. "She loved it. Like you'd love it. Detective Rock, bouncing on my cock."

How original. Juliette Rock had only heard *Rock on my cock* about a million times in her life. "I bet she did love it. And she deserved a slap. A bit of rough."

No verbal reply. A knowing slant to Joshua's mouth.

"A jury will understand you didn't mean it," Rock said. "A powerful businessman, driven to violence by a disrespectful slag of a woman."

Joshua half-nodded.

"My client has no comment," the solicitor said.

"There's no other way for the blood to get on those boots," Rock said. "The spatter on your trousers. The mud. We know you beat her. We know you liked her. You didn't mean to kill her. Just tried to mess up her looks a bit."

Joshua watched her again.

"It'll go easier than if we convict through other means," Rock said. "Murder or manslaughter. Your choice. Minimum of fifteen years, possibly as much as life. Or, if you swing it to manslaughter by reason of loss of control, you might scrape four-to-six, out in three if you're lucky. You'll still be young. Still be able to keep your businesses, impress the women…"

Rock had seen the look in a hundred psychopaths, not only during her time with the police, but around the world. They wanted you to know. They wanted you to know that they knew you know. And Rock had dumped all she had. Accuse, accuse, accuse; tease out a hypothetical motive; show understanding and demonstrate compassion for his crime; emphasise others would understand too; ramp up the worst consequences a final time, then offer a way out at the last.

It was textbook.

"I…" Joshua glanced at the solicitor who gave a tiny wobble of the head—*No*. But Joshua said, "Gabby, she—"

The door opened without a knock. Moses jumped to his feet, ready for the intruder, Rock spinning to meet any threat, but there was no need.

It was a small, balding, fiftyish man in a tan suit carrying a brown briefcase.

"What is this?" Moses demanded.

Interview room doors didn't fly open on their own. It took real sway to access without permission, and this man had no one with him. He was a shade over five feet tall, a crochet thicket of black hair gracing the sides and back of an eagle's-egg-head, a thin, precise moustache on his top lip.

"My name is Silas Bonaparte." The man offered a business card—notably to Moses, not Rock. "I am Mr Sevan's solicitor."

The other legal rep stood, the tall, hawkish man plainly as confused as the detectives. "I think you will find he is already represented."

"Get out, Mr Bonaparte," Rock said. "Now."

The little man, Silas, chuckled. "Oh, I don't think so."

He all-but glided over the floor. Rock moved to intercept him, but Moses stopped her with a gentle hand on her shoulder. Silas Bonaparte then beckoned to the frowning solicitor. When the taller man bent over, they exchanged unheard words for perhaps ten seconds. The existing solicitor paled. He gathered his papers, then exited in a hurry, speaking not another word.

Rock hadn't thought it possible, but Joshua's smug leering escalated to yet another level of slapworthiness.

"Excellent." Silas took a handkerchief, brushed

the seat Joshua's solicitor had used, then sat there himself. Hands clasped before him, he addressed Rock. "I need time to confer with my client, please. A minimum of one hour. Thank you."

11

Moses and Rock ate sandwiches in the pub opposite the station—Rock opting for steak with Moses choosing a low-fat nut fritter thing that was surprisingly tasty. Moses paid and kept the receipts, with little hope of claiming the cost, but he'd try. They chose not to discuss the probable reasons for Silas Bonaparte's presence, agreeing to roll with whatever hit them next. Joshua Sevan had nowhere to go, but something was brewing. Something they'd have to push back against, and Moses was concerned at how much Rock seemed to be up for the challenge. When they returned to the vacant office allocated to them, DCI Wearne was waiting.

She held the signed envelope. "You left this behind."

Moses made no move to accept it. "Was going

to pick it up later. Once I saw how the day panned out."

"It's panning now." She lay it flat on the desk. "Silas Bonaparte?"

"He has a firm," Rock said, having done some internet-based research on the way to the pub. "Rarely goes to court but his barristers have a better than fifty percent success rate."

"That's correct," Wearne said. "He doesn't make it to court often."

Moses pointed at the envelope. "That's his name in there?"

Wearne nodded toward the door. "You don't get to see this yet. But you're about to learn why you're here."

"Enough with these stupid games." Moses reached for the envelope, but Wearne was faster, whipping it back and holding it up—a playground bully taunting a rival. Moses stuffed his hands in his trouser pockets, not caring that much about rumpling his suit. "Okay, have it your way. We'll nail Joshua, then I'm gone—"

A knock sounded a second before Silas Bonaparte entered. He had the look of a mole without glasses but the bearing of a man projecting a force field of pure, unstoppable energy. No courtesy, no handshakes offered. He closed the door and held his briefcase in front of him. Moses thought he should be sweaty and rumpled, but his skin was dry, his clothes pressed, and his head perfectly still, almost predatory.

"Mr Bonaparte," Moses said, stepping forward. "Are we done?"

"We are." Silas moved aside, freeing the door. "We have finished our conversation and a kindly custody officer has returned my client to the interview suite. If you'd care to join us?"

"It's our decision whether we reconvene," Moses said. "I won't be strong-armed—"

"I want a quick result, Inspector," Wearne said. "I'd strongly suggest you conclude matters today."

Moses worked the tension out of himself, replying with a respectful, "Yes, ma'am."

Rock departed the room first, a frown as deep as the one Moses sensed on his own face. He followed, pausing to glance back at DCI Wearne. She waved the envelope and raised an eyebrow. Silas bade her goodbye with a shallow bow, and they all congregated back in the interview suite. Moses had already decided to adjourn the interrogation and hold Joshua as long as possible, but no matter Division 43's extrajudicial access to intelligence, they still had to go through the motions in case a not-guilty plea reached Crown Court.

Rock recommenced the formalities robotically, having agreed with Moses to assess the CCTV footage that was being gathered to piece together Joshua's and Gabriella's movements more thoroughly. They might even have the murder on film. It would meet Wearne's demand for a *quick result.*

Silas said, "My client would like to make a statement."

Moses sighed and whirled his hand. "Make it quick. We have evidence to pull in."

Joshua sat straight, staring at Moses. "I'm sorry I could not recall my movements last night. I had consumed a lot of alcohol and indulged in some narcotic use, for which I accept full responsibility if you need to charge me."

He'd been informed they'd found small quantities of marijuana and ecstasy in Ashley's flat, including a couple of tabs in Joshua's clothing. Personal use, so unlikely to raise the heckles of the Crown Prosecution Service.

"I also acted badly toward my girlfriend, Gabriella Childs. We experienced an argument during which—under the influence of alcohol and drugs—I struck her in anger. She in turn struck me several times, and bit me, drawing blood. Thank you for helping get this patched up, Detectives."

Rock made a nasal sound that was open to interpretation, which Moses read as derision.

Joshua switched to her, stumbled over his rehearsed words a moment, then coughed and returned to Moses in that forced polite tone. "At that point, I lost my temper and wanted to hurt her. I laid hands on her in a way to make her think I was strangling her. Looking at the video, I expect it hurt more than I intended, but I again accept full responsibility for that. I am glad Gabby's friend halted me before it went too far."

"You're glad she hit you with a bottle?" Rock said.

Joshua's jaw jutted, his brow low and eyes narrowed at Rock. "Yes. It helped me see I may have a substance abuse problem." He couldn't sound less sincere if he'd been winking. "After, when we had all calmed down, I apologised and my friend, Ashley Mars, called a taxi and the three of us left the high street. I have since remembered the exact destination. The Hampton estate, where Ash lives. But I did not go straight there."

Rock's hand jigged, silently tapping the desk. Moses would have preferred she didn't; it was on camera. But he couldn't move to stop her either, as that would also be captured.

"During the evening, before the argument, I came across information that might be of use to the police."

"Oh, no, we're not doing that," Rock said. "You're not getting away with this by grassing on—"

"*Constable*," Silas Bonaparte said, his voice booming in the small space. "Please do my client the courtesy of listening without presuming you know the outcome. He has no intention of trying to squirm out of a crime in exchange for information on illicit activities. He is about to provide an alibi."

Joshua's respectful manner zipped back into

smug mode. A *hmm* from Silas switched him back to what would play better in court. “I came across information that might interest the police, so I called a contact I have in CID.” Grin-time. “Someone who has accepted my tips in the past.”

Moses couldn’t help a tut. “Oh, come on, you’re telling us you’re a CI?”

“I arrived at our usual meeting place—on the edge of Hampton Park—at one-twenty-three a.m., at which point I got out of the cab with Ashley Mars. Detective Sergeant Cole Mainey was waiting with another detective, whose name I believe is Burns. I forget her rank. I’m sorry.”

Moses’s heart thumped. A pulse popped in his temple. He kept his hands still.

“But DS Mainey waved to Gabby, and the taxi left all four of us. For the next hour and a half, I explained what I’d seen, and then me and Ash went for a kebab.”

Moses seethed inside. “What did you see?”

“I don’t believe I can say. DS Mainey told me to keep it confidential for my own safety. Lots of leaks these days. He recorded it, though. You’ll be able to hear it if you have the authority to do that sort of thing.” A wink directed at Rock. “I’m sure you can talk him round. He’ll back me up, no question.”

Silas placed a hand lightly on Joshua’s arm, his mole-like features serene. “What my client means is the recording was made on a secure device which is time-stamped, and as long as you or your chief inspector has the clearance, DS Mainey will furnish you with proof of my client's whereabouts at the time of his girlfriend's unfortunate demise."

Moses stared at Joshua.

Rock exhaled, glaring at the table. In his peripheral vision, Moses saw her fists bunch then flatten, likely realising she shouldn't show that above the table.

"Now, if you'll be so kind," Silas said, "release my client immediately. He would like to grieve in private."

"Grieve?" Rock said. "Are you kidding me? He killed this girl, and you—"

Moses twisted a quarter turn in his chair, a big enough movement to cut off Rock's outburst. "We'll release your client as soon as we verify his story with the detective in question. Mainey, you say? Which station? I'll head right on over."

Driving over gave them more time to hold Joshua, and Moses predicted Division 43 could unpack the confidential informant file on Joshua Sevan. He also had no doubt that his anger at the little turd murdering his girlfriend was about to be redirected at DCI Morgana Wearne.

"Well?" Moses said, holding on Joshua.

Joshua looked at his lawyer for an answer.

"No need for that," Silas said. "DS Mainey arrived in this building shortly before we reconvened. He is waiting for you as we speak."

Rock suspended the interview. She and Moses

were up and out of their seats, pulling open the door and locking it behind them to the sound of Joshua's laughter.

They rushed over to the spare office, shouldering past local constables and even a plainclothes detective without apology. A storm raged over the pair of them, united as they barged into the office where DCI Wearne hosted another male-female pairing.

"DI Moses, DC Rock," Wearne said in a pleasant tone, "meet DS Cole Mainey and DS Clara Burns."

The newcomers were already standing. Burns was short with a weightlifter's build and close-cropped hair and a tight t-shirt and jeans, while Cole Mainey was as tall as Moses with hands like shovels and a solid girth over which his jacket would be unlikely to fasten. Mainey extended one of those meaty hands toward Moses.

"Good to meet you," the detective sergeant said. Gruff, gravelly voice. He returned the unshaken hand to clasp it before him. "Sorry about the collar. I understand the frustration. Really. I've been there myself. But he was with us during that period."

"Gabriella Childs was one of our cases," Burns added. "When we saw her with Joshua, we were concerned, but didn't expect her to be in danger."

"It's possible the gun dealers Joshua was informing on killed her as a warning." Cole Mainey gave a big, slow shrug. Addressed Wearne. "I'll have the evidence log, the recording we made, and a formal statement sent over ASAP. Once our DCS signs off on it."

Wearne smiled, slid the envelope to Moses. "Of course, Sergeants. Thanks for your time."

Mainey and Burns gave sombre nods and, dismissed, made for the door.

"Wait, I want that recording," Moses said. "The one you supposedly made last night."

Mainey paused, rounding on him, a blank expression on the surface, but Moses read it as a challenge, a dare for Moses to push him further. Like some semi-respectable mob enforcer hoping Moses might strike him. "I don't have it on me. And our superintendent needs to hear it before we release anything. Although I suppose you could appeal to the Deputy Chief Constable. Rumour has it she's really slack on data protection when it comes to confidential informants."

Moses squared up to him.

Mainey, as big as Moses but softer around the belly, accepted the prompt and mirrored the wide-shouldered stance. Aggressive without being obvious about it. As close to getting his dukes up for a fight as a copper could risk inside a station. "Or… is it the complete opposite of slack? I think maybe I mixed up being 'slack' about releasing CI evidence with 'tight as a duck's arse'." A step forward, daring Moses again. "Unless you'd like to call her up."

"That won't be necessary," Wearne said.

Burns spoke to Rock in a deadened tone, serious, like an imitation of sincerity. "I'm sorry, honestly."

Mainey disengaged with a nod, but then turned back again as if he'd forgotten his keys. "Hey, do you mind if we take the little weasel with us? We have some follow-up."

"No way," Moses said. "We need to—"

Wearne waved it off. "He's yours, DS Mainey. Take good care of him."

"Thank you, ma'am." Mainey exited behind Burns, closing the door firmly.

Moses snatched the envelope Wearne offered and ripped it open. The note inside read:

CID detectives from MisPer will provide an alibi for Joshua Sevan.

Moses scrunched up the letter and threw the ball at Wearne.

"Darren Vaughn," she said, nonplussed. Neutral. "Gurinder Singh-Bahia. Monica Argall. Tajinder Hunjan. All people who this team have given an alibi. All people who should be in jail. What you need to do is—"

"*Angel pen ffordd, diawl pen tân,*" Moses said.

"Boss said no foreign languages," Rock said, a lighter tone than was appropriate here.

Wearne translated for her. "An Angel on the road, a Devil at the fireplace."

"In other words," Moses said, "a two-faced bitch," and strode into the corridor.

Sensibly, nobody came after him as he stormed out, jumped in his car, and drove into the street, heading for home. It was a solid ten minutes until the flashing blue lights tore up the road behind him.

12

Moses hadn't been speeding. Except at first. He'd hit 58mph in the 40-zone immediately outside Lichfield station before his car's satellite navigation system pinged at him. But sirens, blue lights, and finally the vehicle itself presented his pursuer as a marked traffic car.

He pulled into the dual carriageway's next parking bay, the police vehicle zipping in behind. Regardless of whether this was the MisPer guys sending a message or a regular uni who clocked a black man in a nice motor and thought, *drug dealer*, he was in no mood to kowtow to it, so used what he had, stepping out before anyone could tell him not to. His height, his bulk, his mean-face overrode the fine clothes. At least he was out in the open with trucks, commuters, and other road users rubbernecking at the scene. He put his hands on his head for dramatic effect.

DC Rock climbed out of the driver's seat, set her face to neutral, and slammed the door.

Moses lowered his hands. Waited.

She strolled to the front and leaned back on the bonnet, legs crossed at the ankles, arms folded. She had to shout over the traffic. "If your tantrum's over, we have work to do."

"I was already a hair away from quitting," Moses replied, also loud, his accent stronger even in his own ears as his temper rose. "And I'm not gonna be persuaded to stay by hunting other coppers."

"They're criminals, Moses."

"Doesn't matter. I was tricked."

Rock scanned the asphalt before pushing to her feet and approaching Moses. "I was pissed too. I was. I mean, I didn't throw my toys out of the pram, but—"

Moses pivoted and made for his car. "I'm done."

"Wait."

"Nope."

He didn't see it, but her elbow slammed into the base of his spine. Thrown forward, he used his forearm to stop his face planting into his car, but by then Rock had already swept one of his feet aside—an action not approved by UK policing—and hoisted one of his arms up his back.

She said, "Listen for five minutes."

Moses, though, could still move the hand he

buffeted with. He needed to transfer the pain from the shoulder of his clamped arm into strength for his other. “Let. Go.”

“She told me these guys are serious.” Rock’s knee depressed the back of Moses’s thigh, pinning him harder.

Juliette Rock was tall, approaching six feet, but not close to Moses’s bulk. Equally, there was definitely strength there, but if she hadn’t taken him by surprise, he’d have been able to swat her aside. He just had to gauge how to break her hold without hurting her.

“A protection unit for criminals,” she said. “Bad guys. Not stopping at alibis. There are witnesses recanting at the last moment, so a trial collapses. Or worse, disappearing. Bad guys breaking bail and getting out of the country. Accounts of them clearing the way for large shipments coming in. They even use the pretext of missing persons crossing jurisdictional boundaries to operate over county lines, with nothing more than a courtesy call to locals to announce their activity.”

Moses moaned, shifted his weight as if complying with Rock, but squeezed his free hand millimetres under his chest. “Not my problem.”

“If they’re around, they’re helping out someone who needs them. An alibi with a certified time-and-date stamp, or accompanying them on a raid, or taking out some rival OCG by hanging child molestation or trafficking charges on them.”

"That's such garbage." Moses had his hand all the way under his chest. He lowered his elbow to complete the angle. "You think it's some shadow police force within the real one? A… what? A shadow close protection unit?"

"Why not? Shadow CPU would be a money spinner for—"

"Because, for one thing, no way they could hide it that long. People'll get suspicious. And two…" Moses muttered a children's rhyme too quietly for Rock to hear.

"Pardon? What's two?"

He repeated the words at the same volume.

Rock cocked her ear, which displaced her bodyweight. Moses thrust his free arm straight, flinging both of them back. Rock let go, releasing his other shoulder, and stumbled toward the traffic. Into the road. Moses used his aching arm to grab her by the lapel and drag her back to safety, a split-second before an articulated lorry unleashed a mad honk and its air brakes squealed to life—too late to avoid hitting the detective. Or would have been.

She landed against Moses, wide eyed and dishevelled, while the truck dropped a gear and carried on.

"Jesus." Rock gasped, checking herself over. When satisfied no part of her had departed with the angry lorry, she held up two hands and weaved around the safe side of the Lexus.

Moses followed.

She gathered her breath; in-out, quick, sharp. “What the hell did you do?”

“Don’t push me, Rock.”

Rock ran her hands through her hair. She dropped her arms, still breathing hard but with fire in her voice. “What I described, Moses. What’s their primary trait?”

“Bent coppers.” Moses shrugged, a dismissal, but he needed to work out the ache from Rock’s hold. “They’re taking back-handers. Same as a handful of other cops in every other force up and down the country. Probably all over the world. Not what I signed up for. I’m sorry, I can’t do it.”

“This isn’t only about police. Wearne gave me the bigger picture.”

“Then why isn’t she here?”

“She’s the authority figure. You’ll obviously resist her harder, because you’re such a big baby. But *I’m* still on this, and I’m staying on it.”

“Guilt trip?”

“No, I’m hoping to push your sense of justice. Like you did in Plymouth, and like you did with DCI Baines.”

A bolt struck Moses in the chest. He hadn’t heard that name spoken aloud in years. “How’d you learn about Baines?”

“Wearne said to bring him up if you got stubborn. Remind you about it.”

“What’d she say?”

Rock took several breaths, shallower, slower, the

adrenaline of almost being crushed starting to wear off. "Wearne said he… she said he tried to lead you astray. But you did the right thing in the end. She also said to hammer home the point that this division isn't only about corruption in the police."

"That's why she kept it from me. Because she knew I'd say no. But you say…" Moses put his hands in his trouser pockets, again risking the rumpling of his nice suit. "Not *just* police?"

"No. She promised me the unit looks at *all* deep-seated corruption, not only cops. It happens to be cops *this* time." Rock watched Moses, but he gave nothing away. "Your next case might be a religious institution, a high society family, a corporation."

"Why me?"

"Because…" Rock fluttered a hand. "I don't know. I guess because… like me… you'll do the right thing. Like you have before."

"What'd you do to earn that level of trust?"

"You first. Tell me about Baines."

Moses had no intention of revisiting that wound. It was still as raw, if not more-so, than the dead kid in Plymouth. "Nice try. But no thanks. I've been down that road. I'm not going there again."

He showed her his back and took his first step toward the other side of the car. Rock hurried toward him. He spun, prepared this time. She pulled up short and held out a phone. It was already dialled, already connected at the other end, the speaker function active. The time running on it said three minutes had passed.

"DCI Wearne," Moses said. "You've been listening."

"I picked up some of it over the road noise," came Wearne's voice. "But not all. Enough to know it's time for me to stop pussyfooting around. Unless you are planning to forfeit every ounce of goodwill left and are prepared to look like an insubordinate employee to any constructive dismissal tribunal, I suggest you follow my orders to the letter."

Moses chewed his own teeth. Rock remained still, phone held out to him. He said, "Ma'am? What are your orders?"

"If you want a clean record when you transfer out, you will do everything in your power to bring the killer of a twenty-three-year-old girl in, along with anyone who might protect her, no matter what their job is. Clear?"

Moses shouldn't have needed reminding about Gabby Childs. *Gabby.* Like Joshua referred to her. Like she was Moses's friend. "Fine. I'll nail this kid to the wall. The coppers, they're your problem."

"Oh, no, Detective Inspector. This is a package deal. I want the lot of them. That's why I yanked you out of the sewer you've been rotting in. That's why I gave you this opportunity. You will perform your duties to the best of your abilities, or you'll be right back in there. With the other rats."

Moses couldn't tell if she was referring to his

past, his decisions relating to Malcolm Baines and the fallout from over a decade earlier, or if she was simply saying she'd discard him like a turd. He was ready to walk and piece the rest of his life back together as best he could.

"Moses." Rock drew closer, bringing the phone with her. "How about this? We go where it takes us, no matter who is involved in a conspiracy to prevent the course of justice, or even the murder itself. They're people. Criminals. We aim for Joshua Sevan. If bent coppers go down as a result, that's their responsibility, not ours."

Moses mused over the plan. It allowed him to follow orders, and if police officers on the take got swept up in their investigation, it was on them. Their stupidity. Not Moses choosing to harass them.

"Fine, but when I'm done with that," Moses said, "I'm finished here."

Wearne said, "Your choice, of course," and hung up.

"Where now?" Rock asked.

"Time for a code 99." Moses resumed his march to the driver's door. "Follow me."

13

Like the Army, the police had its own language and hailstorm of acronyms and codes, and it was only through usage that they stuck. Even after two years, Rock hadn't mastered them all. One of the first such terms a rookie learned, though, was *Code 99*. Which translated as *tea break*.

It wasn't usually meant literally, though.

The TinPot was a quaint tea shop within what appeared to be a section of an old cattle shed, set amid a tiny grouping of shops built into former farm buildings. What Rock guessed was once the main house—a sturdy, blocky construction—played host to an oak furniture shop whose wares claimed, via a chiselled sign, to be 100% handmade. Other outbuildings had been sectioned off into smaller stores, flogging overpriced boutique clothing, local artwork, and even a shop dedicated to whisky and gin.

Moses waited at the door to the TinPot. "Neat, huh?"

"For a man operating under duress, you seem rather pleased with yourself."

Inside, the walls were exposed brick and wide windows, and trade was as slow as it appeared for the rest of the miniature retail centre. Two elderly ladies nursed a glass teapot between them overlooking the rear fields, and a woman in yoga pants and a loose sports top had a slice of cake and a cup with what looked like a built-in tea leaf strainer.

"Hey, Moses," called the punkish-looking girl at the counter. "Usual?"

"Yeah, thanks, Holly," he answered. "And whatever my colleague here wants."

Holly raised her head to assess Rock. "Frankie know you're running around town with an Amazonian?"

"Not yet. Only found out myself this morning."

"What can I get ya?" Holly asked Rock.

"Just a coffee, thanks," Rock said.

Chuckles from Moses and Holly.

"We don't do coffee," the girl said.

Rock found the board on the back wall and was dazzled by the sheer array of tea available. Chamomile, elderflower, earl gay, black leaf, mint, Turkish cream, blackcurrant fusion, even a banana leaf. "Who would drink banana flavoured tea?"

"About four regulars," Holly answered.

"Got any Tetley? PG Tips?"

"Black leaf, I reckon," Moses said. "And two slices of that orange and almond cake."

Before Rock could voice concern over the "vegan" label on the cake, Holly accepted the order and Moses led her to a dark corner with a view of the courtyard. The pastel coloured wooden chairs were marginally less comfortable than they looked, which was very.

"Okay, full disclosure," Rock said. "I had you down as a black coffee, hard liquor type."

"I gotta admit I don't say no to a bit of liquor now and again. Coffee is poison."

"Is this a punishment? Because I could shout for a vodka if that's easier."

Moses took in the shop as if seeing it for the first time. "I bring my daughter here for our daddy-daughter dates when Frankie has to work weekends. Of course, she's outgrown me using the phrase 'daddy-daughter date' but she still comes with me."

"That's nice."

"You have kids?"

"No. No husband, no boyfriend. And no wife, no girlfriend if you were wondering. Why are you being nice to me all of a sudden?"

"I've been nice all morning. Until you assaulted me, and I almost got you squished. But, heh." He wrinkled his nose. "It's done now."

"And you're okay with seeing this through?"

Moses looked a little sheepish, then Holly brought the two glass teapots—both big enough for two cups each—and presented Rock with what looked like regular tea leaves swirling within, the water darkening around the filter in the middle, and Moses with a lighter version. She offloaded a tiny milk jug, two cups in saucers, and a sugar bowl. "Enjoy."

Rock thanked her and once Holly was gone, she waited on Moses.

He said, "I'm not gonna lie, I felt crappy leaving when Joshua Sevan is walking free."

Rock wasn't sure he was being truthful, suspicious the change occurred after mention of DCI Baines. Or it could have been Wearne's order stripping him of any decision making. She played along. "Me too."

"So—evidence."

Rock hadn't checked her PAL since losing Sevan to the DS pairing, but it had bonged a couple of times. She checked it, looking over the prelims from DNA. "They haven't conclusively matched the clothes to Joshua yet—that will take time—but we are getting them rushed through at maximum. They confirm the blood on them is Gabriella's."

"He fought with her. Both took a cab to the park with a third guy—this Mars fella. Then DS Mainey steps in and learns about… what?"

"Gun deal, apparently. Still sketchy, but from what they told Wearne, they see Joshua Sevan as a *former* gang operative, who remains close to that scene. As part of his penance to his community, he occasionally helps the police with their inquiries. He gave some names and they passed them on. National Crime Agency is taking the tip seriously."

Moses poured his tea. "The alibi stands up?"

Rock poured her own. "The recording devices are CPS approved but wouldn't be used in court as direct testimony of the crime reported. They digitally encode the statement, but the time stamp is dependent on the operator setting it up correctly."

"Meaning it could be set for last night and recorded in the car straight after they left with him."

"And the time could easily be spoofed on the recording if they had something pre-prepared." Rock moved to add milk, but Moses extended fingers her way.

He said, "That might not be necessary. The milk, I mean."

"Seriously?"

"It's not normal tea. Try it."

Rock sipped the hot water. Tasted bitter. Pretty much like tea without milk, but with an undertone of something flowery. She did well not to scowl. "I'm going to add milk. Unless you want to cuff me to the chair."

"I still owe you for the arm-lock."

"I think you repaid that debt with a speeding lorry."

Moses rocked his head from side-to-side and

sipped his own milk-free infusion. He put it back down with a, "Mmm."

Rock added milk to her cup.

Moses got serious. "With Mainey and Burns claiming they met Joshua, *and* saw Gabriella leave alive and well, all the witness statements, video, and physical evidence are now circumstantial, possibly even redundant. How do we collar him?"

Rock tried the tea. Better with milk, but weaker than PG Tips or her preferred Yorkshire Tea variety. And not a patch on a decent coffee. "We need to break that down."

"How?"

"Are you testing me, Inspector?"

"Until someone tells me otherwise, or until Joshua Sevan passes the CPS threshold for prosecution, I'm going to mentor the detective constable under my care. Bouncing ideas off a colleague helps me think and the mentoring side feeds my macho ego." He sipped the tea again.

"Break the alibi," Rock said.

"How?"

"Figure out how they arranged the meet, knock holes in that."

"They're police officers. *Decorated* police officers. If they say they arranged it through something like WhatsApp, then deleted the messages, they'll be frowned upon but believed. Even an elite CrimInt division can't serve a warrant on servers abroad."

Rock pushed through the obstacles, seeing the

endgame first, working backward. "CCTV of the meet. Find out exactly where they went, and when they don't show, we prove they're lying."

"Unless they say they stuck to places without CCTV. No traffic cams, no proof. Remember—police officers will know what to say."

"Then…" Rock stared into her cup, suddenly angry at the concoction. Angry she had no choice of coffee. "Someone needs to admit what they did."

"Joshua was close this morning," Moses said. "But with this… 'shadow protection unit' in his corner, is he likely to crack?"

"You seem very certain he won't."

"I am."

"How are you so certain? How can you be so pessimistic?"

"Mainly because I've seen it happen plenty of times. Plus, it's what I'd do in their position. Use everything I know as a copper, every trick that's gone against me in the past. And this looks as tight as any I can remember. Like I said earlier—I've been down this road before. It's bumpy, and full of decent people who'll hate you for riding like Professional Standards."

Rock being relatively new to the police had never experienced a run in, and had never understood the animosity toward PSD, or their equivalents in different counties. She knew officers who refused to watch TV shows that cast such divisions as protagonists because it glamorised "the enemy."

She said, "We *can* find the chink in this armour."

"I'm really, reeeally sorry," Holly said, rushing to deliver two slices of cake with forks. "I forgot all about these." She presented Rock with hers, then Moses, virtually curtsying as she left.

Rock stuck her fork in the cake and sliced off a chunk. Popped it in her mouth, where it melted in a sweet goo before she lay the fork down. "I need an honest answer."

"Okay." Moses put his hands on the table, finger-to-finger. "Sounds serious."

"It is." As instructed, Rock had followed Moses here, pulled into the car park, but then conducted as much research as she could in the minute she didn't think would arouse suspicion. The Division 43 phones operated on 5G so there was no lag, but some information was still redacted. "DCI Baines."

Moses stabbed into his cake. Ate a chunk. "Mmm, lush, right?"

"Reading between the lines, it looks like Baines was more corrupt than anyone could prove," Rock said. "Is that the 'road' you're talking about?"

"It was eons ago," Moses said. "And another life entirely. Petty stuff. Must be, what? Fifteen? Coming up to twenty years?"

"Petty stuff? They convicted him of seventeen counts of misconduct in a public office, and one count of *murder*. Taking bribes, looking the other way, even tipping off criminals who cooperated with him. But murder too?"

"Yeah." Moses was chewing as he spoke. "All of that."

"But he corrupted other officers who were investigated but never convicted. People he'd mentored."

Moses ceased chewing. "Baines went to prison. Not me."

"No, not you. But here's my question, Moses."

With his mouth full, Moses said nothing.

"If you helped convict your own DCI on 'petty' charges, which led to them uncovering a murder, how come you're so reluctant to do the same with these guys?"

Moses swallowed. "Two reasons."

She recalled the *two reasons* from the roadside, a trick she was still embarrassed about.

"First," Moses said, "there's a lot about the Baines case that folk don't know. Stuff that'll affect people who've been legit ever since. And I can't talk about that without implicating them. Two…" He hung his head over the cake, a skewered piece on his fork. When he lifted his face to Rock's, his entire body looked deflated. "I can't go through it all again. Baines, Plymouth. Doesn't matter that they're guilty. Coppers close ranks. They make your life hell."

"Like a cult. I know. I've heard how—"

"It's more like a gang. Some of it is cultish, sure, but even with the big stuff, it's the other people who get caught up. A DI goes down for murder, racketeering, witness tampering, there's a bunch of others who'll get shafted along the way for not seeing him. They get tainted by association."

Rock understood where he was coming from. "So, they bury their heads. Don't want to know. Or actively dissuade you from taking action and sweep it under the carpet."

"I've seen corruption go unpunished. And I've seen brass cover up for their officers. With something like this shadow protection business… that's how it'll go again."

"You can't know that."

"I just want to get on with my job and let the anti-corruption units do theirs. If I can't do that here, I'll do it elsewhere, even if I have to find another profession. But all hunting fellow cops gets you is grief. Let's try to get around them instead of punching through. Concentrate on the Sevan clan. Anything else is collateral damage."

14

"Division 43 is an intelligence division set up to counter a threat that isn't clear in the literature," Rudolph Kortenberg told the MisPer team gathered in the Safe House. "From the in-person interactions with local police that Agnes and I have found, it looks like an advanced organised crime initiative. I expect they're trying to get to Kaspar through Josh. Meaning we need to make sure Cole's backup to that alibi is air-tight."

"It will be, Rudy," Cole Mainey said. "Count on it."

There were few places in the world where Barney Gray trusted they could speak openly. The Safe House was one of them. In terms of brief chats, they might converse in the open or in a noisy bar or even in their own homes, but never frankly or in minute detail. Even though they all swept each property, personal vehicle, and their workspace in CID every two weeks, it was prudent to have somewhere like this, especially since Professional Standards got so close the previous year.

Always assume they're watching you. Always assume you'll be caught.

Regular sweeps weren't enough. This house was. They'd even used it for legitimate police business when extreme circumstances dictated, refusing to enter it into their logs and blindfolding even the victims they were protecting. Only five months ago, they rescued a girl of fourteen who had taken up with a man she believed to be seventeen, a boy she loved with all her heart after a two-week romance, but who turned out to be a twenty-four-year-old baby-faced primer for a six-strong ring.

She'd believed paedophile gangs in the UK were mostly Asian men, the majority of Pakistani origin, such was the blanket media coverage, so hadn't even suspected her white, British-as-British-can-be lover might be less than he claimed. While Gray hated politically correct language and softly-softly treatment of suspects from "other" cultures, he detested even more the British press's explosions of coverage whenever brown paedophiles got exposed, yet fell silent when white, British gangs—who by far made up most groomers and abusers—were identified and arrested. This girl—*Cindy*, Gray recalled—might never have needed their protection had her perception of perverts like these not been corrupted by sensationalism and—*yes*, although he hated to admit it in an overly politically correct world—downright, blatant racism.

He partially blamed the press, but tried not to, since that meant he had to partially blame the victim for her decisions, and he would never do that. It was the abusers who were responsible, and that one of them suffered a fatal fall from the apartment they stormed to arrest him—when he "attempted to flee" as the report and witness testimony put it—caused Barney no sleepless nights, not even a sleepless minute.

Gray's MisPer team hadn't been able to smash the ring all at once and, prioritising Cindy's life and wellbeing over the thrill of arresting the gang, they handed over the reins to the Public Protection Unit who'd backed them up on freeing the girl. Afterwards, they brought her here. To the Safe House. If Gray's team felt safe here, Cindy would too. And she did. Especially after the gang's leader swan dived ten stories into the canal beneath his apartment, killing him on impact.

Weird how these memories surfaced so readily. Weird how Gray was waiting on Agnes Marsh's report. Agnes Marsh, the youngest and most recent member of their team, a new detective constable whom Gray had hand-picked as a replacement for the sacrificial lamb to the PSD investigation. She was a young constable when they'd met on Cindy's case, who should not have been present at the back door to witness the struggle on the balcony, but who'd kept her mouth shut until she approached Clara Burns and asked what they wanted her to say when the time came. She'd asked them for nothing. No favours, no money. Just told them their secret was safe. When the coroner's report was finalised, five thousand pounds in cash found its way into Agnes's possession, unprompted.

In his way, Gray supposed, he'd groomed Agnes Marsh. Tested her. Getting her to do things that would not be tolerated by an undercover from the Professional Standards Department; disposing of evidence, pressuring witnesses to alter statements, delivering to dead drops. Her background had been one of relative poverty, an absent father, and teenaged years spent dodging a formal criminal record. Perfect for his purposes.

"Now we know names, we can see who the bad guys are," Agnes said over a beer, despite it only being a few hours past noon. The group liked the ritual of mixing beers with business. "Although I keep getting anomalies from the male's name. Moses Glynn, Glynn Moses, seems interchangeable. Mostly seems to go by Moses Glynn."

"Right," Kortenberg said, the beer bottle in his hand sweating, keeping his attention as he rolled it back and forth in his palm. "His police file says Glynn Moses, but people who know him and his online presence say Moses Glynn—and there's not much beyond an active friends-and-family Facebook page, plus Twitter and Instagram accounts that he hasn't touched in sixteen months."

They were relaxing in the lounge which looked like any upper-middle-class home. Perhaps something you'd expect to be owned by a judge or politician. All creams and greys, a gilded mirror over the fireplace. There were no residential phone lines, internet or other access points that a digital warrant could tap, the windows bulletproof and coated with a resin that repelled radar microphone technology.

"What about him?" Burns asked, her beer drained. "Who is he exactly?"

"Welsh, IC3, forty-three," Agnes said. "Twenty-one years on the force. Moves around a lot. Recently suspended after a UC op he was involved with resulted in a shooting death. His statement contradicted those of the AFOs and the other witnesses, and also much of the physical evidence. There's no record of his suspension formally lifting until two days ago, then this morning he shows up at Ashley Mars' place."

Gray didn't drink alcohol but sipped a tonic water to include himself in the ritual. "Mars isn't our principle. If we need to feed him to this Division 43, we can. Is Moses vulnerable?"

"Tapped up some of my pals in the region," Cole Mainey said. "They reckon he was on the verge of quitting. Filing for damages. Lawyer wife in the upper tax bracket, tween daughter. Really dodgy past. Can you believe he was once part of *Malcolm Baines'* crew?"

"Baines?" Kortenberg said. "That wasn't part of his résumé."

Gray grew cold at the mention of Malcolm Baines. Not something he wanted to discuss in depth, but he started seeing Moses Glynn as something more than a blip in his day. He needed to be cautious. "We all know about Baines," he said slowly. "If DI Moses is part of something aimed at us, we can probe it."

"He ain't a part of Haven Maker, is he?" Mainey asked.

"I doubt it. Pretty sure we'd have heard his name before now if he was." Gray turned to Agnes Marsh. "What about the girl?"

"Hardly a girl, boss," Marsh said. "Former Army captain, fifteen years' service, joined us two years ago."

Marsh sounded tough, her voice having dropped an octave in recent weeks, belying her youthful looks. She always wore jeans and informal clothes. In part, Gray suspected, it was to compete with Burns, who never needed to *act* in any way except how she chose. But Agnes had her own qualities, however she chose to project that *toughness.*

She added, "Juliette Rock was a constable for eighteen months, pushed to detective six months ago. Straight to Force CID. One of the Major Investigations Teams."

"Fast track bitch." Burns popped the lid from another beer.

"And the rest of us have to work for our promotions." Agnes Marsh sounded understandably bitter, as most people who'd pulled themselves up from below-working-class lives would. Couldn't be easy seeing yet another privileged officer accelerating their career thanks to nothing more than quirks of fate. It left people like Agnes Marsh, of equal ability in Gray's opinion, trailing in the dust. "But screw her," she said.

"DC Rock is a dead end," Gray said. "Forget her. Leave DCI Wearne, too. Big chums with the police and crime commissioner."

"Moses?" Burns said. "Can't be a coincidence one of Baines' guys is on this. Need me to… lean on him?"

"Not yet. I think a bit of alternative pressure might work."

Cole Mainey finished his beer. "Make him understand we're on the same side."

"You think he's corruptible?" Marsh asked.

Gray placed the quarter-bottle of tonic water on one of the coffee table's coasters, the bubbles sitting uncomfortably in his stomach. "Everyone is. We just have to find a way in."

15

Late afternoon. Before schools kicked out, but after the pubs' regulars had commenced drinking in earnest. Still, the Hampton estate didn't bode well in terms of welcoming the police. A trio of school-aged children roamed on bikes that looked too small for them, observing the borrowed blue-and-yellow chequered BMW park up on Gabriella Childs' street, Moses having chosen not to bring his own car here.

"Five-oh!" came the deep-throated call of a boy whose voice had not yet fully broken.

"Go do your jobs!" came another.

"You let that bastard go!" the third added.

All from a distance, all standing on their pedals, ready to bolt if the detectives went for them.

Moses and Rock ignored the chorus and convened at the front gate of Astrid Childs' yard—a postage stamp of concrete with an empty rabbit hutch decaying against the back wall. It was a terraced house, so all the yards were identical, and Moses knew from his digital recce they all had slightly larger patches of land around the back that were designated as gardens. The door opened and DS Chloe Jackson greeted them, closing the door behind as she trotted out to check their IDs.

DS Jackson had been assigned as the Family Liaison Officer who was ostensibly there to support the bereaved relatives, the link between them and the investigation. Although Division 43 had taken charge, they'd kept her in place since she'd been embedded with the family a few days and they trusted her. Trust and communication weren't the only purposes of a FLO, though.

"Anything out of the ordinary?" Moses asked.

"Nothing we haven't seen a million times before." Jackson hadn't asked who they were. No question as to why this wasn't being handled locally. Perhaps she'd been briefed. Perhaps it was because her shift was almost over. "They didn't want us searching the place, but that was for the usual reasons."

"How much was found?" Rock asked.

"Personal use only. We had to bag it, but you know how it goes."

Moses did. The CPS would look at the seizure

and quietly file it as *not in the public interest* to prosecute. "Who's present?"

"The mother," Jackson said. "She's proper cut up. Mother's boyfriend was here until they heard you were coming. Gary Hopeland."

Rock picked up on the other occupant. "Anything on the boyfriend?"

"Nothing of interest to the investigation." Jackson shook her head. "He was angry, but sad. They were both home last night, claimed to be together. Unless they did it as a pair, they're clear. Besides, didn't you pick up that Sevan lad? He walked as usual, but—"

"The mother," Moses said. "Is she cooperative?"

"To a point. Unhappy at the detective being switched out on her."

Moses, again, knew how that went. "Thank you."

"Pigs!" came a bolder cry from the trio of non-schoolchildren. "Leave them alone."

Another: "Go find who killed her, you lazy bastards!"

Rock's hand shifted to her hip where a sidearm might once have sat, but there was nothing waiting. She sucked in a breath and turned to the little gang twenty yards away.

"I'll watch the car," Jackson said.

Rock pulled herself away and entered the yard with Moses. "Little shits. Need a good kicking to set 'em right. Get 'em back in school."

"It's not that simple with these kids," Moses said, approaching the door. "Mitching's just a symptom."

"Mitching?"

"Skipping school." Moses hadn't used the Welsh expression for truancy in years. Surprising how it had popped back to him.

"What about vandalism? Assault? General disrespect?"

"It's instilled at an early age. Almost impossible to shake."

Rock looked at him, one raised eyebrow. "Really? You think if they got some real discipline, they'd still be shouting that stuff? They wouldn't be chucking bricks at the car if we didn't leave the sarge?"

"To be continued." Moses knocked and opened the door.

Inside, the first room was a large kitchen-diner, where Moses slipped off his shoes and kicked them to the side. A courtesy he always offered and only forewent if the householder told him not to.

Astrid Childs was sat at the dining table, smoking. A near-full ashtray before her. Half a cup of tea to her left. It looked cold. Her eyes were hooded, with dark circles that dated to before news of her daughter's death reached her. The place smelled stale, like many houses where the occupants didn't work, filling their days with one narcotic or another —booze, drugs, computer games, usually accompanied by cigarettes, despite their constantly spiralling prices. Moses read true grief, restrained but nothing to snag his suspicion, yet this step was still necessary.

He introduced himself and Rock and said they were from a specialist unit who'd been assigned to Gabriella's murder.

"So, you're who they've sent," Astrid said. Her voice was slow, but DS Jackson didn't mention she'd been drinking, which she should have if it was true. "Grab a seat. Go ahead. Ask me the same questions all over again." She gestured to the chairs at the round table, straightening her back and showing no signs of inebriation. "Leave the shoes, hon."

Moses checked on Rock, who was struggling with the zip of her ankle boots. Rock nodded thanks and joined Moses at the table. They both had notebooks, although Rock asked if they could record the session, to which Astrid agreed with no more interest than she'd referred to the footwear situation. Rock started up the app that fed audio into her PAL and announced who was present.

"I'm sorry to go through this again," Moses said.

"Weird hearing a black fella speak Welsh," Astrid replied.

Moses was about to tell her he was speaking English *with a Welsh accent*, but it didn't serve much purpose. "I get that a lot. As I said, though, I'm sorry to take you through all this again."

"Me too." Astrid blew a column of smoke upward, elbow propping her on the table. "Go for it, though."

Moses led, establishing the things they already knew, while Rock played the less switched-on role, moving Astrid back and forth through the chronology. It allowed them to stay alert to any inconsistencies, the brain a remarkably creative tool when creating linear lies, but if tasked with shifting the timing around, it often faltered. Astrid didn't falter.

Two days ago, three nights, Gabby didn't return when she said she would. Since Astrid had learned Gabby's latest boyfriend was a man of ill repute—"a tosser who'd knifed someone last New Year's," as Astrid laid him out—she got worried. Yes, it was out of character for Gabby; yes, she was involved with people known to be violent; no, she always called or texted when she was staying out longer than planned. The police opened a file on her, which Astrid admitted surprised her, but they explained the "twenty-four-hour waiting period" requirement was largely a myth, especially when circumstances showed behaviour to be out of character.

During the worst forty-eight hours of her life, Astrid endured the rumours of Joshua Sevan's reputation, not only the mouthy idiot he stabbed at six minutes past midnight on New Year's Day, but several women who'd fallen at his feet, only to emerge broken and scarred. Her friend Veronica headed out with mates, checking the haunts Gabby had been posting about on Instagram and TikTok, and sent Astrid a text message that calmed her nerves no end. It would've been much harder to read before her daughter went missing, but the contents no longer mattered.

She bin high for 2 day straight. That Josh has her holed up in his flat.
Don worry, she safe. Gonna bring her back t nite.

Astrid had slept that night, her and Gary. "It was nice to have the company, looking forward to cooking a greasy fry-up once Gabby was fit to eat it." She stubbed out the cig. "Now all we could hope was the bastard gets his bollocks bit off when he's banged up. But you let him go."

Moses watched as she lit up another cigarette, accepting her anger, her disgust, channelling it into fuel inside himself. He waited an appropriate amount of time before changing the subject. "Do you have any of Gabby's belongings that the police didn't take this morning? I don't mean computers, tablets—"

Astrid snorted. "Like we can afford that."

"If there's anything, anything at all that could establish she was having problems with Joshua. Or anyone else who might have hurt her…" He left it open, something that was automatic, despite the howling knowledge they all held that Astrid was correct: They'd let the killer go.

"She was wrong from the start," Astrid said. "Wrong friends at school. Wrong boys. Wrong men later. Never thought about what she was doing. Proper pain in the arse. Figured if she put out right, gave them something other girls couldn't, Mr Right would take her away from all this. Give her the life of luxury we all reckon we're owed growing up."

"There'd been other men, then?" Rock asked softly. "Others who'd hit her, perhaps?"

Astrid shot Rock a knowing look. "If they were nice, she kicked 'em to the curb."

Moses noted Rock pull a pained expression, as if the pair had shared something. He said, "We're going to go back through every name, everyone she came into contact with. We'll dredge every bit of footage from this area. If your daughter's killer is identified, we'll do everything we can to bring him in."

Astrid sucked hard on the cig, the orange tip glowing for longer than should have been possible. She spoke as she exhaled. "Who are you trying to kid? That gangster shitweasel killed her. You got your backhander or whatever, and he's out on the street. No one's going down for what happened to Gabby. You know it, and I know it. Now, piss off the both of you. Got some friends coming around. Say goodbye to Gabby properly."

There wasn't much else to ask. She saw Moses and Rock as part of the problem, and Moses figured she had no more to add. Background was useful, though. On the way out, Moses warned DS Jackson there was company coming.

"A wake," Jackson said. "It's going to be messy."

"Hanging around?" Rock said.

"I grew up around here." Jackson twitched her head toward the empty street where the three kids had circled but were now conspicuously absent. "I can handle these things."

Jackson returned inside. Rock and Moses got back in the car.

"Still want to chance hitting up Veronica Meda?" Rock asked.

In the passenger seat, Moses clicked in the seatbelt. "Any reason you sound like you'd prefer not to?"

"More damaged goods by the sound of it. Doubt she'll be helpful. And we already have her statement."

Moses agreed in a sense, but this was their case; regardless of the side-issue of bent coppers, Gabriella deserved a result. "Might seem old fashioned to you youngsters—"

"Again, I'm thirty-two."

Moses grinned. "Youngsters. Sometimes, you need to see things for yourself. To understand everyone involved. If you can get past the surface, and see the people underneath, you'll be a better copper for it."

"Like those yobs? Who need nothing more than a hug?"

"Who lack the same building blocks you and I have. Trust is a physical thing you learn. When you're rejected by society, kids like that survive by rejecting society first. If they had shitty parents who never taught them urge control, understanding consequences, or any sort of empathy, that's how they end up. If someone like Gabby had a mum who shagged around and got through life that way, that's all she'd known. It's natural she'd be unable to form regular relationships; it's always a transaction."

Rock faced front, hands on the wheel without starting the engine, breathing through her nose.

"You disagree, Cap?"

As if realising suddenly it was okay to question him, Rock said, "You really are one of those hug-a-thug softies, aren't you?"

"Start the car." Moses kept his tone light as the engine fired, but he hated terms like *hug-a-hoodie* or whatever. "It's biology, Captain. But get me here and be very sure you absorb this. Just because I understand what goes on under the hoodie, that doesn't mean I won't punch my fist through them if my life or welfare gets threatened."

Rock's shoulders relaxed as she turned the car around, seemingly relieved her partner would not launch into a rendition of *Kumbaya* should they end up surrounded by yobs.

"There's understanding a rotten kid and there's stupid," Moses added. "Stupid means dead, no matter what they've been through. If that's put your mind at ease, let's go find ourselves a witness."

16

Agnes Marsh had been to some seedy dives in her time, usually in uniform backed up with a warrant, but the Shaggy Dog Gentleman's Lounge had to be in the top ten. Or bottom ten, depending how you slanted it.

As if modelled on the dimensions of a bus, the through-route narrowed so much that she and Clara Burns marched single file as they traversed the flesh show. Whenever a lingerie-clad waitress happened by, Marsh had to turn sideways, forcing her to view one of the booths along the side in which a variety of women danced to deafening R&B. That the place was so busy at four-thirty in the afternoon should have been a surprise, but it was not.

Marsh didn't judge, though. Judgment required her to act, and acting in these circumstances was not advisable. Even a word of encouragement in the ear of one of these girls to have more self-respect would end badly. Like too many situations, this was about surviving the day. Getting through it unscathed.

Story of my life.

At the end of the bar, she proceeded toward the STAFF ONLY door, Burns at her heels. One of the two women serving—in lingerie—called out to stop her. Marsh fired her the sternest expression in her repertoire, but it wasn't easy with freckles and naturally long-lashed blue eyes. She'd pulled her blonde hair tight, make shapeless jeans work for her, and her tops were always one size too big to give the impression she didn't give a single toss about her appearance.

Marsh flashed her warrant card. "Police."

"Warrant," said a gorilla in a tux who'd come up behind without them noticing.

The two detectives presented their IDs to him and to a second chap who sidled up. Both men were twice Agnes's size, likely steroid induced and extremely similar in appearance. Twins?

"Hey, Travis, we're here to see the big man," Burns said, voice raised over the din. She pushed into the back room, where Marsh followed her with the apes hustling to keep up.

The back room was actually a corridor, with toilets and a door closed to a staircase. For some reason, they'd installed a red bulb. The four faced off.

"He isn't available," answered Carl, the one who appeared to be in charge.

"Make him available," Burns said.

"What about lawyer?" the other asked, his accent more pronounced than the first. *Travis*, Marsh assumed, having been told Travis and Carl were Kaspar Sevan's muscle.

"He advised against this," Marsh said, hoping so much that they didn't get violent. No one except the MisPer team knew they were here; no backup if it came right down to it. "But we've no time for go-betweens."

"*If* Kaspar wants to keep his son out of prison," Burns added.

Carl retreated down the corridor, out of earshot, speaking on a lapel mic. When he returned, he held up his first finger. "*One* of you."

"He'll see us both," Burns said, moving for the staircase.

"One." Carl barricaded the way, brandishing the digit again. "The new girl. He hasn't met her yet."

Burns glanced at Marsh.

"I'll be fine," Agnes said. "Time to earn my keep."

Burns relented, and Travis led Marsh through the door at the bottom and up the metal staircase beyond into a gloomier section.

It was the first important task they had assigned her, the first time she didn't feel like she was trying to prove something to Barney, yet the first time she'd been nervous about screwing up.

Get through it. Prove yourself.

Again, story of my life.

Like much of her career. Like much of her life. Playing catch up to the big kids. While Barney Gray was dodgy as hell, this team did great work for the victims of crimes. Perhaps today he'd get off her back and accept she really was one of them.

Travis escorted her into a room straight off the landing without a door, a space yawning out of the shadow, decorated with movie posters in frames. The man himself, Kaspar Sevan, sat behind a desk, working papers with the kind of stressed out speed Marsh had seen detectives employ right before they were due to commence a period of annual leave, tying things up so no one went free on their watch. Turning his attention on the approaching pair, he looked like granite.

"This her?" he asked.

"You can address me directly," Marsh said.

Cannot show weakness. Must impress the others.

Kaspar Sevan tossed his pen on the desk and leaned back in his swivel chair. "Our facilitator friend advised against face-to-face."

True. And Marsh didn't *want* to, either.

"We don't usually meet the clients," she said. "It's easier that way. No dirt. A firewall. But in this case, we wanted to make sure you understand the level of risk we're taking."

"I paid the fee. You're not shaking me down for a tip."

"No, this is an add-on. We did what we're paid to do, but there may be more to the arrest."

It didn't take Kaspar long to see where she was going. "Me?"

"You, your op. Possibly a link going back further. We think they're going to press Joshua."

Kaspar probed the desk with one finger, then his gaze found Travis. "My son is dumb as shit. There'll be more evidence than what we've found."

Travis shuffled on his spot. "I think you might be right, Mr Sevan."

Kaspar shifted to examine the desk, as if expecting to find a hole where his finger had explored. "Maybe a spell inside will do him good. Teach him he has to be more careful. We can get it down to manslaughter."

"That won't work," Marsh said. "If they break his alibi, they'll know our people lied for him—"

Kaspar stood, chair flying back, his face red. "*That's why you're paid so well!*"

Marsh could not help stepping back, coming up against the brick wall of Travis.

"It's the risk you take in this business, honey. Especially coppers who cross the aisle." Kaspar's natural skin colour blanched back from the red, but his contorted features remained a mask of anger. "I'm prepared to let my son go to *jail* so he can come out *stronger*. You should have contingencies in place for—"

Thunk.

An object the size of a sausage landed on Kaspar's desk and bounced wetly, rolled once, and came to a halt against one of the bound files he'd been working on. Legal papers, most likely. A red stain spread on the sheaf, a puddle forming.

Kaspar scowled, redistributing the pile to investigate the item. He dropped the papers, his face draining to pale.

It was a finger.

"Like my associate explained," Clara Burns said, emerging from the gloom of the stairwell, "that doesn't work for us."

Accompanying Burns was the big man from below, a knife at his throat. He limped alongside Burns, a gash in one leg, trailing blood, and cradling one arm against his other. A wad of something that might have been a spangly G-string performed a poor job of stemming the flow from the stump where his digit was missing. Burns kicked him in the leg-wound, and he toppled to the floor with a grunt.

Carl's brother drifted away from Marsh, but Kaspar said, "I wouldn't do that."

Burns held the bloody weapon by her side as casually as someone might an umbrella—a Gerber 06 combat knife that folded into its hilt, the twin of a gift the woman had made to Agnes after their first Enhanced Pension job together. She barely glanced at Travis. "Kaspar, Kaspar, Kaspar."

She strolled to the desk and, careful to stay out

of the blood, sat on it in a pose Marsh imagined the hookers and other skanks he kept around the place might, all crossed legs and elbows in. Except Burns' short stature made her muscles expand in such a way that a casual observer might think her fat.

Kaspar held his ground, but his tough guy act dissolved as Burns placed the tip of the razor-sharp blade on his chest.

Her amused smile fluttered to life. "You are not throwing us under any bus. See, if we go down, we know how to cut deals. We know all about you, your clubs, your routes in and out of Europe. We have suppressed a *lot* of evidence, thanks to our mutual friend. No prosecution will pass up that deal."

"What do you want from me?" Kaspar managed to say, almost without a tremor.

"And not just from you." Burns twisted the blade on the man's tie, teasing a thread loose. "Other people in your line of work. How do you think they'll feel about *you…* "? She jabbed the point through the tie but stopped short of piercing his skin. "Making us reveal all we know in order to serve as little time as possible? Because yeah, we do have contingencies. Cash on standby, and papers. Plus, all that bounty you're charged with safeguarding, we can take that too. Anytime we like. But we don't want to go yet. Our pension scheme hasn't matured fully."

Marsh hadn't noticed when she moved her own hand, but she clutched the small aerosol, a travel-sized canister that looked like a lady's deodorant but actually contained an illegally potent dose of pepper spray. It wasn't the way this was supposed to go down. She'd been ready to go it alone, show she was capable. Yet she was glad to see Travis ignoring her, having pulled a first aid box from somewhere and tending to his twin.

"Moses Glynn," Burns said.

"Moses *Glynn*?" Kaspar said.

"You know the name?" Burns eased up on the pressure with the knife.

"If it is the same man who moved away from here..."

Marsh found her voice. "We need you to take care of this."

Kaspar showed both palms to Burns. She lowered the knife. Kaspar breathed again. "He was involved in the DCI Baines business a million years ago."

"We know," Burns said. "That's what worries us here."

"Rumour is, he traded old Malc for an expunged record."

"He was dirty?" Marsh said.

"Who knows?" Kaspar righted his chair but did not sit, resuming a fraction of his former confidence. "But he's tricky."

"Vulnerable?" Burns asked.

"A bribe?" Marsh said.

"I do not think he can be bought," Kaspar said,

his Eastern European accent stronger. “I heard he turned on Baines due to pressure on him.”

“A threat, then.” Marsh couldn’t read Burns—approval or annoyance, it was hard to tell.

Kaspar nodded. “I’ll need you to be there with your warrant cards. And your assurance you’ll take care of my girls if it goes bad.”

Burns hopped down, held Kaspar still with one hand, and set the blade at his throat. He swallowed but held her eye. She wiped the blood from his employee on his shirt, then folded the knife closed. “This needs to work, Big Kas. Or it won’t be a finger I remove next time.”

17

Veronica Meda shared a flat with her boyfriend, James. Not Jim or Jimmy, but James. He made that clear. He had a speckling of hairs on his chin that he stroked occasionally, indicating either a contemplative man, someone who indulged in herbal remedies in the afternoon, or a twenty-year-old knob head who took himself way too seriously. Within seconds of entering the flat a couple of miles outside the Hampton estate, Rock settled on the most likely option.

Veronica invited them through to the lounge and the four of them—Rock, Moses, James, and Veronica—settled around the musty-smelling room. It was a small place: one bedroom, lounge, kitchen, bathroom, the front door opening onto a walkway shared with others on the second floor of the low-rise development. There was no back door. The rear of the flat shared a wall with a property facing the other way, with its own front door onto its own walkway.

"Moved off that dump soon as we could afford it," Veronica said, by way of uninvited explanation. A hint of pride. "I got a job. Like, a proper one. Doesn't pay much, but me and James do okay. No tax credits, neither. Pay for this place ourselves."

"The taxpayer thanks you." Rock intended the comment to be humorous yet complementary, but the sudden chill in the room implied they had taken it as sarcasm. "What is it you do?"

"I work in a hospital," Veronica said.

Rock turned to James. Moses did too.

The long-haired man contemplated the question with a finger-and-thumb beard-stroke, blinked in slow-motion, and said, "I, too, work in the health-care profession."

They knew this already; Veronica was a health care assistant, someone who helped with patients but didn't administer treatment, while James worked as a porter. Good jobs, but Rock resisted commenting on that in case it sounded insincere or patronising.

"I'm parched," Moses said to Veronica. "Any chance of a cuppa?"

"Why address the question to her?" James asked.

Moses held himself still, his eyes moving to the other man. "Habit? She's who we're here to see."

"And a female." James placed his hand on his

chest and rose. "I shall make the beverages." He bowed his head toward Rock. "Is tea okay?"

"Do you have coffee?" Rock asked.

James made an affirmative movement with his head and crossed toward the hall.

"Why don't you go and help?" Moses said to Rock.

Rock concentrated on a neutral tone. "Pretty sure he doesn't need—"

"Please." Although it was a pleasant word, the hint of a frown gave her little choice.

Rock stood. "Because I'm a female?"

"No, because I'm a senior officer giving you an order. No milk in mine, thanks."

Rock exited, catching up to James. He seemed surprised to be joined in the kitchen as he spooned Gold Blend into a cup.

"Volunteered to help," Rock said.

He added milk to the instant granules. "No, you didn't. I heard. He gave you an order."

She noted the cheap tree where the cups were kept and added a couple to his counter beside the boiling kettle. "Did you know Gabriella?"

"Indeed. She was a troubled soul. Needed a guiding light to help her through the dark."

Rock forced herself to concentrate on the oh-so-important tea run and accepted the wooden box James slid to her. Opened the lid. Plucked out a pair of tea bags. "She made bad choices."

When he closed his eyes and swayed, then reopened his eyes as if that constituted an answer, Rock read it as *yes*.

"And Joshua Sevan was a bad choice?" she said.

"The worst." The kettle clicked to say it was ready and James poured the coffee first. "He is more troubled than Gabby was, but he also had the most agency to control his own life. He has chosen to indulge only himself, though."

"Yep, that's what we're hearing." Rock sidestepped as James added water to the two cups with tea bags. "You not joining us?"

"I only drink green tea or mint. And I just finished one. Thank you."

"Did you witness the altercation between Veronica and Joshua, and the build up?"

"I did. I filmed it. Evidence. Veronica and I both knew Gabby would not pursue her abuser through the legal system. But if we present evidence of a crime, it requires no approval from the victim to demand action against the criminal."

"You were going to hand over the footage of Joshua strangling Gabby anyway?"

"We are not afraid. What will be will be. If they hurt us in revenge, at least Veronica's friend—and many other women—would be free of one bad man."

Rock thought about that as she mashed the bag. "Veronica was willing to take the chance?"

"It was her idea."

"Did you think Joshua would kill her?"

James sagged, adding milk to one tea mug seeming to drain him of energy. "Eventually, perhaps. But we did not believe it would be that night."

"Did he know what you planned to do?" Rock asked. "Did you tell him you were going to the police?"

Again, with the pause. This one with an added chin-stroke. "Veronica said she was. After I ceased recording the crime. She said it was all they needed to set her friend free."

"How did Joshua react?"

For the first time, James's hesitation seemed real, not some manufactured hippie-lite image that he'd cultivate over time. "He laughed, Detective Rock. He said he'd show Gabby exactly how scared he was of the… quote, *pigs*. End quote."

He blinked dampness from his eyes and finished the final mug of tea.

Rock said, "You shouldn't blame yourself, James."

"I don't."

"You were right earlier. When you said Joshua would probably have killed her eventually."

James returned the milk to the fridge. Held the door open. "But if we hadn't bragged, rubbed it in his face…" He closed the door and picked up the two teas. "Let's get these to the famished pair, hmm?"

. . .

After they got Veronica and James to give fresh statements, again returning to check facts at random points in the chronology, Moses and Rock thanked the pair for the drinks and for their frankness and reassured them they'd done nothing wrong. Other than Veronica and James threatening Joshua with the video evidence, there was nothing new to add.

Outside, Rock and Moses wandered along the low-rise Housing Association path back to the road. It was not an affluent place, inserted amid a network of community buildings and sheltered housing for elderly and infirm people, but it lacked the yobbish accessories and intimidation hanging over Astrid's street. She wasn't concerned, pulling out her mobile and reviewing the autopsy's initial findings that Davina Mishkin had updated while they were inside.

"He killed her as a screw-you," Rock said.

Moses made a similar gesture to James's chin-stroke, the DI's finger following the line of hair along his jawline to meet the thumb at the end. "Sounds like it may have triggered him, yeah."

"And then the Shadow CPU comes in and he gets away with it."

"That's what we're calling them? The Shadow CPU?"

"A close protection unit operating out of the shadows of the police. Makes sense."

Moses didn't object.

"I'll get the surveillance set up," Rock said,

mind thundering ahead. "Wearne can get digital warrants on detectives Mainey and Burns, and their boss—DI Barney Gray. We'll get financial data, personal movements, investments, side-businesses. Then we pick up on Joshua Sevan, his dad... his lawyer might be a step too far—"

"And illegal," Moses said. "DCI Wearne said we stay on the white-hat side of digital surveillance. But can all that. It won't help."

"Why not?"

"Because they'll be alert for it. Especially now."

"But we can piece things together. Even if we get nothing we can use directly, it doesn't mean—"

Moses came to a halt six feet from the police car, parked in a residential spot on the roadside. "Why did I ask you to help make the drinks?"

Rock had been annoyed at first, but concluded there'd been a good reason. "To establish your authority? Even with a white-knight male feminist, you don't want to be limited by accusations of sexism."

"No, simpler than that."

Rock wasn't that bothered, so gave a lazy answer. "To separate them? See if there's any dishonesty?"

"Simpler."

Rock pressed the key fob to unlock the police car and left Moses in place. "I give up."

A wry smile poked at the corners of Moses's mouth as he climbed into the BMW. When Rock got in behind the wheel, he said, “It was so you could make sure he didn’t spit in my cuppa.”

Rock started the engine. “What makes you think I didn’t let him?”

“Keep things simple, Captain. The target is Joshua Sevan. We break the alibi in a way that the Shadow CPU doesn’t need to fight, that might be a solution that doesn’t land us in police purgatory forever.”

“So, they get away with it and we break Wearne’s orders.”

“Unless they want to confess and end up in a cell next to Joshy, Wearne can pass the file to Professional Standards. Once Joshua Sevan is behind bars, and Gray’s people can’t pretend anymore, that’s our job done. And we have nothing else to worry about.”

18

There were some days when Clara Burns was more confused than she'd like. As the sun drained away behind the school she and Agnes Marsh were watching, she tried to work out if this was turning into one of those days.

She'd always found certain situations hard, like when people were expressing themselves in a particular way but said words contrary to that and expected her to understand and—more to the point—act as if the original point was obvious. When it wasn't.

Barney had told her to keep an eye on Agnes for this reason, although Burns had to admit she wasn't the best candidate for babysitting an untested subject. Apparently, Agnes was not always being honest when she said things like, "I'm okay with that," or, "No, I'm not worried."

Burns thought Agnes handled herself as well as she could have back in the Shaggy Dog, considering she didn't have much more physicality to her than an above average constable. It was logical that Burns stepped in when she did. And the pain in Carl's face as she slashed his leg, the sheer panic as she flattened his balls into his groin, then the disbelief as she cleaved his finger, were etched into her memory and made her feel warm inside.

Sometimes, reading faces *was* fun.

"There she is," Agnes said.

From the car registered to their station, Burns and Agnes observed a girl called Eko leaving her school. Late. Some after-school club or another.

They'd logged a bogus yet plausible reason to be here in case Kaspar's stripper, an ex-con with a preposterous name, messed it up or if a teacher got suspicious.

A woman in expensive trainers, hipster jeans and a leather jacket, her frizzy hair still flashing with glitter, speed-walked to catch up with the schoolgirl.

"What sort of a name is Buttercup?" Burns asked.

"A stripper name," Agnes said.

"You don't like strippers?"

"I have no opinion on the matter." Agnes kept her eyes forward, jaw tense—a sign of dishonesty. But not the sort designed to deceive Burns; it was to deflect something Agnes herself didn't want to acknowledge.

Probably.

Burns again struggled to be sure she'd got it right. The tension might have been because Agnes disagreed with targeting the girl. Maybe her guts were chewing her from the inside out, the thought of one precious hair on Eko's perfect little head ruffled out of place.

Perhaps Agnes wasn't right for this type of work. They could cut her loose, siphon her share of the Enhanced Pension Fund to secure her silence, and ensure she knew they'd kill her if she blabbed. She needed to work on the physical side and learn to not flinch when some aspects turned personal.

Buttercup caught up to Eko, asked her the time, and while the girl checked her phone, Buttercup surreptitiously slipped a blue envelope into one of the outer pockets on her schoolbag. They couldn't hear, but Eko clearly grew sceptical about what should have sounded like an innocent question. Buttercup nodded thanks and as the stripper tootled back the way she came, Eko watched her until she crossed the road, then went on her way.

"Mission accomplished," Agnes said.

Burns read it as bravado. The detective constable was not happy. But she'd done what needed to be done. And, after all, wasn't that what the rest of their team did? All they could ever do?

It hadn't been such a bad day after all.

19

Driving through darkened streets, the lights popping on and flaring through the BMW's windscreen, Moses felt like a coward. He read in DC Rock that she concurred. Neither said so.

It was after six by the time they arrived, but Moses asked DCS Cleland, the team's supervising detective, to hang on for them. He was on a different floor to the MisPer crew—or the *Shadow CPU,* as Rock insisted on calling it.

In the 1970s concrete block of a building, they had to walk up four flights of stairs because the lift was out of order. "*Again,*" the duty officer said.

On the first flight, Rock voiced her objection once more. "We don't have to do it this way. Sir."

"Sometimes, discretion is the better part of valour," Moses said.

"Whatever that means, I doubt the person saying it knew much about valour."

"Can't go throwing tanks through every wall we come up against, Cap."

Rock sighed as they hit the second floor. "I don't want a tank. Just a chance."

"Go at them too hard, they close ranks. We lose Joshua too. All because you wanted the big win."

"And the Shadow CPU goes on to protect more killers, more criminals because you were too c—"

Moses stared hard.

Rock said, "Because you were too *cautious*."

Third floor.

Moses was sure they both knew which C-word she was going to use there. "If there's more to it, the DCS will push it up the pole. We'll get Josh. They get the Shadow CPU." He cursed inwardly. "Damn, now you've got me saying it."

Fourth floor. Neither of them breathing hard, which Moses would expect from himself, although most of his colleagues struggled.

Moses grasped the door handle without opening it. "They've been *relentlessly* careful."

"They're not invulnerable."

"Neither are you. Are you really prepared to fight off the Armenian mob *and* a corrupt police team?"

"Yes."

Moses was about to comment on the arrogance of youth but remembered she didn't consider early thirties to be "young". Instead, he released the door and said, "If we swing and miss, we stumble. Division 43 is the bad guy. *You're* the bad guy."

"*We* are."

"Yeah. Difference is, I've been there. And if we push too hard, and they push back…"

"I'll be ready."

She was set. Obviously believed they could bludgeon through.

"Stay in line with me tonight," Moses said. "That's an order."

"Yes, sir."

Once out of the stairwell, they located DCS Sidney Cleland's office, one of a series of small private rooms for senior officers within what looked to have once been a larger workspace. All the lights were out except Cleland's. The door was open, and he stepped out; must have heard them arrive.

"You're Division 43?" the detective chief superintendent said.

"We are." Moses introduced them both with a handshake.

Detective Chief Superintendent Cleland stood about five-eight and held himself with authoritative poise. His hair had aged gracefully too, remaining full and thick, the mid-fifties for Cleland being of the silver fox variety rather than the saggy spread that hit many as they advanced.

"Let's go through this, then." He showed them inside to two chairs he'd prepped. "I'm intrigued by what Division 43 can bring to the region, and even more intrigued about why you'd want to speak with me. You already received the case material in full."

"Thank you for that cooperation, sir," Moses said as he accepted the chair. A bit miffed, the DCS remained standing. Gravitas, he supposed. "We need to ask about something that I hope won't be a big deal."

Rock crossed her legs, hands clasped in her lap. Shoulders stiff. "In a massive coincidence, the team who were investigating the Gabby Childs murder has also provided the killer with an alibi."

Cleland appraised her without speaking, hooded eyes cast toward Moses. "Hardly a coincidence. That team is familiar with the landscape, investigating her disappearance. Stands to reason they would encounter persons of interest."

"What she means, sir," Moses said, "is that we took over from DI Gray, then someone under his supervision—"

"Mainey and Burns," Rock put in.

"Supplied an alibi. However, we think this alibi may be…" A lump bobbed in Moses's throat. Double-speak was never easy. "May have been an admin error in there."

Cleland remained neutral and cleared his throat. "Admin error?"

"When we get past midnight, date stamps can sometimes get mishandled. Two a.m. on the 27th can sometimes be input as the 26th because that's when the shift started, and vice versa."

"I see."

"Sir, the evidence is overwhelming," Rock said. "Joshua Sevan beat Gabriella Childs. He kicked her in the head, twice, and left her to die. As a joke—a *joke*—he left her in the pond at Hampton Park, where she'd be found quickly."

Cleland adjusted his tie and the neutral face grew strained. "Are you insinuating that one of my officers—"

"Two, actually. Sir."

Cleland addressed Moses. "Are you insinuating that *two* of my officers lied to set a murderer free? Two *decorated* officers? Two detectives with exemplary records, who've remained in their posts despite opportunities for advancement because they are so dedicated to what they do?"

Or staying in the same squad to avoid being separated, Moses thought. He pushed the suspicion away, sealing it off from his conscious brain. It wasn't the focus here. He checked his watch and tapped it. "Detective Constable Rock, can you give us the room?"

Rock glanced at his watch, then up at him. "If you don't mind me adding to the PAL that you ordered me to." Forced a smile. "Sir."

Moses had nothing to lose with Division 43. He wasn't the person they thought he was, but adding that sort of conflict to the official record—*if* she meant it—might lead to problems in court. He pressed on, his words firm and clear. "We're just sayin' here, sir, with the physical evidence we have, witness statements, and we are still gathering CCTV, if anything contradicts Mainey and Burns' account, it might lead to embarrassment if they have to explain things. It *could* be a case of a CI asking a favour, claiming he wants to get out of a lesser incident, but then… they can't erase what they did."

Cleland remained stone-faced.

"Sir, all we're asking is that your detectives check they applied the date stamp correctly. We're so close to beyond reasonable doubt that it might become academic, anyway."

"Beyond reasonable doubt?" Cleland said.

Moses didn't want to go into too much detail but had to give something. "The autopsy showed that death resulted from a blow to the head consistent with the spatter pattern on Joshua's shoes and trousers. Sir… if that physical evidence was made public, and you were seen to be backing those detectives…" Moses splayed his hands as if to say, *over to you.*

Rock snapped her head up. "Unless, sir, you'd rather we made that side of the investigation official. I mean, if you want Professional Standards reviewing every conviction—"

"That's enough, Juliette," Moses said.

She fell silent. The first time he'd used her civvy name.

Cleland chewed it over, checking one fingernail with another. He found nothing amiss and again addressed Moses. "If it's an error, and they did get the dates wrong, they'll still be in trouble."

"Sir, I've been through that kind of thing myself. We won't make it any harder than it has to be. They'll walk away with a minor misconduct rap on the knuckles."

"Then it'll be over?" Cleland said. "Joshua Sevan goes to prison, and it spares my team the embarrassment of fighting PSD over an… oversight."

Moses nodded firmly. "And I get to go back to proper policing."

Cleland gestured to the door. "I'll speak with DI Gray first thing."

"You could have told me," Rock said on the way down the stairs.

Second floor. Moses's feet lighter than on the way up, and not because of gravity.

"Told you what?" he asked.

"That you were playing him."

Moses laughed. "What makes you think that?"

First floor.

"No superintendent would go for what you pitched, Moses. You couldn't have been more obviously dodgy if you'd slipped him a grand in an envelope."

Moses halted. "What exactly do you think I did in there?"

"You proved that Cleland either knows or suspects them of wrongdoing. He's either with them or looks the other way when rumours surface."

"Because they get results," Moses said, resuming the trek. "Minor infractions are the cost of doing business in this world. And he doesn't need the embarrassment of a corruption investigation."

"Plus, we'd be fighting Cleland as well as the Shadow Unit."

Ground floor, ready to exit.

"Yeah." Moses opened the door. "But he'll clear the way for us. We nail Joshua Sevan. Let DCI Wearne decide what to do with the intel on DI Gray."

"But you were so close to doing what we're supposed to be." Rock stepped through. "We can dig into this unit and—"

"And we don't need to make an enemy of DCS Cleland."

"You want to root it out, Moses. I can tell you do."

They walked side-by-side toward the front desk.

"It's not good enough," Rock said. "And I think I know why you're acting like such a *coward*."

"Watch the tone, Constable."

"I'm off the clock, I'll say what I like." She

stopped and faced him, her coffee breath on his face. "You don't want to dig into them because you're afraid of them digging right on back. 'Been through it yourself.' That's what you said to him. I don't think you mean you've investigated other officers yourself. You've got baggage, big time, and you don't want it out there."

Moses didn't want the aggressive gesture caught on CCTV, so flexed his fingers. "I'm clean. I always was. Anything they found would be rumours and lies."

"But they'd still find it. And you're scared, Moses. Admit it. We could nail them all, but you're scared. This case is your last chance, and if you blow it by accusing other coppers of something you can't prove, you're finished."

Moses had an answer, but it wasn't something he could voice.

"First thing," Rock said, "I'll get Wearne to transfer this entire investigation to me. Joshua needs taking down for Gabby, but he isn't the real case—DI Gray and his crew are. If you're not going to do your job, at least have the guts to quit and retire." She strode away, tossing the BMW's key fob to him. "I'll get a cab back. You can explain the expenses to Wearne."

Then she was gone. Moses would have chased after her, told her she was wrong, explained *why* she was wrong, but… he'd be lying. He *was* scared. Wearne did pick him for a reason. And now he was certain what that reason was. And he wouldn't play that game.

What we're supposed to be...

He wanted an easier life, to slip back into his role as a DI, supervising others, solving cases, and going home at night to his family. Rock was correct about one thing: If he was going to achieve his aim, be the person he wished to be, he couldn't face that level of scrutiny.

It looked like tomorrow was going to be his last day on the force after all.

20

Moses never used alcohol as a crutch, but sometimes he needed to surrender to the call to shave the edge off the day. Tonight, arriving home at nine-thirty, he wound through the ground floor passage, past the lounge with the TV going, removed his shoes before progressing over the dining room's deep pile carpet and into what was originally designated a "smoking room" circa 1920, when the house was built. A similar size to an average dining room, he and Frankie had tried to rename it something more appropriate, but all sounded either too posh or too hillbilly. A "reception room" or "pre-dining area" or even "the tap room" named after the spit-and-sawdust area that British pubs used to reserve for working men completing their shifts at jobs that attracted much in the way of dirt and stains. Despite his wife forbidding smoking in their home, she and Moses and, eventually, their daughter all circled back to its original name: The Smoking Room.

Here, he went straight to the quarter-circle bar, filled a hi-ball glass with ice, cut a fresh lime and squeezed it over, then added a massive slug of rum. He took a can of Coke, but didn't crack it, instead sipping the rum almost neat. His father's big legacy passed to his son as his father passed it to him.

A Windrush migrant, his dad was proud to forge his new life in the UK, to support England in the cricket, and to swap his football allegiance to Wales when they moved to the Swansea area before Moses was born. But he never gave up his love of the Caribbean sauce. And it had its moments. Like burning away whatever had burrowed into a person's gut that they wanted to forget had ever existed.

Moses brought the glass to rest on the countertop and added the Coke.

Alcoholism was a cop cliché thanks to the commonality of real-world issues that police experienced when self-medicating this way. He'd seen others fall, get help, rise, only to fall again. Some ultimately hit the lowest depths and got sucked under. Others, those frequently with the least to lose, sprung up higher than before. Stronger.

Strength was never an issue for Moses. And only now was he questioning his bravery.

But what if…?

What if the reason they chose him for Division

43 was to back him into a corner? What if they thought he was dirty enough to delve into this Shadow Close Protection Unit and offer something others in the intelligence division and Professional Standards could not?

What if… they were hoping he'd fall in with them? Entrap a suspect as they'd attempted to before…?

"Hey."

Moses found Frankie at the door, their eleven-year-old daughter in front of her. There was more of Frankie in her than Moses, both ladies advocates of "natural" hair, frizzed into similar styles, although Frankie kept hers trimmed closer to complement her slight frame. Moses's height was virtually all he'd passed on to his daughter, Frankie's hands at the girl's elbows rather than shoulders.

"Sorry," Frankie said. "Couldn't stop her. But we need to talk."

"It's okay," Moses said, and meant it, the edge of the day melting into a blunt curve.

His daughter offered him an envelope. Powder blue. No name. They had opened it.

The drink sat uneasily in his stomach. The longer he stared at his second mystery envelope of the day, the less he wanted another sip.

"Dad, I think this is for you."

"Thanks, Eko." Moses accepted the envelope and fished out the note by the edge, a habit despite it having been handled already.

It read:

Your daughter is doing well. She might even make it into that grammar school.

"*Gotsan.*" Moses scrunched up the note, held it tight in his fist for a moment, as if squeezing it harder might make it bleed, then tossed it in the waste bin under the bar.

Frankie said, "Please don't swear like that in front of Eko."

Eko sighed and shrugged lethargically. "I've heard them in English and Welsh, Mum."

Moses strained to obey his wife's request calmly. "Why didn't you call me straight away?"

"It was seven o'clock when we read it," Eko said. "We thought you'd be home sooner."

"Why didn't *you* call when you knew you'd be late?" Frankie asked.

Moses leaned both hands on the bar, his head bowed. The note could be read one of two ways: bribe or threat. He wasn't sure which was making his head pound, which brewed the most anger.

"It's nothing," he said. "Attempted bribe."

Frankie remained a vision of concern, her brow a series of wrinkles usually absent. "You're sure? It's something to do with the new job?"

"Probably. But nothing to worry about. I'll report it in the morning." He added more rum and more Coke to the ice, figuring if he forced more down it'd ease the tension ruining his earlier buzz without getting him proper dizzy. He picked up the remote, and hit the music, Jack Johnson queued up from the last time he secluded himself in here.

Frankie met him as he rounded the bar and kissed him, arms around his neck. Stilted at first, still worried despite Moses's reassurance. Her body pressed against his and he wrapped his free hand around her waist, the kiss softening.

"Ugh, gross." Eko beat a hasty retreat.

Frankie grinned as she disengaged. Backing out, she left him with a little wave. "When you're done decompressing, I'll be waiting. Upstairs."

Moses sat in his preferred reclining chair, sipped his rum, and imagined he was anywhere but here, and that he didn't need to face the morning. Except he knew that he did, and that he had a choice to make.

Step up or back off.

One option was far more inviting than the other. But not as easy to live with.

THURSDAY

21

Rock's phone blasted her awake two minutes after seven a.m. She was hungover, but not horrendously so. There wasn't much choice the previous night, getting home late and opening a bottle of wine. The pizza she ordered took almost a whole episode of Stranger Things to arrive, and she'd started a second glass whilst munching the food, which meant the rest of the wine soon followed. She also needed to let the food settle before lying down, which led to a third episode of the nostalgia-fest of a series, and promptly fell asleep a quarter of the way through. She stirred around one a.m. and slinked off to bed without tidying, pausing only to don pyjamas before dropping off again.

She answered the phone. "Yeah."

"Rock, it's Moses."

"Morning, guv." She teased her mouth open and

closed, parched. Blinked against the wan light through the curtains.

"I'm outside. Need to talk."

Rock fumbled for a glass of water but hadn't brought one up with her last night. "Okay, one sec." She sat upright, checked herself, and figured her clean pyjamas were better than the stained robe on the back of her bedroom door. "You're outside my place? Now?"

"Yeah, I gotta do something before we head to the HQ. If you want in, you're in."

Rock left her bedroom and checked her vision before venturing downstairs. She opened the front door to where Moses had parked his Lexus behind her Prius on the single driveway. He looked fresh, like he'd stepped out of a men's grooming parlour and been dressed in a slick three-piece by some kind of butler.

"Come in." She stepped aside.

As he eased himself in, it made her house look incredibly small. Since she started living here, it had felt much bigger than necessary, plenty for a single gal moving out of the larger place she'd shared with her husband for eight years. Whenever she'd had romantic partners around, like Sam, they had filled it for a time, but it had never been cramped. Moses moving through it made her question that perception.

She directed him to the kitchen where she blearily turned on the kettle. "Coffee?"

"Tea, if you have it."

Rock reached on tiptoe and opened the cupboard above where she kept the coffee and rummaged, coming out with a battered box of Yorkshire Tea. She came back to her regular height to find Moses with his gaze averted. Realising she was in short pyjamas which had ridden up a little, she adjusted herself but said nothing and shook the box. "This okay?"

Moses looked. "That's great."

While she worked, Rock kept her back turned. "I know you're used to the gourmet stuff. I guess this is like eating a MacDonald's instead of a Byron Burger."

"It's cool. We have that brand at home. I'm not a tea snob."

"How do you like it?"

"You have hemp milk? Or oat?"

"Just cow."

He offered a reluctant smile. "I'll take it black, then."

Rock thought little of the request and delivered the drinks to the counter where she'd dumped Sam the previous morning. Moses checked the stool before sitting.

"It's sturdier than it looks," Rock said.

He settled in, sipped his tea, then gave an approving "*Mmm*, lush," and stared for so long it seemed he was waiting for her to speak. She didn't.

He said, "It's worse than we thought."

"How so?"

"They're not police officers accepting back handers for protection."

Rock was classy enough to refrain from an *I-told-you-so*. Besides, she detected a tenderness in her stomach which she was certain would turn to hunger in a few minutes. "What are they, then?"

"They're criminals, Cap. Criminals who happen to be coppers on the side. But I need to see if there's a weak spot before I'm all in. And if I'm going to include you, you have to understand how deep it goes. This morning is strictly off the books. No PAL updates, no calls to DCI Wearne, not a word to anyone. Clear?"

"Does this early morning call come with breakfast?"

"Actually, it does. If you don't mind me checking something out first, my contact owns a cafe."

"Then I'm in."

22

Theo Goodman looked and sounded like the epitome of a jolly African-Caribbean cook, all belly and net-contained grey beard and stained apron, a booming Jamaican accent completing the picture. He was jollier than the last time Moses spoke with him. Perhaps it was to do with his vegan cafe being so busy before eight a.m.

"Vegan?" Detective Constable Rock almost gagged on the word. She'd scrubbed up fast before leaving and had carried herself with real authority until the deadly notion of a plant-based breakfast seemingly shocked her to her core.

"I didn't know, I swear," Moses said.

"Thought you'd come over to the side of the angels," Theo Goodman said through the wide hatch to his kitchen, which also served as a counter for his café.

"I have," Moses assured him. "But my partner was hoping for some cooked flesh."

Theo pulled a sour face. "I can do Fake-On. Like bacon. Without the murder."

Rock frowned more deeply and with more contempt than when she was accusing Moses of cowardice yesterday. "You're a vegan?"

"Accidentally, yeah. My daughter cried for, like, three days when she learned the lamb she'd been eating was literally a lamb. A baby sheep. Then she was shocked to find chicken was actually once *a* chicken, and sausages used to go 'oink.' We basically went veggie overnight with two sneaky bacon sandwiches when she wasn't looking. Then she learned all about climate change and how farming was worse than car factories, so…" He gave a bashful shrug. "We saw the logic. She had a point. We're vegans now. And healthier for it."

"And Fake-On is…?" Rock asked.

"Truth be told, honey, I'm not too sure," Theo said. He leaned close over his counter as if sharing a secret. "No animals, though. Some sort of protein, I guess. Seeds, plants, mushed up—"

"As, umm, *lush* as it sounds, I'll wait, thanks." Rock sidestepped and swept her arm, inviting Moses to get down to business.

Moses filled Rock's spot and, once Theo dropped his smile, hit him with the question. "What do you know about people in your former line of work getting in trouble, only to go free pretty quickly? Big hitters? The kind of arrests that usually stick?"

"Maybe pre-emptive action ahead of a raid?" Rock added.

Theo dropped his head, lips tight behind his beard. While Moses could never claim to read people's reactions like some psychic, the melding of disappointment and fear in Theo's reaction did not require a supernatural talent. "And there's me thinking you came in for an avocado on toast." He lightened his tone, finger raised as if he'd surprised himself; a deflection. "Although, not all avocados are considered vegan, you know? Mass produced ones use captive bees to pollinate more rapidly, so it's animal labour. Mine, I get from a place that certifies them cruelty free. I guess they're legit, but…"

"He can't help," Rock said, repositioning to leave. "Come on, I need bacon."

"Just wait." Moses tugged her jacket sleeve and produced a small wad of cash. A couple of hundred of his own money. Kept it close, so the dozen-or-so patrons didn't see. "Let's talk in the back."

Theo eyed it and his hands went to his hips. "I don't need that."

"Still. Can we go somewhere without eyes?"

"You that desperate? *Lucas!*"

From a door to the side, which Moses had assumed led to stairs or an exit, a man emerged. A thinner, younger spitting image of the man in the apron. Part Brummie accent, laced with Jamaican. "Dad, I'm working."

"Take over." Theo opened the hatch, lifted his apron over his head and handed it to his son. Gestured to two men entering who looked like they were on their way to an office. "Take care of these two."

"Dad, I'm not—"

"I have to talk to my old friend."

For the first time, Lucas Goodman appraised Moses and Rock. "Police? Dad, you don't need to speak with them."

"Police?" came another voice from the same direction. A woman poked her head out; young, black, as pretty as the last time Moses saw her. A young lady, not a girl. When she put her hands on her hips, she conveyed the assured nature of her late mother. "Is that *Moses*?"

"The one and only." Moses opened his arms, and the girl Moses recognised as Fiona—Theo's twenty-year-old daughter—rushed into them. "You've grown."

Fiona pulled back. "You got skinny."

Moses rocked his head back and laughed.

Fiona giggled. Spotted Rock. Watched her for a moment.

"Fiona Goodman," Moses said, "this is Detective Constable Juliette Rock. Be nice."

Rock offered a nod in greeting. "Nice to meet you."

"You too," Fiona said.

Moses stood back a step, taking in both Lucas and Fiona, closer to Theo's hatch. "Fine kids, Theo." He pointed at Fiona and said to Rock, "I used to bounce this one on my lap. Chased her around with footballs." He laughed again when Fiona bashfully swiped at him. "You know, when I think about it, that was about the point I started getting broody. Talking to Frankie about having kids."

"Yeah?" Fiona said. "I'm your inspiration?"

"Something like that. Hey, you remember—"

"Dad," Lucas interrupted, "why are they here?"

Moses offered a calming hand, extended only from the elbow. "It's nothing major. I hoped to get Theo's input."

"What kind of input can he offer?" Fiona said. "He's been out longer than I can remember."

"I know. But I'd like to ask his advice. About some rumours. Maybe our history."

Lucas faced his father, weight to his right side. "You don't have to."

"I want to. This one…" Theo reached over his counter and clapped Moses on one shoulder. "We go way back. You and Fiona, too, like family. Maybe you don't remember."

"You're legit now. *We're* legit." Lucas made a point of ensuring Moses bore the brunt of the comment.

"What a beautiful morning, Simon and Paul, my friends," Theo called to the pair of newcomers who'd taken a seat and picked up a menu apiece. "Got a mean butternut squash and jerk sweet potato sausage in this morning."

Rock pulled a gagging face.

The two customers nodded appreciatively. One said, "Sounds good, Theo."

Theo answered with a booming, "My son will be with you in a moment."

Lucas spoke through gritted teeth. "Tell them, Dad. Tell them."

"Tell us what?" Rock asked.

"Yeah, tell them what?" Fiona said.

Lucas delivered a withering look, as if repeating himself to a child for the seventh time. He made sure only his family and Moses and Rock heard. "That we make more from our cafés and restaurants than we ever did when Dad was involved in that small-time dealing shit."

"Seriously?" Rock mimicked his "withered" delivery. "Vegan food is more valuable than cocaine?"

Lucas shook his head, a glance at Theo that turned into a smirk. "My Dad never made it to the big leagues. Didn't have the stomach for it."

"Lucas," Fiona hissed, hitting her brother on the arm.

"Good job I never made it, too," Theo said. "Or you and Fiona wouldn't have nothin' to inherit when I drop off this Earth. So, look after our business while the grownups talk."

Fiona returned through the door to the stairs or

wherever it led, departing with a wave. Lucas watched on as Theo led them through the kitchen.

Moses had expected an office, chairs, something, but they moved to the back of the pristine cooking area while Lucas manned the hotplate. It looked like the sort on which people fried bacon, sausages, eggs, but there were several stacks of vegan favourites nearby. Bowls for mixing, limes, lemons, avocados—with their certified natural pollination—bread, vegetable-based spreads.

"Hey, so you're craving fried pig flesh?" Theo said to Rock. "Stop by my friend Jacob's place. Four doors down. You wanna ask for a bacon sandwich like a Jamaican?"

"Why?" Rock said. "Doesn't he understand the Queen's English?"

Theo laughed and selected a can of San Miguel from the fridge. "What's this?"

"Beer."

"And what is the container around this delicious beverage?"

"A can."

"Making it…?"

"A…" Rock frowned, side-on to Theo. "A beer can?"

"Now ask for it between two slices of bread."

"May I have a… beer can sandwich?" Then she heard herself. "Oh, my god."

Theo hooted a big—yes—*jolly* laugh. "A beer-can sandwich! Bacon sandwich, yeah, honey. You speaking like the old country now!"

"Bacon sandwich. Damn it." Rock couldn't help slipping into the patois that made *bacon* sound like *beer can*. Her cheeks flushed, catching Moses's eye.

Moses laughed too. Had been holding it since Theo started his little joke. White girl talking with a comedy Jamaican accent. A white police detective, no less. Then she laughed too. Seeing the joke was more than an accent, more than a play on words; Theo wanted to embarrass her. But not too much.

"Don't worry," Moses said. "He does that with every new white person he meets. If he likes them."

Rock took the San Miguel. "Is this for me?"

"After your shift," Theo said. "Or before. No bother to me. Now…" He grew serious again, a glance at his son taking Simon-or-Paul's order through the hatch. "You talkin' about the protection racket."

"Sure," Moses said. "Let's call it that."

"Why you interested?"

"I'm not. My boss is."

Theo hooked a thumb at Rock. "She's your boss?"

"Not yet, but give it a couple of years, I reckon she'll overtake me. No, my DCI. Thinks I'm the guy to bring them down."

Theo ran a hand over his bristly head, stopping at the back of his neck. Rubbed it. "I don't know much. Just stuff I heard before… before Lucas and

Fiona saw we made plenty of money, even before we laundered our cash." He dropped his hand, addressed Rock. "A little weed here and there. Not big things. Not…" He mimed injecting himself. When Rock waved him on, he resumed. "This police force inside the police… cops for criminals, my friends used to say. They started like Malcolm, helping keep the peace."

He petered out, a glance at Rock.

"My partner knows DCI Baines is in prison for his corruption," Moses said. "But go on."

Theo paced a small circle. "You know, they are very similar. Police and criminals. In here." He tapped his head. "I think they are in the same boat. Facing odds in life you do not wish for but accept. Working-class people, mostly. Doing what they do to get by."

"I know the psychology," Rock said.

Theo ceased pacing. "For the right price and in the right circumstances. Yes, whispers of a contact. Someone whose number you pick up through referral. In person. No adverts, even on the night web."

"Dark web, Dad!" Lucas called over the hot plate sizzle of a patty that looked like meat but smelled like mushroom.

"None of that," Theo said.

"Word of mouth," Moses said. "No paper trail, no digital fingerprints."

Theo brightened, as if waking from a power nap. "Why you?"

"Why me, what?"

"Why you so eager here? Don't it sound… dangerous?"

"They put a note in my daughter's schoolbag, Theo." Moses couldn't help watching Lucas a moment, the lad with the hearing of a bat. "Worded so I could take it any which way I fancied. Bribe to get Eko into a good school, or a threat to say she'd never make it."

"Would you have done that, back in the day?" Theo asked. "If someone got too close?"

"Baines was dirty," Moses said. "Not me. I never needed to do that."

Rock looked like she wanted to speak but held herself in check.

"This is different, anyhow," Theo said. "What I hear, it ain't pocket money for underpaid, hard-workin' public servants like you two. So I'm gonna do you a favour."

"You have a name?" Rock asked.

"No, better." Theo switched his gaze between the pair. Twice each. "I'm gonna tell you nothing. The less I say, the less trouble you'll be in." To Moses, he said, "You *or* Mr Baines, neither woulda gone for a copper's family. Even if they got close."

"No. Even Baines had standards," Moses said. "And even though they've stepped over, I don't think they'd do it."

"You think it's a bluff? At that level?"

"I just need names, Theo. Someone they've used. Someone I can use to get to them."

Theo wrung a towel between his hands, a big huff accompanying his sigh.

Moses said, "I only want to chase them off, not bring trouble on me. Or you."

Theo pulled the towel he was kneading tight, then let it drop in one hand. "You riskin' your family for this."

"I'm not." Moses had worked it out last night, lying in his bed, perspiring in the dark beside his naked, sleeping wife. "I won't risk them. Which is why I need to know more before I decide whether to take them down or not. For the sake of decency, Theo… you know there's a right way and a wrong way for criminals to behave. This is wrong."

Theo nodded. "Yeah, man. I see it. But I'm outta touch. You heard Lucas. We got four restaurants. Make more money from this vegan shtick than I ever did with drugs."

"You never made it so big," Moses said. "Because you had a conscience."

"The customers we get in the late-night cafes…" Theo used a finger to close one nostril. "Yeah, there's a few who like to inhale the white stuff. There are routes, failsafes I heard of."

Rock offered a smile, a flick of her hair. Almost a flirt, but not quite. "If there's anyone keeping pet detectives on retainer, you can get a line on it? Maybe someone who's used them before?"

"As a favour," Moses pressed.

"I'll ask around. Subtle. But if I can't find anything, you leave me alone. Clear?"

"Clear."

After Theo's place, Rock refused to talk to Moses, trotting along the busy high street to Jacob's Happy Pig Café four doors down. She ordered one very well-enunciated bacon sandwich—or "cob" as it's known in the Midlands—and dug in as they trod the street back to Moses's car.

"Better finish that before we set off," Moses said.

"Not a problem." A squirt of ketchup jetted unnoticed down Rock's chin. "You think Theo will come through?"

"He was nervous."

"What he said. About you not warning off other coppers with threats... Is that something I should know about?"

She was halfway through the bap. The *cob*.

"No," Moses said. "I got tarred with Baines' brush. But I told you. I'm clean. Wearne wouldn't have me here otherwise, would she?"

Rock took a bigger bite, couldn't reply at first. "We have to give her something."

They arrived at the car, but Moses didn't deactivate the alarm. The sauce was still clinging beneath her mouth.

Rock said, "Let's get Wearne to contact DCS

Cleland. Call him off. At least prevent him from alerting the MisPer guys until you decide if your balls are big enough for this."

Clear insubordination. But she was keeping Goodman a secret from their chief, so he let it slide. She swallowed the last bit of cooked flesh and bread.

"Agreed," Moses said. "For now." He unlocked the doors. "By the way, your chin…"

23

Barney Gray was in DCS Cleland's office at eight a.m. sharp, per the senior detective's request texted last night. He'd tried to keep it breezy, two colleagues who needed a chat, but the specific time instead of "pop up when you're free" as he did for casual updates had set Barney's paranoia tingling.

"It's this alibi," Cleland explained, again in a more formal manner than the pair usually conversed. That there was no union representative or note-taker present suggested it hadn't gone as far as it could, but there was something not right; the narrowing of Cleland's eyes, the stiffness in his hands.

"Yes, sir." Gray had read the notes Cleland offered moments earlier. "My detectives were in the company of Joshua Sevan during the window estimated for the time of death. They also witnessed the victim depart Mr Sevan's drop-off point."

Cleland lowered his voice despite the closed door. "You know I didn't land this job through some raffle. Or because of who my parents were."

Boy, did Gray know it. Cleland voiced it every opportunity he got. Comprehensive school, single mother, no money, pulled himself up through uniform, with years on the streets both as detective and uni when being an out gay man was a source of much ridicule.

"I do, sir."

"You understand that *I* understand what it's like out there. You keep your CIs happy. You keep them safe. Occasionally…" Cleland's voice wobbled a touch as he seesawed his hand. "Occasionally we do favours. Small things to get them out of fines, or keep them sweet with a wife, perhaps. You understand?"

"I do." Gray needed more information before he decided whether to concede or double down. "Joshua isn't married, sir."

"No, no, I know he isn't." Cleland let the hand fall and his eyes found the desk, plainly considering how to approach this with enough subtext that Gray wouldn't take it as an accusation, even though that's what he was dancing around. Cleland sat up straight again. "I'm going to bat for you. I always do, Barney."

"You do, sir."

"Even when I probably shouldn't. But I need to know for certain there'll be no blowback. If your detectives are sure they have their dates right, that's something I'll support. However, before you answer, please have a chat with them. Consider the physical evidence. That Joshua Sevan may not walk away from this, so we may have an issue with those date stamps regardless."

Gray had indeed seen the notarised version of the evidence that Cleland had shown him, but the bulk of it—the thorough detail—was with Division 43 and that pathologist, Davina Mishkin. Inaccessible without clearance.

"Mistakes happen," Gray said. "But I'm not sure they'd confuse one night with—"

The phone on Cleland's desk rang. Cleland sighed, shot Gray an apologetic look, and picked up. "Donna, I asked for no— Oh, hello, DCI Wearne. Yes, I'm going to take care of— Okay, I see. I understand. Thank you for letting me know. If there's anything else we can—" Cleland pulled the handset from his ear. Replaced it. "That was DCI Wearne. Apparently, she can dial my phone directly."

Gray waited. Watched Cleland's thoughts manifest in a bluster that he tried to fob off as no big deal.

"That part of the investigation is done with," Cleland said. "No need to worry about admin errors. DCI Wearne has set the investigation along a different path." A subtle squint narrowed his eyes. "Looks like the error was theirs."

"Looks like it."

"Thanks for your time, Barney." Cleland rose and offered his hand to shake, and Barney stood to accept it. "I'll let you get back to work, then."

"Thank you, sir."

DI Barney Gray convened the team, all present in the squad room at his urging. Although the workspace wasn't busy yet, and the glass partitions offered a degree of privacy, they always spoke around the genuine issues, in ways they wouldn't be concerned about others overhearing.

"There will be no further investigation." Gray remained standing while the others kept their seats —acting casual, like all was normal. "They're dropping it."

"The note worked?" Agnes Marsh said.

Gray had considered that all the way down the stairs. Now, he scanned the faces of his team: Mainey as grim as ever, Burns expressionless, Kortenberg the only one showing concern. "You wonder if that's the case, Rudy?"

"From what we know about Moses so far," Kortenberg said, "it's possible. But that Rock chick? And DCI Wearne? We hadn't even got started on them. Would a unit like that drop it?"

"Cutting their losses?" Mainey suggested. "Come back at the Sevans another way?"

"I don't think they'd drop the Childs murder entirely," Burns said. "If their posh-nob intel division didn't want it and didn't trust us, they'd punt it back to another homicide squad. There's a certain… empathy when a girl gets killed like that. Emotions come into play."

"There's another possibility," Gray said. "I'm still suspicious of Moses's connection to Malcolm Baines."

Kortenberg was nodding, as if predicting Gray's concern. "What if the focus isn't the Sevan family?"

Agnes Marsh sat up sharply, regarding her teammates in turn. "You mean…?"

"Calm it down, Constable," Burns said. "There's people around."

Marsh forced herself to slump back again, waiting on the DI to speak.

"They're coming for *us*," Barney Gray said.

"That's why they called off the dogs regarding the alibi," Kortenberg added.

Mainey shook his head dismissively. "They won't find anything."

"There's nothing to find," Gray said, remembering the rule—act like they're always listening, always watching. "But they'll throw everything at us." He rapped the desk with his knuckles. "Prepare for war."

24

By midday, Rock was fried. With the rest of Division 43 out on other assignments, she and Moses had the run of the place, and spent the morning on the mundane tasks of backgrounding DI Barney Gray's missing persons team. Unlike most detectives, they had full access to sealed files and to places normally shielded by the Data Protection Act.

"But should we?" Moses had questioned.

"You should," DCI Wearne insisted. "If you need me to make it an order, I will. Use everything at your disposal."

Rock had indicated the doors at the end of the room, which her pass still didn't open. "Do we get to go in there yet?"

"The electronic surveillance section can't be disturbed." Wearne tapped Rock's computer monitor.

"Bring me everything you think so much as hints at these people slipping up. We can use the autopsy and blood patterns. But I want this bulletproof. Those detectives need taking down."

"And Gabriella Childs?" Moses said. "She's written off as collateral damage?"

"We get the Shadow Close Protection Unit," Rock replied, "we also get Joshua Sevan. It all slots into place." The opposite of what Moses wanted.

"Shadow Close Protection Unit?" Wearne said. Considered the phrase. "Okay, I like it."

Then she'd left them to it.

Rock and Moses split up the work, using powers intended for combating terrorism and major organised crime to access closed investigations, cold cases, registered confidential informants, and personnel files in a way that would blow the unions' brains out of their ears. Bum-numbing work, but without another physical lead, they needed to lay the groundwork.

Ready for a quick lunch break at their desks, they agreed to pool their knowledge afterwards. Rock took out a ham and cheese sandwich with a box of Pringles and a carton of orange juice, while Moses consumed a sushi box comprising rice parcels, peppers, and avocado, along with carrot sticks and two pieces of fruit.

"How, exactly, do you stay… this size?" Rock asked.

Moses rolled his big shoulders. "With my weedy diet?"

The way he dressed, Rock hadn't been able to determine whether he was bodybuilder big or if he was naturally that shape. He appeared to have a normal neck.

"You get the same nutrition from a plant-based diet as one with processed meat," Moses said. "Better, actually. But I don't lecture, and I'm not militant. It's just right for me. For us."

"Because your daughter cried."

"It was a trigger. Made us reconsider our choices."

"Right. Because farming is killing the planet?"

Moses lay down his chopsticks, comically small in his hands. "Do you really want to discuss this? Because I know how much people *love* being lectured by vegans."

"You know how you can tell someone's a vegan?"

"How?"

"You don't have to. Give 'em thirty seconds and *they'll* tell *you*." She smiled as if awaiting a fit of laughter from her one-man audience.

Moses retrieved his chopsticks. "I don't lecture, Cap. You brought it up."

They went through the rest of the lunch break chit-chatting. Personal stuff they hadn't touched on during the whirlwind first day. Because that was what partners did—personal stuff; her divorce shortly after leaving the Army, the recent break-up with her first proper boyfriend since the split, with Moses filling in details of his own family; wife, Frankie, a part-time barrister, daughter Eko doing well in school, sitting the 11-Plus exam soon to see if she's worthy of a grammar school place… which recalled the note slipped to her by persons unknown. He didn't sugar-coat the recent operation that saw him suspended, but recited it without emotion, as if testifying in court.

Rock almost probed the situation with DCI Baines, but figured it'd result in more denials. There was more to what Moses was saying, but could it get him booted from Division 43? Or was his involvement with a corrupt detective the main reason they had selected him?

Having cleared the food containers away, they got down to it.

"DI Gray," Moses said, "was under a Professional Standards investigation two years ago, which got dropped. DS Cole Mainey and DS Rudolph Kortenberg were interviewed as witnesses. Evidence tampering—or fitting up suspects, as it used to be known. There wasn't enough to charge him, not even as a screw up to give him a formal warning."

"Does that happen a lot?" Rock asked. "Police corruption getting covered up as if it was an error, not an intentional crime?"

"An officer accepting a disciplinary offence rather than a criminal one means no one gets fired, the brass don't get embarrassed, and PSD get a result that doesn't need dragging through court. Like us, they only have limited resources." Moses glazed over a moment, as if cautious about what he should say. "Some corruption is inevitable in this job. Whether it's looking the other way, losing a speeding ticket, or tipping off a CI about a drugs bust… Little things get tolerated when it's for a greater good."

"Should it be inevitable, though? Is it acceptable that we shrug off old clichés like 'a few bad eggs'?"

"Probably not. But let's look at this the way things are, not how they should be, okay?"

"Mainey got his own file, too," Rock said. "A paedophile killed during an arrest. Struggled, attempted to throw Burns from a balcony, but in the altercation—apparently—the suspect flung himself over rather than be arrested. Maybe he thought ten stories into a canal would end like the movies—swimming away without a mark on him."

"Murder is a hell of a step up from making speeding fines disappear. How'd Mainey walk?"

"Witnesses. Including one Constable Agnes Marsh."

"Same Agnes Marsh who failed her sergeant's exam? The newest member of DI Gray's team?"

"Correct." Rock had taken Marsh as one of her research subjects. "She's clean, though. No suspicious incidents, although she's only been with them six months. Same with DS Burns. She's the only one who's escaped any trouble."

"DS Kortenberg was accused of hacking several witness accounts," Moses said. "Police files, as well as their social media, which he—allegedly—used to post a couple of compromising photos. Oddly, those witnesses backed off their complaints, so PSD dropped it. He's got a background in computer sciences. Degree in criminology, masters in forensics. He's the brains of the operation."

"And Mainey is the brawn?" Rock said. "What does that make Burns?"

"Makes her careful. And Gray is the leader, keeping it all together. PSD went at him and missed, then monitored the group. Tried for Mainey with the dead paedo, but a clean officer, Marsh, testified for him—a bribe to make her DC?"

"Timing fits."

"Kortenberg looked at Gray before him, but if the accused copper is better, cleverer than the PSD goons chasing him, it'd never end well."

"So they're on Professional Standards' radar. Beaten them every time?"

Moses's face went blank, turning to his screen. Typing. "Doesn't have to be a current member of the team."

"What are you looking at?"

"Dismissals, disciplinaries, internal inquiries. Anything with DI Gray's name attached, but no fault attributed to him..."

Moses scanned his screen for so long that Rock switched position to behind the DI.

He pointed. "Okay, here. This guy, Ratan Walar. DI at the time. Gray was above him in the pecking order, but they were both inspectors. That was over two years ago. Disciplinary. Not a complaint by the public. Looks like he screwed up something that cost a conviction. Botched chain of evidence. Ended with a demotion to sergeant."

Rock was reading faster than Moses. "DI Gray supported the action, didn't fight it. We should go to PSD. Get more."

"Why?"

"If they're investigating these guys, they might have more we can use. Stuff they can't admit as evidence."

Moses pushed the keyboard away. "If PSD are already on the case, then we can't be seen collaborating with them."

"But Theo Goodman is fine?"

Moses checked Wearne's office was closed, lowered his voice. "If PSD have heard of this, they're investigating the team already."

"It's our case, Moses. And I'm under the impression that Wearne can bypass PSD, get their investigation nixed."

"We can't be seen collaborating with them," Moses said again. "If we do, and we need cooperation down the line for something else?" He clapped his hands once. "Boom. Gone."

"Fine, you want to go in circles here? Then let's talk about Theo Goodman." She also checked on the office, kept her tone low as she perched on Moses's desk. "Maybe you see corruption as inevitable because you're a part of it. Willing to compromise with drug dealers like that."

"He's not a drug dealer."

"No, but he *was*. And whether you were involved with Baines' protection racket, you're not going to deny looking the other way for him, are you? Because that's still corruption. No matter how nice a guy is."

Moses pinched his chin, rustling the bristles of his sculpted beard. Thinking. "If the Shadow CPU has evaded PSD for this long, they'll keep on doing so."

"If you don't want to go through them directly, we won't. But we could make use of their background, even if it's unofficial." Rock pointed at the computer. "Maybe Walar was just a crappy cop, not as compromised as the others, but there has to be more than what's on file."

"It's my way," Moses said. "My case. You're still the junior detective, so I get the final say on tactics."

Rock spun what they knew so far through her mind, checked off the points they could pull on later, even if she had to go to Wearne directly. One of her biggest frustrations with life outside the Army was the civilian instinct to go against superior officers, yet it had taken her two short years to go full circle; questioning Moses, insulting him, planning to go over his head.

She said, "I can live with that. If we're going to handle it on our own, and I'm under no illusion this is as much your ego as concern for our reputation, then we need everything tightened up. Including the note from Eko's bag."

25

While Rock thought she'd done okay with her Army salary, partial pension, and settlement from the divorce, Moses's house was far grander than her own two-and-a-half-bedroom new-build semi. This place boasted a drive big enough for three or maybe four cars, a patch of grass large enough to call a front garden, and a palatial aspect to the smooth, white-painted, three floors before her. There were even miniature columns at the entrance.

Inside, the hall was wide with walnut floors and sedate colours throughout.

Moses must have spotted her impressed expression, as he seemed a little embarrassed. "My wife is part-time these days, but she's a partner. She founded the firm."

Was that his ego twisting and turning, or was he

worried Rock would see the wealth and question his honesty?

In his wake, Rock passed into the kitchen where an attractive middle-aged woman was gathering bread onto a tray alongside some bottled beer and cider.

Moses said, "My wife, Frankie. Frankie, this is Juliette Rock."

Frankie had a wide smile and an easy manner. Her classical hourglass figure wouldn't grace a catwalk in the modern world, but she'd have given the beauties of the sixties and seventies some healthy competition. Juliette bent at the waist to reciprocate the hug that came her way.

"Lovely house you have, Mrs Glynn," Rock said.

To which Moses's mouth fell open in a silent "no" and Frankie's hand found her hip, her eyes widened, and her own mouth formed a crescent with no humour to it; fake shock. It turned into an annoyed glare aimed at Moses.

Rock suddenly wished she was somewhere else. "Did I say something… wrong?"

Frankie melted back into pleasantness that had greeted Rock. "No, Juliette, you didn't. But my husband is still playing silly buggers with that name of his."

Moses reached out a hand but retracted it. "Hey, it's with good reason—"

Frankie cut him off with a brief glance. "His parents, Mr and Mrs *Moses*, moved to Wales. They had a gorgeous bouncing baby boy and wanted a local name. They chose Glynn. Glynn is a Christian name in Wales. Glynn Moses. Not Moses Glynn."

Rock worked back to remember his warrant card. "It wasn't a mix up by the police in the printing?"

"That's what he's selling you?" With a tut, Frankie picked up a tray and made her way to the open patio door leading to the garden. "Ask him why. That's always good for a laugh." She stepped through.

"Why?" Rock said, a grin flickering. Unsure if she should be concerned about the lie.

Moses huffed and shrugged. "It's a long story."

Frankie called back from outside. "It's not a long story. Tell her."

Rock leaned on the counter, head cocked. "Well?"

"Sorry, Cap, my wife talks like a peppermill. Frankie, we're here to talk shop first." Moses shook off his jacket and beckoned Rock to follow him.

They passed into a dining room fit for an ambassador's reception (probably) and then to a nook marked *The Smoking Room*. It did not smell of smoke, nor even booze, although there was a bar in one corner, a big TV on the wall, and a few chairs arranged—Rock supposed—for conversation. Like a miniature pub. Moses went to the bin in the corner and pulled out the screwed-up note. Passed it to Rock.

Your daughter is doing well. She might even make it into that grammar school.

She agreed it could be read any which way and dropped it into an evidence bag. Sealed it. Not that it'd do much good, having passed from the person who left it to Eko, then Frankie, Moses, and now Rock. Anyone could have written it, and it was proof of nothing. But it might help as a tiny piece in a larger jigsaw.

Back in the kitchen, a girl, taller than the ten-year-old she'd been expecting, was on her way outside, calling, "Oh, barbecue, cool, what's the occasion?"

"Eko," Moses said.

The girl, exceeding five feet already, had her mother's pleasant smile. "You're Juliette? Wow, Mum is gonna be bummed."

"*Eko*." Moses's tone carried a fatherly warning.

"Sorry. But I think we're almost ready."

"For what?" Rock asked.

"Dinner."

"But I'm not staying, I—"

"Of course you are. That's why Dad brought you by, isn't it?"

Rock held up the note. "Just collecting this."

Again, Moses's lips parted in a silent denial.

"Okay," Rock said, "we have to work on our communication. When a bit of warning is needed, speak. It's called conversation." Rock noted Eko's hand to her mouth, giggling behind it. "You want me to pretend you're not a jackass about your name, you need to say so. You want to hide this as evidence, you need to let me know the play. If you want to—"

"What's that?" Frankie asked, returning inside brandishing a long-handled spatula.

Rock and Moses held their tongues. Moses again huffed with a big exhalation, his shoulders rising and falling as he showed Frankie and Eko his palms—an open gesture, but one doomed to failure.

Rock slipped the bag into her pocket. "Okay, guv, I'll leave you to sort this." She made for the exit.

"Where are you going?" Frankie said. "Dinner's nearly ready."

Rock's chest felt empty all of a sudden. "Home?" Which was a lie. She was going to trail the forty-five minutes back to Division 43, log the note, then go home, which was the opposite direction to Moses's place.

"Oh, I don't think so. We're going full Lethal Weapon on this one. Come on, Riggs. Eat."

Rock appealed to Moses for help, but he shook his head and gestured to the patio. Fearing what might await her on a vegan barbecue, she obeyed out of politeness.

Moses took the spatula from his wife and joined her in the cool evening of a garden with a green, tidy lawn with a channel of wildflowers down one side and an extensive vegetable patch on the other, ending with an allotment-sized square at the end along with a shed and greenhouse. She couldn't help saying it out-loud: "Nice."

The barbecue itself was a gas model, which Rock had always considered pointless—coals were the way to cook outside, otherwise you may as well grill everything the conventional way and carry it to the garden to dine. She said nothing, though; it was the least of her worries.

"What is that?" She poked at a sausage that looked orange.

"I'm not gonna tell you." Moses had donned an apron and took up the cooking tools. "You'll try it. If you don't like it, you can leave it."

"Sounds like your philosophy for most things."

"I just know the length of my horns, is all." Moses's smile wasn't warm, likely for the benefit of the other females in case they came out. "The way I see it, if I'm not comfortable in the job I'm doing, I'm the wrong person for that job. It don't benefit the taxpayer, or the community, to have me going through the motions."

"And you're doing that because, what?" She

patted her pocket containing the note. "Corruption is always inevitable?"

"Some, sure. Technically. But not all corruption is bad." He turned the sausage-shaped things on the grill and checked the progress on the burger-shaped things.

"Seriously? That's what you're going with?"

Moses turned a flat object that looked somewhat like a beef burger. "When I was a snot-nosed detective constable—"

"Like me?"

"Even snottier." He smiled, and she smiled back. Then he went back to the sausage-like things. "I'd arrested a rapist. My DI was distracted because the victim was a prostitute. Didn't give it priority."

"He still with the force?"

"*She* is, yes, but much more twenty-first century these days. But my point is, I messed up a technicality. Evidence handling went by way of someone who didn't sign the right sheet. I shouldn't have done it, and my DI should have spotted the error. But before the suspect's lawyer could pick up on it, the lawyer's legal secretary pulled me to one side. This hot piece…" He mimed either the shape of the woman's buttocks or her breasts; Rock wasn't sure and honestly wished he hadn't. "She pulls me to one side. And I'm a hot piece, too, and this is the nineties, girl power and all that, so I'm thinking she wants to ask me out. I'm ready to give her the 'alright or wha?' treatment, y'know, turn on the charm, but I know I gotta say no 'cause of conflict of interest. Instead, she gives me the anecdote. A story. From a different case. She described, in detail, how some other DC had made the exact same mistake I had. She said it with a wink, not literally, but I had enough about me to see the similarity, take the hint and, well…"

Rock deadpanned him. "You faked the chain of evidence log."

"And a rapist went to prison."

"A lawyer's employee does something that'd get her struck off, you do something that'd get you fired and probably charged, a man goes to prison, and all's well in the world."

Moses switched his tool to tongs and squeezed the orange sausage-ish object. "The guy is still in prison. And I ain't ever regretted what I did."

"What happened to the lawyer's assistant?"

Frankie wound one arm around Moses's waist and handed him a bottle of fruit-laced cider with the other. "She became a lawyer herself and married the sharpest, *hottest* young detective on the force…"

Awkward wasn't the word.

"He still hasn't told me about his name," Rock said.

"Like I was tellin' you, it's a long story," Moses said.

Eko joined them, carrying a bottled beer in one hand, cider in the other, neither open. "It isn't a long story at all. Juliette, can you have a drink if you're driving?"

"One." Rock accepted the San Miguel. Read the label. "This okay for you guys?"

"Lots of stuff is accidentally vegan," Moses said.

Eko passed the cider to Frankie. "You're a meat eater?"

Rock used the bottle opener on the barbecue to remove the lid. "Afraid so."

"It's okay. None of us will be one day." Eko checked on her dad's cooking and selected a hot dog bun. "That one's ready."

Rock didn't want the philosophy hanging over them, so offered, "It's admirable. Especially your generation. Really fighting for the environment."

Eko carried her sausage-alike in the bun and added sweet chilli sauce, presenting it to Rock. "*And* it's cruel."

Rock reminded herself she was a guest, so she refrained from pulling a face and replied as politely as she could. "Farming is cruel? In Britain? I don't think so."

"How do you feel about fox hunting, Juliette?"

"Eko," Moses said. "We don't lecture."

"I'm not, Dad. She brought it up. I'm curious about fox hunting."

Rock could smell the sausage-shaped plant, and it didn't make her want to vomit. "I… don't like fox hunting."

"Why not?"

"Ripping apart an animal for fun, it's—"

"Wrong? Inhumane?"

"It's not the same thing as farmed meat, Eko." Rock glanced at the parents for approval to continue. Neither stepped in. "We have laws. We treat farm animals well."

"You're happy to ban fox hunting because... Why? Killing an animal for pleasure is wrong?"

"Yes."

"Do humans need meat to survive?"

"I do." Rock offered a casual, open expression.

Moses held the cider towards his daughter—*this is her thing.*

"Factually?" Eko went on? Not unpleasant or petulant, but firm. "You *need* it? You'd *die* without it?"

"Fine, no," Rock conceded. "I don't *need* meat to survive."

"Then you're eating meat for pleasure. Killing animals. For pleasure. No matter how comfortable they are while they're alive, it's the same thing."

"It's not the same—"

"Isn't a fox enjoying a cushy life until the hounds come along to rip it apart for the amusement of people in red coats blowing a horn?"

"Fine, I'm a sociopath. Can we talk about something else?" Rock bit into the end of her sausage-thing and her mouth filled with flavour. The sauce wasn't too hot, although the substance was looser than meat. Not bad, though.

"Are we in danger?" Eko asked.

Moses swallowed and Frankie disengaged. Rock turned her body, taking another bite.

"If I believed you were, we wouldn't be hanging around here," Moses said. "But we're taking the note as a precaution."

"*The* precaution?" Frankie said.

"We're not at *the* precaution stage yet."

Didn't take a genius to work out "*the* precaution" was a code for what to do if the family was in danger. Better she didn't know about it.

"A precaution against what?" Eko asked.

"I think we need to trust your father," Frankie said.

Moses took a long pull from the bottle. Rock chose not to speak. This was his family.

He lowered the bottle. "It's *a* precaution. Nothing more." To his credit, Moses then went through all he could without naming anyone or going into graphic detail. He wasn't exactly *honest* with them, though, saying the same things he'd said to Rock, with which Rock disagreed, namely that he believed the note to be bluster, that "these people" don't go after the families of police officers. He insisted the group sticking their heads up that high would get them taken off.

It was his choice to say that. Rock would have made a different call.

After, they ate in earnest. Eko didn't seem put out by their exchange and happily listed the ingredients of each foodstuff. It wasn't so great that Rock would have turned down a pork sausage or a bona fide hamburger, but the meal went quickly, and conversation switched to Rock's time with Moses, her career, even her hair, which she had long considered her best feature. Frankie poked fun at her "peacock" of a husband for dressing and grooming so fine when his new partner was a flame-haired "Amazon warrior" as a café waitress had called her, and Moses made mention of Frankie's "superior fuller ass" which earned him a playful slap from his wife and a gagging sound from Eko.

Soon, it was time to go. Rock still intended to log the note on the way, but it was later than planned.

At the door, Rock got the sense that Moses's three ciders to her single beer and a cup of coffee had left him relaxed, a little buzzing.

"I'll find out eventually," she said.

"About what?"

"The name. Why you switched it."

"It's not important." Moses moved to close the door behind Rock.

But then Frankie joined them. Two ciders. A bit buzzy too. "He's embarrassed by it."

Moses bowed his head. "Not now."

Rock waited, addressed Frankie. "Go on. If we're going to be partners…"

"It *sounds* cooler," Frankie said.

"Thanks." Moses tried again to close the door.

Rock stopped it. "Cooler?"

"My peacock of a husband," Frankie said, "prefers the way it sounds. 'Moses Glynn' sounds *cooler* than 'Glynn Moses'. Moses is a cooler name for a cop than Glynn."

Rock looked Moses up and down: the expensive suit, the suave shirt, impeccable hair on both his face and head. "Image is that important, is it?"

"I like what I like," Moses said.

Frankie's grin became a laugh. "Goodnight, Juliette. See you again soon."

She closed the door, and Rock made for her car. Within seconds, Moses had caught her up, tiptoeing as if Frankie wouldn't know where he was.

"I mean it," he said to her, any sign of inebriation vanished. "I know it looks like I'm playing loose, but I swear, everything I do? I do it for them."

"Even the dodgy stuff?"

"Everything."

"And if it loses you your job, or gets you hurt? Or hurts them?"

"If I didn't think it was the right thing, I wouldn't do it. Believe that, if nothing else. I won't risk my family. Not for anything."

Rock did believe him, although didn't all criminals think they were doing the right thing in the heat of the moment?

"Okay," she said.

Driving off the property, Rock wondered if she'd made a mistake in coming here. If Moses turned out to be dirty, if she had to go behind his back for any reason, would she have the strength to tear that all apart? She hoped she would. For now, she'd have to play it by ear, and gamble on there being nothing in Moses's past that would jeopardise the assignment, otherwise she'd never prove herself worthy to DCI Wearne.

FRIDAY

26

Early mornings didn't agree with Rock, something she thought she'd left behind in the regimented barracks and dusty camps of Abroad Someplace, and latterly the shift work as a uniformed constable, but if she was going to be partnered with DI Moses for the foreseeable future, it looked like she'd have to get used to it all over again.

He'd texted at six a.m. to say he had a name and wanted to meet up with Theo at eight, but Juliette put him off until nine. Not because she was lazy, but because she already had an eight-a.m. appointment in Force CID headquarters. Namely, the Professional Standards Department.

Okay, it wasn't an appointment, exactly, but she'd used her Division 43 access to check the names of those involved in the attempted disciplinary proceedings against DI Gray's team and Gray himself. She then found that, like most police divisions, PSD had gone computerised to keep detailed headcount, overtime, and working time directive records, meaning she could see the shifts of her colleagues as scheduled across all forces under Division 43's purview.

DCI Clinton Flood headed up a team of four who'd delved into the mess left by Barney Gray's rescue of brother-sister twins whom the father, Harold Minsk, was attempting to smuggle to Ukraine, a country the twins had never even visited, but where he'd been deported thanks to his preference to burgle his way to riches instead of working a regular job. Essentially, DS Cole Mainey had allegedly arranged the deletion of CCTV footage that showed him entering the workplace of one Yanick Colgrave, the same Yanick Colgrave who retracted his story of police brutality during the arrest of Harold Minsk a few hours after the visit.

PSD occupied an isolated area of the third floor, accessible only to those with special permission. And guess what? Rock's pass thunked open the locks, and she waltzed straight in. Striding through as if she belonged, she found Clinton Flood was a DCI without an office, his own superintendent reserving that privilege for a glass cubicle almost identical to but smaller than DCI Wearne's. He was ensconced within a square horseshoe of a workstation at the head of the room, while the other desks were L-shapes, all but one of them empty. Close to the exit, a woman used that one—around Rock's age with light brown skin, black hair bound in a tight ponytail, and a simple white blouse, she watched Rock approach DCI Flood, but the woman soon vanished from Rock's peripheral vision.

Flood rose to his feet. "Can I help you?" White, late forties, possibly early fifties, head perfectly smooth but for a wild shock of hair clinging to life support in a half-circle from one ear round the back to the other; a similar pattern to Silas Bonaparte's thatch, but while the lawyer's pate played host to a manicured lawn, Flood's last strip of hair looked like a meadow of wildflowers. He was heavyset, not slobbishly fat, just what happened to men of a certain age.

"Detective Constable Rock. Division 43." She presented her ID, which he checked studiously.

"I've heard of that. Intelligence, right?" He handed back the ID.

"Need to make a call to verify?"

"Depends what you need to know."

"Detective Sergeant Cole Mainey. Detective Sergeant Rudolph Kortenberg. Detective Inspector Barney Gray. DS Burns too if you have anything on her, but I didn't see an official ticket in her name."

Flood studied Rock as he had her warrant card. "Yeah, I'll make a call."

As Rock took a seat before his desk, Flood used the phone without masking his conversation, presumably with his absent DCS, asking what he was allowed to say and what he couldn't. Nodding. *Hmm*-ing. Nodding some more. Thanking his boss for their time.

"Okay," Flood said. "I can talk to you. I will require warrants for any materials to be copied or removed."

"I only need background for now." Rock opened her PAL recording app and announced the presence of herself and Flood, but he waved a hand and slashed it across his neck. She switched off the app and showed him it was dormant. "Problem?"

DCI Flood laced his hands in front of him on the desktop, as if cupping a small bird. "In my professional opinion, Detective Constable, a voice recording constitutes material being removed. I'd rather keep this above board."

"This is an active investigation, sir—"

"Look around."

She did, catching the eye of the woman in the corner before returning to Flood. She kept her face blank.

"This is Professional Standards," Flood said, eyes deepening, either sinking into the bags beneath them or the bags themselves expanded. "We have to be whiter than white. If this makes it out and the recording isn't backed up with an official order for me to reveal the facts of a particular case, we might compromise not only this, but several ongoing investigations."

Legalese. Blocking. Excuses.

Flood's hands tightened, crushing the bird in Rock's imagination. She wondered what Moses would make of the change in demeanour. Was his earlier breeziness the act, or this assertiveness?

"That's fine, sir." She put the phone away, but not before thumbing the record button, the bottom end sticking up. She'd destroy it later if Wearne concurred with Flood.

If Wearne concurred...

Only two years earlier, Rock wouldn't have dreamed of disobeying an order from a senior officer, no matter how arse-headed the order may have proved.

She shoved that notion aside, concentrated on where she was, not where she'd come from. "Can you outline your conclusions regarding DI Barney Gray's team?"

Flood's hands separated, palms up. "There's not much to say. I mean, we had them on our radar after their first blip resulted in DI Ratan Walar's demotion, but DI Gray was very cooperative in that matter. Others... not so much."

Again, the animosity toward PSD made little sense. Why be upset if you had nothing to hide?

"Which other matters?" Rock asked. "Cole Mainey?"

Flood leaned in before cupping the bird again. "Cole Mainey, yes. We were concerned about him, about a withdrawn statement, which resulted in a complaint from a kidnapping suspect, and—which made us take notice—the kidnapping victims' mother. She didn't make the complaint, but when asked about it, she called Mainey a hero. Wanted to thank him and… DS Burns, I think, who brought her kids home. Said… I can't remember exactly, so I'm paraphrasing. With a warrant, I could…" Open hands, fingers spread.

"Paraphrasing is fine, sir."

"She said she wished DS Mainey had given Yanick a proper thrashing instead of just roughing him up."

"What did you make of that?"

The cupped hands returned, Flood's gaze finding them, then flattened them to the desk. He met Rock's eye. "There was a tussle, and perhaps DS Mainey imposed himself strongly, but Yanick Colgrave retracted his version of events whereby he was attacked. He admitted he tried to flee, but when Mainey blocked his way, he pushed the man to the side. In reaching for Yanick, Mainey inadvertently clotheslined him, and the suspect fell, striking his head. He slipped as he tried to get up, breaking his nose and rupturing his eye socket."

Rock pictured a Keystone Cops scene, or something out of a Carry On movie. "You believed that?"

Flood's shoulders slumped. "There was no evidence to proceed further. And with the complainant admitting dishonesty, then backing up DS Mainey's and DS Burns' version of events, there was little to do. DI Gray emphasised Mainey's exemplary record."

"And Kortenberg? Gray himself?"

DCI Flood adjusted a stapler so it sat perpendicular to a pen. "My instruction this morning is to cooperate to the point where I'm comfortable volunteering information. Beyond that, I should ask for official paperwork."

Rock never flirted intentionally, not even when it was advantageous. It was demeaning. That didn't mean she couldn't soften her tone and play the innocent. "My boss is riding me for this. If you missed out on them, you've got to let us try."

"I really don't, Detective *Constable*." His face hardened as he stood. "I'll be happy to give you whatever else you need on production of the correct paperwork."

The conversation was over, and Rock couldn't push any harder; she wasn't sure how much sway Division 43 had, but she doubted Wearne would encourage insubordination to the degree Rock was considering. "Thank you for your time, sir."

Rock went through the usual ritual of handshakes and painted-on smiles, before departing through the now-empty room. She scanned herself out of PSD and made for the exit, preparing a text to give Moses her ETA, all whilst rehearsing what she'd say about DCI Flood. Moses would be pissed. But since Moses was dancing around the issue in a way she found confusing—and more than a little suspicious, if she was honest with herself—she was absolutely right to pursue this angle.

Again, she had to chase that unease away, ignoring her supervisor's instruction. But having emerged from a semi-successful conversation, she wondered if she'd have had an easier time toward the end of her military career had she acted closer to this way than submissive and accepting the wrongs of her superiors. And she'd learned more than Flood had said, that—

"Hi."

Rock looked up from her phone to find the Asian woman from PSD slinking out of the ladies' room. The word *slinking* seemed appropriate because the woman glanced up and down, before twitching her head toward the toilets and disappeared back inside. Rock followed.

The bathroom was empty, the four stalls wide open.

"Who are you?"

"DS Hopkins," the woman said. "Reeva Hopkins."

"You were one of the investigating officers on—"

Reeva Hopkins slapped Rock hard across the face. Rock barely moved, but the blow stung. She set her feet and prepared to retaliate, but Hopkins held a finger to her lips and widened her eyes. They were wet, panicked.

"I won't name names." Hopkins backed away, the finger trembling.

"What the hell are you doing?"

"Sorry." Hopkins lowered her hands. "Don't push him. Please."

"Why not?"

"Because he'll help you in the end. And that'll finish him off. He's only got a few years until retirement. Let him see his pension."

"Is DI Gr—"

"No names!" The detective sergeant stepped backwards. "You don't get it. They have him. Which means they have *us*. If you pressure him too much, if you break him, I don't know what will happen."

Rock worked her jaw, the slap burning on her cheek.

"Sorry about that," Hopkins said. "But we can't risk—"

Rock punched the other detective in the stomach and backhanded her across the face. Hopkins stumbled to the floor with a whimper, scrambling back as if expecting a kicking.

Rock held her ground. "I *was* going tread lightly before, but I'm sure as hell not going to after this."

And Rock exited, leaving the warning behind, paying as much heed to it as the imaginary bird in DCI Flood's hands. If they'd scared off PSD, this unit in the shadows needed dragging into the light.

And Moses's worries about the future would not stop her.

27

Moses received Rock's text that she'd be with him in half an hour, but that wasn't good enough. She'd been the one who pushed him to go all in, and he'd waded as deep as seemed logical. He texted back that she should meet him at the crime scene where he was headed.

He'd exited Theo's place with a free mushroom and Fake-On cob, satisfied Theo was telling the truth. At least as far as Theo knew. It was third-hand information at best, and Moses hated working on that assumption, but he'd tracked down the guy whose name they'd come across during their review of DI Gray's PSD encounters, and researched him whilst munching on his cob in the car.

Ratan Walar was a detective inspector working across two regions when he was unceremoniously dumped from the MisPer unit—and the so-called

Shadow Close Protection Unit—with a demotion to boot. While the intel from Theo was likely to be out of date, it was still worth following up.

Moses made some calls and learned the intel was gathering dust, Walar having since kept his head down and got himself promoted back to DI within a social care unit aimed at protecting vulnerable persons. Walar ran a group of sergeants and constables focused predominantly on "people who worked in the sex industry."

What they'd have called "vice" in the old days. Some places, like Moses's old CID squad, still did. Unofficially.

Ah, the old days. Not as good as people liked to pretend.

Moses drove to the crime scene in a run-down residential shopping district, where two female sex workers had double-teamed a horny man the night before but sought to drug and rob him once their primary duty was complete. The bulletin Moses read didn't have names yet, only that three people had been admitted to hospital: one man with narcotics-related complications, and two women with broken bones, trauma to their bodies, and possible brain injuries. A section of the street had been cordoned off, tape enclosing the area between the side-entrance to a flat and a john's car which was parked outside. Dark clouds had rolled in since dawn and threatened rain in a big way; if the heavens opened, it would make evidence gathering difficult.

Moses intercepted Walar as he exited the property.

"Didn't dose him enough?" Moses asked as Ratan Walar accompanied him over the street busy with techs, uniforms, and a half-dozen people craning to see what was going on.

"Opposite." DI Walar was a skinny British-Indian bloke in his thirties, with a large nose and thick hair and an off-the-rack suit of manmade fabrics that would not only make him sweat excessively on hot days but also appeared too big for him, like a teenager wearing his father's clothes. "They gave him too much. Reacted with the guy's steroids and turned him into a rage machine."

"Damn."

"*Damn*, yeah. Understatement. Neighbours heard a lot of banging and—quote—howling. Took four unis and a Taser to subdue the guy."

Moses would have liked to have been here. Taken a shot himself. But no, that wasn't his way anymore.

Walar raised his pen to his forehead and saluted with it to a pair of white-overalled people approaching from inside, held up two fingers on his other hand. The pair diverted to a police community support officer who had arrived with three coffees in reusable cups. "Sorry to rush you, DI Moses, but as you can see, we have to determine what happened here and in what order. Figure out who to arrest for what. So… what can I do for you?"

Using the same skirt-around language he laid on Cleland, Moses explained about Gabriella Childs, skimmed over how the investigation concentrated on a potential "mistake" on the team's part, and emphasised how he'd hate for an admin error to be the reason Joshua Sevan went free. As he was coming to the end, as Walar's head bobbed in understanding, Rock drove up, parked a couple of yards from them, and Moses made the introduction as she rushed over.

Looked like she'd just got out of bed, her hair draped over her face, a tilt to her head suggesting a headache. Had she carried on drinking last night?

Walar picked up where they left off. "I see what you're saying. And I wouldn't put anything past Barney Gray. Or that big lump Cole."

"Ha, lump of Cole," Rock said.

Moses remained stone and Walar ignored her.

"You were tight with Gray," Moses said.

"I respected him," Walar said. "We were both DIs in parallel units, but he had the years and the senior rank. He lost faith in me. A mistake. Minor, but fair. They merged mine and Barney's and cut back the scope—like they do every opportunity these days. I accepted a backwards step to a different division. Six months back in uniform. But it allowed me to climb back to the dizzy heights of DI." He spread his arms. "And look at me now."

Moses heard more sarcasm than bitterness and

let the silence hang for a moment, watching Walar until he dropped his arms.

"PSD investigated you," Rock said. "How was that?"

Moses squinted her way, but she kept her eyes on Walar so couldn't receive the hint to take it easy.

Walar shuffled foot-to-foot, glancing at the coffee-carrying PCSO. Back to Moses. "It was frightening. That I might lose my job over a mistake. And it *was* a mistake. Not like the scenario you seem to be hinting at. In the end, they were fair, Gray was fair, and it worked out okay."

"And that was the last you heard of it?" Moses said. "Rap on the back of the hand?"

"Until Flood came back to ask the same things you are."

Rock tensed, and Moses twigged something was up. She said, "You met with DCI Flood?"

"Twice more," Walar said. "Wanted me to grass on Barney and Cole, Rudy too. But I couldn't have done even if I wanted to."

"That's three," Rock said. "You said twice."

Walar turned a slow pivot, ruing his mistake. "PSD wouldn't go after them again. And I would never say anything either."

"Why not?"

Walar opened his mouth but closed it again. A vein showed on his temple, and Moses wasn't sure if it was there before. "The case is closed. And I have work to do."

Moses grabbed his arm before he could turn away. The man glared at Moses's fingers wrapped entirely around his upper arm, but Moses didn't let go. Rock touched Moses's shoulder.

The three stood there, connected. Silent.

Moses strengthened his grip, twisting the pain in Walar's face. He couldn't quite understand why he was doing this, only knew it had to be done, and he would not be the one to back down.

"You don't understand," Walar said. "I *can't.*"

"You *will.*" Moses clung to Walar's arm as he tried to pull away, the vice detective's teeth gritted. "Don't make me do something I don't want to."

"Moses…" Rock applied pressure to the hand on his shoulder.

Moses jerked Walar inches toward him. "He can tell us more."

"He won't."

Two detectives, around fifteen yards away, noticed the three of them. Although Moses's body shielded what he was doing to Walar, the pair watched without hiding it, the taller of them taking a step forward. Walar gave a small shake of his head, indicating they should hold fast.

Moses redeployed his focus onto Rock, loosening but not relinquishing his grip. "How do you know he won't say more?"

Rock steeled her lips, not meeting his gaze. "Because they got to Flood."

Moses let go of Walar, seeing that Rock had

more information than he'd realised. It wasn't the time to ask why or how.

"What did they do?" Moses demanded.

Walar rubbed his arm, gesturing to the two detectives, who'd ignored his *hold fast* gesture and progressed halfway to him, that he was fine. Now they did back off.

"I don't know," Rock said. "Hoping DI Walar can shed a little light."

Walar shook his head. "If Flood's your best bet, forget it."

"When we dig, when we expose them, we're going to find a *lot*." Moses towered over Walar. "And if that blows back on you, we can make sure it either gets added to the charges or it exists as background."

"You won't get anywhere," Walar said.

"Then you have nothing to lose. What do they have on Flood?"

Walar put his hand on Moses's chest and Moses was tempted to break the man's thumb. He didn't, the placement of the hand submissive, not aggressive, otherwise he might have taken issue. Both men turned from the scene, facing Rock, as if the curious detectives might lip-read their conversation.

"It was about eighteen months ago," Walar said. "The man's mother died. Hit-and-run."

"Wait, what?" Rock said. "Are you saying DI Gray—"

"Not him. The people who pay into their enhanced pension fund." Walar pulled his shoulders up tight. "That's what they call it. Enhanced pension." Hands in his pockets.

"Talk to us," Moses said. "What were you into?"

"Look, I was always on the outside. I had other responsibilities. I dabbled, sure, but I kept out of the heavy stuff. That's why Gray was happy to drop me under the bus." Walar's throat sounded dry, his speech halting. "I'm not proud of my time there. But you can connect the timeline yourself. They go after Mainey and miss. Then Kortenberg, but the case is too complicated to prosecute. Then Gray himself. It looks to their clients that maybe their protection inside the police is under threat. Then Flood's elderly mother dies in the middle of an investigation, a hit-and-run that was never solved... then within two weeks Gray is in the clear?"

"Since then, there's been nothing," Rock said. "Not one charge, not one disciplinary like yours."

Moses ticked the events off, the timeline they'd gone through the previous day. It matched. "The Sevans?"

"The Sevans aren't their only clients."

Moses took that and crushed it into his gut, ice running up and down his arms, and in behind his eyes. "They'd go that far? Murder a police officer's family? Could Gray have given the order?"

"Like I said, I can't be sure. I doubt it. I never thought they were killers. But if they are, you should leave this whole thing alone. *Now* I'm definitely done." Walar proceeded toward his detectives and the waiting coffee. When no one stopped him, he called back, "Good luck with your case, Detectives. Be careful. *Very* careful."

Moses didn't know what to say. He'd underestimated their reach, their will to survive. He imagined Frankie and Eko, cocooned in the armour of his earlier denial, exposed and vulnerable. He had to address that, and soon.

But maybe it wasn't only the cops they needed to worry about.

28

Moses gave Rock a head start as they drove in their own cars to the M6 northbound, the air charged with rain, not yet falling. He was surprised when it didn't descend during his journey.

Before departing, he'd paced and breathed deep, controlling the anger raging within, still in control enough to see he'd be foolish to report to Wearne, seething as he was. It wasn't only Rock he was pissed at, either. His own indecision factored in, swinging between pulling the trigger on The Precaution and thus panicking Frankie and Eko, and holding tight, confirming the Shadow Unit was a danger. Crying wolf helped no one.

The anger and fear didn't dissipate, but he channelled it into a semblance of officialdom and, forty minutes later, both he and Rock stood before the seated DCI, Moses with his hands clasped behind him, Rock pretty much to attention, a soldier on parade.

"DC Rock has filled me in on her approaching a witness without permission," Wearne said. "You have an objection to this?"

"Ma'am, I told her to wait on my instructions." Moses heard his own robotic tone, recalled many-a detective acting this way, and him being tempted to punch the offender in the chops. He pressed on anyway. "I wanted to interview another witness first and would have been able to put a better picture together, before approaching DCI Flood."

"The PSD guy who you think is compromised?"

"He is intimidated enough to back off the Shadow CPU." Again, Moses regretted his words. He sounded like Rock.

"The situation appears to be reciprocal," Rock said.

"I haven't finished, Constable," Moses said.

Wearne deferred to Moses.

"Ma'am, if DC Rock is correct and the groups under DI Gray's protection are protecting him in return, if we go after the MisPer team directly, the Sevans, and God knows who else will come for *us*. For my family."

"That's the job, Moses," Rock said.

Moses lowered his brow, maintaining his respectful tone with Wearne. "And now, if Flood is compromised, under the influence of one of the OCGs, he'll report this. They'll know your name and Rock's name. Which means they'll soon know *my* name, and they'll go to Gray. Then they'll know what he knows, and that includes where my daughter goes to school."

Rock's chin jutted, eyes defiant. "Big, strong, DI *Glynn*, scared by the bad guys."

"You're damn right I am. This is serious."

"Then quit."

"Detective Constable Rock." Wearne rose to her feet, steel in her voice. "You are addressing a detective two ranks higher than you. A senior, highly experienced inspector, and you are under his tutelage."

Rock's defiance turned dour. "Yes, ma'am."

Wearne remained impassive, only… not. Her intent was clear. "Well?"

"I apologise for my outburst." Rock looked up at Moses. "Sir." Back to Wearne. "If you need to remove me from this case, I'll understand. But I'm the one who wants to go where the chips fall. No politics, no favours for friends, no fear."

Wearne relaxed only slightly, a sigh as she assessed the pair. "No one is being removed. But you, Juliette, will respect your DI, and show you can follow orders as you did in your distinguished Army career."

Moses wasn't sure, but he thought he detected a hint of subtext there. That maybe *distinguished* wasn't the correct word.

"And you, DI Moses," Wearne said. "You will go where this case takes you. Focus on the Gabriella

Childs murder, but if that leads to police officers' arrests, including compromised PSD individuals, that's where you go. If there is any sign of a threat against you or your family, we will take steps to protect them. Preservation of life will always take priority over arrests." A nod to Rock. "Understand?"

"I do," Rock said. "Ma'am."

Wearne sat. "If PSD are aware of us, we must make them understand the confidential nature of our work. We'll haul them in formally if needed."

"We should keep it on the down-low," Moses said.

Rock appeared wary as she objected. "The boss said we pursue it, *sir*."

Moses eased his formal stance. "And Division 43 has more extrajudicial powers than most, doesn't it?"

"What were you thinking?" Wearne asked.

"Full surveillance of PSD. All the names who've clashed with Barney Gray and his people."

Wearne thought about it. "That would be unwise. A blanket phone tap…" She shook her head. "I don't think we can justify that."

"Then metadata only. Their office phone, police issue mobiles, personal mobiles. See who they're calling. Cross reference it with known OCGs and other suspected criminals. If they place calls to unregistered numbers, like burner phones, at least it's confirmation."

"And Gray's team is already under such an order," Rock said.

"To what end?" Wearne asked.

Moses had thought about this all the way here, rehearsing his lines, his approach. Pushing the fear for Frankie and Eko to one side, but never forgetting it, never losing it entirely in the fog. He'd never planned to kowtow to Wearne, but as he'd told Rock the previous day, he couldn't risk his family. "We find enough on one of them. Just one. And we turn them."

Rock almost smiled. "How?"

"Walar knows more than he's letting on. Flood obviously does too."

"Reeva Hopkins as well." Rock stroked her own cheek but perked up suddenly. "You're not killing time with this?"

"And Agnes Marsh," Moses added. "She's new to Gray's team. Might not have done anything too bad so far, but I'd bet real money she watched Mainey pitch that guy off the balcony. If we catch her in the conspiracy, she might turn."

DCI Wearne appeared satisfied, glancing between Moses and Rock as if watching a tennis match. "But you need to plug any potential leak. If it hasn't already been sprung."

"You'll sign the orders?" Moses said.

"Metadata surveillance of all parties. A gagging order on Flood and his people, and a warrant for them to hand over any and all materials relating to DI Barney Gray's team. And pull DCI Flood in to formalise it all, to be sure he understands where he stands."

Back out in the squad room, Moses met the stares from DI Xian and DS Ellingham who'd been watching the exchange through the glass.

"It's normal to take a while to break the back of this place," Xian offered.

Ellingham pumped a fist, miming the breaking of an imaginary back. "On your way somewhere?"

Rock faced Moses, seeming smaller than before. Waiting on him.

He said, "Not there yet. But yeah. Working on it."

29

The boutique art gallery on the edge of Birmingham's city centre wasn't due to open for at least another hour, although the timekeeping was slack enough to keep its high-paying clients happy. Not that anyone was buying this morning, but the casual browsers were used to the odd hours and tolerated them. Fans of movie poster and comic book homage artwork were a funny bunch.

Kaspar Sevan liked the fan-art but would only purchase something if it had been approved and signed by one of the luminaries of the superhero and movie world, such as the late Stan Lee. He owned a six-foot-high original, painted in oils by a young girl from Phnom Penh, featuring the Hulk fighting Wolverine and Spider-Man, which was signed on the back by one of the heavyweight artists from Marvel comics along with the legend, "This is one of my favourite works anywhere in the world." He wasn't sure if it had increased in value, but he'd been happy to part with £100 for it several years ago.

The poster he stood before in the hushed near-silence was a print of the Exorcist, a replica of a rare misprinted one-sheet that had been displayed in Pensacola for two weeks upon release of the movie. He identified other flaws too, but dismissed them as being unworthy of his attention. Shadowed by Travis and the patched-up Carl, he paced to the next, a Terminator 2 poster, which didn't seem old enough to be designated a "classic" given that Kaspar felt it only came out a few years ago, but doing the maths he realised it was over two decades since the movie's release. If it was an original from a famous cinema or movie theatre, he'd consider buying it.

The lawyer made not one sound. Simply glided to a position by Kaspar's side. Travis and Carl appeared surprised too.

"Silas." Kaspar squinted to check the grain in the poster's paper behind its glass panel. "You said it was urgent."

"Our mutual friends need to talk." Silas Bonaparte kept his hands clasped, rocked on his heels.

"We already talked. I did as they asked."

"I know, but this has gotten slightly more complicated."

"How?"

"Let's go somewhere more private." Silas strode noiselessly away.

Kaspar followed, understanding that the gallery was not a secure location. An associate who wasn't blessed with the options facilitated by Silas had recently been indicted and imprisoned based on recordings made via bugs planted in her legitimate place of business and from radar microphones aimed at the untreated glass of her windows.

The gloomy back room was cramped, lined with even more artwork on shelves and in cages, through which Silas passed until they came to a loading dock with an insulated door. It was better lit, had more space, and contained the male detectives this time, the white and the black one—Mainey and Kortenberg. It was highly unusual for the cops to meet like this, especially so soon after sending a delegation to his club, so it must have been serious for an in-person get-together. Kaspar expected it concerned his son, Joshua, who was sat on the edge of the dock, legs dangling over the lower level where vans pulled in to load or unload, kicking his heels on the wall like a bored four-year-old.

Mainey said, "We're clear." He put away a wand, with which he'd been scanning the bay.

Kaspar signalled his son to stand, and the lad obeyed, coming shoulder-to-shoulder with Kaspar, Carl and Travis behind them. Mainey and Kortenberg faced the four men, with Silas in between.

The fat, balding lawyer seemed to ooze something invisible yet viscous and fragrant. "May I remind you all that meeting like this is very foolish?"

"Noted," Mainey replied. "But you're a facilitator, so facilitate."

"We need to come to an arrangement," Kortenberg said. "About Joshua."

Joshua virtually danced on the spot. Fingers raking his hair. Pupils dilated. He was on something. Again. "Hey, don't talk like I'm not here. Speak to my face." He pointed at his face. "Here. Here's my face."

"You never told us about all the physical evidence you left," Kortenberg said. "We need to know these things before going to bat for you."

Silas nodded, accepting. "We did not have all the facts. We were not to know this 'Division 43' would take over."

Division 43. Kasper expected trouble, but hadn't expected them to be such a pain in the arse. If Gray was worried enough to send his senior enforcer in Mainey…

"Wait." Kasper patted Travis on the shoulder. "Search them."

"Aw, really?" Mainey said. "You want to touch me up?"

As Travis advanced, Kaspar said, "Your last messengers threatened to sell me out for a reduced sentence. This is a small inconvenience."

"And, gentlemen," Silas said, "do not forget our

ongoing agreement. Searches like this are not personal. And we submit to them at any point."

Mainey grumbled but acquiesced, arms raised to the side so his gut hung over his belt. Kortenberg did the same. Travis made a thorough pat-down of Kortenberg first, feeling all the way along his arms, the torso, legs, and showed no embarrassment at feeling in the corners of his groin.

When he finished, Kortenberg said, "Got a cigarette?"

Mainey barked a laugh and waited for the same treatment. At the groin-probe, Joshua piped up, "Shame the girls aren't here. Would've liked to see that."

"Be glad Burns is taking care of something else right now," Mainey said. "You saw what happened to your pal there."

Carl claimed his hand still throbbed, the pain managed by products normally supplied to the public at a premium price. The surgeon had been unable to save the severed digit, which they told the NHS doctor he lost in a cooking misadventure, so he would be forever hobbled by its absence. He'd discharged himself against doctors' orders, mainly so no one looked too closely at who he was, and what might have happened to him.

Travis's hand lingered in the crease of Mainey's groin, much deeper than Kortenberg's. He said, "That bitch took Carl by surprise. Tries that with me, I stab her in pussy and rape the wound."

Kaspar wasn't sure what happened next. A snap. A thump. A grunt. All seemingly at once. Whatever it was, Travis was lying on his back, cradling a broken finger, his nose bleeding all over his face.

"If you can't stop me doing that," Mainey said, "you ain't stopping Burns from cutting your dick off and raping *you* with it first, all before you even get your knife out of its hilt. Comprendez?"

"Comprendez this." Joshua whipped out a gun.

Before he could raise it, double wires sprang from Kortenberg's hand, their pins embedded in Joshua. The boy pulled into a snarl, but Kortenberg held up the Taser handle, finger on the button. "Ah-ah."

"Crappy search," Mainey said.

"Gentlemen, gentlemen." Silas appeared unruffled, even amused, by the exchange. He followed the wires between the cop and Kaspar's son. "Is there any need for that?"

"Is there any need for a gun?" Kortenberg retorted.

Kaspar snatched the gun from his son, an old Browning replica retrofitted to fire live rounds—likely procured from the very people he'd grassed up to save his own skin. "Is that thing loaded?" He checked it. Yes, it was. He handed it to Carl. "Dispose of this carefully."

"It hasn't been used," Joshua said.

"That you know of, Josh. What kind of an idiot—"

"*Gentlemen*," Silas tried again. "Any firearms are against the rules. Our police friends cannot help if they catch you with this. With any unlicensed gun."

"I need it." Joshua flailed his arm in the general direction of Kortenberg. "Look at this. Look how they're treating me."

"Why are we here?" Kaspar asked, resigned to his son being a moron.

Travis pushed himself up to sitting, then heaved to his feet, circumventing the wires to retreat to one side.

Silas said, "I am here to remind you of the rules. The terms of the agreement, should it prove necessary." He plucked the two barbed ends of the Taser wires from Josh, drawing a painful hiss, but doing it as casually as sweeping aside a spider's web from an eave. "And to, hopefully, maintain the peaceful entente that has served us well so far."

Kortenberg wound the wires back into the Taser's housing.

"And?" Kaspar said.

"And to remind all parties that there is a system of mutually assured destruction in place. If one betrays the other, they implicate all." The lawyer exposed his teeth through a slimy, fishlike smile. "Except yours truly, of course."

Kaspar loathed the lawyer for his smug attitude, but he was too efficient to cast loose for a few quirks. "Okay. What's the other 'and'? Why do I care?"

"And, this intelligence unit is tapping up some people we don't want tapped up," Mainey said. "Which means you have to provide some manpower."

"You need to take this old school," Kortenberg added. "We'll cover our alibis. You make sure your boy has one in advance this time. Keep him out of the way."

"What do you need?" Kaspar asked.

"Oh," Mainey said. "This is going to be messy. Fun. But messy."

30

With rain clouds somehow transitioning to an ever deeper shade of grey as they roiled in from the south-west, Moses selected Lichfield as the station to summon DCI Flood—a posting where no one knew him, where the people there had been co-operative last time they descended, and which sat roughly equidistant between Division 43 HQ and Flood's own building. Rock voiced agreement with this, although they didn't talk much while they waited in reception. They'd driven separately in case they needed to split their efforts afterwards and didn't relish imposing on Lichfield any more than they already had.

The order to attend the meeting—*meeting*, not an interview—was delivered via email to Flood's superintendent, verified up the chain, then Flood was driven to meet with Moses and Rock by one p.m.

The DCI had tamed his ring of wispy hair and smartened himself up with a tie and suit jacket. They convened in a meeting room set up for between eight and ten people, where a union rep called Tessa Glass joined them, although Flood waived his right to full legal counsel. Moses informed him he was not under arrest but was required by legal order to cooperate with the investigation. Flood stated he understood.

"One moment," he added, before conferring in whispers with Tessa Glass. The rep nodded along, whispered back, and then Flood whispered some more before resuming his interaction with Moses and Rock. "When will the appropriately ranked detective arrive?"

"I'm sorry?" Rock said.

"A detective of appropriate rank. When interrogating a serving officer, the interviewing detective must be at least one rank higher." Flood waited. Nothing happened. "I have been on the other side of this table many times. I know the rules. Better than either of you."

"You're not under arrest and you're not even under a yellow notice," Moses said, figuring he could play the officialdom game too. "It's not that type of conversation. We're executing a legal warrant, obtaining privileged information about a sensitive case. You're required to cooperate."

"But information I have might implicate other detectives. That makes it a Professional Standards matter, and as such, I may be in breach of regs if I'm seen to have acted improperly."

Moses hoped Rock continued her silence on this. She had a fast mouth, but it seemed their truce established in Wearne's office was holding.

"DCI Flood declines the invitation to interview," Tessa Glass said.

"He can't," Rock said.

So much for her playing the game.

Moses said, "DCI Flood is under orders—"

DCI Flood took over his own defence. "When those orders go against police regulations, I can refuse them."

"With a legal warrant?" Moses handed the signed paperwork, which his super had verified by phone.

Flood hunched over the desk to read the sheaf. "I need a few moments to confirm this document's authenticity." He fished a pair of spectacles from inside his sports coat, but the stutter in his voice, the forced frown, and dots of sweat beading on his head betrayed the lie; he knew full well he was compelled to talk. "In private."

Rock suspended the interview, and they headed out into the corridor. At the end of the passage, Rock plainly recognised someone and picked up her pace, prompting Moses to accompany her. Down there, in a communal area with tea and coffee making facilities, the Asian woman saw Rock and froze with a cup halfway to her lips.

"You drove him here?" Rock said.

"Yes." The woman had a dark smudge under one eye, which she touched with her free hand. The badge hanging on a lanyard around her neck ID'd her as DS Reeva Hopkins. "He deserves some support."

"You can't help him by covering for him."

Moses had no clue what was going on, but remained stern, exuding the impression he and Rock were in sync. He said, "It'll go easier if we don't have to suspend him. Or anyone else involved."

Two local detectives were making brews, pretending not to listen in.

Hopkins grimaced, lowering the mug of tea to the nearby counter. "Just back off. He'll give you the materials you need, but please don't box him in."

"Why?" Moses said. "What's he hiding?"

Tessa Glass came strolling by, ignored them as she spooned coffee into a mug. Rock and Moses watched her until she looked up. "Help you?" she asked.

Rock adopted the fist-on-hip stance she seemed to use whenever someone was being obstinate. "Is DCI Flood done with his reading?"

"Comfort break." Tessa Glass continued making her coffee, accessing the fridge for milk.

"The toilet?" Moses said.

Tessa nodded.

Moses convened with Rock, Hopkins in the middle, their backs turned to the union rep.

"Hopkins," Moses said. "How deep is he? Really?"

Hopkins shook her head. "You'd have to ask him."

Rock pushed into Hopkins, chest to chest, as if about to start a fight in a pub.

"Cap," Moses said.

Rock backed off a few inches, but the bar brawl threat continued to simmer.

Hopkins looked away, holding in what Moses read as tears. About to breach. "If you pressure him too much, if you break him, I don't know what will happen."

"Why…?" Rock narrowed her eyes, holding Hopkins as if in a physical vice. "His mother. Is it to do with what happened to her?"

Hopkins tore herself out of the vice. "How did you learn about his mum and son?"

"Son?" Moses said.

"Son? Oh, shit." Rock snapped toward Moses. "We need to find him."

"What?" Hopkins looked to Moses.

The other two detectives observed, twitches of amusement at this departure from the regular goings on. Tessa Glass paused to watch too.

"You said it," Rock told her. "In the bathroom."

Son? Bathroom? Moses had no clue, but again acted as if he knew all he needed. "What did you mean by that, DS Hopkins? You 'don't know what will happen'?"

He couldn't stop thinking about Flood's nervousness, the flop-sweat, reminiscent of a suspect boxed in. About to confess.

"I..." Hopkin's eyes roved side to side, mouth half-open. "I didn't mean he'd... Or maybe he... Oh, God, no!"

Moses took off, sprinting up the corridor. Past the now-empty office. Didn't know where the gents was but followed the sign at the next corner. With Rock right behind him, he burst through the first door, yanked open the second, flew inside.

A shoe on the floor. A broken mirror. Drops of blood on the sink.

Moses checked the first stall. "DCI Flood, are you in here?" He slapped open the second. "*DCI Flood.*" The third one was locked. He battered it with his open hand. "Anyone in there?"

No reply.

Moses kicked it at the lock. The flimsy mechanism snapped with ease and the door slammed open, revealing DCI Flood sat on the toilet lid, fully clothed, with a shard of glass in one hand. He pressed the edge against the flesh of the opposite wrist. Blood coated both of the man's hands and arms.

He sobbed, his hand shaking. "I... I can't..."

Rain pattered on the roof, starting as a tap-dancing mouse, then expanding in seconds to several buckets of nails being poured from a great height. No eyes were drawn upwards, though. All remained fixed at ground level.

"We don't need to make this official." Moses couldn't tell if he'd cut the wrist, or if it was the hand holding the triangle. "But I need you to put the shiv down."

"I'm such a… a coward. I couldn't do it. Couldn't stand up to them—"

The sound of the outer door opening cut him off. Moses clicked his fingers at Rock, and she intercepted whoever was coming in, saying, "Closed. Bit of a mess. Seriously, you don't want to be in here."

Placated, the person must have left, as Rock locked the door from within and came back inside.

"Come on, sir," Moses said, hands out, calm, soothing. "We can work this out. Keep it off the books. We'll help."

Flood screwed up his face as if he'd eaten something foul, leaning sideways on the stall. "And now I can't even do this." He lifted the shard millimetres from his skin.

Moses saw an advantage. Couldn't help himself.

He snatched the wrist with the glass and turned the arm. Flood's fingers opened. The glass fell to the ground where it broke into three. Moses hauled him out of the stall, grabbed the man's belt, and threw him along the floor. He skidded to a halt beneath the basins.

Rock approached, stopping short. "Moses…"

But Moses was already upon Flood, pulling him

up by his scant hair. "You know what? No matter what happens next, I'm gonna say you helped me."

The DCI yelped and moved one hand to toward Moses's.

"Nope." Moses pulled Flood's head back. "Get blood on my suit, shirt, or socks, this goes even worse."

Flood made a hacking noise, eventually saying, "Worse? Worse than what?"

Moses planted an open hand against his chest, throwing him back on his arse. Flood turned on his side, covering his head, saying, "No, wait, please," but Moses could barely hear.

"Even a rumour," Moses said. "Spreads quickly on the street. I wonder how long it'll take to get to Kaspar Sevan. Or whoever's got you bricking yourself."

He gripped Flood by the collar, heaved him to his feet again, and hurled him into a hand dryer. The DCI banged off it head-first, the device humming momentarily, before he staggered aside. Moses strode toward him, but Flood cowered, his back to the wall.

"Silas Bonaparte!" he cried.

Moses froze. "Talk."

Rock pulled up alongside him. Face stern. Eye-flit toward Moses, but otherwise resolute.

"I can't give you everything," Flood said. "I destroyed a lot. But if I give you even a little…"

"We know about your mother," Rock said. "I'm

sorry."

"I still have my boy." Blood in his mouth, his eye swelling, Flood coughed a humourless laugh. "I'm done, one way or another."

"Looks like it," Moses said, fighting back a sense of pity, an instinct he should let this broken man be.

"You're done, too. You just don't know it yet."

"Silas. He's the lawyer who sprung Joshua."

Flood dipped his head and shoulders. Moses held him up straight.

He closed his eyes for a beat before opening them, blinking. "I was close. So close. We'd done one guy, but we were short of the threshold for a criminal case."

"Ratan Walar," Rock said.

Flood didn't need to confirm. They knew. "I used the other cases to build bridges into their network. I knew they needed help to cover up so much. To keep doing what they were doing. And the lawyer, he was the pattern. I got so close to finding their safe house."

"A safe house?" Moses said.

Flood held one finger and thumb an inch apart. "This close to turning Walar. Three, four months after I turfed him out of the team." The hand dropped, too weak to remain in place. "They needed somewhere to stash cash, blackmail material, fake IDs for themselves, including passports—which Walar confirmed by accident." He half-groaned, half laughed. "I was bluffing that I knew, but I'd guessed, and he confirmed they existed. Presumably if they have to run. I found a chain of property deeds. One good contender that I wanted to raid was owned through a trust run by Silas Bonaparte." Again with the thumb and finger and an inch apart. "I was that close to finishing them all."

"Wait, so it was the Sevans' lawyer?" Rock said.

"Served him notice of the injunction. As he was appealing, his clients turned up at my lad's primary school. Took him for a ride." He gestured up and down as if appraising himself. "I know, I'm an old dad, right? Second wife. Younger." He moved his jaw, working the words out. "They picked up Stevie, showing police ID. Ten years old, he was. They were police. His dad's friends. No stranger danger. Took him for a ride. Long ride. Talked about sports. School. Careers, that kind of thing. Mundane stuff. Then, when my wife was going nuts 'cause he'd not got home yet, they dropped him off. Unharmed. But the message was clear. They could get to me. Or him. Anytime."

"You don't have to lie down for them," Moses said. "We can protect your boy."

"That was *before* they killed my mother," Flood said. "They waited six months, but they did it. I had detectives under me looking at Gray. Not by my order. But I couldn't demand they back off."

"Reeva Hopkins," Rock said. "She was investigating."

"They killed my mother. Eighty-eight years old.

Outright killed her." Flood gazed into space, at nothing in this room. "No warning at all. That came after. They don't enjoy hurting kids, they said. But they would."

"How did you spike the other investigation?" Moses asked.

Flood shrugged like it was the simplest thing in the world. "I told them the truth. Reeva and Blume, they came to my mum's funeral. I did it there. At the graveside. Told them everything. And I told them the worst of it."

"Which was?"

"That they'd given me the addresses of every detective under me. Everyone was in danger. They all noticed people following them in the next few days, and… it was enough." Flood had ceased sobbing. He had nothing left inside him.

"Who?" Moses pushed Flood harder into the wall. "Who did it? One of Sevan's goons?"

"Who's Sevan?"

"Kaspar Sevan. Barney Gray works for him. Or with him. Through the lawyer."

Now Flood's laughter echoed off all the walls, and someone was knocking on the door. A deep voice demanding to be let in.

"It wasn't the gangsters who picked up my boy," Flood said. "It was the cops themselves. Mainey. Burns. Not hiding. Not giving a crap I'd know."

Rock had to raise her voice, the clattering rain echoing off the tiles. "They threatened your kid to back you off. Killed your mum to back your team off. Then threatened the whole team the same could happen to them?"

Moses went cold, his hands numb. He let Flood slide to the floor where he sat, legs spread. No attempt to get up. His bones had turned to rubber.

"You almost turned Ratan Walar," Moses said, a touch dazed himself. "He's the weak link."

Rock said, "Not the first time his name's come up."

Moses stared at her, frowning, thinking, a dark cloud at the back of his head. "Eko." He turned around and made for the door, unlocked it, and barged past the pair of uniforms gathered there with Tessa Glass. As he took out his phone, still moving, he heard Rock forbidding entry, thankful she was so damn headstrong. Taking no crap. Using her authority despite her slight rank.

He dialled. Frankie answered. "Hey, you know what we talked about? The Precaution?"

"The Precaution?" Frankie said. "Are you sure?"

"Yeah. Take Eko. And tell no one. Just do it."

31

When Rock caught up with Moses in the car park, it was raining even harder than she'd expected. Really sloughing down. Hammering like God was angry at the asphalt covering His perfect creation. Unis and civvy-dressed detectives ran from cars to the station and vice versa. Umbrellas buckled under the onslaught.

And DI Moses Glynn stood out in it, his suit soaked as if he'd swum the English Channel. He held out his arms, face to the heavens—a martyr communing with a wrathful deity.

"I've known men like you," Rock shouted over the din of the rain on her hood, a waterproof poncho borrowed from the duty sarge's staff. No danger of being overheard, the racket of water on metal roofs a drumbeat drowning out everything else.

Eyes closed, Moses opened his mouth, drinking in the rain.

"All my life, I've known men like you."

Moses lowered his arms and bowed his head. Through the streaming torrent, through the rivulets running over his face, he opened his eyes to her. "You think you know me?"

"You try to be good. You try to behave in a way society accepts. But you're constantly battling with what you *feel*. A need to succeed, whatever the cost. You're not afraid of Barney Gray beating you, because you always win. You're afraid of what you'll have to do to get there. What you *know* you have to do."

Moses tilted his head back again, hands dripping at his side. "I never wanted to come back to this."

"Sometimes, it's necessary."

"On the battlefield, Captain, maybe. This is a society." Moses faced her again. "Decent society. We shouldn't have to play by their rules to bring them down. We should be able to tackle them without this. For fifteen years, I've stuck to the law, succeeded within it. But today…? Today, I conspired with a criminal, and beat a man for information. It was like the old days were yesterday."

Rock recalled his earlier words to her, words she hadn't believed, but they resonated now. "Some corruption is inevitable, boss man."

Moses pointed his chin at the station. "What's the story back there?"

"Flood's playing along with our version of events. He was caught, tried to kill himself. When you fought to stop him, he went for you with the glass shard. You defended yourself using minimum necessary force, and then he tried to kill himself again by lunging headfirst into a wall. You stopped him. Saved his life. We're heroes, you and me."

Moses laughed, deep and wholeheartedly, arms out again, embracing the non-stop downpour. "Not all corruption is bad, Cap. Saved a life, got a lead, and people think we're awesome."

"When you've finished…" Rock waved her hand in his general direction, "whatever this is… I'm ready to get back to work when you are."

Moses tore himself away from praising the sky, and there was no mistaking the steel in him. "You don't know me, Juliette."

"I know you've got more to lose than a career. When will Frankie and Eko be safe? The Precaution?"

"In about two hours."

"Then you've got time to change. Get ready for tonight."

"What makes you think I'm not going with them? What makes you think I won't turn tail, protect my family? Hiding out until this is over?"

"Like I said, *sir*, I've known men like you." She

took her hood down, soaking her hair, her face, a cold stream running down her back. “And because some women are like that too.”

32

A simple instruction: *Make sure you have a damn alibi for tonight.*

"Fuck you, Dad," Joshua said to his absent father.

"You what?" Ash said.

Joshua was cold and the marijuana buzz hadn't been as strong as he'd hoped. Weak stuff. He paced under the rain-lashed smoking porch of the Dancing Lion, where he and three friends had made sure to start drinking around six, being loud and brash but not causing any trouble; enough of a rabble to be remembered but not involve the police. It was almost ten, and Ashley Mars smoked the joint Josh had rolled for them, leaning on the rail that overlooked the trash end of the beer garden.

Passing their own spliff between them were Sabazio Molinelli, who looked as Italian as his name suggested but was about as Italian as Joshua's left testicle, and Markar Aviet, a distant cousin to one Sevan or another—Kaspar or Joshua, no one was quite sure. Both did occasional work for Joshua and, like Ashley, wanted more from lives shot through with poverty, having being trampled over by a system designed only for those born wealthy.

They wanted some of that. And Joshua was giving it to them. Without being demeaned by Kaspar Sevan's demand for patience while employees ascended. Recalling the leeway he'd given Gabby, Joshua decided he needed a demonstration of loyalty from his crew.

"Let's go see Halime," Joshua said.

Sabazio passed his joint to Markar and spat toward a bush. "Halime. Come on, we got better places than that."

"Dogs in there, man," Ashley said, and he'd know; he ran the place for Joshua. "You want a whore, I vote for Julia's."

"That's one of my dad's places," Joshua said. "No, it has to be Halime's."

Markar stubbed out the joint on the rail. "At least let's use the Kingfisher Boutique. They got Jacuzzis there."

The Kingfisher Boutique had cost Joshua more to set up than any other whorehouse in the region. He funnelled his best girls there, kept it clean and air-conditioned, and even employed someone his dad fired three years ago for popping Viagra and speed like smarties.

"So, Kingfisher?" Ashley said.

"No. I'm paying. I say where. And I say Halime's."

He booked them an Uber—on Joshua's account to cement his alibi—chattering non-stop to the driver about a show he'd watched recently concerning socialism.

Stay out of trouble.

Be memorable.

Halime's occupied several back rooms of a former independent cinema. They used to rent it out for social events, business meetings, whatever, but thanks to a bit of strong-arming the owners, it was Joshua's for a bargain price. He planned on renovating the main theatre one day, perhaps a burlesque show, something classy like that, but for now it was a dark whisper among the lower end of the "incel" market. Involuntarily celibate men who yearned for female company, but who were too inept to conquer regular girls and couldn't afford the Kingfisher Boutique.

At a door off the alley, a tall and wide black man with an umbrella appeared surprised to see Joshua and his three friends. Joshua shook his hand and called him Colin, as if that was his name, and thanked the man as he opened the door.

Inside, the air was musty, like getting into a car in which an apple core had gone bad but couldn't be located. Sabazio's curled lip would earn him a broken nose in the near future, but Joshua wanted them to be a part of this.

Behind an old-fashioned booth, like those where people used to buy tickets as they entered the cinema, Halime herself waited cross-legged. She wore too much makeup and the lingerie with a corset pushed her fifty-year-old boobs into a wrinkly cleavage, but she still pitched in with the girls on busy nights. She'd have seen Joshua enter on the monitor, security being one feature Josh didn't skimp on.

The menu was clear behind her: *£10 hand, £20 oral, £30 full.*

"I want the ugliest one working tonight," Joshua told her.

Halime uncrossed her legs. "Are you sure?"

"I'm sure."

"We have a… nice girl. Just arrived from Congo. Not pretty, but…" Halime mimed a curvaceous body.

Joshua had had enough of her blocking him. "Let me through. I'll choose."

"I can bring her for you to see—"

Joshua punched the Plexiglas between them. "*Now, damn it!*"

The three men with him shuffled foot-to-foot, as if embarrassed by a parent trying to act *cool, man.*

Halime pressed a button under her counter and the steel door buzzed. Joshua pulled it open, seething at her disobedience. She was good at what she did, though, so he'd only frighten her. Maybe demand she swallowed his jizz at gunpoint.

Later, though.

Now was a time for something else.

The lounge was like a dimly lit pool hall, with only one table which no one was using. It smelled faintly of body odour, a miasma of perfume and deodorant and cheap soap masking it with what Joshua thought was a worse replacement. There was a bar that served cans of beer and cider, and a few bottles of whiskey and vodka, served in plastic cups. No ice. He calculated that a freezer was an overhead too far. Besides, no one came here for the quality of his booze.

The women were largely ugly, with fleshy hips and either small breasts or ones too massive to hold a pleasing shape without scaffolding. This was where those women came who needed cash, who were unlikely to make money in the classier joints, and certainly couldn't strip for a living.

"Hey, Josh, what are we doing here?" Ash asked.

Joshua glanced back at the crew. "You lot want to make your way up? Then you stick with me. Through everything."

Nods. Gazing around. Maybe they were worried he was going to demand they screwed one of them. The girls all averted their eyes, as if some animal instinct told them they did not want to be selected tonight, not by these men. Not for any amount of cash.

Halime sashayed in, directing a particularly hideous troll to replace her through the security door. She had the manner of a drunk aunt in a saucy mood. "Perhaps Helena would meet your needs tonight?"

She indicated a woman who looked sort of Greek. Definitely Mediterranean. One of those with a wide arse and massive, pendulous tits.

"Who was that?" Joshua pointed to the door where Halime had directed the troll.

"That? She's Nadia." Halime patted Joshua's chest, that saucy smile painted wide. "She's new. I am still breaking her in. Let me introduce you to Monique. She's another new arrival… but very experienced, if you know what I mean."

"I don't want experience." His voice verged on a growl. Frustration at another person trying to manipulate him threatened to spill over into his fists. "Bring me Nadia."

Halime blinked rapidly, a deep breath, struggling to keep her outer shell looking happy. All around, tension dissipated from the women, relief that it wasn't them.

"If you insist," Halime said, heading for the booth.

"I'll need a car, too." He was drunk and high. Again. As were his crew. Getting stopped on the way to his hideaway would mean his dad brought more embarrassment down upon him.

Not that Joshua cared. He needed this.

Halime emerged with the lingerie-clad girl, a tanned specimen with dark frizzy hair, a crooked nose, and no chin. She wasn't fat, but her face sort of merged with her neck, as if she was made of wax.

"Perfect," Joshua said.

Quietly, beside him, Markar asked, "Perfect for what?"

Joshua slapped an arm around Markar's shoulder and gripped the back of his neck, outwardly friendly, but he knew it'd hurt. "For what I'm planning on doing—and you guys are gonna pitch in—I don't want a *pretty* face begging me to stop."

33

DI Ratan Walar was committed, Moses had to give him that. After a shower at his empty house, changing into a looser, more casual suit and shirt, Moses had calmed down enough to form a plan in conjunction with Rock and Wearne. Specifically, continuing Flood's tactics from before the Shadow CPU broke him, to turn one of them against the others, or persuade a former member of the inner circle to confess in exchange for full immunity and anonymity.

According to the phone trace authorised by DCI Wearne, Walar had relocated from this morning's crime scene to the hospital where he'd lingered for an hour and four minutes, before spending five hours back at his home station—a few miles east of Birmingham—where he no doubt carried out his responsibilities as a supervising detective and juggled his department's caseload. He travelled to two more crime scenes and then, after a period of downtime at a local eatery which his Wi-Fi connection identified as part of the Zizi's chain, he came out to this morning's address where two women had been beaten to within an inch of their lives. That was nine p.m. It was now ten-thirty.

"This will work," Rock said.

Moses bristled at the third time she'd said this. He watched through the drizzle, their car tucked between a banged up once-blue Fiesta and a white transit van outside a closed carpet shop. "I have no idea what he's doing."

"I don't either. But if he's this dogged about the job, maybe he's not like the others. Maybe it won't be that difficult."

"Did you just use the word 'dogged' without irony?"

"I did."

"Right you are. Each to their own." Moses had lost sight of Walar, a solitary uniformed sentry on duty outside the shop in his waterproofs, drenched despite the let-up in the rain. "I'll probe this, Juliette. If there's a chance to get them all, fine. I don't think there will be, but I'll look. It's all or nothing."

Rock gave him a quick once-over before resuming her eyes-front observation. Probably her time in the army, but Moses found her disciplined in the act of surveillance; no drinks to make her pee, no stinky snacks, no complaining about being bored. She said, “Leave no one to take revenge?”

Moses scanned the street for Walar, all-but deserted this time of the miserable night. “Exactly. The criminals we can deflect. Even the worst ones, the major players. They know it’s not good business to come after us alone. But other cops who’ve gone all the way to the other side, or if the big boys still control coppers on the inside, not so simple.”

“What’s Walar doing?”

“Maybe crime scene techs are still on site.”

“Seemed more open and shut than that.”

She turned her head to him. “Like Joshua Sevan was a slam dunk?”

Moses shifted his weight, his lower back starting to complain. “And it will be again. Gabriella Childs will—”

In a sudden explosion of noise and diamond specks, the driver’s side window shattered. The glass sprayed, biting Moses’s face and neck. He lifted his hand in a futile attempt at shelter, but Rock’s side also disintegrated in a shower of glittering shrapnel.

If it hadn’t been for the episode with DCI Flood this afternoon, Moses might still have been rusty, out of sync with the violent world in which he cut his teeth. He could have leaned away from the attack, scrambled to get out of reach. He might even have assumed this was a mindless act of vandalism, or robbers who’d picked the wrong car. But because he was amped, his brain on red alert for danger, because of all he'd seen and heard today, he knew what this was.

It was a hit.

As the attacker tried to grab him through the gaping window, Moses reached across his body and tugged the door handle. Slammed it open hard. The person who'd broken the glass took the car door in his body, thudding loud, but not moving as much as Moses expected. He shoved again, dislodging the obstruction, and planted his foot on the road.

Rock had attempted the same but wasn't strong enough. She sprung the opposite way to follow Moses out of his door, when a gloved hand clawed at her. Found a hold on her leg. Dragged her backwards.

Moses couldn't help yet. A dizziness at the back of his eyes narrowed his focus. Necessary—no, essential—or he'd be no use to Rock. They'd both be dead.

Out of the car, he angled his hips to strengthen his gut, one elbow in, one raised. The assailant was a man in a ski mask and leather jacket, wielding a crowbar. Big, brutish, perhaps a steroid abuser, but it was hard to tell.

Moses said, "If this is a robbery, you gotta know, we're police. If it's something else, come on and dish it out."

The guy rushed with his empty hand extended, the heavy, industrial grade crowbar low down in his other, meaning it'd have to swing upward at an angle. Moses would need to duck backward to evade it, but the car made that manoeuvre impossible.

He stepped inside the swing and brought his knee into the man's groin, not messing around, so hard it should have made him vomit up his own balls. Instead, a crunch emanated.

He was wearing a box.

Still, Moses's blow damaged the protective garment, meaning he'd mangled its contents some, too. He wound up a punch that flew straight into the man's sternum. The attacker's eyes bugged as the air flew out of his lungs, and the blow propelled him backwards. He bounced, rolling twice as if he'd fallen from a speeding motorbike, then lay on the tarmac, sickly yellow in the streetlights.

He wouldn't be getting up anytime soon.

Rock's cry pierced the night—of anger or pain, it wasn't clear. Moses ducked to see inside the car.

Rock had been pulled backwards by her collar. Rightly gripping the hand behind her, not pulling with the clothing against her throat, one foot braced backward against the door for added strength. But her head was halfway out the window. That assailant's crowbar—near identical to the one Moses had faced—raised high, slick in the rain. She'd be dead in seconds.

Moses leapt over the car bonnet, sliding on the wet metal, but already knew he'd be too late.

The man brought the weapon down. Rock's head exposed.

Moses landed the other side.

The attacker lunged forward, his head striking the car before the crowbar could connect.

Moses was already reaching for him.

Rock had unbalanced her foe, the motion of raising a heavy steel bar displacing his bodyweight, so even with Rock's lighter mass, she'd summoned enough strength in her legs to tip him. Moses planted his forearm through the guy's head, throwing him backwards and onto the pavement.

However, even all-but down for the count, the guy had hung onto the crowbar. Which made him a viable target in Moses's eyes. A thug willing to cave in a woman's skull. Who'd have done the same to him.

Moses rushed him and—much like he'd pictured Joshua Sevan aiming at Gabriella Childs—swung a kick into the guy's midriff. A wet snap. A pained grunt. Moses grabbed the back of the guy's coat, a heavy wool number instead of leather, and heaved him up.

Thankfully, he swung the bar at Moses, who accepted the gift. Blocked the looping attack at the crook of the thug's elbow. Returned the favour with a reverse jab that took out his opponent's nose.

"Moses, he's done," Rock called, out of the car, rubbing her neck.

"Not yet." Moses slapped the hand with the crowbar, the weapon clanging to the ground, then backhanded the thug so he clattered into the carpet shop's shutters. He grabbed the man, lifted him so he was on tiptoes, and ran him toward the road, legs pin wheeling.

Rock shouted, "*Moses!*"

Moses threw the man, aiming for the partner struggling to his knees in the middle of the slick road. Lights reflected in the damp sheen. The wool-coated attacker slid more than rolled, a few nasty grazes in his future.

A car rode toward them, but Moses strode out, the drizzling rain fresh on his skin. Blood scenting the air. The car halted and honked once before pulling around them and—seeing Moses wind up a kick to the first guy who was trying to get up—tore away into the night.

The kick landed, pinging at least one tooth out of the man's mouth.

Rock caught up. Pulled on his arm. "Moses, stop!"

"They weren't dicking around." Moses again advanced on the pair, now soaked, bleeding, scrambling backwards so slowly it was as if their joints had rusted. "This was a serious thing. Trying to hurt us. Big time."

"That's not what I mean." She tugged again, this time in the direction of the shop where Walar had disappeared. She was holding her warrant card toward an incoming body.

Moses prepared for another threat.

No, not a threat; a police constable.

The sentry on duty.

"Police," Rock said. "We're making an arrest."

The uni was young, Caucasian, a calming hand outstretched as he'd been trained, his other holding a truncheon, ready to flick it out if needed. He wouldn't be able to see the ID clearly from where he halted. "On the ground. Both of you."

Someone else brought up the rear at a jog.

Moses fought the pulsing inside his head, the stretch of muscles at the back of his neck and forced breath into his lungs. Finally, he produced his own warrant card, fingers shaking with the adrenaline surge. "Police. DI Moses Glynn. Like the lady said, this is our collar."

The uniformed constable risked a look at the two broken men, water pooling around them, a darker cloud spreading in the puddles. "No kidding."

The second arrival stepped up beside the uni, DI Ratan Walar taking in the scene. Moses pictured it from Walar's perspective: the two bedraggled detectives, a pair of beaten civilians, a terrified constable.

"It's okay, Gary," Walar said. "I know them."

"Sir…" The constable gestured to the pair of fallen men.

Moses processed several things at once: First, that he'd gone too far in regards "self-defence" or "minimum necessary force"; second, that he'd gone way, *way* too far in terms of arresting a suspect; third, that if Walar wasn't entirely free from DI

Gray's influence, this was something they could use.

While his clarity and speed of thought frightened him with the possibility of swimming upstream into the corruption from which he'd once escaped, he had to convince Walar not to paint Moses and Rock as the bad guys here. Plus, there was an advantage in the offing.

"They were here for *you*," Moses lied.

Walar sagged in place, as if the rain had soaked him through and made his bones bend. "What the hell are you talking about?"

Moses stepped between Walar and the two thugs. "We have viable intelligence that Barney Gray sees you as a loose end. But we got here first. They had to take us out before getting to you."

"Barney?" Walar's brow curved low, eyes focused on the two fallen men. "He wouldn't. He… *can't* do that."

"We can protect you." Moses jabbed a finger at the pair on whom Walar had focused. "But you have to come with us right away."

Walar pulled himself away from the men lying in the drizzle. Hand to his mouth. Nodded. "Okay. What do we have to do?"

34

The woman had suffered. No "probably" about it. She'd been through *torture*. Not a long period, but torture, nonetheless. Not long, because Kortenberg had pegged Joshua Sevan as impatient, easily excited, and likely a touch premature in the bedroom. They'd also tailed him for the early part of the evening, ensuring he honoured his promise to stay out of trouble, so had observed him make his way to the brothel. Unfortunately, they lost him soon after. Hadn't picked up the van he borrowed, nor followed him to the secluded forest track where he and his friends had indulged in… whatever they had indulged in. Kortenberg was glad he hadn't witnessed it.

Beneath the canopy of his umbrella, pulling in the wind, DS Rudolph Kortenberg was almost isolated. It was better that way, analysing events with a trancelike detachment, swallowing the sour tang of the mistake they'd made in not keeping Joshua closer. The woman: Whipped, strangled, even some burns. And the final indignity lying spread-eagled, naked, in woodland.

If they'd gone with Kortenberg's first idea to arrest Joshua and keep him in a cell, that would have sufficed, but the tantrum he threatened had persuaded his dad to go the *out drinking with friends where there's plenty of CCTV* route. Joshua, as Kortenberg expected, went off-script.

Now, the four boys—not men, *men* wouldn't do this—stood in the rain, shivering. Only Joshua showed no emotion, no anxiety over the scene. He wore a sneer like other people wore hats.

"Make it go away," he said.

Agnes Marsh had come out with Kortenberg, a two-person job for which he wished Burns was present. Marsh had shown herself to handle most situations with stoic calmness, but violence on this scale was a first for her. He'd expected a bit of a mess; injuries, sexual assault, drugs. This was way beyond their remit, beyond what any of them had signed up for. It was rare they covered up a murder at all, and that was usually scum-on-scum violence. Their actions were intended for the aftermath, when they had all the facts. They never got involved in the initial crime. Never got ordered around as lackeys.

If Burns was here, being spoken to like some cleaner, she'd have cut out the little twerp's tongue.

"We're not your mop-up crew," Kortenberg said, stepping back from the corpse.

"You're what I say you are." Joshua was acting the big man in front of his friends, showing off. Earlier, he'd been slapped down by his dad, and this was his way of regaining control, picking on the weakest of the weak.

"Who is she?" Kortenberg asked.

"No one who'll be missed."

"I asked for a factual response, not your opinion. Who is she?"

"Was," Agnes Marsh said.

Kortenberg wiped his face, rain having sprayed in as the wind picked up. "Who was she?"

Joshua's mocking laugh led to him turning his body to his friends, encouraging them to force their own laughs, but their hearts weren't in it. One of them, Ashley Mars, called out in support, "You're here to help sort this. So sort it."

Like Joshua, these boys were striving for control. A lack of direction, unable to grasp their own destinies, led to a life in the scuzziest business imaginable. Unlike a scant few Kortenberg met, none of these chav pricks would have survived in the real world, none of them intelligent enough to progress in regular jobs. Only paths lined with vulnerable people, and only then if they avoided crossing someone who could fight back.

Like the police.

Joshua clicked his fingers. "Hey, hey, you with me?"

"I'm with you."

"I *said*, she's nobody. Some Russian or Kurd or something. I dunno. Halime kind of liked her, but she always latches on to the orphans. The ones with no friends. That's why I picked her."

One of the boys whose name Kortenberg didn't know made a gun gesture. "Not the only reason, ugly bitch."

Forced laughter.

Nothing from Joshua, tracking between Kortenberg and Marsh, the dead, nameless girl, then back to Kortenberg. "Well?"

With every passing minute, the chances of a stray patrol car passing by and spotting lights in the woods increased. Five men and a woman stood debating what to do with a corpse was not something they could talk their way out of. Barney Gray would never put up with this. They weren't about disposal; they were about protection.

"Dig a ditch," Kortenberg said. "Put her in. And her clothes. Add paraffin. Burn her. Cover her back up. You did this out here? In the rain?"

"Some. Got a van too."

"Burn that out in the next county. Plus, your clothes—all of you. Go over to West Brom or Derbyshire, make sure the van's reported stolen first thing in the morning."

"Then what?" Marsh asked. "We need to provide an alibi?"

"We'll provide evidence we've been tailing him," Kortenberg said. "We'll make logs of him in several places along with these…" He struggled for a synonym for Joshua's hangers-on, those boys with more self-entitlement than self-control. "These friends."

Marsh chewed her bottom lip, watching the girl, as if she was thinking about trying to revive her.

"Problem?" Joshua asked. "Because one phone call to my dad and you and me can get cosy. Know what I mean?"

Hooting laughter from the crew. Less forced than before.

Again, Kortenberg wondered how long it would take Clara Burns to disembowel Joshua had that been directed at her. Marsh didn't flinch, once again *acting* the way Burns did, but not quite selling it. Constantly trying to prove herself an equal.

"I have a better idea," she said.

"What sort of idea?" Kortenberg asked.

"The risky sort. But we can deal with two birds. One stone."

"I'm listening."

And it was a good idea, but yes—risky. He'd have to run it by the boss first.

35

After ten minutes in the bathroom at Wednesbury Town station, Moses reappeared, smooth and collected. No shake, no anger lingering in his eyes. Like he'd been rebooted through a minor pampering session. Rock was sure she detected a subtle cologne.

"Ready?" he said.

"Can we do this?" she asked. "Morally? Legally?"

"Deceive a suspect to elicit information?" Moses said. "I'm not going to lose sleep over it. Will you?"

Moses didn't wait for an answer, just ambled down the abandoned corridor toward the sergeant's office where Walar waited. Voluntarily. Rock followed, annoyed at herself for allowing the DI to push her so easily into this course of action.

Wednesbury was close enough to the West

Bromwich prostitutes' place to make the journey palatable, but sufficiently far away that no one knew Walar, and the Shadow Unit would not pick up on it. A uniformed sergeant and PSCO were required to man the building while they were here, and their top-secret reasoning seemed to excite the two local coppers rather than annoy them. Walar had called in to log off for the evening, so as far as anyone else was concerned, he'd gone home to his wife and three children. He'd cooperated with the detectives, talked the constable—Gary—around, and explained who the beaten men were.

Cop killers.

There might be blowback, but they had made Wearne aware, and she confirmed she'd do all she could to ensure no excessive force charge reached Moses's desk. Moses had seemed grateful but nonplussed, if a little bedraggled.

Now he'd resumed his usual pristine outward appearance, a lightning switch from rampaging beast to thinker, to pursuing the Shadow Unit via a weak link in an already-damaged chain… it chilled Juliette Rock almost as much as the attempt on her life.

But he was the Inspector. She was the constable. If it went wrong, she was following orders.

The sarge's office was a cubby-hole with only essential furnishings—a desk, chair for the sarge, two chairs on the other side, computer, metal-grated window, and a fan. There were shelves too, stacked with archive boxes. Walar had taken the chair behind the desk, the sergeant's seat, and Moses accepted one of the lesser positions without complaint. Rock did too.

She activated the secure interview app for the PAL and narrated the official spiel of how Walar was not under arrest but they were making an official record of the conversation for which Walar may be held to account if he was found to be dishonest.

"Talk to us about Barney Gray," Moses said.

"My old DI back in MisPer." Walar had loosened his tie, placed his hands on the desk, one on top of the other. His hair was mussed, and he looked tired. Other than that, he was as calm as Moses.

"And the side business. Your force inside the force."

"Is that what you call it?" A hint of a smile. Glance to the phone. "I don't know about any side business."

"You're under obligation to be honest," Rock said.

"Thank you, Detective Constable. But remember I'm here voluntarily, waiving my right to be interviewed by someone of senior rank."

"You're here," Moses said, "to save your own arse."

Walar sat back, hands in his lap. "There's no reason to come after me."

"You think it's a coincidence? Come on." Moses

spoke with such conviction he almost convinced Rock he was being truthful. "We pick up Joshua Sevan, Barney Gray's Shadow Unit breaks him out, and our intelligence division snags that something is wrong. The evidence is damning for Josh, but in order to convict him, we need to break Gray's people. Break the alibi. They reject the out we give them, an admin error, and as we dig deeper, we find you."

Walar rubbed his eyes and yawned. "I left Gray's team *two years* ago."

"And not been involved since?" Rock said.

Walar again eyed the phone. Rock read this as being uncomfortable with the recording.

"Give us something," Moses said. "Look after yourself. If you want protecting, if you want us to cut you an immunity deal, give us everything. Everything you did while you were with them."

Walar shook his head. "There's no such thing as immunity deals. Not with criminal cases."

"Don't pretend you haven't looked us up. An intelligence unit probing deep corruption. You know we come armed with Home Office powers. Above regular police divisions."

Walar considered it, side-on to Moses. "I want it in writing."

"Give us something to take to the boss."

Again, Walar shifted position, shoulders low, head cocked as if listening for intruders. "Like any investigation, *if* DI Gray is guilty of the things you say, you follow the money. Which is the gangsters themselves. Solve the dead tart murder and see what turns up."

"Gabby wasn't a prostitute," Rock said.

"Whatever she was. Solve that, and Gray's house of cards comes down. Along with the boss himself."

Rock and Moses looked up, their eyes snatching at one another before both spotted their own tells.

"Oh, you didn't know that?" Walar said. "You thought Barney was the big man running things?"

Moses recalled what Walar said at the scene, how he seemed more confused than scared. *He…* can't *do that.*

Can't.

Moses pressed his palms onto the desk. Silent for the recording, but expanding his shoulders, showing Walar his bulk. "Who?"

"You know I can't offer any suggestions without a formal agreement."

"It'll take days. Even with the enhanced court access. We kick you out of here, you won't last long enough to get it checked over by your lawyer."

Walar took a breath, which he released slowly, steeling himself for a battle of wills. "You'd cut me loose? Let me die? Instead of offering me and my family protective custody?"

"They'd really go after your family?" Rock said, snagging on DCI Flood's mother.

The increased tension in Moses wouldn't be obvious to anyone who didn't know about the threat to Frankie and Eko, but Rock spotted it. He said, "A name."

"Not on your life," Walar said. "Or mine."

"Then there's no agreement." Moses terminated the interview, switched off the app, and handed Rock her phone. He stood.

Walar stood too, looking skinnier somehow, his eyes deeper in his tired face. "What, that's it? You let them go?"

Moses paused by the door, turning his head and shoulders. "I've been wanting to lie back and relax since this whole thing started. If you're going to dead-end us, then that's exactly what I'm planning. Unless you want to add anything."

"I can't give you the magic bullet until I see immunity."

"But you can give me something to speed that up."

Walar squinted, glancing about the room as if expecting rescue at any moment. Rock considered the uniforms out front, dismissing them as a threat because of the randomness with which she and Moses had picked this location. A direct raid, perhaps?

Nothing happened.

"I was essentially a go-between," Walar said. "Before they got involved with that Facilitator guy, the lawyer—"

"Silas Bonaparte," Rock said.

"Yeah. Before then, we took it in turns. But I only ever dealt with one guy."

"I need a name." Moses said. "If Gray isn't running this, then who?"

Once again, Walar shook his head. Repeated himself. "I only dealt with one guy. One who had any say over things."

Rock saw where it was going. "Kaspar Sevan. He organises the protection racket."

Walar gave a single laugh. "Nah, not him. Someone under the radar."

"Stop playing games," Moses said.

Rock fumbled with the phone in her pocket, again trying to thumb the recording app to life, but couldn't remember which way up it was.

"It goes way back to small time favours," Walar said. "Small favours that grew. The guy who gave the orders back then, whose lead we followed, was Theodore Goodman."

36

From the moment Barney Gray met Constable Atkins, he liked the kid. Studiously official, unflinchingly honest, and happy to help root out police brutality wherever it reared its ugly head, he dispelled any worries Gray had allowed to worm into his thinking about the Division 43 investigation.

With all digital ears to the ground, Gray had made preparations in case the hospitalisation of Moses and Rock went wrong. At Gray's insistence, Kaspar had urged the pair of thugs he'd brought in from Chester to make nice with two of his girls who were mainly dancers but who'd doubled up as prostitutes in the past, kissing and cuddling through three costume changes to create a trail of photos and give Kortenberg access to the men's cloud files. Here, their tech expert—Kortenberg—manipulated the date stamps and metadata to show the four had known each other for several months. Long-distance relationships meant a strained time, but the girls had been looking forward to seeing their men for dates that evening. When the boyfriends didn't show by six p.m., one hour late, the girls filed a missing person's report.

With Barney Gray's team.

All set up in advance. If the sting went well, they would drop the missing persons case; if it went badly, well… it went badly.

When the pair arrived at Sandwell General Hospital, beaten and damaged with one of them having exploratory surgery on a suspected burst intestine, it flagged with Gray's MisPer team. Since they'd taken on the girls' report, it was acceptable for Gray, Marsh, and Cole Mainey to venture into West Brom's turf and attend the hospital, where they could scrutinise the statements by various witnesses. Marsh had arrived afterward, sent by Kortenberg to run her idea about Joshua's mess past Gray in person, not over the phone, and Gray liked it; he had a twist in mind, though.

That a constable had lingered to watch over the two men on the ward had set off a trickle of enthusiasm in the DI. Over an early morning cup of coffee laced with a special slug from Barney's hip flask, shared between the three MisPer detectives and the constable in an empty canteen, Gary Atkins confirmed how events unfolded.

"And then the ambulance arrived?" Barney said.

"Yes." Atkins again consulted his notebook. Not something many constables used as much anymore. "Twenty-three-oh-six. They called two, because the injuries appeared to warrant it."

"And the man claiming to be a police detective tore through both?"

"Correct, sir." Although he addressed Barney, the lad had the gift of speaking to all three of them. "And he struck the suspects several times after the point at which I would have deemed them no longer a threat."

Barney exhibited his "disgusted" face, a slight shake of the head, as if he couldn't believe a fellow officer of the law would stoop so low. He heard a tut from Cole Mainey, but it was becoming more inevitable that Cole would be the one to deal with Moses eventually. Cole would have finished off Kaspar's idiot brawlers and put them in the ground, making it look accidental.

"Detective Inspector Walar," Barney said. "He vouched for the man and woman?"

"He said he knew them, sir, yes."

"How did that make you feel?"

"That… If DI Walar knew them, he should have taken them into custody pending a referral to the Independent Police Complaints Commission."

"But he didn't do that," Barney said, offering the hip flask again.

Atkins politely declined. "No, sir. Once

someone showed up to relieve me, I escorted one of the suspects in an ambulance with the paramedics, and a second constable, Sarah Lawlor, arrived to go with the other. DI Ratan Walar went with the detectives from Division 43."

Which was what Barney Gray had feared. Now it was confirmed. "Thank you, Constable Atkins."

Eager to return to the thugs' bedside and finalise his report that would likely never find its way to the IPCC, Atkins departed, leaving Barney with Agnes Marsh and Cole Mainey taking turns to drain the hip flask neat.

"Who's Ratan Walar?" Marsh asked, passing the flask.

Mainey accepted the final drip of whisky. "Someone who won't be a problem."

37

It struck Rock as an anachronism, sitting in a car across the rain-washed street, watching Goodman's most popular restaurant. A stakeout for nothing more than the sake of it. Unless Gray himself showed up to shake hands and speak his confession to Theo in a voice loud enough to be recorded on their phones from twenty yards away. Behind glass.

According to the hastily acquired digital warrant, Goodman and his two grown children, Lucas and Fiona, were all present in the Kind Vine Fusion Café at two a.m. It doubled as a cocktail bar, although Rock couldn't see the chap she met this morning manning a grill from the crack of dawn, then putting in a full shift into the early hours. Not without some help. Perhaps of the chemical kind.

On top of being pointless, the surveillance was

also inconvenient, but DI Moses had only given her a choice on the surface.

You go home, I'll do it myself.

No, Rock didn't leave people hanging, even when their logic proved flawed. She had nothing except sleep to do otherwise, but she liked sleep. Sleep was her friend. Sleep kept her alert, sane.

"What do you hope to achieve?" Rock asked over the cup of McDonald's coffee.

"Fresh eyes." Moses brought the McDonald's black tea to his lips. "I went in this morning thinking I knew stuff. Now I know more stuff. Watching with that new context…" He let the comment hang, but Rock understood.

The café-bar was doing scant trade, but those inside the tiny establishment, little bigger than the café in which Rock had met Goodman for the first time, appeared well oiled and spending. Goodman had said a few of his clientele indulged in the white stuff, meaning they likely had money, and cocktails were a money-suck on any night out. Profitable, too.

"You think I'm going to believe you?" Rock asked.

Moses eased his head around to stare at her. "What d'you think I'm lying about this time?" Back to the café-bar.

"The coincidences are too stark to ignore. I think she brought you in specifically for this. Wearne said she usually paired newbies to the 43 with a more experienced detective, but she was letting us find our own way. I think she lied. I think she *did* pair the newbie with the experienced detective."

Moses sipped his tea. "I'm the more experienced detective?"

"Maybe not in Division 43. But in this? Yeah." Rock extended her coffee-arm toward the café and back again. "If DCI Baines started something that you witnessed, that you have more insight into than you let on, you have to tell me."

Moses kept his bland, impassive mask in place. "I *have* to?"

"Think about it. How many years ago was Baines running his miniature protection racket? From the odd backhander, to… whatever Barney Gray is running."

"Except he might not be running it."

Rock watched through the glass frontage, unable to make out faces, but pegging Goodman as the main man behind the bar.

"It was small stuff," Moses said. "Baines and Theo. I was part of Baines' team, a detective constable, on secondment from uniform, ambitious. They looked at me, this big black guy, and they thought 'undercover.' And they were right. I was the best guy for it. Didn't look like a copper, didn't speak like one, and with my background I didn't act like one."

"Your background?"

"Second generation, African-Caribbean,

working class. Experienced racism but…" He bunched the fist not holding his cup of tea. "I boxed, I was an athlete, I worked hard at school. No one fucked with me more than once."

"Carried that chip into the police?"

Moses lowered the fist, eyes on the Kind Vine Café. "You call it a chip. On my shoulder, presumably. But aren't chips on shoulders unwarranted? Something teenagers carry around 'cause they feel hard done by? The racism was real. I was the gorilla in my high school. And my college. And for about five days through police training until I put a stop to it."

"How did you put a stop to that?"

"The usual." He didn't elaborate. "I got involved when Baines suspected I lifted some cash from a drugs sting. Yeah, I was their pet UC officer, and I played along in exchange for some personal mentoring. I got it, too. Baines and Vaughn and Peterson, they were good teachers."

"Vaughn and Peterson. New names."

"They ain't on the force anymore. Retired. Forget them. But Baines. He thought I'd been tempted. Introduced me to what he called the 'real scene' they were dealing with. Introduced me to Theo in particular. Told me all about the help he'd given, the tips he'd dropped us. I thought he was a CI, but no. Theo gave us a name and an address and slipped Baines a bag that contained a sandwich and five grand. Baines gave me one thou."

Rock's coffee tasted bitter. It was going cold. "And you took it?"

"I was so shocked; I didn't know how to say no."

"*No*. Like that. No *thanks*, if you want to be polite."

"You and me, Captain. We went to Theo this morning and left, knowing he might be up to illegal stuff. That's corruption on our part, especially when he ain't an official CI."

"That's—"

"Different? Sure it is. And what went down with DCI Flood in that bathroom? I smacked him around and you—"

"I had my partner's back, Moses. Flood is compromised, you—"

"Did what you needed to. And I'm your supervisor, not your partner."

Rock thought she heard rain patter on the roof, but it was just the wind kicking up. "And I suppose you think I shouldn't have?"

"You did the right thing. And when we have to explain my excessive force with the dunces who came at us earlier, you'll confirm they refused our clear instructions, that they displayed incontestable intentions to kill us, and that I was justified in the licking I dished out."

"You lost your temper, Moses."

"I was thinking clearly. Not dispassionately, but clearly." He forced a breath through pinched lips. "I wanted to do it."

Rock didn't know what to say to that.

"I didn't keep the Baines money for myself," Moses said. "I knew it was wrong. I stashed it. I gathered information on Baines and on Vaughn and Peterson. They liked Theo because he was sane. He had manners, and he kept any… disciplinary issues in-house. Never spilled over into random violence. No bystanders. No witnesses. Only people who got hurt were folks in the drugs trade. In exchange for keeping him in business, and sorting out his boys whenever we could, Theo gave us names, places, intel."

"You were wiping out his competition."

"Baines said we were doing our jobs. Keeping the streets safe for decent people. Getting rid of the psychos and the worst of the worst. Said if we took out Theo, someone would jump into his shoes, and that person might not be so cooperative."

"How big was he?"

Moses put his tea in the cup holder. "He did okay. But he started pushing harder. Wanted Baines to do more. He got more and more stressed. Made evidence disappear. Perjured himself in court. One dealer killed a punter, for no other reason than he thought the kid was a UCO. He wasn't. Dealer was high, unstable, but Theo wanted him back on the street. Baines made it happen and doled out cash to us all to keep it hushed."

"More cash. That you didn't spend."

"It's all in the official investigation." Moses lowered his eyes, both hands on the wheel. "I thought I was doing him a favour."

"Who?"

"Baines."

Rock's coffee was cold. Too bitter to drink. "What favour?"

"Going to Professional Standards. I thought… I dunno, I thought he'd made a mistake, screw it, they'd listen. They'd help him get out from under Theo, reprimand him. That Theo was the big fish, the *drug dealer*. But they just saw it as a bust."

"You were implicated too."

Moses nodded. "I returned the money. Testified in exchange for a new posting and a clean record."

"Theo got away with it."

"Not really. With Baines in prison, Vaughn and Peterson retiring, Theo wasn't protected anymore. He got pushed out. In his way, Baines was right. Theo was a good one. Kept order, with our help. He didn't have the stomach for the big time. I moved on, heard nothing from him."

"But it worked out. His cover businesses are doing well."

Moses remained blank, a slate without a twitch, without a single identifiable emotion. "More luck than judgment. And being on top one minute, forced into years of legitimacy. What does that do to a guy who thought he was untouchable? Untouchable because he was doing the right thing for his community."

"If he found a way back in…?"

"Brokering deals, a go-between. The process he knew from the old days."

Rock had weathered the fatigue of the late hour, now more alert than if she'd shot the coffee straight into her veins. "And Wearne needs someone who knew the setup, knew the players. Someone willing to go the extra mile, punch his way through to get the truth. That's the real reason she brought you in."

Moses appeared more crestfallen, more tired than she'd seen him since they met mere days earlier. "Christ. And now I'm stuck. I've seen what they've done."

"And if you took down your boss for what he did, Wearne figures you won't stop for this."

Moses stretched his jaw, his voice strained. "After, when I got my new posting, I was fine for a while. But word got around about me cooperating with PSD. That I grassed to save my own arse. I got frozen out. Dog shit in my desk, a dead rat delivered once a week every week to my home, eggs smeared on my windscreen. My DCI picked up on every minor misstep in every case I took. I landed shifts with PCSOs and newbie uniforms on jobs. No one would work with me willingly. The whispers got around that *I* was the dirty one, who traded my friends for freedom."

"Which was why you didn't want to work against the Shadow CPU."

"I got through it, Juliette. I got my head down.

I worked every case with not one slip up. If I had to bend the rules to survive, to get the result, I did it. I made sure no other copper was involved. That it never got back to my family. I told myself I'd stick around long enough to get something else, to push myself to DS or whatever. Then Frankie was pregnant, and I had no choice. I worked OC, a couple of undercover assignments no one else wanted, I moved around. In time, I got the stink off me."

Rock hooked her fingers into the handle and opened the door a crack. No light came on, nothing to alert their subjects to their presence. "I'm going home, Moses. You do the same. We'll pressure Goodman tomorrow. Okay?"

Moses nodded. "Late start, Cap. Get some sleep."

Rock got out and wandered to her own car, both vehicles present so they didn't have to share a lift only to part ways again. She waited for Moses's Lexus to leave before she started the engine.

Rock still had to wonder if Moses was being honest with her. Even if he wasn't, she trusted him in the here and now. Whatever else might creep out of past woodwork to taint the present, she'd handle it. She could not afford to trust the wrong person again, but she needed to start somewhere. A formerly dirty police detective might be the right place.

38

Ratan Walar was not in danger. That much he was certain. Even as he spent a full hour travelling the circuitous route home from Wednesbury, checking for tails, for anyone who might take more than a passing interest.

He was not in danger.

Few people knew of his time with Barney Gray's team, and even fewer knew the real reasons he left. It was, in its way, understandable that someone like Kaspar Sevan would go after him with thugs or even killers, believing Walar would spill his guts to that intelligence division. The thing that had rankled with Walar was the timing.

Would some criminal, even one as up his own arse as Kaspar Sevan, really send out a hit on him?

And how would they know where to find him?

Heck, how did DI Moses track him down? He

hadn't logged his plan to visit the scene, just popped in on a whim, revisiting the place after someone back at the station commented that the hookers deserved what got dished out to them, robbing a paying customer like that. Wasn't it their job to prevent "regular" women having to endure men like the suspect the responding police officers subdued? Walar wanted to remind himself of the sheer inhumanity of the crime, pressuring himself to see past the females' illicit intent and view only the resulting pain and injuries.

It wasn't hard.

And no one was following him.

He was not in danger.

A mile from his home, Walar decided to shore up his end of the deal, what he'd agreed with Barney Gray, and called his number on the hands-free, stored in his phone as Nancy Blue.

He picked up after three rings. "DI Gray."

"It's Ratan."

"Ratan." A pause. "It's after two in the morning." He was feigning a sleepy voice, but he'd sounded alert moments earlier.

"I won't say anything to Division 43. I won't sell you out. Convey that to whoever you need to."

"What are you talking about, mate? Have you been drinking? Look, I have to get back to bed."

Walar didn't believe Gray was anywhere near a bed. "Barney, this is not being recorded. I'm not setting you up."

A nasal sigh came through the earpiece, impatient and annoyed in the same breath. "If this is a prank, Ratan, it's not very funny."

Walar pulled into his road, a winding street so long it boasted access to two train stations. A busy thoroughfare lined with trees and bus stops but gave the impression of being in some middle-class enclave. "Barney, I—"

Blue lights flashed in his rear-view mirror. No siren. But the car, a powerful responder like a BMW, settled in behind him, a clear signal for him to pull over.

"Are you there, Ratan?" Barney asked. "Are you okay?"

"There was no tail," Walar said. "I should have remembered that. Why bother when they can wait for me instead?"

Barney again emitted an exasperated sigh. "It'll all be fine, Ratan. Whatever you're going through, whatever your real reason for calling me at this hour, I'm sure you'll work it out."

Barney Gray hung up and Walar pulled over. About ten doors from his own home. His phone went dark, both hands on the wheel, forehead easing down to join them.

A knock at the window. An officer in uniform, gun on his hip. Black gloves. A tattoo on his forearm: The words *Utrinque Paratus* under what looked like a diamond with a rounded top and a pair of wings. Something familiar about it.

Authorised Firearms Officers did not make random traffic stops. Nor were they given to politely knocking on windows if they suspected the occupant was someone worthy of AFO response.

None of this was right.

Walar sat up, keeping his hands in sight. Opened his door.

The AFO stood back, hand near his hip should he need to pull his weapon. His chin square, nose flat, his eyes dead and narrow. Ex-military type.

Utrinque Paratus.

Ready for anything; the motto of British Paratroopers. The tattoo wasn't a rounded diamond, but a parachute. With wings.

Climbing out of the vehicle, Walar spotted the man's partner, aiming an MP5A submachine gun as cover from the responder—yep, BMW estate; real muscle, not a random stop.

"I'm a police officer," Walar said. "May I present you with my warrant card? It's inside my jacket."

"Slowly," the man facing him said.

Walar followed the directions, exaggerated, deliberate movements. Handed over his ID.

The AFO examined it. "Thank you, sir. However, I need to check your car."

"My car…"

Walar had been afraid of an execution, something set up to look like he'd been conspiring with undesirables and either took his own life or did something to deliver a hail of bullets. All the energy seeped out of him, his feet and hands so heavy he wasn't sure he could move them. It wasn't an attempt on his life. It was a different kind of setup.

He said, "Boot's open."

The AFO strode to the back, his partner maintaining a bead on Walar from twelve feet away. Nothing Walar could do, except await the inevitable.

The officer put his hand on the release, pulled up, and the back hissed open. Walar didn't need to look at what was in there. He knew it would be enough to arrest him, and to achieve what Barney Gray was aiming for.

SATURDAY

39

The waiting room to HMP Dovedale was comfortable in a generic way, and the coffee machine hummed, offering generic instant coffee, generic tea with powdered cow-milk, and sparkling water on the side. Moses had finished his own brew picked up at a service station on the way, but wished he'd bought more as their wait tipped over the hour mark.

"I had a Lieutenant-Colonel during training who called me Foxy Rocksy," Rock told him out of the blue.

"Yeah?" Moses said. "Bet that went down well."

"I didn't have the strength or nous to stand up to him as a private. And if I did, even a few years ago, it wouldn't have got me anywhere. Later, when I was a Captain and he was a Lieutenant-Colonel, I ran into him on a base in Germany. Lieutenant-Colonel Jefferson Thorebourne."

Rock let the name hang, as if percolating it on her tongue, a nasty dose of medicine she didn't want to swallow.

Moses said, "Prick name. Jefferson Thorebourne. Not bein' funny, but he sounds like a guy worth a slap."

"He was worth more than a slap. He used the nickname more than once. A Lieutenant-Colonel. In front of six witnesses. Two of them women. Used in front of a bunch of other people too, later, and a bunch of others. If it was a one-off, I'd have shrugged and moved on. Annoyed, but forgot about it in time. Didn't seem like it was going away, so—being a big girl—I plucked up the courage to file a complaint."

"Didn't get anywhere?"

"I got a 'clarification' on how I must have misheard him and a promise from the LC to enunciate more clearly around me. A non-apology. I fought as long as I could, within the bounds of the Army's procedures, but in the end, they beat me. Not even the women backed up my claim."

Moses sounded bored, even to himself. "Hearing loss?"

"Sudden and short-term." Rock put her hands together, hunched over. "No one called me a liar, but no one backed me up either. It was a small thing, but it's one of a hundred little things that build up. Minor incidents that go unanswered. Not only the sexist stuff, but I saw more than my fair share. And while our paths are all different, small things become big things. For everyone."

"You did something about it?"

"The usual. Isn't that what you called it?" Rock smiled, although it was tinged with a sad edge.

"You slapped a Lieutenant-Colonel?"

"It was a *punch*, Moses. It was the Army, not a Love Island cat-fight."

"What'd they do to you?"

"I could have been dishonourably discharged. But they saved face and let me go. I hung onto my pension and the excellent references the police are looking out for."

"You think you should've hung on? Fought it?"

Rock shrugged, but not casually; more like she was redistributing the weight rather than shifting it. "They were eager that the sexism and harassment allegations didn't see a court martial. Prosecuting me would have brought them out."

"Still a shitty thing. Boxing you in like that."

"It's the natural order."

Moses wanted to exercise his hands, something other than drumming them on his leg. He considered helping himself to a drink, but he'd neck the water and didn't want to pee in this building. "'The natural order.' Like you think my taking the money might have led to other stuff? If I hadn't turned Baines in?"

She pulled a pained expression. "No judgement, Moses. It's over."

As ever with Detective Constable Rock, Moses was unsure if she was being straight with him. The maxim of keeping one's enemies close applied here, although he hoped *enemy* was too strong a word. She plainly harboured some suspicion of his time in the thrall of DCI Baines, and Moses had plenty of reasons to lie, reasons he had accepted long ago and would accept deep into his old age.

And yet.

He had to admit, as they chitchatted, awaiting admission to this male category B prison, the woman had qualities he'd found useful. Her ridiculous enthusiasm, her insistence that all would be fine if they had the courage to face down the dragons ensconced within the underworld, had infected him, forced him to glimpse the ghost of his old self, where nothing was impossible if he just stayed the course. Events had also brought to the surface long-repressed anger, his survival instinct kicking in and overriding police regs, jettisoning a decade and a half of studious analysis, of holding himself in check.

Perhaps this was what he needed. Perhaps Division 43 was the place for him after all. They'd even got him into this prison with a minimum of fuss.

Maybe he should tell Rock the whole truth.

"Ready." The mid-twenties guard was a private employee of the company who'd won the contract to run the prison. As Moses and Rock followed the young man through another security scanner, he said, "Sorry about the wait. There's a bout of flu going around so we're short-staffed."

"That's okay." Moses softened his tone with the kid, having been a touch grumpy when they arrived, which he attributed to a fitful night sleeping alone. "How did he seem?"

"Annoyed. Wanted to refuse you entry, but I explained you had a court order to attend an interview. He seemed surprised then."

"Yeah, he would."

"Why?" Rock asked.

"I tried to visit a few times," Moses said. "But he wouldn't see me."

"He isn't obligated to."

"No. But now he is."

At the room set up for lawyer-client conferences, the guard opened the six-inch-thick slab of a door. Inside, a grey-flannel-dressed man in his late fifties sat in the middle of the room, cuffed to a bar on a table. His flint-hard eyes stared at them from under white, bushy eyebrows.

He said, "Detective Inspector Glynn. Or is it DI Moses this week?"

"Hi, Malcolm," Moses replied. "Prison life clearly agrees with you."

"Come in, son. Make yourself comfortable." Malcolm Baines jerked his chin toward Rock. "Your filly stays out there, though. And this stays private.

No recordings. Or I no-comment my way through whatever you're here to discuss."

Rock waited a full three seconds after Moses locked himself in with his former DCI before presenting the young guard with an order. "I need to hear what they say."

The guard, whose name she learned was Dirk—after some fictional action hero—insisted it wasn't possible. The rooms were designed for protected conversations, but she highlighted the court order was for Baines to attend a formal police interview, which—by law—were recorded. He stuttered and ran his hands through his hair, and said he'd have to speak to his supervisor.

"And it might take some time because, y'know."

"The flu," Rock said.

"Yeah. It's like the start of the zombie apocalypse or something."

"Then go speak to your supervisor. I'll wait."

"In the corridor?"

Rock spread her arms. "It's not an active part of the prison. I'm authorised to be here, right?"

"Of course." The wet-behind-the-ears guard departed, glancing back at Rock before exiting through another security point.

Rock sat on the floor and removed her left shoe, essentially a flat but with a chunkier sole. HMP Dovedale wasn't an airport, and they had attended with authorisation and court-approved papers, so the prison stopped short of x-raying the detectives' footwear. Something Rock had banked on.

It meant she was able to smuggle in a listening device. Designed to absorb vibrations through walls, she'd liberated it from Stores the day she received her non-apology—sorry, *clarification*—from Lieutenant-Colonel Jefferson Thorebourne, but never found the right time to catch out the sexist officer and present incontrovertible evidence of his unsuitability for command. Admittedly, that was largely down to the bloody nose she presented him with, so she couldn't complain. Proof it had sort-of worked out okay dawned as she unwound the wired device from her shoe's hollow sole, unhappy at being frozen out but pleased she'd been proved correct: Baines didn't want to speak with her, and Moses had no choice but to play along.

Although neither had voiced it aloud, Rock would not object to Moses doing this were the situation reversed. Conversing in private with no record of the conversation was dumb, and he'd know it.

Rock plugged the mini-USB end into the matchbox-sized flash drive, earbuds into the headphone jack, then with her back to the wall placed the flat end against the interview room door like a doctor listening to her patient's heart.

• • •

Moses considered all the techniques taught him over the years, the subtleties he worked out for himself, the tricks and micro intimidations that often proved the difference between a no-comment and a confession. Despite being out of the game so long, Baines wouldn't be tricked.

Which left honesty. Sitting at eye level. No bullshit.

"Theo Goodman," Moses said. "I need to talk about your relationship with him."

"Theo." Chuckle. Snort. "He's nothing more than a supplier for phones and other shit to get into Dovedale. Sometimes, when I'm desperate and they up security here for a time, he passes on messages and instructions." Baines grinned wide. "Am I prettier since you last saw me, or what?" He'd lost a couple of teeth, his skin was dry, and blue prison tats stained his wrists, likely roaming up his arms. Unclear words had faded on his neck. He'd aged more than Moses expected, grey hair long and thin, streaked with its former black—a slick badger, but meaner. "Theo'll make a suitable partner. Best of luck with that."

"I'm not partnering with him. I need to know how much deeper he ran."

"Deeper?" Baines bent right over to scratch his head in a piss-take of confusion. Sat up. "I trusted you, Moses. You were like a son to me. An illegitimate son, but a son, nonetheless. Or my wife cheated on me with the local pimp. I'm not sure. Sorry, bad simile."

Moses noted the dig at his ethnicity, but it washed straight off him. Little jokes about black people's hair, the size of his cock, drug-dealing and pimping were all in a day's work for the old-school guys. Or it had been. Less-so now. Up-front, anyway.

"How did it work?" Moses asked. "I knew our end, the bits you passed on. I never got deeper. Never saw the mechanics."

"Why would I tell you? Old time's sake?"

"Yes."

Baines licked his lips, moved his shackled hands as if about to rub them over his face. "You know how I live, Moses?"

"I'm sorry, Malc. They knew it all already. You'd have gone down whether I stayed schtum or not."

"It's the principle, though. That's what rankles. After all I did for you. Spoke up for you when the Russians wanted you gone."

"Because I wouldn't do what they asked."

"No." Baines scowled. "I ended up with that shitty stick, thanks very much."

Baines set his lips taut and thin, the gesture of a person unwilling to say more.

"Theo Goodman has resurfaced as a person of interest," Moses said. "I thought they forced him out after you came in here. But I'm wondering if he was hibernating."

Baines laughed, a single barking breath. "He always lands on his feet, that guy."

"I'm wondering if he's the one running it."

"Running what?"

"Your old protection racket."

Baines lost his swagger, gaze stuck on Moses. "What makes you say that?"

Moses watched for deception, for manipulation, both skills at which Baines had proved adept. He calculated how much was safe to say, how much the former DCI would have inferred already. "We've seen an increase in failed prosecutions. Disappeared evidence, witnesses failing to show for court, even alibis offered for killers who're bang to rights. Guy called Barney Gray seems to be top dog on the copper side."

Baines' eyes twitched, pupils dilating. He knew the name.

Moses gambled, pushing rather than waiting. "PSD detective lost a family member a year and a half ago and got threatened with more deaths if he didn't cooperate. A DI called Ratan Walar used to be involved in the game, was ready to cooperate with us. But we learned this morning that a prostitute called Nadia turned up dead in the man's car. Tortured to death. He's under arrest. I'm guessing they'll find plenty of DNA to link the pair."

Baines stretched his toothy smile, the gaps black and deep. "You know how many ex-coppers get to live in General Population?"

"Not many."

"But I do. Know why?"

"I was curious."

"Because I *run* this place. With my connections, I get stuff in, I get stuff out. That made me a lot of friends, and now those friends are my foot soldiers. No one fucks with me." He jabbed a finger as hard as he could, given his restraints. "Don't think for one second your threat scares me. Barney Gray doesn't scare me. And Theo Fucking Goodman doesn't scare me, either."

"You can't help." Moses stood.

"You telling me you haven't dabbled since?"

Moses controlled his anger, his indignation. "I've been clean. Perhaps too clean. I could never turn into what you became."

"Why are you here, Moses? Actually, don't even bother to answer that. I know the reason. It's for *her* benefit, isn't it?" Baines' mouth curled into a smirk. "You *know* it was go-betweens. Blind drops. Messages passed through lawyers. You're here for the theatre. So that redheaded strumpet doesn't know how involved you really were."

Rock's heart drummed a hard, fast beat against her chest.

Moses lied to her?

Right to her face?

A door clunked open. Out of the corner of her

eye, Dirk the guard returned, horrified to see her in position.

"Nasty business," Baines said. "But profitable."

"You ran more than the protection racket, Malc. Didn't you? I suspected, but never said."

"You make out like you did me some favour. Like that wasn't the right thing to do in the first place."

Dirk rushed forward and Rock had to scramble to her feet, losing her connection to the interview, advanced on Dirk, whose horror morphed into fear.

"Did you speak to your supervisor?" she asked pleasantly.

"Not yet. He'll be in touch." Dirk's head switched between the interview room door and the entrance he came through. "You can't do that."

"I can, and I will, Dirk." Rock retreated to her former position. "If you interrupt me, or try to stop me, I'll break your arm. I'm sure your supervisor will be happy with another person off sick."

And Dirk could only watch as Rock resumed her vigil.

"Don't make out like you're an angel, Moses. You did okay out of me."

"I was never like you," Moses said. "I just wanted to be a decent copper. I'd never turn all the way like..." He waved his hand at the room. "Like this."

"You think I shat my career away."

"I think you're the cleverest copper I ever met. Before or since. You could have been running things from the right side. Instead of the shadows."

"And you'd have liked to be there? My right-hand guy?"

Moses meant it when he said, "Yes. I wanted to bring *down* the bad guys. Not work with them. No matter how much pocket money they slipped us."

"Pocket money?" Baines said with a growl of ridicule. "Maybe to you. But to me, it was my pension. My future."

"Hardly that, Malc."

"Hardly?" Baines shook his head, again that note of ridicule. "I know you saved up most of what I sent your way. Dropped a hefty deposit on that nice house of yours. But while you were busy laundering your share through the casinos and Theo's cafés or whatever, I danced with the big boys. Bought a whole fucking *house*. Place I'm either gonna sell up or live in when this sentence is up. And I'm not gonna want for funds, neither."

Moses touched his face, tracing the lines of his thin beard, which he'd trimmed this morning, an odd urge to impress his old boss. "Bragging, Malcolm? That's not like you. Hoping you're not jealous of your heir apparent. Know DI Gray and Theo are piggybacking on the business you set up… Does it bother you? Them profiting off your enterprise?"

Baines hooted with laughter, the cackle of a mad

old hillbilly in a rocking chair cradling a banjo. He'd probably slap his thigh if he'd been able. "You think I'm jealous of that kid? That's what you're taking away from this?"

"He's running your scam, Malc. He's expanded it, improved it. He's—"

"You know why I'm glad you're here? Really?"

"Why?"

"Look at me, Moses. Look at me properly."

Moses closed his mouth and laid his hands in front of him, inches from Baines' reach.

"I told you, boy. I'm the daddy in here. I can get anything in and anything out. Except people. That's an ask too far. But phones, itty bitty tablet things? All here. Means I can e-commute." His grin turned wicked, the gaps in his teeth a deeper black than before, his distorted tats morphing, almost taking on a life of their own. "Gray ain't doing nothing I don't approve first. He didn't *take over* my seat at the table, you prick. He's keeping it warm for me."

"You're lying," Moses said. "Your protégé turns up with a warrant, forces you to do something you don't want to, and you've got to brag. That's why you didn't want this recording, why you didn't want my constable in here. So you could brag to your heart's content and intimidate the student who's gonna take your big project down." Moses pushed away from the table. "I'm not gonna learn anything here. Nothing except the strong guy I knew is just a little boy overcompensating for his failures. Who thinks a stash of phones keeping him in touch with the outside world equals an empire."

Baines got lower, close to the tabletop, the cuffs pulling on his skin as he strained against them. His face glowed red.

"Be seeing you, Malc." Moses made for the door.

"I'm happy to see you here 'cos I get to tell you in person. See the blood drain from your face with my own eyes. Or it would do if… y'know…"

Moses sighed, glanced back, but stayed on course to exit. "What do you gotta tell me?"

Baines grinned that awful chequered grin. "That I know all about your 'Precaution'."

Moses stopped dead. Remembered. "We all had our own Precaution. Mine's changed since the old days."

"Yeah? Then you won't mind that I already gave the kill order."

Moses's pulse thumped in his neck, his head. His face was hot. He turned his whole body toward the man bound to the table, no longer red, no longer angry, as if something had sated.

"Yeah, Moses, that's the old rage machine I remember. Let me light that fuse. I do love the fireworks."

Moses waited. No words. No movement, or he'd throttle the guy.

"Last chance to back out, Moses. Slot that fiddle

back in the roof… isn't that the saying you sheep shaggers use?"

"Close enough."

"If I don't call off my attack dog today, that pretty rose-lined cottage in the Cotswolds is gonna be redecorated with your wife's blood and entrails. I haven't decided what to do with the ten-year-old yet. But it'll be nasty, Glynn Moses-Moses Glynn. Nastier than anything you and I saw on the job."

Moses didn't have time to crush the man's skull, as much as he wanted to. He ripped open the door, found Rock leaning on the wall.

"What'd he say?" she asked.

"Road trip," Moses said. "And I need Gloucestershire plod on the line. No questions asked."

40

"Should've known. Should've known. Should've known."

It had become a mantra since screaming out of HMP Dovedale and tearing through traffic to the M6 southbound. Moses returned to it every time he or Rock got done with one call or another. They were flying at 100mph in Moses's Lexus, a blue light on his dashboard, a siren clearing the occasional knot of traffic, something he must have paid to install himself since this wasn't a vehicle approved by the police for personal and business use.

What else had he bought with money undeclared to Professional Standards?

Rock used her authorisation code to mobilise the Gloucestershire police, but the location of Frankie's mother's cottage was remote. Even at the best of times, cuts to policing meant difficulty in assembling even a pair of constables to back up a colleague being overwhelmed by wrongdoers in an urban location. The Cotswolds village of Nipping Haven was never home to a police station, community constables doing the occasional round, with PCSOs utilised to deal with the occasional drunk who didn't want to leave a pub at kicking out time. Nothing much ever happened in Nipping Haven. It didn't allow property owners to rent their homes as holiday cottages, and the businesses only advertised on tourist sites when a festival or special market popped up. It didn't appear on some maps, with even Google Earth missing it for at least two years.

Which was why, Moses said, they hadn't sold his mother-in-law's cottage after the old lady's passing. It was both family holiday home—for the extended cousins, nieces, and nephews too—and an off-the-record retreat should the Moses family ever need to flee. It came equipped with plenty of security, including a licensed shotgun, as around 75 percent of residents had, so it wouldn't blip on any digital sweeps of the area.

Rock watched the needle push over the 100mph mark, hanging up after contacting the assistant chief constable to emphasise the emergency a police officer's family currently faced. "They're on their way."

Moses slapped the wheel. "Should've known."

"That Baines was still running things from inside? How could you have known?"

"There were hints that it was a bigger setup. Someone coordinating, probably through that lawyer guy, the one they call the Facilitator."

"With the creepy name and face."

"Yeah, Theo isn't the Facilitator. It's the lawyer. Silas." As the motorway snarled up, Moses hurtled down the inside lane, easing off to 70 mph, then as the vehicles ahead pulled over to the middle, he sped up to 90, crossed into the hard shoulder, and switched motorways to the M5. "Whatever his role, whoever's paying him, they must have ready money."

Rock agreed but didn't need to say so. She did, however, need to voice the other thing. "I heard."

"Heard what?"

"Everything." She fished the sensor end of her array from the pocket where she'd stashed it as the conversation neared its conclusion. "I listened in."

Moses ground his teeth, this early section of the M5 almost deserted. He sped up.

100 mph.

110.

"Thought we might need it as evidence," Rock said.

"It's not me." Moses spoke as if someone had wired his jaw shut. "I had no choice back then. Welsh. Black. Poor. Built like this."

"But you took the money. More than you let on. You took it, enjoyed it, and you're still enjoying it."

"I used it to jump start a decent life, yeah. Frankie thinks I inherited it. And you're not telling her anything."

The thought hadn't entered Rock's head. Nothing had. "I don't know what to do with this."

"Trust that I'm not that person anymore. That I won't ever go down that path."

Rock palmed the sensor, held it out of the way. "That's the real reason you didn't want to go so deep. In case it all came out."

"No. I didn't want to go so deep in case I wrecked my career all over again. If I'd known about Baines… if I'd known how far this group could reach…" He slapped the wheel, coming up to road works where the mass of cars before them obeyed the average speed cameras' commands to limit their speed. "Should've known."

"What happens next?"

"What happens next is, you can't trust me. I can't trust Wearne. She knows more than she's letting on, and Baines knows even more still. About me. I can't protect what I've got, and I can't protect Frankie and Eko." Another slap of the wheel. "Everything I ever did was for them. Even before I had a family, it was for the future. Every wrong thing, from that first bonus Baines gave me, to ploughing through those arseholes last night, I knew I was protected, and I knew it was right for them."

For them.

For my family.

The cry of every corrupt police officer, politician and public servant ever. Rock refused to feel sorry for him. "And the case?"

"It's over with. Wearne tricked me. Brought me on board because of Baines. Because I was connected. You were right—the coincidences are too much for it not to be manufactured. Soon as I get Frankie and Eko back, I make it clear I'm done."

"And if they come for me?" Rock asked.

Moses concentrated on manoeuvring through the thick roadwork traffic, honking and whooping the custom siren. "I haven't taken a penny, haven't looked the other way, haven't let one thing drop since Baines went down. But I have to let this go, stand aside."

"Laying down for the bad guys? Putting your fiddle back in the roof? Isn't that what Baines called it?"

"An old Welsh saying. Learning the fiddle is hard. Putting it back in the roof is giving up." Moses shot her a glance filled with conflict. "Even if we take down the people we got in our sights, Baines will carry on."

"So it's Barney Gray, his team, Joshua? We leave Theo? Leave Baines?"

"I never should have said yes to Wearne. Should've trusted my instinct. These guys, sure, they need to end, and I'll end them, but this isn't for me.

I'm not some pawn. Soon as I can, I'm quitting this unit and getting back to my life."

They spent the rest of the journey in silence. And even at the speed Moses managed to re-establish, it was a long drive.

41

DCI Wearne rarely questioned herself. It was unusual for someone in her position to hold such confidence, but she possessed an uncanny ability to see all the threads at once, growing annoyed when her peers failed to keep up. As a child, her parents once tested her for autism, the conclusion being that she may have registered somewhere very low on the spectrum, but her problems were predominantly "personality led." In other words, she could be a bit of a dick.

And bright. Very bright.

Puzzles were a distraction for her. Something to keep her mind active while other kids flailed with simple algebra and physics calculations. In high school, teachers tried to avoid placing her in a group project except where the curriculum demanded, and it was for this reason she avoided university altogether, pursuing a vocation where her problem-solving and analytical skills would be most appreciated. At a time when GCHQ and even MI5 preferred degree-laden candidates, the police appealed to her.

During her early days, she hid her short temper along with her contempt for slower minds, and even resisted advising detectives whilst she was in uniform. She found, though, that on top of her analytical talents, a slew of that same logic applied to people, picking the right candidates to work alongside and under her even when conventional testing suggested otherwise. She could also discern which people she'd be happy working *under*. This, more than anything, had propelled her to DCI at a relatively young age.

Understanding people.

Predicting behaviour based on previous data.

"Did I get it wrong about Moses?" she asked Zachary Shepherd.

The police and crime commissioner had stopped by unannounced, something he was entitled to do since he was held personally responsible for Division 43 by the Home Secretary, but not a power he'd exercised since the early days of its inception. In fact, he'd asked specifically about Moses. Locked away from the main squad room in the digital monitoring station, unmanned and soundproof, Wearne had detailed the investigation so far, confirming Moses had committed an act of violence, but Rock had backed him up to call it "an extreme self-defence measure."

"I don't know," Zachary said. "It's hard to say. Is he utilising his specialist knowledge of this matter or slipping back into old habits?"

They'd known his past, suspected he'd committed more misdemeanours than he'd admitted to, that he'd been a part of several illicit interrogations, and even conspired with criminals. Yet a deep, non-redacted dive and a thorough wiretapping during his period of suspension confirmed he'd been a total boy scout for many years; a rough diamond, but one who'd applied much polish, and left the filth behind.

"But if we missed something in our sweep," Wearne said, "he might be covering up old crimes."

"It was always a possibility."

"That's why I paired him with Rock. She won't take any crap. Won't hesitate to turn him in if he goes too far."

Zachary gave a warm smile. "She's loyal, too. Her psyche profile is equivocal on that."

"I don't think they've worked together long enough for him to switch her loyalty from me to him. From the force to a corrupt officer."

Zachary ran his eyes over the computer banks, the painted-black window. "He's a good-looking guy. They've spent nights in one another's company."

"Oh, pu-lease, Zach. Rock is a decorated Army

vet, a captain. She refused to back down in the face of bureaucracy, corruption, and the old boys' club. She's not going to let her lady parts change who she is."

Zachary held up both palms in surrender. "No, no, I'm sorry. Of course. But they have dug in hard together. Even if it's platonic, it could still be a distraction."

Wearne's phone vibrated and she picked up. An electronic voice told her, "Detective Constable Juliette Rock. Authorisation code used to deploy authorised firearms officers immediately. Address…" The location was a place called Nipping Haven with a GL postcode. She guessed it was Gloucester region, but had to Google the place—a village in the middle of nowhere. She relayed this to Zachary, then placed a call to Rock. "Voicemail." Then she tried Moses. "Again."

Zachary paced. "Get hold of the locals and find out exactly why the hell they're out there. Then we can ask why they're doing this without *your* approval, and maybe we'll get an answer to your question."

"Which question?"

"Were you wrong about Moses? Let's hope the answer is no. Because it won't be me who loses his job over this."

42

Throughout their marriage, and for some time before, Frankie Moses spent much of her day worrying about her husband. That he was concerned enough for her and Eko to enact the Precaution had left her reeling, panicked, and it had taken a full day for her to settle into Prose Cottage on the edge of Nipping Haven. She felt safer in the evening than in the daytime, trying to act normal for Eko's sake. At times, the ten-year-old seemed so grown up, like a teenaged know-it-all, when talking about the big issues of the day, of climate change and plastic waste, of school uniform policy and approaches to bullying. Then there were days when she spent her time perfecting a cartwheel or her latest kata from her karate class, as she was now doing on the lawn of Prose Cottage while Frankie shared a G&T with their near-neighbour, Joan, on the uncomfortable patio chairs she'd been meaning to replace since last summer.

Prose Cottage.

With a P. Not *Rose* Cottage as thousands of such retreats were named up and down the country. Frankie's mother had been a poet and aspiring writer who made no money from it but loved to come here to compose, anyway. Frankie had penned many-a story too, copying her mother's mannerisms and thoughtful expressions, staring out the window at the view. Atop a hill, with the only neighbours a ten-minute trek down the lane, a person could see for miles in whatever direction they faced. Like defending a fort.

Which made it ideal for Moses's paranoid assertion that one day an enemy might come for him, for *them*, and they'd have to make do until the powers that be mobilised. At night, and when the sun chose not to shine and they remained inside, deadbolts and steel-lining secured all the quaint-looking doors, while laminate-strengthened glass in the windows wouldn't stop a high-velocity bullet at close range but would limit its lethality, and an emergency line connected through a satellite phone, accessible from every room including the panic room constructed in the former coal store off the kitchen. Not to mention the shotgun which Frankie kept hidden but close at hand. Currently, it was in the umbrella rack in the porch, a coat slung in a sloppy heap hiding the stock.

The pre-noon G&T helped with Frankie's nerves, her new neighbour having introduced herself last night after they'd settled in, and Frankie was thankful of the company. She figured it was safe. The woman was short with grey hair, of indeterminable middle age, but clearly the sort who favoured the company of cats over humans.

As the pre-noon drinks morphed into post-noon, they watched Eko attempt a complicated 360-degree spin-jump, which Frankie could not imagine being of any help in an actual fight, and shared limited personal information—the name of the city they lived, ages, careers, Eko's school year. Joan's major revelation came that she was a widow of eight years and recently bought the next property over after she grew tired of "city life" in Cirencester.

Frankie had visited Cirencester more than once, a nearby medium sized town, so if Joan had tired of that "city" it suggested she'd never ventured far from this sleepy, affluent region.

"What about you?" Joan asked. "Did your man leave you?"

"Not yet. But who knows when he'll come to his senses." Frankie's flippant answer made her ponder whether three G&Ts this early in the p.m. meant she should reacquaint herself with the coffee pot. "He's working. We're out here having a bit of a break before Eko's Eleven-Plus."

Joan tilted her head as Eko swept her arms slowly over her wide-legged stance, hands forged into blades as they crossed one another. "Do you fight?"

"That? No. Her dad insisted she start when she was seven, almost eight. She's a brown belt now."

Joan chopped the air with her hands. "And does he do all that chop-socky stuff?"

"Oh, no, nothing like that. Glynn learned how to handle himself the old-fashioned way." Frankie was going to leave it at that, but at Joan's querying squint she elaborated. "Trial and error. Brawling as a youngster, in and out of trouble. Boxed for a while. If he didn't stand up to people, he'd have been trampled underfoot. And being built naturally like a grizzly bear helps."

"Will he be joining you?"

"Maybe. I haven't spoken to him in a day or so." She didn't see the need to say the mobile reception was down at the moment. It was unreliable at best, but she hadn't been concerned, not with the sat phone in the house. "But I'll be sure to remind him about what he's missing once I do."

Joan laughed. A bit too hard. "Oh, my, I think this has gone to my head."

"Me too." Frankie stood, watching Eko as she steadied herself on the table. "I'll make some coffee."

"That would be lovely."

Frankie went inside and boiled a kettle, then filled a stone cafetière and let it brew, watching Eko's kata progress through what looked like a series of small wooden-framed panes but was two sheets of near-bulletproof glass with the wood sandwiched between. All around, the garden had been trimmed by a guy they paid to come in once a month, who mowed twice a month in summer. She pictured Glynn out there, in his scruffs, digging out a square of grass to convert to a vegetable plot.

During his suspension he'd seemed so peaceful in their own garden back home, spading chicken manure into trenches to rot down in preparation for peas, broad beans, and other crops. He'd be happy here, glancing up occasionally to help correct Eko's posture despite not training in the discipline himself, maybe indulging in a beer or one of those flavoured ciders he'd taken to during the sunshine months. It'd be good for him. Months, not weeks. Maybe even years, if they could find a school for Eko.

Rural Gloucestershire needed policemen, didn't it?

She brought the cafetière outside on a tray along with two chunky mugs and an orange milk jug with a sugar bowl that had lived here as long as she could remember. Eko had gone still, while Joan's gaze had settled on something that fascinated her more than the fresh beverages. Frankie placed the tray down and, curious, followed Joan's line of sight and crossed to Eko, who was staring at the same spot.

That same spot beyond the wall held a man with

a gun rushing sideways. A machine-gun. Helmet. Body armour.

Frankie squeaked rather than screamed, whipping her head all around, spotting another intruder perpendicular to her and Joan, aiming their way. One hand extended, patting the air to say, *get down, stay still.*

Silent approach. Armed to the teeth. A full unit.

"Glynn," she said, and gestured for her daughter and neighbour to follow her lead, sinking to her knees, hands on her head.

And then the rest of the firearm-equipped officers descended, announcing their presence in yelled orders, and storming into the little cottage, as if a cadre of terrorists had taken them hostage.

"Glynn," she said again, and rehearsed how many new arseholes she was going to tear her husband when he finally arrived.

43

While Moses had expected fireworks, he didn't think he'd be the bad guy in this. With minimal privacy in the kitchen due to the AFOs in the garden and front path, he faced down his fire-breathing wife with equal parts apology and relief that they'd got here in time.

"In *time*?" Frankie said. "Your stormtroopers scared the hell out of Eko and probably induced a stroke in poor Joan."

"A stranger, Frankie?"

"She's a fifty-year-old widow and was living next door when we arrived. Unless you think your big bad enemies are playing the long game? Installing sleeper widow assassins everywhere you might consider hiding?"

Moses conceded it seemed unlikely. "Your cell phone wasn't connecting."

"It happens from time to time around here. You know that."

Moses again conceded the point. He roamed the kitchen more than paced. Although the locals had declared it clear of intruders, bombs, or anything else that might do harm, he was certain Baines wasn't bluffing. The threat was real. Something was amiss.

He'd been less than enthused to learn Frankie had isolated Eko in her room with an iPad and headphones to blot out the goings-on below, and although she'd launched into a big hug when he showed up, she also scolded him for this "overreaction."

"I wouldn't be surprised if Joan files a complaint," Frankie said. "I mean, *seriously*, Glynn? Couldn't you have called the house phone?"

"When I couldn't raise you on your mobile, I was worried they were already holding you hostage, or…" He didn't want to say it out loud. Tears pricked behind his eyes at the very hint of a thought. "Or worse."

The word calmed Frankie for only a moment. However, she recharged, regrouped, and relaunched. "That's no excuse for all *this*." She swung an arm at the back door, to the once-neat garden trampled by the armed police whom Rock had commandeered. "You and your bloody paranoia. What was it that made you send us away? If it was that dangerous, why don't we have around-the-clock protect—"

A new voice intruded. "Umm."

"Oh, hey, Juliette." Frankie switched tones, as if an old friend had popped by. "Just having a chat with Serpico here."

Rock pressed her lips together, an apologetic shrug. "Boss?"

"It's okay." Moses wound his hand through the air. "I won't get to keep anything from her. Let's hear it."

Rock held up a small box that looked like a rectangular flowerpot. She clicked a panel which fell away to reveal what looked like a walkie-talkie. "Jamming device. It was behind a drainpipe out back."

"Inside the property line?" Moses crossed the room in four strides and accepted it from her. "The cell phone issue was intentional."

"Moses…" Frankie held onto his arm.

"Short range, a hundred yards maybe," Rock said.

Moses thought it through. "It had to be on this property, or close by."

"Given the additional security in the house, they wouldn't take any chances. That's why it was against the wall of the house, not out in the field."

"But the motion detectors," Frankie said. "We'd have heard anyone at night."

If anything bigger than a rabbit entered the garden, the physical movement activated a bright light and buzzed loudly enough to wake someone in the master bedroom.

"Meaning they planted it in the daytime," Moses said. "Someone you saw."

Frankie's face creased, hand to her mouth. "There was only Joan."

To Rock, Moses asked, "Where's the neighbour?"

Rock was already moving outside, Moses jogging after her. She said, "The team cleared her ID. I sent a female officer to take her home."

Home was down the back lane, a single-track dirt track wide enough for a compact car that ran along all the cottages dotted along the back of these farmers' fields.

"Constable Dawson," Rock called into her radio.

She and Moses hastened through the garden, drawing looks from the other AFOs—six here, all but one male. The sergeant in charge fired them a frown at the question that needed no words: *what's going on?*

"Dawson, respond," Rock said again. "Position and status."

"She's with the woman," the sarge said, keeping pace as they passed into the lane.

"How far to Joan's property?" Rock asked.

"Three minutes if we hurry." Moses took off at a jog.

The sarge beckoned two more to accompany him.

Moses called back to Frankie, "Stay inside!"

Their run lasted two-and-a-half minutes, the armed officers taking point as they came up on the property. Much like Moses's cottage, it was the epitome of "quaint" but large enough to boast a sizeable nest-egg. Unlikely it came equipped with the same features as theirs, though. And the back-patio door was open, slid all the way on its rail.

The sarge positioned them all by the dry-stone wall, using it as cover, and tried again. "Constable Dawson. Nicola, this is Edgar. Come in."

No response.

Moses eyed the AFO beside him, crouched, ready for action. The officer prepped his MP5A, but also carried a Glock 17 on his belt. Moses reached for the Glock. Was about to snatch it for his own use, to take down the person who'd been prepared to disable or even wipe out his family, when the sarge, in a breach of protocol that might have got him fired if it went wrong, called out, "Breach! Breach now."

The two AFOs leapt into action without questioning the order. A colleague in trouble. A friend, most likely. They rushed in.

Unarmed, Moses kept to the rear but didn't slow. Stupid move, stupid gung-ho ego, but he wasn't prepared to wait, either.

All piled through the open door, the sergeant

first inside, positioning to the left side to cover the second, the third knowing the routine and following through. Moses hesitated at the doorway, sense taking over—not wanting to startle the police into shooting him—and finding Rock immediately behind.

A cry of, "Oh, Jesus H. Christ," resonated.

No one could hold position.

Moses bundled through, the veranda clear, the next room—a book-lined lounge musty with cat smells—also empty, but past the stairs and into the bright, wide kitchen, he found the bodies that had caused the AFO's blasphemy-laden shout.

An older man and a woman about the same age —late sixties—whose faces Moses vaguely recognised lay slumped on the dining table, blood having spread from their throats and sunk into the wood. It had dripped on the floor and dried over several hours. They had started to rot, although the stench was not yet overwhelming.

The third body was dressed in police-issue body armour, a woman with her neck cut open, eyes wide, and her weapons and radio missing. The sarge had already laid her down, ripping off the armour, the other AFOs scrambling to help.

And they would try.

They would stem the blood, which Moses could see had ceased pumping already, and they'd do all they could. He suspected they understood the futility as he did, but instead of stopping them, he took up his radio and relayed the news no copper wanted to hear. Someone had cut down one of their own, and the suspect had fled.

Rock breathed through her mouth, deep and steady, frayed to the core as she contained what was clearly a boiling anger, ready to spill over into one almighty grease fire. "You know the area. Which way would they go?"

"They're long gone." Moses sensed her fury as it was coursing through him too, fiery and gritty in his veins. "Too many variables. But we'll get this one. We'll get it for sure."

"One of Kaspar Sevan's people?"

"They better hope so. A real cop couldn't do this to one of their own. No matter how far they've fallen."

They watched the futile attempts to revive PC Nicola Dawson, her teammates daubed with her blood, each of them radiating false hope, verging on denial. All anyone could do was find who did it and dish out as much punishment as they could get away with.

"Get a proper description from my wife," Moses said. "Then scramble a chopper. We're gonna get this murdering bitch. That's a promise."

44

Clara Burns ran. She hated running. Unfortunately, the 450cc Kawasaki motocross bike she'd stashed would have been too loud and drawn the attention of her Gloucestershire colleagues, so after killing the AFO she'd legged it on foot. And when she did things she hated, she hoped no one got in her way, because it rarely worked out well for either party.

It had been half an hour since the raid. Her cover had fooled Frankie Moses and, more importantly, the police who'd stormed the place. A bit of makeup to age her eyes, the grey wig, the frumpy clothes. She'd never worked undercover professionally, but this one had been a doddle. Screaming, crying, dropping the only glass with her fingerprints and trampling the shards underfoot as she retreated, playing the damsel in shock, then citing a need to ingest a heart pill. She'd said she didn't need an escort, and if the regs-heavy sarge hadn't lumbered her with the girl to get her back safe, if the young AFO had let her be instead of insisting on clearing the house as a precaution, she'd still be alive.

It wasn't Burns' fault. She had no choice.

The call to execute the wife and girl never came, and with the police arriving en masse she guessed something had gone wrong, that Moses Glynn or Glynn Moses—whatever—had learned that they knew about his family retreat. She wasn't even sure how *they* knew about it, but it wasn't her job to ask those questions. All she had to do was kill everyone who'd seen her, wash her hands, and get out with her go-bag, grateful neither Rock nor Moses dwelled long upon her.

Running.

She hated it but was good at it. She kept herself fit, and then some; had even braved marathons in the past. Her preference was for strength, for muscle, which she could feel rising and falling, sense its expansion as she exercised, isolating certain groups for a deeper burn. The process broadened her shoulders and widened her thighs, making her look chubby in the wrong clothes, but one of the many emotions she'd jettisoned long ago was vanity. Besides, when fleeing a crime scene, it was an advantage looking like this instead of like Agnes Marsh or that bloody Olympian-built detective constable with the red hair.

Burns' cross-country jog brought her out in the village of Nipping Haven with only a light sheen to her brow and around a twenty percent elevation to her heart rate. She blamed much of the sweat on the rubber-lined wig that fit like a bathing cap to prevent her real hair—and therefore DNA—from shedding. Maintaining the older-lady image, though, wouldn't be out of place, even if the knapsack she'd grabbed before departing might seem a tad unusual.

There was little in the way of eye contact here, although it wasn't unfriendly, and she hadn't made her face known. The mostly older population, a scattering of people out and about, browsed the antique shops and traditional butcher's, the two bookshops, and an assortment of other buildings Burns thought long extinct in modern Britain: a church with its doors open, three pubs, community centre, a town square featuring a war memorial, the surrounding walls dotted with teens—the kids behaving well; no booze or joints in sight, although their heads stayed buried in phones. That suited Burns.

Then out the south end of town, she diverted off the main road and took a dog leg dirt trail that traversed a public footpath, sheltered for ten minutes in a barn where she snapped off the wig, drank some water, and changed into hiking gear. She stuffed her old-lady clothes and hair into her bag and followed the backup route—again, at a jog—

overtaking a party of ramblers without allowing them to see her face, returning their polite "hellos" with a wave and a "hi there" before forging on.

Rather than continuing to the pub-lined loop that would bring her back to Nipping Haven, she followed a less-worn public footpath between two fields which had become overgrown through lack of feet upon it, redolent with scents of lavender and wild garlic. Within fifteen minutes, she arrived at a secluded spot in an orchard, shielded from the road by thick bushes where a BMW 3-Series waited. It was where she'd intended to set the bike alight, along with everything else that linked her to the cottage neighbouring Frankie's, had she not been forced to go with the backup escape route.

All she could burn now was the backpack and its contents, which she did using lighter fuel, checking off her precautions in the house: touched nothing except in gloves, hair secure in the bathing-cap-wig-contraption, seen only by Frankie, Eko, and the dead people, plus a handful of AFOs whose attention remained on an external threat.

From the BMW, she retrieved a grey business suit and white blouse, and changed into it with a spritz of flowery-smelling deodorant, then dropped the old hiking gear onto the fire, adding some twigs to keep it going while the boots caught. She'd be wearing low-rise heels all the way home. Then she climbed into the car, started it, and flicked on the police scanner. She was ten miles from the crime scene, and only five minutes from the M5 that would take her north back home.

Technically, she had not failed her part. No call came to execute the pair, and she hadn't been caught. No one would be able to ID her except for unreliable witnesses, and her alibi in the Midlands was as tight as it could be—both digital signatures and eyewitnesses. It was only as she was merging with the M5 traffic that she heard on the scanner a police helicopter was being scrambled. The description they issued was that of her old persona, and the thin blue line had claimed another life.

She mourned the loss of a fellow police officer, but again reiterated it wasn't her fault. If they'd listened to Burns, left her be, the girl who'd escorted her would still be alive.

Forty-five minutes after fleeing the scene, Clara Burns was a ghost, on her way to being a very wealthy ghost indeed. "Love this job," she said aloud, and wondered what she should cook for dinner.

45

As soon as the situation filtered through to DCI Wearne, she recalled Moses and Rock all the way back to the Division 43 base. Partly, Moses suspected, to bulldoze Wearne's authority over them. It was easier to chew them out face-to-face, so even past eight in the evening, after hours of searching for the person sent to monitor or possibly assassinate his family, Moses stood ready, unrepentant. Hands behind his back, chest high, eyes front.

"So they win?" Wearne said, almost spitting the words.

Her office was dark, a single lamp illuminating the space, the main office lit only by Moses's and Rock's computer screens, the motion-activated lights having clicked off behind the pair as they delivered their summary to the chief.

"It's not about winning or losing, ma'am,"

Moses replied. "It's the preservation of life. Which is the prime concern of all police investigations."

Wearne wound up a response, but restrained it, switching her focus. "Zachary Shepherd." Wearne moved her gaze from Moses to Rock, then back again. "He doesn't have much authority in the traditional sense, as I'm sure you know. He's about policy, budgets, allocation. But he has influence. Influence enough to persuade the Home Secretary that Division 43 is not only needed, but a boon for policing. If he is to maintain that influence, which I shouldn't need to remind you is very important to him, he has to deliver. *We* have to deliver. And yes, as you've alluded to, part of your selection to this team *was* your unproven but widely acknowledged former connections to organised crime. I make no apologies for that. Or that I assigned DC Rock to be your conscience and my eyes and ears—in case your connections weren't quite as *former* as believed."

"Ma'am?" Rock sounded offended, if not a little confused.

Wearne waved her off. "What happens when this case collapses thanks to a detective going off the deep end? What happens when this case collapses because the opposite happens—a detective conceding defeat after a setback?"

Again, Moses fought the pressure inside his head to keep his frustration in check. "We were hours, maybe *minutes*, from them being killed."

"Nicola Dawson." Wearne hit her remote and the face of the dead AFO appeared on the screen on her wall. "Twenty-six years old. She had a dog, a cocker spaniel called Jinx. Bought it after moving in with her boyfriend, Danesh. Her mum and dad paid for the deposit on their flat. Nicola liked old Ealing comedies, surfing, and had a unicorn tattoo on—"

"Ma'am, I wasn't aware I had another assignment," Rock said.

Wearne rounded on her. "Are you interrupting me, Constable?"

"It appears I am, ma'am, yes. You implied I had additional instructions on this case. But I want it on the record that I was unaware of any such order." Her eyes flitted to Moses. Clearly for his benefit. He'd made it clear how coppers looked down on snitches, and he wouldn't wish that guilt on anyone, even if it wasn't real. "Was I supposed to check in more often?"

"You were *supposed* to do what you did when the Army refused to back you. When your senior officer undermined you, against Army regulations; when you believed senior officers were covering up the disappearance of military hardware from Stores; when you learned US troops had killed civilians, despite British intelligence warning them of the potential error; not to mention a dozen other incidents in which you displayed the moral fortitude I require in a detective." Wearne peered, unblinking, at Rock. "I expected you to do *the right thing*. That's why you're here. Because you don't waver when things get tough."

Wearne hung her head back, breathing deep, before righting herself, composed and collected.

Calmly, she said, "Zachary Shepherd. He can't protect us from the Home Office axe. Especially now a police officer is dead. Gloucestershire are demanding answers, and their brass aren't exactly disconnected from the Westminster machine. Why were we able to commandeer them so easily? Did we give them sufficient intel to secure the welfare of Nicola Dawson against a… what are we saying? A hired assassin? One of Gray's team?"

"We have an open mind on that, ma'am," Moses replied. "We hope it was outside. Otherwise, we have a stone-cold psychopath pulling a wage from the taxpayer."

Wearne resumed the officialdom. "Was her death brought about because we forced them to go in ill-equipped? Poor intel from what purports to be an intelligence division? Or hot-headed impulsiveness? Slack supervision in the field? Or an unforeseeable consequence of a well-planned assassination attempt, interrupted?" She touched her desk with all her fingertips, her hands arched like two spiders testing a new surface. "Because someone needs to answer for that, and quickly."

"I'm the scapegoat," Moses said. No anger, just

understanding, even accepting his fate. "I should have known more."

Wearne clasped her spider-hands before her, straightening and fixing on Moses and Rock in turn. "If we get a result, an arrest not just for our case but PC Dawson's, it's over. But it needs to happen soon. Either Barney Gray's cops go down, or Joshua Sevan and, preferably, his dad need to be blamed. If not, DI Moses, you're out on your ear, and DC Rock? Your fast track to command is stuck in the bog."

Moses didn't need long. He'd already talked it through with Rock and they were in agreement. "Ma'am, we came too close this time. To losing Frankie… and Eko. Please reapply pressure on DCS Cleland to get Joshua Sevan's alibi revoked, in exchange for which we will not pursue disciplinary proceedings against the detectives in question. We'll chalk it up to human error. Joshua goes down, maybe we tie his dad in somewhere, try to get DI Walar out of jail when we link the dead girl to the Sevans, and justice is served. At least, the best we can achieve at this stage."

Rock lowered her head, stiff in the movement. "And we'll come back to the Shadow CPU the next time they surface."

"A postponement," Wearne said. "It keeps us safe and staves off the political pressure. Fine. Joshua Sevan will do for now. Go get him."

46

They could have gone home, picked it up first thing, but where was the fun in that? Rock was single, and happily-so. While they stuck around Division 43's HQ, Moses's house was ringed with blue—protective custody composed of thoroughly vetted personnel.

Rock still rankled at losing the bigger fish, though. Held out hope something might shake out of the office-bound re-examination of Gabriella Childs' murder.

If DCS Cleland was to get Gray and the team to recant the alibi, they needed evidence that tipped the balance of risk the other way. If they pushed it, they had to prosecute, in which case the police would close ranks and unions would obscure the facts, and the public would call it a witch hunt. Political pressure, the threshold demanded by the

CPS for a prosecution, and the question of how far these tentacles wound, might prove an obstacle too far.

"We can still make the case," Rock said, leaning back in her chair, feet up on the desk, shoes off—a luxury of civilian life being the tolerance of sloppy appearance when shifts overran.

"Not before someone dies," Moses countered. "We'll get them. Or someone will. But it's a long-game. Take what we can, come back for the rest when we're in a stronger position."

Rock tilted her head. "Think about it objectively. How we can push it back to the threshold."

Moses, who'd begun to tire for the first time since Rock met him, leaned his head on one hand, waiting for her to take him on that magical journey to *the threshold*.

Juliette Rock planted her feet on the floor and counted off on her fingers. Thumb: "The witnesses. We know for sure Joshua and Gabby argued. They clashed physically. He threatened her. Had threatened her in the past." First finger: "The video evidence. The mobile phone footage of the altercation backs up the witnesses. CCTV shows him and Ashley Mars getting into a car with her, the driver of which has been located."

Not by them, Rock knew. Unis had been sent out in the hope of another witness, but it hadn't worked out well in terms of evidence.

"Lost his dash cam SD card," Moses said. "Confirms Joshua's statement that the men got out and he dropped Gabby at a later stop near the park."

"We're either wrong about all of it, or they got to him."

"And we know how much leverage they can exert."

Rock's second finger: "Blood. Which…" She tapped the keyboard and clicked her mouse, bringing up the report on the bloodwork. Returned her thumb and two fingers to attention. "Matches Gabriella's blood type from the initial tests, but full analysis is still pending. We're sure it'll come back as hers, and when it does—"

Moses leaned heavier on his hand, as if about to fall asleep. "That's odd."

"What is?"

Now the opposite; he woke up as if ice cold water had splashed him. "We had a rush on the DNA. Should've been in by now."

Rock checked the records. He was correct; the autopsy should have been completed, but nothing had been uploaded to her PAL.

"Don't we have our own team on this?" Moses asked.

"No, Division 43 dictates where the examinations take place, but rely on the force pathologists. We picked Stoke's NCA base because it has someone Wearne trusts and was close to HQ."

"They stiffed us? Gave something else priority?"

Rock lowered her thumb and two fingers. "The

physical evidence is what will make this case. When we one hundred percent link the blood on Joshua's clothes to Gabriella's killing blow, that will force them to reconsider. If they have the right lawyer, someone who can chop up the science and lay some doubt with a jury, it won't be enough to convict Gray's people for the cover up. Time of death could be disputed, say he did her in later. They get off Scott-free, and maybe Joshua does too, given their testimony. If the physical evidence is questioned." Rock drummed the desk. "We need to shore up that side of it."

Moses's eyes narrowed as he looked up an entry. "Davina Mishkin was in charge of the blood work." He checked his watch. "I don't think it'd be too rude to pop by."

"She'll be working now? On a Saturday night?"

"It's only nine." He fired off a grin. "And we have a lot more access to personal information than we should."

Rock was already tapping at her phone, reading Davina's home phone number off her screen. Held the phone to her ear and locked eyes with Moses. Enthused at last. Moving quickly.

The enthusiasm folded into a frown. "No answer at her house." She read the screen again. "I'll try her mobile."

Again, she listened, the trilling going on and on, until the automated Vodaphone voicemail message butted in. She tried the house again, then the mobile again, and grew irritated at Moses not asking what was wrong, instead working his own station across from her.

"Voicemail again," she said.

"It's turned on, we can find it." Moses spun his screen to Rock. "And here it is." A map took up three quarters of the screen, coordinates, the post-code, and an option for directions listed down the other quarter. A red dot radiated from the street map. Moses tapped it with one thick finger. "It's sat at Davina Mishkin's home address."

47

Within twenty minutes, Rock pulled up on a neat, leafy street, three houses down from Dr Mishkin's, and Moses got straight out of the passenger side. Three houses down because there were so many cars parked. She joined Moses on the pavement, both walking with hands in their pockets, assessing Dr Davina Mishkin's house: a whitewashed semi-detached with a single driveway, garage, and a patch of grass out front, its border populated by roses. A little bigger than Rock's own place and in a nicer area, yet it was not the kind of swanky pad Rock associated with doctors; but then, not all medical practitioners could dwell in the world of the truly elite.

There were lights on. Three cars in the single drive. More cars in the road, which Rock figured were close enough to the Mishkin house to suggest visitors.

"What do you think?" Moses asked.

"You know what I think," Rock answered. "You sure you don't want to wait?"

"If she isn't dead or being held against her will, I'm guessing you're worried about the same thing as me."

"I am?"

"Yes."

"Go for it. Impress your supervisor."

He was right, but it annoyed her as he approached the door ahead of her. Music emanated from within, muffled, something classical.

She said, "It's a bloody dinner party, isn't it? That's why she isn't answering."

"But…?" He twisted to her, arching an eyebrow.

"But the report is still late. She should have produced the evidence we need by now."

"And she hasn't."

Moses knocked. Rang the bell. Twice. Both got their ID's ready, held out for whoever answered.

The door opened. The man staring at their warrant cards had a red tint to his cheeks, the slack smile of someone who'd imbibed more than a couple of sherries. He was tall and trim, athletic for a fifty-something. The slack smile faded, and the redness spread.

"Police." Moses lowered his card. "I'm Detective

Inspector Moses, this is Detective Constable Rock. Is Dr Mishkin available?"

"I'm Dr Mishkin," the man said.

"Dr Davina Mishkin?" Rock said.

He stiffened, as if waking from a power nap. "My wife." He called into the house. "Davina, may I borrow you a moment?"

"Can we come in, please, sir?" Moses asked.

Male Dr Mishkin stepped aside but eased the door closer to the jamb. "We have company. No offence."

Moses glanced at Rock. Returned attention to the door. Shrugged. "If we don't get what we need from your wife, sir, we're coming in."

The athleticism apparent in the man evaporated as he pulled back his shoulders. A shake in his voice. "I hardly think so, Detective…"

"Moses."

"Detective Moses. I'll be making a note of both your names—"

Rock shoved open the door but didn't enter. "It's Detective *Inspector* Moses and Detective *Constable* Rock. We're not in America. *Sir*."

"Excuse me?" The doctor left his mouth open in faux-anger, Rock having picked up on the same bravado as Moses plainly had.

Rock peered into the softly lit home, candles featuring somewhere. "Is she coming, or doing a runner?"

Davina Mishkin appeared from a flickering

room, a tight dress clinging to her ample frame. "I'm here. What is it?"

"Police, darling," the man said. "Rather rude police. I suggest you report them first thing Monday—"

"The Joshua Sevan evidence," Rock said. "We need access to the results. Now. Please come with us."

Dr Davina Mishkin strolled forward, as well greased as her husband. "It's a Saturday night and we have guests. I can't—"

Moses stepped into the door frame, pretty much filling it. "If you don't, a very bad man gets away with murder. Some very bad people stick two fingers up at the law."

In the gap between the jamb and Moses, Rock watched Davina Mishkin blink rapidly, glance at her husband, then focus on Moses. "I am under no obligation to do anything of the sort."

"If you don't, I'm going to break into your lab and search it myself. Where's the DNA result? The link between Gabriella Childs and the suit Joshua Sevan was wearing? The hairs that prove he was wearing that suit—"

"Everything okay?" called a voice from the candlelit room.

"Murder investigation," Moses called back.

"Everything's fine, yes," the pathologist replied in an airy tone. Then to her husband, "Go back and reassure them it's just a work thing."

Male Dr Mishkin departed, frowning at the detectives as he went.

Once he was gone, Rock said, "We need to see the results. Can't wait until Monday."

"I shelved it," female Dr Mishkin said. "There was nothing that helped, so I thought it'd wait. Plus, I heard you had freed the suspect. I'm sorry if that caused problems, I have a heavy caseload."

"We appreciate that, Doctor," Moses said, stepping back to the outer step, less intimidating. "But recent developments mean we have to move forward. Tonight. We need the DNA results before Monday. An arrest is imminent and—"

"No, you don't understand." Dr Mishkin shook her hands at them. Waited for them to listen. When satisfied, she said, "The blood work won't help you. It wasn't human blood."

"It wasn't... what?" Moses said.

"We know it was human," Rock pressed. "We know it was Gabby's blood type, but the full DNA workup takes time. It should have been complete before tonight."

"No. The people conducting the preliminary analysis made a mistake." Mishkin fixed them with wide eyes, any drunken sway or cant jettisoned in favour of earnestness. "The blood on the trousers and shoes came from a *dog*. It was canine blood."

Rock couldn't help herself. She pounced. Gripping Mishkin by the arms, squeezing. "I'm gonna need those items, Doc. We're gonna get them tested ourselves, and—"

Mishkin yelped and Moses touched Rock's shoulder. She released the woman, who recoiled in fear.

Moses no longer bore the manner of a police officer demanding cooperation. His shoulders had drooped some, and his eyes looked sad.

"What is it?" Rock asked.

"They're gone, aren't they?" Moses said.

Dr Mishkin held her ground. Weeping tears down both cheeks, hugging herself, rubbing the marks left by Rock's grip on her arms. "I was ordered to release the clothes back to the suspect. Someone from his lawyer's office collected them this morning."

The back of Rock's neck tingled. She felt cold. "They got to you too?"

Mishkin gave no hint of guilt, of regret. Wet eyes, bobbing throat. But she wasn't about to relent. "The initial tests were contaminated. The blood on the clothes was canine. The release paperwork was all in order." She bent slightly at the waist as if she'd been punched. "There's nothing else to say. I'm sorry you wasted your time."

Moses heaved himself around, making for the street. "Goodnight, Dr Mishkin."

Rock hesitated a second. Disbelief freezing her in place. Shocked at Moses letting it go like that.

But he was the senior detective here, so she trotted after him. Caught up. "What was that?"

"That, Captain, was the sound of us losing. If they can intimidate a National Crime Agency pathologist into going along with them, we've got nothing. And we'll have nothing in the future."

He kept going, his pace slower than usual but his strides just as long. He wanted more. Wanted more *from her*. From Rock.

"Whatever you're thinking, I'm in," she said.

He walked in silence. Stopped at Rock's car. "Don't make promises like that before you can read minds." Hand on the roof. "Anything?"

Rock mimicked his position, her palms flat on the metal opposite him. "You never planned on letting them go."

Moses allowed a wry smile.

The truth then dawned on Rock, blooming into a clearer picture, something that gelled more coherently than the things he'd been saying to Wearne. "You can't see a way of getting to them within our current rules. Even the enhanced powers."

A twitch of confirmation joined the subconscious hint of a nod.

"You didn't want to implicate me or the chief."

Moses's head dipped, breaking from her gaze.

"It's an old-school situation, isn't it?" she said. "Come on, Moses. Hit me. What would you have done in the old days?"

"Switch the rules," he replied with a tap on the

metal. "How does one gang eliminate another? It's not by wiping them all out."

Rock tried to see where he was going, but it was hazy. "The leadership?"

"Close. But not quite." The shovel of a hand on Rock's car roof clenched. "But this will be messy. No grey areas. Nothing Division 43's extra judicial powers can shelter us from. It's street rules. It goes wrong, we get fired. Maybe worse."

When Rock left the Army, she'd been lost. She joined the police almost by default, because there was nothing else to do. As she rose in the estimation of her fellow officers, she caught the eye of senior management, and her fast track to command was cemented in the next eighteen months. She worked hard. With her no longer on deployment, spending so much time with her husband and pushing on in her career, her marriage broke down—the arsehole rekindling an affair he'd sworn was in the past, something she suspected he did purely to initiate the proceedings, to sabotage all they'd tried to build. She was free, though, in both her personal life to explore career options as well as her sexual preferences, muddled in her pre-army life and resurfaced before meeting Sam during that climbing session, free to go where she chose. And she had an aim now, ambition: To ascend through the ranks and positively affect the police from that lofty position.

Return discipline.

Root out dishonesty.

Kill off the corruption that had stained law enforcement for so long.

Ego, perhaps, but she believed in what she was doing.

"Rock?" Moses said. "Are we doing this?"

"Yes," Rock said. "Whatever it takes. I'm in."

48

Cole Mainey used to object to working Saturday nights, but he'd joined MisPer because the good a copper sought to do in narcotics or even CID had been stymied long ago. He'd figured why not do something for himself, first under Baines, then Gray. He never expected to find fulfilment in the day-to-day job. Finding runaway kids, as well as vulnerable people ranging from the mentally ill to trafficking victims, sent him to bed with a warm sense of pride. It more than offset the actions he took in order to enhance a pathetic police pension that kept getting smaller and farther away.

And Saturday nights were good hunting.

He'd been stiffed with Agnes Marsh, the girl still learning the ropes of both the legitimate Missing Persons gig and the Enhanced Pension Scheme. He was still unclear whether Barney had recognised a kindred spirit in her or if she'd engaged in a spot of light blackmail. Cole had learned she'd witnessed him flinging that pervert out of his window up north and said nothing. At first.

Did she press Barney later? Did Barney let her in without mentioning certain threats to save face?

No, not Barney's style. Besides, it wouldn't have been his decision.

"Tip off's a dead end," Marsh said, returning to the corner of Broad Street in central Birmingham.

"No sign of Billy Toxteth?" Cole asked.

"Nor Drake."

"Okay." Cole checked his watch: midnight. "Guess we'll call it a night."

Agnes Marsh nodded, downcast, and was already heading back to where they'd parked their cars. Cole wondered, too, if she was cut out for the official part of the job, let alone the extracurricular business.

Agnes Marsh was glad to hear DS Mainey declare the long day over. Not only the stress of covering bases in the Sevan business, but this had been a tough missing persons case, which she'd thought was about to end happily. She'd explored a squat tonight, an old electrical store filled with homeless people strung out on heroin and meth, on the back of a tip that came in from a flyer offering a reward for information on Billy Toxteth's whereabouts.

The fourteen-year-old had met and formed a relationship online with someone who became his boyfriend in real life. A guy known only as "Drake", reputedly a seventeen-year-old, but Agnes had her suspicions about him, since no one in Billy's family or circle of friends had met the lad, and the MisPer team could detect no electronic signature for him, Drake having used a powerful virtual private network to exchange messages.

Agnes was sure Billy was either dead or embedded as a slave for some appalling individual, possibly smuggled abroad. It was depressing, but then so much of their work was.

"Hey, lady!" A boy's voice. The same boy's voice who'd directed them to the squat.

She turned and found the gangly kid with a pudding bowl haircut jogging toward them. He was out of breath, eyes sunken, aged anywhere between sixteen and twenty-one. Or younger. A blanket hung around his shoulders. Rotten trousers. New boots, probably from a charity.

Cole Mainey stepped between them.

"It's okay," Agnes said, moving aside. "You're Toby?"

He nodded, halting, breathing hard. "You came to my place."

"You were in the… building? With the others?"

"My friends, yeah."

Cole flexed in place, his mouth a grim line. "Ya lied about the kid?"

"No, no, I didn't. He's not here anymore."

Agnes allowed hope to spike in her chest. "Billy?"

"Yes, Billy. He moved on." The kid, Toby, beckoned. Jittery. Hopping backwards. "This way."

"Where?" Cole didn't move. Arm out to suggest—strongly—that Agnes didn't follow.

"I'll show you. Hotel. Can't remember the name. A hostel, really." His drug-addle stupor lifted. "This way."

Cole opened his jacket to unstud the extendible baton he always carried. He and Agnes both did. Agnes also kept a canister of pepper spray on another hoop.

Without another word, both went after Toby.

The lad babbled a bit, talking about how Billy and Drake lived in the squat for a while, but some charity came by, something to do with "the gays" as he called them. "Homeless Pride," he said, clicking his dirty-caked fingers at the memory. He led them down the side of a multi-storey parking lot, an upmarket shopping precinct towering to the other side. "They don't care about regular people. Just the poofs and dykes sleeping rough. Think their kind has it harder than me. But, y'know, the rain and cold, it don't discriminate."

Cole's rule for engaging with informants like Toby was to remain silent unless asked a direct question. Agnes had broken that rule only once, which resulted in some drug addict—yeah, you encounter a lot of drug addicts in this line of policing —thinking she was his friend, and begged her for a night or two off the streets; her couch, her bathroom floor, anything. She'd had to say no, and the situation turned violent, and she left the poor guy squirming in pain after a shot of pepper to the eyes.

At least tracking down Billy Toxteth might assuage some of that heartache. Balance her part in freeing a man who'd kicked to death a girl who could so easily have fallen through the cracks like Toby here.

"This is the place," Toby said, arm sweeping toward a grungy building.

Red double doors, peeling paint, the word *hostel* over it with a *full* sign beneath this, a handwritten addition declaring, *Seriously, we're full—don't even ask.*

"In here." Toby opened the door, peeking his head through and checking all around before going fully inside.

Cole Mainey stopped Agnes from following. A stern expression. He took his warrant card from one pocket and hung it around his neck, then removed the baton from his belt. Agnes did the same and gave him a firm nod—ready.

Toby poked his head back out. "You coming?"

Mainey led the way, with Agnes bringing up the rear. Inside was a tiny reception desk, a hole in the wall, with a cage closed around it. The place stank of homeless, that overwhelming stench of filth and booze; an undercurrent of faeces and piss.

Toby shuffled like a hunchback, delighted to help. "Here, here." He directed them past the narrow staircase to a door. "Through there. Communal room. They're in a bunk next to the door."

Cole pushed by Toby and wrapped his big hand around the doorknob. Nodded to Agnes's belt. She exchanged the baton for her spray. Cole nodded the countdown.

3...

2...

1!

He crashed through, Agnes again playing second fiddle. But they weren't in a room.

They were back outside. An alleyway. She only had seconds to register the location before the door slammed shut behind and a hand gripped her wrist.

Twisted.

The pepper spray fell from her fingers. Her assailant converted the arm lock to a choke hold, pulling Agnes back against a female body. Through considerable pain, she craned enough to see she was being subdued by that ginger detective constable.

Juliette Rock.

"Take it easy," Rock said. "This isn't about you."

Eyes-front, she watched Cole Mainey and Moses Glynn facing off.

"I'm letting you go." Rock eased the pressure on Agnes but didn't release her. "No interference."

“Okay, bitch, fine.” Agnes slithered free.

“Behave. And we won’t have a problem.”

Agnes considered going for Rock, but the background Kortenberg acquired suggested high level hand-to-hand training.

“Whatever.” Agnes straightened her jacket and stood aside. “Mainey’s got this.”

Removing his expensive-looking jacket, Moses hung it neatly on the broken bracket from a drainpipe long-since forgotten. He said, “I don’t believe in ‘types’, not when it comes to people. Especially in our line of work.” Rolling up his sleeves. Keeping his waistcoat buttoned. “But you and me, Cole, some things stay the same.” Fists up, sidestepping, Cole following him. “Sometimes, we speak a different language.”

Cole dropped the baton and kicked it away, warrant card heading the same way. He shrugged off his own jacket and tossed it to land on a closed bin. His sleeves were already short. Fists already pumping. He clearly didn’t give this a second thought.

“Okay, then,” he said. “Let’s chat.”

49

For the next ten seconds, the two men circled, bucks sizing up a rival for a doe's affections. In the end, Moses was the one to grow bored first and feinted with his left. But Mainey read the bluff and rode the follow-up kidney shot, his lowered elbow taking the brunt. He returned the attack with a jab that connected with Moses's lip. Luckily, Moses saw it in time and jerked back, the blow glancing his mouth rather than smashing teeth.

Mainey reacted to Moses's next fake attack much the same way, but instead of a reverse punch, Moses stamped on the other's foot and barged him with a shoulder. He thudded into the man's torso. Fat and muscle cushioned the impact, dredging him back only a couple of feet instead of throwing him into the Dumpster-style bin.

Quick change of tactics.

Moses used the momentary lack of balance to land three hard shots in his opponent's midriff, then a solid uppercut to the jaw that flared through his own knuckles. Mainey's head snapped back.

Another opening.

Moses lined up a boot, as if kicking down a door, and thrust it forward. Slammed into Mainey's chest. As Mainey's eyes bulged and he gasped for air, Moses sidled in for a big hit.

But Mainey was acting.

He ducked what would have been a knockout haymaker and with a roar he charged Moses, lifting him off the ground with brute strength and momentum. Moses had no say in their direction, raining ineffective punches at the man's back. A glance over his shoulder identified the danger: a solid steel rail outside the next building's fire exit.

This is going to hurt.

Moses twisted, brought his arm down, and saved his ribs and kidneys from the collision, but the crash into metal brought a thick wave of pain and a loud clang.

Agnes Marsh shouted, "That's it, Cole, fuck him up proper."

"You got him, Moses," Rock countered.

Moses shoved away from the immovable barrier with one foot, raising a knee into Mainey's bulk, but connected with nothing important. He still had Moses around the waist, so Moses tried a hammer-blow with his elbow, but lacked leverage.

Mainey bent his knees, roared again, and lifted Moses like a deadweight.

Stronger than Moses had expected.

He tipped over like a wrestler, Mainey's hold slackening enough for Moses to squirm higher, which played into his hands.

Mainey pinned Moses's arms to his side, a bear-hug in mid-fall, leaving the DI with even less control than before.

"Shiiiiiitt!"

The two men hit the filthy concrete, Moses head-first, rearing up at the last second to prevent a skull fracture. But the impact tore into his face, white flaring as he hit. His shoulder followed into the crash. The movement, though, caused Mainey to take more of the force than he likely intended, the slap of his back like a thunderclap.

Moses rolled away, vision blurred, blinking, trying to orient himself. Lying on his front, five yards from Mainey. He'd ended up in a puddle. Hoped it was only water, but it smelled far worse—diesel, a cocktail of garbage water, the ever-present hint of piss.

DS Mainey lay still. Breathing but moving slowly, a turtle upended. "Ah, for crying out loud." He glanced at Moses. "Damn, you're still going."

"You too." Moses manoeuvred into a push-up position and heaved himself to his knees. Ignored the damp, the prospect of whatever made up that moisture. Blood dribbled down his chin, an unseen trail from his brow warm down his neck. "Wanna give up?"

Mainey shifted himself onto his front, moving like a robot with faulty gears. Onto one knee. Twisted himself at the waist, wound one shoulder then the other, and he turned his head as far as it would go. His neck cracked. "Ah, that's better." He stood fully and adopted a boxer's pose. "I can probably manage round two."

Moses jumped from his knees to his feet, an action intended to show he wasn't in the least bit tired, but in fact jarred his arm. It wasn't broken, but it wasn't in great shape either. "Sure. Round two sounds good."

Rock had been excited by the prospect of seeing Moses rip into Cole Mainey.

How does one gang eliminate another?

She'd thought the crooked detective soft and flabby, but it was clear he was once well muscled, still was, with a layer of fat simply hanging over his frame.

Take out the biggest, meanest guy they have.

The pair threw down again, landing blow after blow, blocking with forearms, neither willing to get too close. It was most definitely a *street fight*, not two artists going at it. Then Moses forged an opening.

Predicting a shot at his face; he grabbed

Mainey's arm, dragged him forward and hit a straight punch into the man's nose. It crunched and blood popped, sending him reeling.

"Is this a new policy, then?" Agnes asked.

"Nah, we just can't beat you within the confines of the law," Rock replied, keeping an eye on her in relation to the spray she dropped. "This is only the start."

Agnes's face contorted in anger. "Get him, Cole. I've seen you take out bigger bastards than this."

Cole Mainey fired back, but he overreached, his sight most likely obscured through the damaged nose, and Moses took advantage, landing a hook that sent Mainey stumbling.

"We're going to get you all," Rock said. "You can't keep this up indefinitely."

"Don't have to." Agnes seemed to find it funny. "You think we're planning on doing this for another twenty years? Get real."

"No, I don't think that." Rock turned her attention back to the fight, half an eye on the pepper spray. "I think you're going down. And guess who they'll cut loose first."

Cole Mainey wasn't done, though. As Moses shuffled in again, he lashed back with his foot, causing Moses to jump aside, then aimed a volley of punches. Most failed to land; blocked, dodged, or absorbed by a meaty forearm. But a couple got through, including one to the face that resounded with a Hollywood slap. And a stagger from Moses.

But Moses came back yet again. Fists. Elbows. Knees. More fists.

"Last in, first out," Rock said.

Agnes rounded on her but didn't approach. "What did you say?"

"You know the rule, Constable. Look at what they did to Ratan Walar as soon as we got a sniff of them. Last in, Agnes, is always first out. We have plenty of evidence, but not enough for the whole team. And when we come for you guys, and..." Rock gestured to the pair of bucks smashing into one another. "And we're going to. Maybe not this week or next. But we're coming. And you'll be the one they sacrifice."

Agnes tried to front it out, but a flicker in her cheek gave Rock the advantage. Marsh's teeth clenched to see it off. "I know we'll beat you."

"Think about it, Agnes. Self-preservation."

"Fuck you." Marsh turned back to the fight.

Both men were ailing, exhausted, bleeding from the face, the knuckles. Moses's darker skin hid more damage than Mainey, but if this was going to be won on points, Rock gave it to Moses. She might have been biased, though.

"It's over," Moses said.

"Not even close." Mainey wound up a haymaker, then thrust a jab instead.

Moses sidestepped it and launched an elbow into Mainey's ribs, casting him several feet away. "I still can't believe humans can do what you do.

Forget police. Forget that we're supposed to be on the same side. Basic decent humanity, Cole."

Mainey spat blood. "Humans are survivors. The apex predators. And all apex groups need their alphas."

"And that's what you are? Deciding who's worth a second thought?"

"Damn right we're the alphas."

"Not anymore." Moses threw himself into the fighting red zone, leading with a gut punch that landed on Mainey's elbows, tucked in just in time, then head butted him. "I'm taking over, y'hear? You're mine."

The punches flew again, hard and fast, and all Mainey could do was make himself as small as possible, which was still pretty big, protecting his tender spots, half-ducking the attack.

Yet, he didn't go down.

"Time, Moses," Rock said. "He's baked."

"Not even close." Moses fired off a triple to Mainey's head, a boxer hitting the speedball.

"You kill him, I have to arrest you. And you know I will."

Moses paused. Long enough for Mainey to swing an arm, on the end of which his battered and bleeding wrecking ball of a fist drifted close to Moses's face, but even to Rock it appeared to be moving in slow motion. All Moses needed to do was step to his right, tug Mainey forward, and stick out a leg. What several dozen jackhammer blows had failed to do, gravity performed with aplomb, Mainey a tree being felled by a sloppy lumberjack.

He landed flat on the floor and moaned. Hands pushed beneath him, ready to rise. "Gimme a sec." Through deeper breaths, he sounded drunk, followed by a groan. "Round three coming up."

Moses obviously saw what Rock did. What Agnes understood too, but contained behind a mask of lip-curling hate. Mainey could probably add a few more licks, could've lasted another round, but continuing meant doling out more punishment than a human body could withstand. Rock worried he might already have done so.

Moses hobbled over to his jacket and draped it over his arm. The rest of him caked in dirt, blood, and whatever else. Ripped shirt, waistcoat, skin. "No round three."

He attempted to walk without a stoop, without the limp, but the hurt was as clear as if it had been painted on. He glanced at Rock. Pivoted to Agnes Marsh, who glared up defiantly.

"We're at war now," Moses said. "No police, no gangsters. Me and you people. Me and Baines, if it comes to it. Me and Theo-fucking-Goodman."

As Moses stepped around her, the junior detective's jutting jaw, the fearless sneer, faltered. It was more than a defiant expression, more than pretending she wasn't bothered by her situation.

Setting out to follow, Rock paused to speak to Marsh. This time softly, allowing the curiosity to spill on her tone. "You want to ask something. Don't you?"

"No," Marsh said.

"You do. And it's okay. I twigged as soon as Moses said it. Something important. They're hiding it from you."

Agnes trudged two paces toward Mainey, still on his back but rolling onto his side. She halted. Faced Rock. She said, "Fine. Who's Theo Goodman?"

That was what Rock had been hoping for. Seeing her angry, then scared, then deflating as she read the situation for what it was.

Rock sidled up close to Agnes. "Like I said…" She replied quietly enough to keep it from Mainey. "Last in, first out. They haven't told you everything because they don't really trust you. And if they don't trust you…? As soon as we get close…? Think about that for a while."

Rock turned from her and ambled out of the alleyway, Moses refusing her offer of a shoulder to lean on. Time to go home.

50

Moses sat on the throne lid in the downstairs bathroom wearing only gym shorts, awaiting Juliette Rock's arrival. Unlike many spare bathrooms, this was a full-sized one, with a toilet, tub, and separate shower—and a full-length mirror. A full-length mirror that the powerful extractor fan kept free of steam, which revealed him in all his glory.

Moses Glynn was a big man. Big-boned, big framed, big muscled. He didn't look like a bodybuilder or even a Hollywood action man, but a slab of lean beef. Square, wide shoulders and a flat stomach, pecs only small mounds on the surface, his general girth hiding their power. His arms and legs, like his body, didn't ripple with bulging muscle, but nor did they wobble; no spare fat, no loose skin. When he flexed, the definition was there, but in everyday life, he just looked… big. It was one reason he'd started grooming so thoroughly—to alleviate that thuggish size, his brutelike mien. And now it was all gone.

He'd expected resistance from Mainey but had gotten his own way in physical altercations too often. Made him slack. Sloppy. This was supposed to be a threat, a slap in the face. And if he hurt this badly having won the fight, his throat tightened whenever he thought of Mainey bleeding internally, dying on a gurney in a Saturday night Accident & Emergency ward surrounded by other victims of punch-ups, stabbings, even shootings. A triage nurse might consider him lower priority than someone holding their guts in their hands from an open knife wound. Then Moses and Rock would be on the hook for murder—manslaughter at best.

He'd left his car in Birmingham and Rock drove him home, managed to get in the house by pretending to the AFOs guarding the place that he was drunk, Rock rolling her eyes and asking them to "keep it quiet, things have been stressful this week", and made it to the downstairs bathroom without waking Frankie or Eko. Once in there, he stripped to his pants. His waistcoat was torn and dirty but maybe salvageable, his bloody shirt a write-off as it slapped to the floor like he'd been running in red gloopy rain. His trousers were ripped in the groin and one knee. It was all going in the bin. Or a fire.

Wasn't that what people did after a crime like

this? What Joshua Sevan had been planning after Gabby's death?

Rock had scooped up the sodden clothes in a bin liner and left the room while he tossed his boxers and socks in the bin. Then he eased himself into the shower—another movement that flared pain through almost every joint. Lifting his hands to rinse his face and hair hurt. Using soap on the cuts hurt. Lifting his legs to wash them hurt.

Then nothing did.

The sting of soap radiated through him. Rinsing out whatever might have mingled with his blood in that alley. Warm water, flowing, embracing. His aching joints creaked and moaned, but it was like he'd over-exerted himself at the gym or a football match or running a marathon. And then he stepped out.

Careful not to stand on the bloody smears on the floor, he'd found the gym shorts in the laundry bin in one corner, which he'd used the day before he learned of his assignment to Wearne's squad, and figured they'd preserve his dignity better than the towel. Then the hurt came back, and he had to sit.

Juliette Rock returned with cleaning products, cloths and tea towels, two bags of frozen vegetables—peas and sweetcorn—and a first aid kit. She said nothing as she sat on the bath side and turned Moses toward her. He let her. She looked him over. Hand hovering over his cuts, his swollen bits, then opened the first aid kit.

A gauze and TCP—a mum treating her kid's grazed knee. Except, not.

She held the back of his head, then applied the ammonia-drenched gauze to the cut over his left eye. A thousand wasps stung his face, the flesh beneath the cut contracting and fizzing. He did nothing but hiss.

"Don't be a baby," Rock said.

She withdrew the pain-soaked gauze and dabbed at it, drying the skin around the wound, then sealed it with four Steri-Strips. She repeated the process with the cut on his bottom lip, needing only one horizontal strip. Then she wrapped a tea towel around the bag of frozen sweetcorn, handed it to him, and made him press it against the right side of his face, which had swollen. The cold penetrated not only the rising bruise but his knuckles on that hand too, highlighting the damage, which hadn't quite hit. His face's left side was also swelling, but that could wait.

Rock then checked him over and sterilised the rest of his cuts and scrapes, although none required the Steri-Strips. She placed a fresh gauze on his elbow and set it with a bandage, and the same with one knee. He let her, although knew he'd remove it first thing in the morning.

Finally, she wrapped up the bag of frozen peas and had him hold it against the other side of his face where she'd sealed the brow and set to work on cleaning the floor. Other than her "baby" admonishment, neither had said a word.

The door opened.

Frankie. Dressing gown. Pursed lips. She leaned on the wall, arms crossed. Closed the door behind her with the flick of an ankle. She watched Rock clean. Eyes roved from her up her husband's form to his face.

Moses averted his gaze from hers, catching sight of himself in the mirror, holding two towel-wrapped frozen veg packs to his head like a DJ with oversized novelty headphones. He lowered them.

Frankie drew a sharp breath but kept her face neutral. "Man, you are the very embodiment of toxic masculinity."

"Frankie..." It hurt for Moses to speak.

Rock paused only a second in cleaning, but kept at it, head down.

"No hospitals open at this time?" Frankie said.

Moses braced himself even as he replied, "Hospital... No, wasn't a practical idea."

"Lemme guess. You did it for us?"

Moses took in his form again. His fingers felt mangled, so gripped the bags harder, hoping to limit more swelling. "It's not that simple, Frankie."

"You're not supposed to be that guy anymore, Glynn."

"I'm not," he said.

Frankie wafted her hand up and down, aimed at

Moses's array of injuries. "Evidence to the contrary, m'lud."

Moses hung his head.

"Is it going to get worse?" Frankie asked.

He couldn't answer fully, not now, not with his mind in this state. "Maybe."

"How bad is it? You, I mean." Again, the hand-waft at him. "*This*?"

Moses tried for a smile, but guess what? It hurt. "If I was a white man, I'd be purple tomorrow."

Frankie half-snorted, half-sighted. "You're not gonna tell me, so I'm not gonna ask anymore. But it's Sunday tomorrow. You won't tell me, you can explain it to Jesus. Yeah, church. No arguing."

Moses was agnostic, closer to atheist than Christian, but Frankie came from a line of ardent churchgoers, and he never questioned her commitment. He wasn't sure where Eko landed on the religion scale, but suspected she was closer to him than her mother. Still, the girl accompanied Frankie most weeks and never complained. This week, he wouldn't either.

Moses put the bags back on his face.

Frankie pushed away from the wall and opened the door. Paused. "Juliette?"

Rock shifted to her haunches, the floor clean. "Sorry about all this—"

"You got nothing to be sorry for. But leave this for Glynn. I made up the spare room for you."

"Oh, not necessary, honestly, I'll—"

"Did that sound like a request?" Eyebrows raised. Mouth set.

"Best not to argue," Moses said.

"Do I have to go to church?" Rock asked.

Frankie's eyes hooded, scanning the floor. "Depends on your explanation for all this over breakfast. Goodnight." She left them to it.

Rock stood, folding the cloths so nothing dripped. "What do we tell her?"

"The truth," Moses said. "For now, I'm gonna rest, try to heal a bit."

Rock nodded and moved to leave.

"Be vigilant, Cap," Moses said. "We've lit a fuse."

"We should tell the rest of the division to be on high alert," Rock said.

"Yeah."

They said nothing more. Just went their separate ways, slipping into the night, hoping tomorrow would bring them closer to the end.

If they stayed out of jail.

SUNDAY

51

For most of her life, Agnes Marsh had yearned for the kind of existence where she could accommodate, in both time and money, lazy Sundays in beer gardens with friends, laughing, drinking a tad too much, indulging in a five-o'clock curry or pizza, followed by an early night—with or without a man—to prepare for a fresh start Monday. Although this afternoon granted her the beer garden, the booze, and the company, it wasn't Marsh's idea of a day off. She still saw herself as a copper, working her second job—the Enhanced Pension Scheme—and after last night she wasn't sure it was for her anymore. It was like the side gig to supplement her retirement was becoming the prime factor in her life, relegating police work to second fiddle. And it was getting more serious every day.

"Did you see his willy?" Burns asked with a titter over a bottle of tequila-enriched beer.

Marsh caught the eye of Cole Mainey, who'd brought his own chair to the Volley Horse, a cushioned folding number that let him sit at an angle not granted by the wooden benches and tables.

"Yeah, no choice," Marsh said, grinning Cole's way. Winked. Humour masking her discomfort at the memory. "Don't worry, big guy, it's all good down there."

Cole made a sort-of *harrumph* noise. It hadn't been pleasant for him either.

Having acted super-macho and strong all the way home, she'd gotten him to his house, sensing the shakes hitting him as they left the alley. He'd vomited twice. He'd told her to go to hospital after the first chunder, but on the way there he changed his mind. It was fine; she hadn't been taking him there, anyway. No way they wanted more questions. Without visual evidence, it'd be their word against Moses and Rock's, which might open the group to more police teams, more probing. As Mainey had passed out on his bed, rumpled and bloody, she reported in to Gray, who had an unlicensed doctor call her back within five minutes. He'd told her to get Mainey cleaned up.

Yes, everywhere. Check everything. The doc said he'd be with them in an hour.

So, she'd run a bath and half-dragged Cole there, him stirring enough to crawl along. She had to undress him, wincing at the purpling of wide swathes of his skin and the smaller cuts peppering his face and extremities. And yes, she glimpsed his penis—and his ball-sack—accidentally; she'd intended to leave him in his boxers, but they were plastered to his trousers so the two garments peeled off as one. She could have afforded him more dignity by pulling the boxers back up, but once the sight landed, it wasn't leaving her brain anytime soon.

She helped him into the empty tub, half-filled it with cold water to help with the injuries, and waited on the doc.

"No internal haemorrhaging," Marsh told the gathered team. "Just looks like the Elephant Man."

Again, the bravado, launching a round of camaraderie-infused chuckles. Mainey struggled to extend his middle finger, which escalated the amusement.

It petered out quickly.

Here, in the generous grassy garden at the back of the pub, as far from the kids' playground as they could get, Barney Gray had gathered them. Alone. No other customers yet, although that would soon change.

"Why here, boss?" Kortenberg asked him.

"I know it's unusual to talk shop outside the Safe House," Gray said. "But given they pegged the two of you…" No accusation, no malice as he indicated Cole and Agnes. "I don't want to take the chance. We can't risk them finding that place or connecting us with Haven Maker. Or the Trembling Alien accounts." Gray lingered on Marsh a little longer, although she was sure it wasn't necessary to speak like this in front of the others; perhaps he was concerned about Marsh's inexperience. Enough, though. Down to business. "We need to do a sweep of our comms, take added precautions. The Safe House is out of bounds until I say. Or until we need to abandon ship. Clear?"

Nods all round.

"I know the landlord here," Gray went on. "He wouldn't let a copper stake it out from inside, and I've swept the immediate area."

Kortenberg checked around as if searching the sky for birds. "It's not overlooked, either."

"Bingo," Gray said. "I'm as sure as I can be in a place like this, they haven't got a radar mike on us."

The pub itself was set back from the road and the garden neighboured only a field of sheep, which sometimes came up to the fence, to the delight of kids when they were present. No place for a nosey plod to hide.

They all waited on the teetotal Gray sipping his orange juice—Agnes, Kortenberg, Mainey, Burns. Beer, cider, a whisky chaser for Mainey. Noon. In the sun. It should have been nice. It wasn't.

Gray said, "I need to know where everyone's head is at."

Unspoken, they waited on Mainey. He refused

to drink his IPA through a straw, despite the two teeth that he'd lost and the stitched lip. Small sips, so he didn't dribble. His speech was slurred but not through drink—he'd rejected the doc's opioids and hadn't got the hang of his new mouth yet. "I gotta get a shot at a rematch."

"I disagree," Burns said. "We don't take the chance. They're not proper cops. No one will care if we kill 'em. Leave something from Moses's past to blame. We're clean."

"They'll have records," Kortenberg offered, his South African accent stronger when he needed to make a point. "Lose the foot soldiers, someone else takes over. And whatever evidence we leave, they're into us deep."

"They found us in the middle of the night," Marsh added. "Used someone from an active investigation to lure us there. That means they were on us. Either with eyes following..." She lifted her phone from the table. "Or pinging us on the network towers."

Kortenberg waved her off. "They are police issue. Not a concern. It is simple to track any copper given sufficient reason."

"People've come for us before," Burns said. "You need to hold your nerve."

"They're closer than we thought," Agnes pointed out. "Too close."

"Nah." The word sounded raw in Mainey's throat as he strained to return his pint glass to the table. "It was a power play. They want us to step things up. *Ahhh—*" He leaned over. One of his injuries must have stabbed up one side of him—a bruised rib, perhaps.

"You can say you fell downstairs," Agnes said. "I'll vouch."

Mainey's reply was a scowl. "Baines knows this guy. He'll know what to do."

"We trust that?" Gray said. "He's a decade or more out of the game."

All paid attention to him. No one spoke. Questioning the man inside wasn't something Marsh had heard before.

"We're running things out here," Gray went on, nervous. "We see what he doesn't. I'm not going against him, just… We're living it. It needs to be our call."

Others nodded, but the atmosphere darkened, grew heavy. Like someone had raised a contentious political view in a group of like-minded activists. Despite Gray's words, Marsh sensed discord, and no one knew where to put themselves.

Gray said, "So let's make a call on this. I'll take any heat with Baines."

"Fine." Marsh let him stew. "But I can't help feeling it. They're still close. We have to consider what Cleland offered. The admin issue."

"No way," Burns said. "That's like an admission."

"But might be the prudent approach." Kortenberg had adopted his thinking pose—steepled fingers against his forehead. Deep voice at a higher pitch. He appeared to detect it himself and coughed, switching back to his normal tone. "Throw Joshua under the bus, and this can all go away. Mainey gets another shot once his body heals."

Agnes thought back to what Juliette Rock had said. *Last in, first out.* She also wasn't sure if Mainey had heard much as he fought. She doubted he'd picked up the exchange, but he was sharper than he looked, not a brawler.

"Take out Moses and put the fear up Rock," Burns said. "Like really scare the shit out of her. Moses was on the verge of quitting when we got close to his bitch wife. But something made him step up. We cut off Moses's head and leave it at Rock's house, and—"

"No," Agnes said. "We start killing cops on purpose, that's… it's…"

Burns' blank expression drilled into Agnes, shutting her up. "What? You think that lass in Gloucestershire was an accident? That I slipped?"

"No." Agnes gulped at her Sol, the lemon tasting stronger than it should have. "It was… you were in a corner. Had no choice."

The others were watching her, too. Not speaking. A sheep baa'd somewhere. A cloud covered the sun. Agnes Marsh sipped again.

"One was unfortunate," she said, staring at her

beer bottle, the lemon slice floating in it, bobbing amid the foam. "Two would be overkill."

All took a turn at their drinks.

All except Burns. Her middle finger traced the rim of her bottle. "You're aware Ratan Walar isn't likely to see a court date, aren't you? Seems that hooker he killed had a boyfriend in the same prison. Awful oversight by… someone." She shrugged.

"Walar isn't our business anymore," Gray said, lasering in on Agnes. "Don't let that worry you. It isn't on us."

Last in, first out.

"Who's it on?" Agnes asked.

"You don't need to know that."

They haven't told you everything because they don't really trust you.

"I'm with you," Agnes said. "All of you." She panned between them, from Gray, over the blank Clara Burns, past Kortenberg who maintained his thinking pose, and to Mainey, who appeared to soften as she landed on him.

And if they don't trust you…?

Rotating the bottle in her hands, almost dancing, she kept her gaze on the table and said, "Whatever we need to do, I'll do it. All the way."

"No one wants to cool off?" Gray said. "No one needs to back down?"

Kortenberg lowered his hands. "Go big or go home, isn't that what they say?"

"Good." Barney Gray took out his phone.

• • •

Silas Bonaparte spent his Sundays in quiet reflection. Sometimes he went to church to give quiet thanks for his good fortune, and for the fortunes he received in kind. Today, he satisfied himself with a stroll around his thirty acres after a plentiful lunch with his wife of twenty years and the three children with whom he'd been blessed—two boys and a girl, each more meticulous at school and in their personal endeavours than the last. Sports, academia, socialising. They'd all excelled, largely—so Silas believed—because of the rigid and unrelenting discipline on which he prided himself.

The phone in his pocket rang.

He normally left all personal electronic devices at home when out for a solitary walk, but this was the emergency phone. The one he only carried when events were sparking too close to the gunpowder. It was rare he resorted to such a precaution, but this week delivered a more pronounced necessity.

"Yes?"

"Moses is closing in," Barney Gray said. "We're in agreement about what to do next."

"I haven't agreed to anything."

"You don't get to agree. You're the help. Our employee."

"My instructions are for the good of us all. Why don't you listen for a moment and—"

"No, you listen," Gray said.

Silas found the indignation in Gray's tone rather amusing. *The help*. He'd heard far worse insults from far worse people than DI Barney Gray. But nonetheless, sometimes one had to listen. And he did. Listened to the events of the previous night, to the risk Detective Inspector Moses and Detective Constable Rock now posed.

"Well," Silas said. "That is quite unacceptable. Do what you must. I will do what *I* must."

MONDAY

52

Frankie Moses drove her new Toyota Rav4 Hybrid through the molasses of Monday morning traffic and onto the A-road toward Birmingham. She was in a better mood today, despite the armed police escort in the seat beside her. The man's name was Graham. At her request, Graham was not in uniform, but wore a high velocity armoured vest under his shirt, a Glock 17 on his hip, and an MP5A submachine gun in his lap. He had a helmet in the footwell, and he called her *ma'am*, despite her telling him not to. It was annoying, but less-so than her husband of late. Time was a great healer, though, and after putting Glynn through the penance of church, of explaining to his daughter—plus God, Jesus, and whoever else would listen—how he got into the state he did, Frankie inched toward forgiving him.

A face-to-face meeting with a suspect that got out of hand.

Riiiight.

It took a little prodding for Moses to admit that *maybe* he'd been hoping to push the suspect over the edge, make a mistake. And yet, she wasn't sure even *that* was the whole truth.

His usual excuse—"for them"—washed even less with Eko than it did with her, but Frankie was no longer bristling with anger. She'd let go of the sort of grudge her mother used to dole out whenever she or her sisters were naughty or disrespectful, and even forewent the typical penalty of banishing Glynn to the couch. Besides, making him climb the stairs was better punishment.

Forgiveness was also a befitting admonishment to his partner, Juliette. Although the previous day's breakfast had been cordial, Frankie still couldn't shake her concern.

Was Rock a beneficial influence, firing up the big man's lost motivation and verve, or was she enabling his worst instincts, allowing him to drag her down to the level at which he once operated? He had supposedly left the scuzzy end of the spectrum long behind, risen above it, a handsome black angel soaring above the storm. He no longer needed to act this way.

And yet.

"Ma'am, the traffic is getting heavy up ahead,"

Graham said beside her. "If you want to avoid it, there's a shortcut—"

"I know it," Frankie said, flicking the indicator. "Friends in high places?"

Graham tapped his ear where the earpiece nestled, connected via a curly cord to a radio that extended to a lapel mike.

They pulled off onto the wide country lane. It led to a second road five miles away, which reconnected to the A-road beyond a turnoff to a different town. Traffic was usually lighter after that point, the road overgrown on both sides, greenery hanging over this early in the summer. They'd need to do something about it if they wanted to avoid an accident in the near future.

Graham jerked around. Frankie saw the blue lights too before hearing the siren.

"What do I do?" she asked.

"Keep driving."

The BMW revved behind her, flashing its lights angrily.

Frankie edged the vehicle closer to the hedgerow, slowing down without stopping.

Moses had warned the team guarding them that there were factions within the police who were seeking to do harm, people he described as "compromised and desperate" so Graham was under no illusions to the danger of a traffic stop. And now a BMW was flashing them with no intention of passing.

Into his lapel mike, he made the call. "This is Bravo Golf Two en route to location six. Currently being instructed to pull over by a rapid response vehicle." He relayed the licence plate. Listened to the reply.

The car behind whooped and honked, flashed its headlights faster along with the blues.

"It's legit." Graham tapped his submachine gun. "Someone reported an armed man in a car."

Frankie again watched them in the rear-view, "Can't you call them off?"

He was listening again. "Anti-terror squad. Need a visual check. It's okay. Pull over."

She slowed, looking for a suitable place, the first being a gate to a field that accommodated her SUV. The responder pulled up behind, swinging across so the police vehicle blocked the road.

Graham unlatched the passenger door. Loud clunk. A creak of the hinges. His ID in one hand, Glock held by the barrel in the other. Slow movements.

Frankie craned back to see.

Two armed police were out of their vehicle, aiming her way. She quickly threw her eyes forward, hands at ten and two on the wheel. Sweaty palms. Dry mouth. "Graham, is everything alright?"

No response from Graham.

Frankie shifted her head centimetres at a time, angling on the mirrors to see the pair of armed police officers, both men, approach Graham. One of them stowed his machine-gun and checked Graham's ID, then spoke over the radio. A quick confab resulted in both officers making safe their weapons and Graham trotting over to Frankie's window. She pressed the button to lower it.

"They just need to do a quick search of the car," he said, relief streaming from him. Nothing like a warning from DI Moses to put the willies up someone.

Still, Frankie hesitated. She was a partner in a solicitor's and knew the law. Okay, she hadn't practiced criminal law in over a decade, but she was sure this wasn't right. "I can refuse."

"Yes, but I don't think we should." Graham twisted back to one of the officers who approached apace, raised a hand to say *okay*, but it didn't slow him.

The officer leaned on Frankie's car, a tattoo on his forearm reading, *Utrinque Paratus,* beneath a pair of wings with a blurred object between them. "Ma'am, please step out of the car."

"I don't have to," Frankie said. Hands staying at ten and two. Holding tight. Breathing deep and long. No shaking.

Graham, of equal size to the AFO, said, "She's correct. You've no reason to pull her over."

The tattooed AFO stood up straight. He was clean shaven with a firm, straight chin, eyes narrowed like a cowboy's as if set that way through a lifetime of squinting at the desert sun. "Is that where you want this to go?"

More macho posturing. If Moses's actions two nights earlier had embodied what people meant by *toxic masculinity*, this pair were candidates for the next poster campaign.

"Oh, for crying out loud." Frankie hooked her fingers into the handle and yanked it open, hoping to "accidentally" catch the squinty officer as she did so, but he stepped out of range. Once out, she opened the back door too. "Be my guest."

"Thank you." A stern look at Graham precluded Squinty crawling halfway into the back and feeling down the seats.

Frankie crossed her arms, leaned her weight on one hip. "And what do you expect to find?"

"Nothing, ma'am. It's procedure." The officer backed up, then circled to the boot. "Can you open this?"

Frankie sighed but complied, pulling it up to reveal the messy contents: three sets of wellies, waterproofs, and hats; boxes of papers; a first aid kit and breakdown pack as required by French law in case they fancied a quick flit across the channel to Brittany or Disneyland Paris. "Happy?"

The armed officer frowned. Reached for the long, green breakdown kit which resembled a small tent bag. The zip was partially open and a bit of clear plastic poked through. He fished it out.

Brown flakes of dried leaf.

He held it before Frankie. "If we test this, ma'am, what will we find?"

Frankie's pulse quickened and her face got hot. Recalling so many clients with the same defence, the disbelief she met them with but still tried to defend them, the laughter Glynn shared when he encountered what she was about to say, what she couldn't help spilling from her mouth. "That's not mine."

"Not yours? We framed you?" The officer wasn't mocking. If anything, he was a little too neutral. He tapped the body camera on his chest. "Ma'am, this had been running since we pulled you over. So has my colleague's." He waved to the chap farther back, who returned the gesture. "It shows we couldn't possibly have planted this."

Graham joined them. "Ma'am?" He frowned at the package.

The AFO held it closer to Graham. "Ma'am, I understand you're married to someone on the job."

Fuming, Frankie barely held her temper in check. "Is that what this is about? You're planting evidence in my car to get at my husband?"

"Ma'am? Of course not. We're all on the same side." The squinty officer with the tattoo grinned. "In fact, your husband being on the job means we won't take this further." He tossed the packet of weed back in amid the wellies and emergency essentials. "What's a little personal use between friends?"

The officer closed the boot.

"Thanks, man," Graham said, and offered his hand.

The AFO shook it and spoke directly to Frankie. "Besides, if we were able to 'frame you' with this paltry amount, imagine how much we'd put in there if someone really wanted to get to you."

The comment chilled Frankie. Even as the man walked away, and Graham resumed his place in the passenger seat, seemingly not noticing the implied threat, Frankie trembled. Anger, fear, impotence. Didn't matter why. All that mattered was she needed to speak with her dumb, macho thug of a husband.

Rather predictably, when he got his blood up, Moses made things worse.

53

At Moses's request, Wearne had gathered the Division 43 personnel and laid out step-by-step his and Rock's case to date. It wasn't normal to do this, Wearne had told them. The squad's brief was to work hard and fast on their own assignments, not draw things out, nor turn it into a scrap that pitched and rolled, advantages seesawing from suspect to investigators like a sports game between two evenly matched teams.

The four who were working locally waited on Wearne to speak, gathered at desks in a loose semicircle, clearly put out: the male pairing of DI Xian and the rugby-battered DS Ellingham, and the two females working on the institutional child abuse charity case, the stocky DI Brienne Archer and the Maori woman, DS Tahana. Banner and Clarke were still out of town, chasing business that extended to several government-funded think-tanks but had been briefed on the phone. All were notified of the attempt against Frankie on Saturday, but this was the first time it had been laid out in stark detail.

"Where's DC Rock?" Xian asked.

"Coming," Moses said.

Ellingham folded his arms. "If we're all under threat thanks to your sloppiness, she could do us the courtesy of being here."

"This is on me," Wearne said, firing his annoyance down with a stony glare. "I paired two newbs together without explaining why. Explaining would have put them on the defensive. Moses because of his history with the practices I want wrecking, and Rock because I knew she'd keep him in line. Or thought she would."

"She's checking out a firearm," Moses said.

While Moses found guns created more problems than they solved, he accepted the need for them sometimes. He still didn't feel he'd reached that threshold, but had not objected to Rock's request.

"She might be a while," Brienne Archer said, the armoury not on site but ten miles away, a facility they shared with the National Crime Agency. "The armoury guys are loads of fun with newbs."

"Anyone else feel the need to be routinely armed?" Wearne asked.

When Moses first arrived less than a week earlier, DI Archer and DC Tahana were wearing shoulder harnesses, but he had seen no other evidence of firearms around the place.

"Increase in hang-ups," Ellingham said, referring to his personal mobile. "Could be coincidence."

"Could be triangulating your position," Moses suggested. "Keeping an eye on you."

"They don't have to call to do that." Xian looked at his own phone screen. "But now you mention it, I've seen an increase in those spammy accident claim calls."

All nodded.

"They won't have a warrant," Wearne said. "But they might have a tech person piggybacking the ISPs or mobile masts."

"Do they need an open channel for that?" Tahana asked.

No one replied.

Moses didn't know much about that side of it, but had sat in on some exercises. "It's easier if you do, but not essential."

"But this morning?" Wearne said. "Are we certain Frankie Moses's stop-and-search was another warning?"

The main door opened, and DC Rock hurried in, an apologetic nod to all as she fell in beside Moses. Her jacket molehilled where the Glock 17 sat on her left hip, a small enough mound to overlook if a person wasn't watching for it, but impossible to ignore now Moses knew it was there. She was right-handed, so would need to cross her body to draw it, which many people preferred.

"PC Kyle Brennan and PC Nick Balls." Moses had researched the officers who pulled over his wife as soon as Frankie called—an eerily calm and collected call in which she recited the facts blow by blow.

Given their professions, neither Moses nor Frankie had indulged in weed for the past couple of decades, and he was sure Eko hadn't discovered its pleasures yet. Even if she had, at such a young age, she'd have found a more suitable hiding place than the back of her mum's car. All they could do was step up the security on her and make the protection unit alert that there may be an approach at some point—to show, to emphasise, that they could get to his family if they chose. This morning showed them declining Moses's invitation, sent via Mainey's face, to back down.

"Brennan is former military," Moses went on. "Honourably discharged following a combat mission that saddled him with a dose of shrapnel in his leg."

"Is 'dose' the right word?" Xian asked.

"I don't care." Moses eyed the group, awaiting further input. None came. "Enough to limit his career in the armed forces, but he managed to pass civilian police tests."

"There's a very fine margin in the Paras," Rock said. "They're strict about that."

"He's also the lucky man who discovered the body in DI Walar's boot." Moses waited for that to sink in.

"What about the fabulously named Nick Balls?" Archer asked.

"Wasn't with him that night," Moses said. "Brennan is a bit of a loner and switches shifts a lot. Means he ends up with different people."

"He's the link?" Wearne said.

"Haven't found he has any contact with Barney Gray or any of his team."

"Burner phones?" Ellingham offered.

"Possible. Could be he's doing favours for mates, but there's no firm crossover as yet."

"I still have friends left in that world," Rock said. "I'll call in some favours, see if there's more to the discharge. Or any rumours about the man himself."

"How's the gun feel?" Xian asked.

"Prefer a Sig, but this is fine." Rock patted the bulge. Waited. She must have picked up on the discomfort. Unless an officer landed guard duty, firearms were for specific ops, not for *just-in-case* scenarios. "I've been attacked directly over this. Moses's family was in the company of a cop killer for several hours. I've seen shadows and suspicious vehicles nearby. And now Frankie gets pulled over by the same guy who got Ratan Walar banged up on remand." Her eyes bore the kind of steel Moses expected from someone who'd commanded up to a hundred or more troops, who'd led ground operations in the heart of enemy territory. "I won't apologise for defending myself this way. You'd all do well to consider the same."

Wearne shifted her stance, scanning her team.

"When will we hear from DCS Cleland?" Xian asked.

"I'll follow up with him shortly," Wearne replied.

"But don't expect much," Moses said. He'd detailed the fight with Mainey but not the background, the duelling aspect; he'd told them the same as he'd told Frankie and Eko. "I don't think they're going for it, given the additional warning."

DI Archer kept her brow low, an almost mocking grin forming then fading as fast. "I don't get it. They move from stationing a killer, presumably ready to get bloody when the big boss man gives the order, to a small bag of weed that's barely enough for personal use? Why move from deadly to subtle?"

"Vexes me too," Moses said. "We can only speculate on it, so I'm not gonna dwell there. It's happened. And I can't keep treading water. I want to meet with our surveillance team, get hands-on with them." He pointed at the sealed door at the other end of the room, which Wearne said he wouldn't be able to access until he was a fully fledged member of Division 43.

Everyone but Rock shuffled awkwardly. Wearne

pulled a strained expression, meeting Xian's inquisitive glance.

"Just sayin', I need this, or I walk away. If we can't take them all down, all of them at once, I have to drop it. I won't put my family in the way. Even if I lose my job."

"All of us, sometime, have felt that way," DI Brienne Archer said. "Me and Kyla recently got done fending off personal threats ourselves. Not family, though. Not as close as they've got to you. I don't know how I'd have dealt with that."

"I've been there before," Moses answered. "There's a big difference between bravery and bravado."

Rock gave him a friendly punch. "More scared of Frankie than DI Gray?"

"You know it. And I ain't even a little bit ashamed."

"All or nothing." Ellingham nodded slowly, thoughtfully. "Totally right. Get 'em all or push it up the chain."

"I need to see everything," Moses said again. "Decide if it's worth subbing to the CPS and charging them all or punt it to a Professional Standards division from outside this region. Somewhere Gray can't have compromised them."

"They go down," Rock said. "But we have to accept it won't be us taking them out."

Wearne rocked on her heels. For the first time

since Moses's initial introduction, she appeared reluctant to say her piece.

"They don't know?" Xian asked Wearne. "Do they?"

Moses turned sharply to Wearne. Glanced between the other four, who returned no eye contact.

"Not yet," Wearne said. "They don't have clearance."

Rock's right hand twitched, as if flexing in readiness to pull her weapon. "Know what?"

Wearne led them without speaking, her manner demanding they follow. Moses wondered what made the four detectives so awkward but left those thoughts behind as Wearne scanned her pass to unlock the mystery door.

The DCI held it open only a crack. "One reason we have the extra-judicial powers is the understanding that people's privacy is not invaded unnecessarily. To listen in fully, as in conversations, text messaging, recordings, we need sign off from a judge."

"So, you don't have quite as much power as a judge," Moses said, recalling what she'd told them on his first day.

"More than most superintendents, but no. Not as much as we'd like." She opened the door. "No humans can listen to those calls, not even the recordings made when keywords crop up."

Moses entered ahead of Rock, his mouth falling open at the sight.

Wearne stepped aside so they could see properly. "We can access whatever metadata this throws out. Pass on suspicious keywords, like bombs, shootings planned, that sort of thing, to the relevant authorities. Counter Terrorism has their own system which speaks to this one, and need their own warrants. Organised Crime has theirs, and we all need approval for actual surveillance. This…"

"It's terrifying," Moses said.

The room was freezing. Full of computer servers, it whirred and ticked, flashed, illuminated with buttons and LEDs.

"It's one of four domestic supercomputers in the country," Wearne said. "We house it. It isn't ours, but one condition of it being here is we can access limited intel at the push of a series of authorisation codes. It can decrypt coded messages, hack private accounts and servers around the world, and all we have to do is say please."

"All the intel we've gathered on their movements," Rock said. "All the connections…"

"One big algorithm," Moses finished. He stared at Wearne. "So, I don't have access to what I need?"

Wearne met his gaze, unwavering. "If DCS Cleland cannot persuade the team to withdraw their alibi for Joshua Sevan, I will apply for deeper surveillance on Gray and his team. And on Kaspar Sevan, as well as Theo Goodman, since he appears to process information for them. We will get what we need. This team won't hang you out. And I don't believe for a second you want to quit any more than I do."

Moses hated to admit she was right. He didn't want to quit. But everything from his corrupt days—every act, every last penny he took—was for the good of him and Frankie and their yet-to-be-conceived child. To give them what he didn't have growing up; financial security, physical safety, a decent future. Justice was secondary.

But, damn it, Wearne was right. He couldn't let this go. The shift from over-the-top assassins with baseball bats and whoever was stationed in the Cotswolds and had killed PC Nicola Dawson, to smaller gestures, to "what if" scenarios.

"It's as if someone else is giving the orders," Moses said aloud.

"Pardon?" Wearne said.

Moses ran through it again, picturing the escalation, culminating in him and Mainey going at it and a final offer to DCS Cleland. "What if Gray isn't behind the thing with Frankie this morning? What if—"

His phone rang. It was in his hand, so he couldn't resist glancing at the screen.

His blood ran cold. "School." He answered. Listened.

And his cold blood turned to ice as he understood that Frankie's stop-and-search was nothing but an appetiser.

54

There had been no stopping Moses. He rushed out, not another word to Rock, his face slack and gaunt, stumbling as if waking from a deep sleep to find his house on fire, rushing to get away but groggy, only propelling himself in the general direction he needed to go. Childishly, he jammed the outer door with a chair so Rock couldn't catch up immediately, although Xian was fast to shift it. He hadn't stopped Moses either.

By the time Rock got to the car park, Moses was already peeling away in his Lexus, so she followed in her personal vehicle. He broke every speed limit, but she kept him in sight. Resisted making it a pursuit and called for any traffic vehicles to ignore the rocketing Lexus with DI Moses at the wheel.

Within fifteen minutes she calculated his destination and ceased ignoring the incoming calls from

Wearne. Answered, "He's heading for the MisPer Unit. I'm sure of it."

"Why?" Wearne asked.

"Can't say. That call from his kid's school set him off, though."

"We rang the school when you weren't picking up. They need to verify my identity before they'll say anything, but they confirmed no police action or ambulances are required and all their students are accounted for."

"Then what did they tell Moses?"

Silence on the other end.

"Ring his wife," Rock said. "They probably called her too. If they didn't, the school will still talk to her."

"You know her, Constable. Wouldn't it be better coming from you?"

"I'll keep trying Moses, guv. Can't have him doing something he can't take back."

Rock hung up. She was the only one who knew the whole truth behind his approach to Cole Mainey, and here he was, pushing himself to the limit of sanity, knowing the team were all present at their home station as Cleland had recalled them for a formal meeting. He was complying with their request, but that didn't mean Barney Gray would go for it.

And Moses knew this.

Within forty minutes of leaving Division 43, Moses pulled up hard outside the station, abandoned his car in the road, and rushed through the front door. Rock took a second to double-park marginally more tidily, then badged the handful of uniformed officers rushing out to see where Moses had come from. She said they were on a job, and to watch the cars, receiving a flurry of "yes ma'am" replies.

Inside, she knew exactly where she needed to go, and her RFID-chipped ID admitted her without a problem. The place was old, like a school, but the signage was clear. The bewildered trail of detectives and unis gave her a good idea which way Moses had barged through too.

He hadn't reacted like this when they placed a killer with his wife. Nor had he flown off the handle when they murdered the constable in Gloucestershire. He'd calculated his response to them compromising the pathologist before going after Mainey. But this… He was like an arrow fired from a crossbow, homing in on its target.

To wound? Or to kill?

She'd caught up in time to see him scan into the CID area housing several squads. "Moses! Wait. Think it through."

He half-turned. The door in one hand open a crack. Blank face, dead eyes. He blinked once, then delved into enemy territory.

Rock dashed forward, caught the door before it closed, and pushed on through.

Moses wound his way through the tightly set

desks, fists bunched, shoulders high, glancing at the placards denoting the different squads, then knifing toward his destination.

The MisPer unit was all present: Gray, Burns, Mainey, Kortenberg, Marsh. All except Mainey stood, surprise blooming.

Kortenberg and Marsh glanced at Gray, but Burns and Mainey stayed on Moses, Burns' grin a slash of pink in a pale face atop a build similar to "Joan's" but Rock couldn't be 100 percent sure of it; could Burns have been the one who murdered a fellow officer? Their assumption it was an outside contractor may have been wider of the mark than they thought.

Kortenberg dodged into Moses's path. "Hey, wait a sec, my friend. Let's talk this—"

Moses's huge hand shot out and his fingers wrapped around the South African's throat. Moses pulled the obstacle toward him, jerked him so hard his feet left the ground, then extended his arm and released Kortenberg across a desk. His head and legs flipped places, and paperwork and a computer keyboard went flying.

The crash and clatter brought more detectives running.

"It's okay," Gray called, patting the air for calm. "Personal dispute."

The incoming saviours pulled to a reluctant halt, their adrenaline shots visibly ebbing.

"Moses, this isn't the right time," Rock said, almost caught up.

Mainey had pulled himself to his feet. Recovering the way Moses was—toughing it out. "Round two already? With an audience?"

Gray shot him a *shut the fuck up* glare, then presented a serene expression to the spectators. Addressed Moses. "What do you want?"

"I mean it," Moses said, heaving in breath after breath, the strain of not pummelling the man before him a clear effort. "Withdraw the alibi and send Joshua Sevan down. Someone has to answer for Gabriella Childs, and it doesn't need to be you sheepheads."

Kortenberg righted himself, patting himself down.

Burns smirked, but otherwise motionless. Hands under her desk.

Rock checked Kortenberg over visually, but other than the shock, he seemed fine. She kept one eye on Burns. "Moses, let DCS Cleland handle it."

"No." Moses pivoted to take in the team. "It's not a trick. You win."

Gray said nothing in reply. He waved the other detectives back. Once the audience withdrew, he said, "I don't have to do anything."

"You don't believe we'll back off. Yet you keep on coming. If you don't believe these tactics will work, why do it? Why go for Frankie this morning? Why Eko's school?"

Kortenberg and Marsh were the antsy ones, unsure who to look at, while Mainey grinned and Burns held as still as a column of rock.

"Let's pretend," Gray said. "Let's pretend I know what you're talking about."

"Let's pretend." Moses absently rubbed one forearm, tilted a few degrees that way—an injury that hurt more than he'd let on? "Sure. Let's pretend I go away. Pretend I was barking up the wrong tree all along and you guys are only on the hook because of one dumb admin error. Let's pretend I can't go through all this bullshit again because even if I gouge you people out of the police, there'll be more along to fill your place."

"You think I can magically present Joshua Sevan to you?"

Rock interjected, "When I started as a detective, I got all the shitty jobs."

They all focused on her.

"Meaning I typed up reports," Rock went on. A pointed glance at Agnes Marsh. "Newbies are sometimes dumped on. Make mistakes. If it's one person in the team, someone who took a while to come forward with her mistake…"

Marsh hooked a thumb toward herself. "I take the blame, and everyone walks?"

"It's the most workable option," Moses said. "And we all go away."

Mainey folded his arms over his chest. "Nope.

No compromise. You leave the slag's murder unsolved, move on."

Rock leaned on the desk Kortenberg got tossed over. "Joshua Sevan is a bloody headache. For you and his dad. After what we think he did to that girl in DI Walar's car… It'll be a win all round."

Without moving a muscle, Burns said, "That's not how this works."

Gray, though, returned to his seat as if dismissing everyone from some meeting. "Not usually."

"Boss?" Burns said, shifting her forehead, lines creasing it as her eyes narrowed.

Gray watched Moses, cast a look over to Rock, then across his team. "Leave me. Without assaulting anyone else. Finish up your day. Call it a truce. A temporary one."

Moses eyed him sceptically. "No more warnings, Barney. Or I ain't a copper anymore, and you don't want that."

"I'm sure none of us do." Barney Gray shivered theatrically. "But in all seriousness, get out of here. I'll see what I can do."

55

The gears inside Moses ground into a sick feeling expanding right through his body. As he marched through the school to the head teacher's office, he couldn't shake that sensation of loss, of defeat. Of the knowledge Barney Gray and his team were going free.

But his original offer of compromise hadn't worked—primarily, he suspected, because they didn't believe Division 43 would back off. They were right, of course, but Moses would have. He didn't need the hassle of being labelled a grass, a snitch, a *traitor*. Going after Frankie and Eko at their hideaway had meant their resources were more plentiful than first thought, killing the AFO showed their ruthlessness, and forcing Davina Mishkin to fabricate bloodwork and misplace evidence proved they had serious access.

How?

Didn't matter. That they were more criminal than cop had motivated Moses to step up a gear, to fight them head-on, but even with his wife and kid in protective custody they'd found a way in. Not through the bodyguards, but through more frightening means.

Stealth.

First, the weed in Frankie's car, then… this. At the school. His switch in tactics had necessitated someone else taking the reins, attacking him from a new angle. With new menace.

In the head's office, Moses affected his softer voice, that of a middle-class white man called Stuart, an invention whom he called upon when he worried his size, deep voice and—yes, unfortunately—his race might intimidate the person in front of him. It was less of a problem in the modern world, and a tactic he detested, but when it came to Eko, to getting what was best for her, Stuart usually accompanied him into these conversations—a higher pitch, more emphasis on his Welsh accent. "I'm so sorry, Mrs Donovan. I cannot believe this happened with Eko."

"She is a bright girl." Mrs Donovan peeked over her glasses at Eko, sat in silence beside her father, Frankie having been informed and on her way. But Moses insisted on getting this out of the way sooner than that. "Never any trouble." As Eko shrank into her seat a little deeper, Mrs Donovan poked her glasses back up her nose and returned to Moses. "But we have had similar issues with youths who also hail from more... urban areas."

Urban areas. White-middle-class language for *black neighbourhoods.* While it was pleasing to see people attempt to retune their word choices to a less offensive note, it sometimes fell flat. Especially since the Moses family lived in an area that couldn't be whiter if they lived on a cloud.

"I understand," Moses said. "I'm tamping over this, Mrs Donovan, but I'm sure it won't happen again."

"Do you recognise it?" The head teacher pushed the knife with a pencil, the eraser poking the handle. It slid perpendicular to the edge of the desk.

"It's from our kitchen." Moses's hand hovered over the utensil, a smaller-sized ceramic blade with a point, the paring knife one of seven multi-coloured items that came in a set.

"The other unfortunate thing," Mrs Donovan said with another swift peek at Eko, "is that your daughter denied knowing anything about it."

Moses faced Eko, who looked up at him with tear-filled eyes. He firmed his own gaze and dipped his chin in a partial nod, trying to tell her to play along. He picked up the knife—his knife. His kitchen knife.

They'd been in his home.

Must have been while they were all out, with minimal personnel covering the front door only.

"Thank you for not involving the police, Mrs Donovan," Moses said as meekly as his Stuart-voice allowed. "I'll be sure to deal with this in the most severe way I'm able."

"Our policy is to add this to the Prevent database, but Eko's grades are easily in the top ten percent. I'd hate to lose a student of her calibre. Or see her fail to snag a grammar school place due to a… Let's call it a blip?"

The woman wasn't quite smiling but was plainly waiting for an agreement. A conspiracy to take this no further.

Not all corruption is bad.

"I understand," Moses said.

"I suggest Eko spends the week reflecting on what she's done. She has a hundred percent attendance apart from last Friday, and I expect some additional revision might come in handy for the end of term."

"Thank you." Moses rose to his feet a little sharply, noting Mrs Donovan taken aback as he loomed over her. He would normally drop his shoulders to mitigate his size, but he found it difficult to shake her *urban* comment. He extended a hand instead and in his own voice he said, "This will not happen again. I assure you."

With what looked like a feat of enormous courage, Mrs Donovan shook his hand.

Moses departed with his daughter, shushing her when she stammered the word, "…Dad." He waited until they were around the first corner, away from the office, then hugged her tight, careful to keep the blade away from her.

"I'm sorry this happened to you." He disconnected and kneeled, hands on her shoulders. "It's my fault. My job. People warning *me*. Not you. Nothing to do with you."

"They… the bad guys…" Eko glanced back toward the head's office. "They put this in my bag?"

Moses nodded. "I don't know how they got in, but it's over. I promise."

And as they wound through the school, back toward the car, Moses couldn't help but wonder how "over" it really was. He'd done all he could, though. All he could to protect his family and do his job.

And he'd failed.

But, as long as Frankie and Eko were safe, he could live with failure.

56

Moses drove home, his heartbeat steady, his breath calm and measured. Once there, he got changed into loose trackie bottoms and an old baggy tee-shirt. He ignored the pull of rum and cider and occupied himself in his other, more effective and more productive distraction.

The garden.

Early evening was Moses's favourite time of day. The sun was still up, but this early in the summer it wasn't unbearable, and the plants got themselves a healthy dose of light to keep the photosynthesis rolling. In the vegetable plot at the end of his land, Moses touched the first pea pods of the year, having planted them early in pots inside the greenhouse, and moved them outside during his suspension. He'd done a lot of gardening during that brief period when he thought his career was over, where

Frankie had put him in touch with employment lawyers, and he planned on suing the force for constructive dismissal.

He'd been admiring the progress of his broad beans when the call came in to report to Division 43 for duty.

In the seven days since venturing into this new division, since promising to give it his best shot, the fledgling broccoli plants had matured under the butterfly netting alongside small lettuces, although the carrots were yet to show any sprig of green. He feared they'd been overwatered by the downpour a few nights earlier.

"Should've planted them inside first," Moses said, sensing Frankie approach.

"Should've thought of a lot of things sooner." Frankie handed him the bottle of Rattler cider, his favourite unflavoured brand since discovering it in Cornwall several years earlier.

As Moses pushed to his feet, every bruise and ache flared in unison. Superficial, but still painful. He accepted the drink and knocked back a quarter, his head spinning as the strong alcohol hit home. "Thanks."

"You going after them?"

Moses turned his back to her, assessing his options in the carrot department. "Replant here, or give 'em a few more days to sprout? Or do a backup batch in the greenhouse?"

"Glynn, I'm serious."

"Me too." He still didn't look at her. "I also need to choose when to put the six chilli plants out. Probably not just yet."

"I need to know, Glynn." Frankie took hold of his arms and made him face her. "How long do we have to live with armed police outside our door?"

"I'm waiting on the all-clear from Wearne. From Rock. She's still on the Gabriella Childs case."

"*She* is." Frankie's eyebrows popped. "Meaning you're not?"

"I sent my resignation by email," Moses said. "Unpaid leave until I find another division."

Frankie's mouth made an "O" as she held something in. Annoyance at him not discussing it, most likely, but hold it in she did. It was what she'd wanted, after all. "Good." She nodded. "Good… I mean, it'll be hard to find somewhere after… Plymouth, and now… this. Still, you know. It's good."

"But?"

"Is Juliette not in danger?"

"I made a deal." Moses again found it hard to look at her. Fighting pressure behind his eyes. Pushing back a bitter swelling in his gut, nothing to do with anything Cole Mainey landed on him, either. "They need to work out the logistics, but we all walk away clean."

"And you can't go back to Division 43? Seemed to… I don't know…" She touched his arm. "For a while, it seemed to do you good."

"A while isn't enough." Moses drew her to him,

a *cwtch*, keeping the cider from spilling. "I only care about forever."

They kissed. Moses never doubted his marriage, his commitment to it, or the risks he took to maximise the lifestyle he felt robbed of as a kid. Watching others grow up happy, while he and his parents scraped along. Seeing his friends assume university was in their futures, while for him it seemed a fantastical dream. His childhood epitomised what Theo Goodman said about police and criminals having similar psyches; struggling to get by, unappreciated, fighting for a better world.

The kiss broke, and Frankie's body relaxed some. Hands still hanging around his neck, leaning into his circled arms.

"We can go back to how things were," Moses said.

"You really want to?"

"Yes." He kissed her again, hoping to bury the lie. He'd be okay with it in time. But to stay like this, knowing he'd hidden from the bogeymen in Gray's team, under Kaspar Sevan's yoke, was too heart-breaking for words.

So, when Frankie left him alone, he lost himself in his garden, and tried not to think about where it all went so wrong.

57

Juliette Rock had hoped Moses would change his mind. He blamed himself for the failure of the operation and had resigned his post only a week into it.

Fear.

It was a killer when it came to families. Rock would have endured the threats if she had her way. Set a trap. Used the former paratrooper Kyle Brennan if she could. Appealed to him as a fellow military veteran.

Seemed unlikely he'd turn in Barney Gray, though. Seemed unlikely they'd even had contact with one another. Then there was what Moses had intimated.

It's as if someone else is giving the orders.

From the direct approach of crowbars used as weapons in the night and stationing assassins in holiday homes to planting a small bag of weed and then, as Moses explained before leaving West Bromwich, a knife in a schoolbag.

Had Moses's altercation with Mainey done the trick, but someone else moved into play? Or had Gray been stood down? Overruled?

If Gray had been called off, ordered to rein in his team, then who gave the word?

Theo Goodman, resurgent but operating from the shadows of legitimacy?

Malcolm Baines, the kingpin presiding over his empire from behind bars?

Kaspar Sevan, protecting a world across which his son rattled like a Tasmanian devil whirlwinding through life without a thought for the consequences?

Although they traced the hang-ups aimed at the rest of Division 43 to three pay-as-you go phones registered as part of the same batch, there was little else of note plaguing them. The team all took some time out of their own cases to lend fresh eyes to the data, and to push the IT division which, like the computer and armoury, they shared with the NCA, and found no viruses or similar on their devices. Satisfied the place wasn't one big listening station for whoever was pulling Barney Gray's strings, she ended up growing annoyed as she ran through the incidents so far.

When nothing new jumped out at her, she went home, an irritating niggle persisting.

It took her the entire drive, pulling up to her house with the AFO pairing stationed in a car outside, before she realised why she was so annoyed: They'd directed almost every threat at Moses. Only when she happened to be present did she end up on the receiving end, meaning they believed he posed a bigger threat than her.

In her house, she checked the Glock on her hip—a foolish Army chick with a gun. Paranoid, almost hoping for an assault.

What if Moses was right about that?

If the Shadow CPU wanted to harm her, would carrying a gun at all times mean they stepped up their offensive and brought in guns of their own? A sniper, perhaps? A drive-by? Her being armed would do nothing to prevent most assassination scenarios.

The house was quiet. She listened for a full minute, to the clock ticking in her lounge on her right, to the fridge in the dark kitchen ahead. The fridge's hum made her think she should dust off one of the cookbooks that she rarely picked up. For a moment, she couldn't recall why she'd never followed through with her plan to learn a new skill.

On the day she was discharged from the Army, she'd vowed to be a good wife—whatever that meant in the twenty-first century—and to find something meaningful to do with her life. She'd bought a ton of cookbooks, since that's what she'd observed "good wives" do in the past and had even delved into a few tomes. But living so close to her husband for the first time, things had gotten tense, claustrophobic even, and she had been considering the police for a while. A lot of ex-service people did. She'd deliberated long and hard, though, as she'd seen two outcomes for former military becoming civilian police officers: Those who adored it and slotted right in, and those who hated it from the get-go, unable to acclimatise to the abuse and lack of actual power the police in the UK hold.

To save her sanity, and her marriage, Rock threw herself into it. Found a career. Forgot about cooking. Yet the claustrophobic tension between her and Pete never abated. The evenings grew dull. At best, they virtually ignored each other. Weekends away to rekindle the romance fell flat as petty squabbles lingered in the background.

It was better they parted ways. It was only later, after he moved out, that she learned he'd been sleeping with an ex, on and off, for the past five years.

Someone in the house adjoining hers thundered up the stairs, snapping her out of her introspection. She kicked off her shoes, clipped off the holster and carried it with the gun into her kitchen where she flicked on the light, and nearly jumped out of her skin.

Her own reflection in the door to the garden shocked her. That hadn't happened before.

And shouldn't happen.

The angle was wrong for that, for her to see herself in the door as soon as she flicked on the light. She would have to shift more to the right for that to happen.

Usually.

Keeping low, beneath the windows that were blacked out thanks to the halogens illuminating the kitchen, she drew the Glock from its leather holster and stalked around each hiding place—the island, the refrigerator, the pantry.

All clear.

Only then did she press herself against the fitted cupboards and crab toward the door that had scared her. The key was in the lock on this side.

Rock reached for it and found it wasn't wide open, just not closed. She was certain she'd locked up that morning, but only after a relaxing espresso on her patio. Yes, she'd rushed out, but she normally removed the key and left it somewhere a burglar breaking a smaller window couldn't reach it.

No, she *had* locked it.

Rock laughed at the spread of appreciation, at her fears of being considered insignificant now dispelled by the evidence before her. Someone *had* broken in, then left, but couldn't get the door to close properly—an issue she'd been meaning to deal with for months, the house still "settling".

Then the reality hit her.

They'd been in her house.

Had they taken anything, or… more to the point… had they planted something? It seemed to be a favoured tactic. Plant something illegal, then have a supposedly neutral officer discover it.

Rock took off, tearing around her house, her military training on clearing buildings of insurgents flashing back as if the past two years had never happened. She chose not to alert the AFOs out front, preferring to use her own methods. Plus, maybe a tiny part of her wasn't sure exactly how many people Gray had in his pocket.

When she could not locate an intruder to shoot, she pulled open every cupboard and drawer, checked every hidey-hole she could think of, including the tiny loft and the toilet's cistern. One big downside of new-build houses soon presented as an advantage, the lack of storage space offering limited options on where to stash a brick of heroin or a weapon used in a murder. After only fifteen minutes, she satisfied herself that nothing had been left behind, nor anything of significance taken.

Then why break in?

And with a patrol car watching, they'd have had to sneak in through the back, which meant the neighbours might have seen. To minimise the risk, they'd have likely come in under the cover of darkness. Meaning it was recent. The sun only set an hour and a half ago, so…

Had they been inside when she came home? Was that why the door was slightly ajar? Because it took a bit of welly to seal it, and she'd have heard.

Rock turned on all the lights, including those to

her tiny, messy garden. She made a sweep of the outside, again as an Army captain, not a police officer. She didn't care a jot if one of the many neighbours who overlooked the patch of ground looked out to find her examining every square inch of the place.

Again, nothing there.

She retreated inside and locked the patio door.

The small, clean house was now a small, cluttered house, and as Rock tidied up, put every last thing in its place and made the bed, the shell of bricks and mortar felt very empty. She gave a loud, "Huh," and half expected it to echo from every wall. The house absorbed the noise instead.

She took out her phone and looked up Sam's number. Didn't call. Instead, she looked him up on Facebook, a quick digital recce before inviting him over. For the company only, no funny business.

Netflix, maybe.

No chill.

Dumped a week earlier, he'd wasted no time in changing his relationship status, and when someone inquired about that, he replied "broke up, no biggie." At least he'd calmed down from his "bitch" comment to her face. Maybe he'd said harsher things in private. He'd posted nothing except a couple of dozen memes whose themes declared how life was short, and happiness needed to be grasped with both hands, and to live life to the full, and look to the future, and move on from the past, and blah blah blah... She checked his Instagram and found nothing except the same memes repeated. No climbing pics, no new women, no angry missives about how shallow women were.

Just life affirming memes posted by a dumped, super-reliable guy.

"Yeah, not happening," Rock said aloud, and looked up the site for the nearest Premier Inn.

She booked online, then packed pyjamas and a change of clothes, and headed out, letting the AFOs know she wouldn't be back, but to keep an eye out. The lights were staying on intentionally.

Seven minutes later, she drove past the hotel at five miles per hour over the speed limit, then got to a roundabout and circled back. She observed every vehicle coming from the opposite direction, trying to see inside, but failing. Only one car—a dark green Mini Cooper—slowed when she eased to the centre of the road, but again could not see in through the windshield.

She pulled into a slot at the hotel. At reception, she gave her booking details and, upon presenting her police ID, requested a room overlooking the car park. She rushed straight up to the first floor and without turning on the light she cracked the curtain as far as she dared.

Most of the car park was visible, along with the entrance. Nothing happened for several minutes.

Then a Mini Cooper passed by from the direction of the roundabout. Could have been dark green, but hard to tell in the streetlights. Didn't mean much, anyway; they were common cars. And she couldn't see even a partial licence plate from here.

More nothing.

Finally, the Mini Cooper returned. Drove slowly by. It pulled in, rolling gradually along the row, pausing at Rock's vehicle, before turning around and exiting.

But not before a lamp built into a bollard gave Rock a flash of the driver's face. The pretty, petite face of their last hope of nailing the group.

Agnes Marsh was driving. She was alone.

Now Rock had to find out why.

58

Moses was getting more annoyed at finding new parts of him that hurt. As one major bruise softened, a new one tightened, and gave him difficulty walking. He'd imbibed two more bottles of the strong cider and started to regret the third as a headache kicked in, and the night-time cold banished the day's heat. Frankie made her authoritative instruction to go to bed sound as seductive as it usually did, and he promised himself he'd make the effort.

Sex shouldn't be painful, but maybe it'd help loosen him up physically as well as mentally. Plus, he really wanted to.

Frankie was an amazing woman. Strong, intelligent, funny, and righteous.

Forgiving.

Perhaps not her best quality, but definitely the

most important when taken in the context of their marriage.

More than once in their time together, Moses had thought about breaking things off with her. She was too good for him, and he was forever letting her down. She suspected his indiscretions with Baines were more severe than he'd admitted, but she'd been instrumental in pushing his decision to turn on the man. Made Moses see Baines was using him, a tool in a machine that included much bigger targets. PSD didn't want Moses, the tiddler of a fish; they wanted the shark.

Frankie went to bed first, telling him she'd make things nice. Massage oils, candles, her "good" outfit.

To pass the time, Moses conducted a final check on himself. His hair, his thin beard, a twist to ease another kink from his back. Then, to pass a little more time, he checked on Eko.

She was splayed on the bed, head on one pillow, a leg sticking out of the covers. Her room was a mishmash of girly-girl and tough-girl: nail polish, hair products, a rack displaying her Karate belts from white through red, the brown worn around her waist during training. Her posters were the usual bland boy bands, although a Korean group had recently entered her collection, these alongside luminaries like Bruce Lee and Jackie Chan, Gina Carano and Ronda Rousey.

Moses lifted her leg under the cover and pulled it over her.

She stirred. "Dad… you're not supposed to do that anymore." Groggy. Turned over, away from him. "I'm not six, Daddy."

"I know, baby." He kissed her head. "I still need to check sometimes. Dads are lame like that."

She said nothing more, so he assumed she'd fallen back asleep, probably wouldn't remember this by the morning. He made for the door, but her voice stopped him. "Dad?"

He paused and rotated back to her.

Eko was sitting upright, watching him with the detached bemusement of a botanist examining an overhanging branch of fauna. "I'm sorry, Dad. About the knife."

Moses ambled back to the bed. Sat on it, his legs supporting as much weight as the bed. "It's okay, baby. Not your fault. You couldn't have known."

"I mean… I did know, Dad."

Moses clamped his throat and listened.

"I took the knife, Dad." She seemed fully awake. Hands in her lap, her face earnest in the crack of light from the hall. "I was scared. All this stuff going on."

Moses shuffled to her and wrapped her in one arm, sensing her fear, her shame, and wanting to hold tighter, but scared he could break her.

"I didn't want to go unarmed," Eko said. "I know we have the cops watching, but…"

Moses's chin rested on the top of her head, his

hand stroking her hair. Despairing for the right words. "It's okay, baby."

She pushed away, the tears she'd held back when they were in Mrs Donovan's office now ripe and spilling. "It's not, though, Dad. You're going to let them get away. I heard you and Mum talking. I know you're scared, but I was ready for them. I'd have defended myself if they came for me, and—"

"I'm sorry." Moses looked deep in her eyes, the light catching the moisture so her brown irises seemed to flicker. He held her arms and recited to himself the reasons he did the job the way he did, took the risks he'd taken in the past.

For them.

For her. Even before she was born.

For Eko.

If it hadn't been for her, Moses would have broken off the marriage. An unexpected surprise, but one that saved him. Set him on the right path. The hardest path he'd ever taken, but he'd done it for her.

Because she saved them.

Before, when it seemed like Baines had him in the hole for all they'd done, when PSD were going hell for leather in their investigation, he'd fought back. He'd taken the hard path, struggled and battled through, and came out the other side.

Now he was stuck in that rabbit hole again. An impossible path before him.

"There has to be a way," Eko said. "There's always a way. Isn't there?"

Moses kissed his daughter again and eased her back to her pillow. Pulled her cover up, and she accepted it.

He said, "I'll take care of it, baby. Daddy promises. We're not out of it yet."

TUESDAY

59

Moses pictured himself moseying. Yeah, moseying. Not walking or striding, but *moseying*. Like a cowboy, or perhaps Richard Roundtree as Shaft or Jim Kelly as Black Belt Jones, or one of the many blaxploitation heroes of his youth; anachronisms that would have no place in the modern world. He'd shaped the narrow line of beard using a straight razor and donned a dark purple cotton shirt, his blue-grey wool suit with the most room under his arms, and shoes that looked formal but came with chunky soles that gave excellent grip. No tie. No waistcoat.

Oh, and small sunglasses for the low morning sun, á la Morpheus in *The Matrix*.

His only precautions were a can of pepper spray in one pocket and an extendible police baton heavy in a pouch he'd had custom-sewn into the lining of his jacket. He still didn't think he needed a gun.

Not yet.

Not on this long, busy road winding to the north of Birmingham. A dual carriageway blocked off from pedestrians by a metal barrier. He'd parked and set off on foot, the exercise easing more kinks from his body. He was almost moving freely again, but this excursion wasn't his choice alone.

He placed a call, a Bluetooth bud in one ear, the mike to his chin, cancelling the traffic noise. Wearne answered, and he asked, "Did you process my papers yet?"

"No, but I understand. I can't pretend I wasn't hoping you'd reconsider—"

"I am reconsidering. Hold off on it. I'm coming in. Just have a stop to make first."

Pause. Breath. *Hmm.* "Is this the same reason DC Rock has said she'll be late today? A 'stop to make' seems to be a common excuse suddenly."

Moses smiled but didn't reply with anything except, "Thank you, ma'am."

He had texted Rock with the arrangements, but also added it might be dicey, so she didn't have to be there. He'd excluded her from enough on this and, like Eko, she hadn't wanted to give up. Admittedly, she had less to lose than Moses, but that made it no less important.

He spotted her on a pedestrian overpass,

stretching from a residential estate on one side of the road to the industrial estate on the other. He waited for her to cross and descend to him. Jeans, flat boots, long-sleeved t-shirt, light coat long enough to cover the Glock holster, which was empty.

"Where's the piece?" Moses asked.

"'Piece'?" Rock replied. "Are we mafia now?"

"Question stands."

"Lock box safe in my car. Even if it gets nicked, no one's getting in without some specialist equipment. Figured it'd be better to leave it."

"Yeah, they'll just take it off you." Moses pressed on toward the lay-by where a static caravan had been converted into a greasy spoon café and two trucks and a van were parked farther down. "You sure you want to do this?"

"You're sure we can trust Theo Goodman?"

"No, that's why I gave you a choice. And you can still back out."

"Not on your—"

"Before you answer, I'm buying you breakfast."

"I have news too," Rock said.

"Good." Moses wanted to listen, but something was more pressing. "Can we grab this moment first?"

"Sure. It can wait."

Inside the café it was as basic as Moses expected, with plastic chairs and Formica tables, and a counter with a manual cash-only till and a grill and hob behind.

"Vegan options are going to be limited," Rock said.

"Tea is vegan." Moses checked out the cartons. "And he has oat milk."

The "he" Moses mentioned was a skinny Mediterranean-looking man in a black t-shirt with a hair net and a big nose, a disinterested manner which suited all as Moses ordered a regular tea with oat milk and a bacon and egg sandwich with a coffee for Rock. They moved outside with their drinks to sit on flimsy aluminium and plastic tables tied to the ground with bricks to prevent them being blown away by traffic turbulence. Rather than face-to-face, they positioned themselves side-on to one another, observing the heavy flow of vehicles.

"I'm not gonna lie to you," Moses said. "I took the money."

"I know," Rock said.

"I mean, a lot of it. At first, it was pocket money. I was new to it all, and Baines and some others, they started me off small. An illegal slap here, a punch in the gut to a mouthy chav there. I went along with it. That was the way of things. Make sure they don't walk all over you."

Rock remained noncommittal, motioning with her head to show she was listening.

"First time I took any cash was on a call to the Hampton estate, where Gabriella Childs lived. Hell, she'd have been a baby back then. It was always a shithole, worse than now, to be honest. We were following up on a stash of drugs and knives some kid found on his way to school, and we figured it was a dump from someone who got their collar ."

Rock's sandwich arrived, dripping with melted pig fat, delivered with the kind of surly ambivalence Moses last saw from a road sweeper. She served Moses with an appreciative smile and said, "Lush."

"The previous day, bobbies pulled up in a marked car, and this kid, Ben, he'd run straight away. Out of sight, he must have dropped his gear and carried on running. When the car caught up, he was clean, so he got kicked. Luckily, red tape and all that meant he was logged. Me and Malc, we bagged the stuff and sent it for printing, then went to grab Ben. He fought, though. He clocked me, and I arrested him for assaulting an officer, but he told Malcolm he'd pay the tax."

"Tax?" Rock said through a mouthful of meat and bread.

"That's what I said. But Ben led us to a stash in a flower bed a dozen yards away. A box like those petty cash tins. Had five hundred quid in it. Malcolm Baines, man..." Moses pictured the incident. "He split the money. Hundred for him, four for me. 'Compensation,' he said. I stared at it for a time, and the way Ben was acting, it was clear. Obvious. This wasn't the first incident like that."

"And you... took it?"

Moses sipped his tea. In reality he preferred a creamy hemp concoction over oat milk, but it wasn't terrible. "Yes. I was a young black man in a predominantly white profession with guys who'd already made fun of my hair and called it 'banter'. References to the size of my dick, which was of course a 'compliment' and pointing out how I didn't act like 'most black fellas.' They weren't threatening, weren't directly abusive, and I gotta say it's not like it was in the seventies, but still. If I kicked up a fuss, I may as well've kissed my career goodbye."

Rock kept eating.

"I took it, yeah. I bought my girlfriend a nice dinner and took her for cocktails. Not Frankie, this is before. But that was the first. I took it to fit in. Small potatoes, but tidy, y'know? A scumbag loses out, I benefit."

Rock swallowed, licked sauce off her bottom lip. "Still criminal behaviour."

"Yeah. And it got worse. A little here, a little there. They let me tag along for six months, showing me the ropes. I was in it for thousands. I'd met Frankie by then, started dating after that tip off about the rapist, and then, eventually, I met Theo Goodman."

A truck roared by, closer than the others had been, faster, throwing papers around, and both covered their drinks and food.

"He seemed nice?" Rock said.

"Yeah. He ran a lot of small-time ops. Heard

about a lot of big-time ops. He never wanted to be a kingpin or godfather of crime. He wanted a way for local people to make a little cash. Because society wasn't giving them a fair lick. A bit of drug dealing, a bit of sex trade, some illicit cigarettes from the continent… It was harmless enough. I suppose… I suppose I sympathised." Moses had stuttered into a zone where he was justifying his actions so switched back to facts. "And whenever anyone threatened to move into his territory, he tipped us off."

"With a little bonus for your trouble?"

"Bigger fish, the bigger bonus. Went on for about two years."

"And you never questioned it?"

"It grew. Slowly. Like an addiction. It was how Baines did it. How guys before me got drawn in, how others came along after I got established. A small tight-knit team, even after Baines got his promotion. We were doing a good job for the police and getting paid through the back door by a grateful citizen."

Moses counted three army vehicles pass by, noting Rock linger on them as they receded into the distance.

He said, "I got enough laundered to provide a deposit on a house, and with mine and Frankie's incomes, we got a nice place in a nice area. I furnished it, did a few renovations, and then it stepped up a gear. Soon, we weren't always arresting these guys, just dishing out beatings and raiding their shit. We burned them out a couple of times, the coke or weed or whatever going up in smoke while we pocketed any cash. But then Baines told us to start confiscating the drugs instead of destroying them."

Hot nausea roiled inside Moses, recalling how close he'd come to being irredeemable.

"I realised Goodman was expanding, not defending. And Baines was more of a partner than a contact or friend. And he was running scams I never got wind of."

Rock sipped her coffee, the sandwich finished. "PSD got wind of it? Prosecuted you?"

"No. PSD got wind of it because I tipped them off."

Rock froze, the mug halfway to the table. "You started it?"

Moses pushed his sunglasses farther up his nose, the sunlight having crept in around the side. "Yep. I'd confessed everything I dared to Frankie one night. She was ready to leave me, but I became an unofficial client instead. Negotiated immunity before I'd tell them anything. Made out like it was petty stuff, but corruption nonetheless."

"Tricked them into giving you a free pass?"

"Yeah. Frankie worked out the legalese, to the point it covered anything I might implicate myself in, with the exception of sex crimes, crimes against children, and murder."

Rock got the mug to the table and exhaled

through a narrow mouth, as if she'd been winded. "I didn't have Frankie down as..."

"Corrupt? She wasn't, not really. She was pregnant, and we both wanted to start afresh. Clean. She didn't aid my crimes, either, just helped me make amends. I had to go confess to God too." Moses couldn't help a brief internal laugh at the memory. "But she helped on the condition that I went clean. Like straight down the line. No more dodgy deals. If I had to go off-book to stay safe, she'd tolerate that, but anything else was on my own head."

"And you sent Baines down."

Moses's gut still churned whenever he summoned an image of his mentor's fate. "Thought it'd be simple, but I had to go undercover. Wear a wire. Get confessions. They had enough, but they made me go in for more. More than Baines, they wanted everyone. I did what I could, but those young lads, some in uniform, others new to detective civvies, they didn't deserve it. They'd been manipulated, almost *groomed*."

A Renault Grand Scenic with its indicator flashing turned off the road, rolling into the layby.

"Six coppers lost their jobs and did a few months inside. Four more forced to retire. And Baines was done for sixteen crimes. Including the robberies, one murder pleaded down to manslaughter, several counts of supplying a restricted substance, collusion, perverting the course of justice... You name it, they prosecuted for it."

The seven-seater Renault slowed and pulled into the lay-by, going past the café to park behind a lorry.

"Without our protection, Goodman withdrew. Others moved in."

"And you got away scot-free." Rock spoke without malice, without judgement. Matter-of-fact.

"Not quite scot-free. When they learned how deep I was in it, the PSD guys were so pissed at me for securing complete immunity that they leaked my name. It wasn't a jail sentence, but they knew the rest of the coppers would treat me so badly I'd have to quit. Rats rotting in my car, delivered to my house. Dog shit on my desk. Only speaking to me when they absolutely had to. And I almost did quit."

"What stopped you?"

"I was depressed, ready to go. Even prepared to divorce Frankie because I felt so useless, so stupid for doing what I did. But like I said, she was pregnant. And I'm not kidding, I wanted that family. That life. It was what I'd saved for, the whole reason I did what I did. To give myself that boost. A start I'd missed out on." He shook his head, a nasty taste surfacing. "I'm not justifying it, I'm really not. But I wanted you to know everything. And this is everything. No more surprises."

The Renault backed up, stopping beside them. There was a sticker on the side identifying it as a licensed minicab. The window rolled down and the Pakistani driver called out, "Moses, yeah?"

Moses and Rock made for the car. Moses opened the door for Rock and she thanked him. He climbed in the back with her and asked, "Where are we going?"

The driver checked his mirror and signalled to pull out. "To see Mr Goodman of course."

60

The cab dropped them without charge at a cheaply constructed building in the middle of an industrial park denoted by a single sign as *Earth Crop Food & Drink*. It was one of dozens of identical boxes, with a huge number 18 above the company sign the only thing differentiating it. Comparing this property with the others, Moses grew uneasy at its lack of activity. While the rest of the buildings nearby had vans, lorries, even sizeable cars moving to and fro, Earth Crop Food & Drink appeared abandoned.

"Why'd he send the cab?" Rock asked. "It's not like he blindfolded us."

"Tradition, I suppose." Moses rapped on the regular-sized door. It was next to a larger, rolling door, big enough for a small lorry to ride under.

"Maybe he didn't want cars parking out front for any longer."

"Or maybe he didn't want our cars nearby so we'd be harder to track."

Moses banged the door harder this time. Waited. "You said you had news too."

"Yeah, it might work out—"

The door opened. Rock stopped speaking and Theo himself greeted them. Jogging bottoms and unzipped top, polo shirt showing his chest hairs and crucifix. Furtive, checking the lot out front, he said, "Inside. Quickly."

Moses stepped into the doorway, hesitating to check the inside for others, then ducked all the way in.

With an office to the left, they were in a storage depot, lines of shelves packed with boxes of dried goods down one side, opposite a row protected by ceiling-to-floor plastic strips holding back the cold of a powerfully air-conditioned section. In here, Moses spotted fresher goods; vegetables and fruit in clear containers.

The door closed, and Theo led Moses and Rock along the aisle.

"This yours?" Moses asked.

"Yeah, man." Theo sounded almost comical, like someone putting on a stereotypical Jamaican accent. *Yeah mhaaan*. "Expanded into distribution. Supply my own stores, send the bill to my accountant in the Isle of Man, and suddenly I'm running a non-profit."

Rock took the place in as she walked. "Tax evasion."

"No, no, no. Tax *avoidance*. Completely legal. The big money people do it. The politicians do it. You can't blame a hardworking guy who came from nothing for trying it too, eh?"

"Why are we here, Theo?" Moses asked.

"You wanted to meet, I'm meeting."

"This place is a graveyard. You cleared it out for us."

They rounded a corner to an open space with pristine kitchen equipment ready to be shipped. Cookers, industrial fridges, dishwashers. A dozen of each.

"I need somewhere I control," Theo said. "Arms up."

"Really?" Moses raised his arms.

Theo patted him down, locating both the truncheon and pepper spray, but allowed Moses to keep them. Then he did the same with Rock, his motion slowing as he clocked the holster.

Rock joined Moses, side-by-side. "Now we do you?"

"He wasn't looking for weapons," Moses said.

"Can't trust a guy like Moses." Theo winked. "Not always, anyway. You know, when you walked in my door the other day, I thought we were back in business. But way you talked, I guessed your little filly wasn't quite up to speed. I get the feeling that's changed?"

Rock said, "I know all about Baines and what Moses did. Your former business arrangement."

"Good, good." Theo's mouth hung open, as if about to laugh, but it never came. "You said you had a proposal, Moses. Something that might help me out?"

"I don't know everything about your current business," Moses said.

"You *do* know everything, my friend. I'm legit." He swept his hand in the direction they came. "Vegan is big business. They even want white goods that have never been near meat."

"You supply a little extra too, Theo. Don't pretend you don't. Passing information for Baines? Packages in and out of Dovedale?"

Theo wafted his hand and shook his head. "A little favour now and again. You gon' deny a guy this?"

"The protection unit," Rock said, pushing the point of their visit. "Convince us you aren't a part of it. Because we've got plenty of hints you might be."

Theo let go of the non-laugh and converted it to a grimace. Perched himself on a chest freezer. "Malcolm had a good thing going. Protection for those who kept their business out of the public eye. Off the police radar. If we weren't shooting up clubs or stabbin' our rivals to death, or any of that New Jack City crap, he was happy. We weren't

Yardies or mafioso. Just a bunch of guys making a living."

"I'm not hearing any names," Rock said.

"Easy." Moses paced, then switched back and eyed Theo. "The process you set up with Baines. It had double blinds, dead drops for money and instructions. But he never gave it up. Not fully."

"There were people working for him you never heard of. He did it well, my friend. Smaller cells. Like terrorists. No one knowing the other's business. Barney Gray was a wet-behind-the-ears detective constable when Baines went down."

"But already had the connection?" Rock said.

"Yep. You smart, girl." Theo winked again. Flexed his jaw as if chewing gum, but his mouth was empty. "They got desperate to hang on. To not get caught. People like Cole Mainey were on board already, spent too much time on the unofficial side of things, so clever clogs like Barney leapfrogged him in the police ranks. Played it well, too. Better than Baines in some ways. Expanded, took on clients with no respect for boundaries. Too much taste for the product. Made them loose. Only way to keep control was through fear."

"The Sevan family," Moses said. "Did they take over?"

"My patch? Yes. And others. They used my guys to get phones into the prisons, lots of them, but specifically Malcolm Baines."

"He was telling the truth," Rock said. "He never stopped running things."

"Oh, I wouldn't know about that. I'm just telling you what I've seen. And what I've seen? It's limited to my legitimate businesses. To hearing rumours, not participating."

Moses remembered the enterprise being clinical, not bloody. Even the beatings they administered were careful and calculated, meant to hurt and intimidate. "In your eavesdropping capacity, then. Let's look at the recent makeup of the business. The Sevans expanded and even the psycho son Joshua got in on it."

"Gray kept it in-house. Kept the circle small. Once he recruited a couple of newbies, he built a good professional rep. A woman came first, I think. Only met her briefly, but never liked her. Scary-ass lady."

"That'll be DS Burns," Rock said.

"And a black fella, too. Equal ops. Get in an ethnic, there's less questions from up high."

"Kortenberg," Moses said, naming the South African guy he'd chucked over a desk. "He's more than a diversity hire, though. He knows his tech. Probably the guy who doctors the records to fit their narratives."

"And an Asian. More boxes to tick." Theo's grin was a rueful one, almost sarcastic. "Walar?"

"Yeah, Ratan Walar," Rock replied. "But they turned on him after he left the group."

Moses pictured them in order. "If it was Burns who Frankie met, who killed Nicola Dawson to get away… She's their trigger person, their assassin. Baines probably identified her as a psychopath early on and picked her up. Kortenberg is their IT wizard, one of Gray's. Mainey's the old school brawler from Baines' day. Brings the contacts and helps with intimidation of witnesses… Like me, he knows where to hit people. And Gray himself is the leader, the thinker."

"What about Marsh?" Rock asked.

Moses thought about that. Shrugged. "A chance encounter with a like mind. She witnessed Mainey kill that paedo and kept her mouth shut."

"Recruited as a reward?"

Moses turned a full circle, watching Theo, taking in their surroundings—dark and impersonal. Didn't feel like Theo at all. "They're going further than Baines ever used to. Coppers' families, killing cops, planting evidence, frame ups for murder."

"No, no, they bad," Theo said. "Brutal. They got more anonymity. Means they got distance. Less they see of the humanity, less they care. More violence. More money. More grey areas."

Rock said, "Killing a police officer isn't a grey area."

"When they don't know the officer, it is grey. *Almost* anonymous to them." Theo shook his head, taking in both detectives. "You don't get it now, you'll never get it. This anonymity, their brutal ways. Even a guy like me, selling weed and a bit of coke here and there, I couldn't cope. I gave it up."

Moses wiped a hand over his face. "So they escalate. The Sevans and a few others are new, ruthless clients. No code, no honour. And, what? Two years ago, PSD come in and start making waves?"

Theo cinched his lips and lifted his shoulders. "I was out by then."

"PSD gets close, and Clinton Flood takes down one of them. A sacrificial lamb in Ratan Walar, but they didn't have enough to prosecute. Just moved him out of the department due to paperwork irregularities. A token demotion."

"Then as he goes after more, DCI Flood's kid gets taken for an unexpected ride," Rock filled in. "And a few months after that, to cement the threat, his mother is killed. He's crushed, his squad backs off after similar threats, and everyone goes about their business."

"See?" Theo said. "Anonymity. You keep the relationships personal, you keep the business clean."

Moses broke from his benign stride and walked right up to Theo. "Anonymity? How does it work? It can't all come from inside Dovedale prison."

Despite Moses's invasion of his personal space, Theo kept up his pally manner. "Moses, Moses. With Baines inside, I feel like I need new partners. Out here. I mean, I tried to help Malcolm where I could, but… he abandoned me."

"So, tell us." Rock came alongside Moses.

Theo bobbed on the spot, still perched on the chest freezer, his teeth showing through the crack formed by his widening smile. "I enjoyed my old life. This business, it is good, but is hard work. I'd like to hand this over to Lucas or Fiona. Or both, whatever. While I work on my pension arrangements."

"You want your old territory back," Moses said, a tingle playing at his fingertips. "We take out the protection group, take out Kasper and Joshua Sevan, and you're free to go back to hocking speed and weed to your clientele."

"Without fear of retribution."

"All I can promise is *I* won't be going after you."

"Moses…" The warning in Rock's voice was deep but lacked conviction. She didn't follow up.

"Deal," Moses said. "What do you have for us?"

Theo stuck out a hand, but Moses didn't shake, too similar to a hundred small cuts that led to him almost ruining his life.

"Okay, have it your own way." Theo withdrew the hand. "Before he went inside, Baines wanted to secure his fortune. He poured it into a number of investments. One in particular growing with every year: Property."

"A house? An apartment?" Rock said. "Where?"

"That, girl, I can't tell you. I was never invited for the housewarming."

"Then it's useless."

"But I know the name of the lawyer who set up

the trusts. Who moved the deeds so it couldn't be traced to him?"

Moses stuffed his hands in his pockets and rocked on his heels. "Keeping us in suspense, Theo?"

"Silas Bonaparte," Theo said. "The lawyer's name is Silas Bonaparte. Concentrate on him, and the rest will slot into place."

61

The Division 43 team had gathered once again, DCI Wearne at the head of the pack, DI Bobby Xian off to the side. Moses mingled with DS Ellingham, DI Archer, and DS Tahana. Rock had said she needed to stop off on the way back, so after the cab dropped them in the same lay-by from where it collected them, she and Moses went their separate ways. She wasn't here yet, and Wearne didn't wait.

"Specialist protection officers will be in place to cover all your homes," the DCI announced, "and digital forensics are monitoring your families' movements and electronics. If they ID any of you, and the multiple hang-ups on your phones suggest they have, they won't make a move while we're in place."

"Which brings us to Theo Goodman," Xian

said, a pointed look Moses's way. "We're a deep corruption unit, and you made a deal with a gangster."

Wearne joined him in the pointed look. "The ethics are questionable."

Moses had expected this response. He had told no one about the background he'd given Juliette Rock, so they wouldn't know more than he chose to give them about Theo. Yes, he'd been on the cusp of growing into the sort of man Kaspar Sevan was, but he'd never tipped all the way over. And Moses had computed the arguments already, trying to talk himself out of it, but the choices came down to the same thing: Take out Barney Gray and the Shadow Protection Unit, or let them go and hope they slipped up in the future.

"Lesser of two evils," he said. "Not a big enough threat to concern us, and he'll be a good contact. We'll have more eyes on Kaspar Sevan when it's time to raid him once and for all."

DI Archer said, "The link is this potato of a lawyer?"

"He's the go-between. Which we knew. But more importantly, he helps them with their accounting through a separate firm."

"According to your pet gangster friend," Ellingham said.

"Depends which is the pet," Xian added.

Tahana stayed silent. Moses pegged her as being new to the team, established but not cemented into the group dynamic.

"I'm nobody's pet," Moses said. Although *pet* was partly a joke, he had to choke back a more robust response. "Until Goodman becomes a problem, I'll assume he's a source. You need to as well. If he oversteps, we'll take him."

"Move on." Wearne checked a text message and swiped to clear it. "The money."

"Silas Bonaparte facilitates several relationships. He's the blind drop, the backup for several crime families, and owns an accountancy firm based offshore but employs people in the UK."

"Laundering their backhanders?" Xian said.

"Laundering or prepping for cash deposits. Goodman also mentioned an 'artist' who costs a pretty penny for 'personal assignments.'"

"Forger," Archer said. Not a question.

"Safe assumption." Moses brought himself back to the lawyer. "So, this facilitator, his clients are the bad guys, like Kaspar and Joshua, but when his regular services don't cut it, he calls Barney Gray to see what they can do from the inside. It's a two-pronged attack of bribery and threats. It explains the change in tactics—Silas taking over the intimidation, switching from Baines' old school threats and the Shadow Unit's brutal methods to something less obvious but with more impact."

"And your friendly bad guy can make the case?" Xian asked.

"Goodman doesn't know, but I can guess how it works."

"How?" Ellingham asked.

"Small favours in areas that have certain access. They'd start by either asking, bribing, or threatening to obtain info that won't endanger anyone. It's accepted because, why would a detective inspector be doing harm? It's just circumventing red tape. Then they keep going, to the point they can get whatever they need."

"Davina Mishkin," DS Tahana said, her first contribution this morning.

"The pathologist, right." Moses heard the door's magnetic seal clunk unlocked, and he assumed it was Rock arriving. "Clearly thought she'd done what she needed to in replacing the results with canine bloodwork, and then when we showed up, she was terrified. The way she spoke, I don't think it was a bribe. I think they issued threats."

Xian was looking at the door. Out of the corner of Moses's eye, Juliette Rock entered. Ellingham was staring too.

Moses kept his attention on the group. "But Division 43 was formed because we have a ton of legal oomph, right? Tracking the money should be easier, given our leeway. Problem is, I'm expecting Silas to have covered most of his bases. We don't know the name of the trust he set up for Baines, and we don't even know if the property he bought is in the UK, so—"

Now Tahana and Archer appeared to be watching Rock's entrance. Not listening to Moses.

He followed their gaze and Wearne did too. When he saw who Rock had brought with her, he forgave their lack of manners and wondered if what he was seeing was too good to be true.

I have news.

Good news for a change.

"No shit," Moses said.

Rock urged the person beside her forward, the young, hard face now a shy kitten, startled by unfamiliar surroundings.

Rock said, "Everyone, this is Agnes Marsh."

"You're cooperating?" Moses said. "To bring them in?"

Marsh shook her head, the kitten bewildered by an unexpected arrival. "I can't help like that. They never let me all the way in. And no way I'm wiring up."

Rock took the lead. "We believe they're going to do to her what they did to Ratan Walar. She's expendable. And while we can't use her against Barney Gray, she's going to help us get to him. Through Silas Bonaparte. In fact, Gray's called a meeting at the Safe House today."

"At the Safe House?" Moses said.

Marsh flapped one hand, then firmed it up, a single digit raised. "No. You're not following me. And I'm not going in bugged."

Moses huffed, his hands in his pockets. "Then what good are you?"

As Marsh hesitated, Rock's expression worked like a visual nudge.

Marsh said, "I heard a name. Something that might help you trace the money."

"What name?" Moses tried to sound interested, but he remained sceptical. "We already know about Theo. About Silas Bonaparte."

"Trembling Alien Entertainment." Marsh's voice hid its timid notes, a firm, confident statement. "Trembling Alien Entertainment Inc. Or Limited. I didn't take it all in. Something called 'Haven Maker' too. I think one of them is a company name laundering their money."

"It's a start," Rock said to Moses, then took in the room, which gave nothing away.

Marsh's throat bobbed, chin low.

Moses nodded, eyes not moving from Marsh for a second. "Looks like we might be in business. Let's check it out."

62

Barney Gray once thought it inevitable that he'd end up like Malcolm Baines—incarcerated, awaiting release so he could raid his stash of cash and fake IDs, then spend the rest of his days tanning himself to a deep mahogany, introducing a Viagra supply to age-inappropriate women, though still of legal age, who were not his wife. That fantasy took a back seat the day he accepted a leadership role.

Why assume prison?

Why not have more contingencies than an enhanced pension scheme?

Why not do more than rely on investments and parole hearings?

As technology improved, so too did the forging of documents to bypass such technology. Waning government budgets meant Border Force cuts, along with the police and NHS, and allowed them to step up their activities. There wasn't a single area of the police that wasn't suffering, and that included Professional Standards. They only had limited time, personnel, and balls.

Gray realised they'd move on once pursuing his team became untenable and even undesirable. Walar was the one to leave, the sacrifice to help them save face. That they'd tried again rankled with Gray, and the action the team decided upon still hadn't sat right. As for the escalation to killing a fellow police officer this week?

They'd crossed a line, and Gray was responsible.

Ultimately, he was responsible for them all—their safety, their actions, their future. A future he believed he'd secured thanks to more contingencies than those Baines had dictated.

Gray was their leader. Not Malcolm Baines. And he'd led them to the Safe House to discuss that future.

"I need an honest answer," Gray said, having gathered them in the usual room, no beer this time; it was too early in the day, and they had a busy one lined up. "Have we gone too far? Do we need to cut and run?"

Silence. Thinking faces.

As was usual in these circumstances, Kortenberg was the first to speak up, his deep velvet voice almost a comfort, but in this case not quite. "There's no evidence to link us directly. But if they get more on Joshua, or bust us here, they'll have everything they need."

"Thought this place was air-gapped," Burns said.

"It is disconnected from us." Gray had checked that over himself. The paperwork was anonymous. No traffic cams for miles, either. And the neighbours were far enough away as to remain disconnected from their comings and goings. "Silas saw to that."

"What if they turn that little shit weasel?" Mainey asked. "Soon as Joshua does something we can't dig him out of, he'll fold."

Marsh, normally feigning a tough outer shell, had spent the minutes here hunched over, hands moving from the chair arm to her knee to her thigh, to tapping a tune on the chair arm again. "I've seen his type. Cole's right. He'll testify."

"I have his clothes," Gray replied. "He turns, gets off whatever petty crap he's done to land him in trouble, and we do him for murdering Gabby. Admin errors can work both ways."

Marsh said, "I thought we already rejected their kind offer."

Burns scoffed, rolled her eyes in disgust. "We're going with that? Rolling over for that piece of shit Moses? I say kill the bastard and his two women, watch the rest of his division run for the hills."

Kortenberg pressed his fingers together. "Hate to admit it, but leading them to Joshua Sevan may be the best option. His dad might even be up for it. Cuts them off from digging deeper."

"Hand over the clothes too?" Gray said.

"Bury them somewhere. Anonymous tip. They'll still have Josh's DNA."

"We hold our ground," Mainey said. "They'll go away like everyone else does."

Gray looked at the scenarios. Holding their ground was the more rewarding option, *if* they pulled it off. *If* Division 43 went away, and Moses with them. *If* Joshua could be controlled, and *if* Kaspar got the nod from Baines to move things up a notch. But Baines was just a figurehead to Gray. Someone they honoured, like the founder of a charity who'd long moved on to other things but maintained the respect and admiration of those left behind. And since Burns had killed Nicola Dawson in the Cotswolds, he was looking at worse than Baines, should it all collapse around them.

While Baines was all but untouchable, comfortable in his Dovedale citadel, this was Gray's op. The only question was which way the loyalty would swing.

To him, or to Baines?

He said, "Hurting and threatening evil scumbags helps us in our daily job. Threatening cops who get too nosy keeps us safe. But we've never actively planned the murder of one of them."

"Killing their chief weapon sends the best message," Burns said. "Dump Joshua's clothes behind his washing machine or some place, it looks like he was in it for the blackmail. That doc will say what we tell her to. It'll look like Joshy did Moses and the fam, but missed the evidence he was looking for." She sat back, tutting like she was the most intelligent person in the room, surrounded by miscreants. "It's the safest option, but if you're too soft, then fine."

Gray couldn't consider his options for too long. Had to assess which way the wind was blowing in the room, if there was an appetite for outright murder. Otherwise, they'd go over his head, ask Baines or even Silas about their next move.

"DCI Flood's mother was a misunderstanding," Gray said. "Nicola Dawson was self-defence." A glance at Burns to reassure her he didn't hold it against her, even though he'd literally thrown up when he got the news. Of all the members of the team, she was the one he expected would slit his throat if Baines deemed it necessary. "We've never willingly killed a police officer. Never planned it from the off."

Burns twisted so she was side-on to Gray. Clear where she landed on this.

"Would Baines approve of this course?" Gray asked her. With no reply, he pushed, "Unless you're suggesting we disobey him. Kill Moses, use the confusion to bail out?"

Burns still didn't look at him. "What if I *am* suggesting that? Cut our losses."

"We what?" Kortenberg said. "Take what we have so far? We'd need more."

Gray sensed a rise in pitch, a stillness to the room. A shifting of loyalties, from the past to the present. Words waiting to be spoken, but no one braving the danger. Perhaps the reverence in which they'd held Baines wasn't all-encompassing, not when the personal stakes were so high.

Might self-preservation trump loyalty?

Gray chose the courageous option, the role of leader. He said, "There are ways. Big risk, big reward. Remember, Moses is close and there are cracks. But Baines is even closer."

The stillness iced over.

Gray held his gaze on Kortenberg, who kept his fingers steepled together without speaking, then shifted to Cole Mainey, who maintained that wide open position—legs apart, one hand on each chair arm—but chewing his lip instead of replying.

"Go for it," Agnes Marsh said.

Gray snapped his attention to her. "Agnes?"

She was jittery, shrugging, that bravado returning, her nervousness plain. But she fought it. "They followed me this morning. I've had a mate say they pulled her over on some bullshit traffic offence, then questioned her about me."

Burns twisted to her, frowning. "Which friend?"

"Sally," Marsh said. "Sally Washington. You don't know her. Works at Marks's."

"Where does she live?" Gray asked.

"Bankshall Street, why?"

"Just a question. What happened?"

Marsh again tapped the chair arm, working her jaw before answering. "I think they were showing they could get to us like we did them. Like a silent threat. Bastards. I say we do them. Both of them."

"Constable Rock too?" Mainey said. "Golden girl on the fast track."

"She'll draw more heat than a disliked negro," Kortenberg added. When they all looked at him awkwardly, he said, "You all know it's true. Young dynamic white girl, or a black veteran cop with a questionable history? Who's going to upset the brass most?"

Mainey stretched his neck, rolled his shoulders, working out a kink. "Doing his family'll launch a bastard of a manhunt. We could do him, but…" A glance to Burns. "Should be a bonus if we get the chance or he pushes us into a corner. Not the main play."

Burns turned to stone for several seconds, before giving a single nod.

Ice cracked. The first stages of a thaw. No one met another set of eyes in the room.

That was Gray's job. "So, we're agreed we don't need to kill them. Just keep them at bay until we finish up."

"And watch for an opening," Mainey added. "I'm finishing him if I can."

Gray nodded. "If we're doing it, we're all in. The

next phase of the Pension Plan is the most dangerous. With Baines out of contact for the time being, we bring it forward without him. We do what I say, or we join him inside."

Agnes Marsh was the first to affirm her commitment.

Cole Mainey grunted agreement.

Rudolph Kortenberg pulled a pained expression, stretching his lips thin. Then he nodded too.

Clara Burns was last. She'd stated she wanted to kill Moses, but going against Baines? Acting without his say-so? It all hinged on her.

"Bailout like this, you're taking a big risk," she said. "And there's still a wildcard in Joshua that needs reining in."

Gray reiterated, "If Baines finds out we went against his instructions, we've no idea what will happen. Who'll stand with him. Against us."

"But if we pull it off, it's the biggest reward," Marsh said.

A spring thaw had come and gone, and the flowers of cooperation bloomed. They were following him. Out of self-interest, but he trusted they'd come together. Mostly. They *could* pull it off.

"Ready?" he said.

Nods from everyone, even Burns now facing him, a mischievous smile replacing her distaste.

Gray stood. "Then why are we still sat here? Let's go to work."

63

Bonaparte and Partners was a law firm based in central Birmingham in one of the many classic red-brick buildings around the courthouses, a landscape of built-up hills and valleys to rival San Francisco. Okay, maybe not quite San Francisco, but Moses found himself impressed with the architecture every time he visited this part of the city. No time for that today, though.

Moses led with Rock backing him up—leaving the gun behind again, to her clear annoyance. It was almost as if she was *hoping* to shoot someone. Although Xian held rank, he was happy for Moses to take charge, with Ellingham and Tahana in tow. Meanwhile, DCI Wearne and DI Archer prepped a station north of the city, clearing out the Police Community Support Officer contingent and leaving behind only a custody officer, as they expected at least one arrest this afternoon.

They arrived at the Birmingham office en masse, rushing through the front, the security measure of locked revolving doors succeeding only in delaying them as a skinny West African security guard who spoke little English admitted them with a mix of terror and excitement. There were three solicitors' businesses here, and Silas held the fourth floor. The doors to this area were locked too, but Moses banging on the wired glass drew a woman's attention, and he slapped both the warrant and his ID on the pane.

Marching through the space, it reminded Moses of a stately home, the original coving along the roof and mahogany bookcases clashing with the ultra-modern furnishings and computers decorating each of the half-dozen-or-so desks. The team broke off one at a time to secure the locations of the array of personnel. All wore formal clothes, manning desks, on phones or working books, but needed isolating to ensure they destroyed no documents. There were two glass cubicles set up as offices for—presumably—private conferences with clients, where people worked with those clients, and Rock emptied them out with the deepest of apologies. Each tracked the thinning group of cops as they strode through, with Moses approaching the final sub-office at the end alone.

With a floor-to-ceiling glass frontage and double

door, it was housed before an arched window, backlighting the occupant—Silas Bonaparte. With the ornate bookshelf, antique desk and wingback chairs, the enclave resembled an MI5 set from a seventies spy movie, or an elite gentleman's club—the type frequented by old Etonians, not the sort where ladies undressed for horny drunks. Moses didn't knock, just pushed open the door with Silas's name upon it in gold leaf.

The lawyer put down his fountain pen and removed his glasses. His thin used-car-salesman moustache crinkled as he sat back in his seat. "Detective Inspector Moses. Inevitable that you'd try to abuse your power through me, I suppose."

Moses said, "You're ordered to turn over any and all documents relating to Trembling Alien Entertainment Limited, their holdings in the UK, and any business records for the past four years." They'd found the *Trembling Alien* references easily enough. Nothing on *Haven Maker*, but they expected that name would crop up again as they excavated the lawyer's finances.

Silas's near-bald head remained motionless, his chest heaving once in a bored sigh. He extended a hand and clicked his fingers. Moses presented the warrant. Silas put his glasses back on and spent almost five minutes reading every word. Moses waited patiently, the power play obviously meant to intimidate.

Rock joined them to investigate the delay. Moses kept her silent with a flat-hand gesture.

Silas returned the papers to Moses. "This is a warrant relating to money laundering."

"We believe Trembling Alien Entertainment is not a console games start-up, but a money laundering front. Which you run through your accounting arm of the business."

"As I intimated, it was somewhat inevitable that you'd come. Very well, take me away." Silas held his wrists together as if awaiting cuffs.

"That's a pretty defeatist attitude," Rock said. "You're not even going to pretend?"

"Pretend what?" A frown formed on the man's forehead, wrinkling the smooth, pale pate above.

"You're expecting to go down for this?" Moses asked.

"I am expecting you to take me away. If you're as committed and somewhat obsessive as you seem." Silas looked at his hands, but when no handcuffs arrived, he stretched to see what the other detectives were doing—securing the files per the warrant. "Trembling Alien Entertainment only. Everything else in this office, or connected to me, is privileged."

"The warrant allows us to seize assets and information uncovered through our investigation into Trembling Alien."

"I assume nothing will indicate I cooperated in any way. If word got about that I was in breach of clients' data, it might be… unfortunate."

Moses tried to read the man: Eyes too small, darting about like a gerbil's, a plaster-of-Paris head, the stiff mohair-like thatch from one ear round the back to the other, his narrow frame that gave the impression of being soft despite the lack of obvious fat. A darting tongue touched his top lip then retracted and a single bead of sweat trickled from a pore beneath the thatch, winding past his ear and to the loose skin at the base of his jawline.

"What do they have on you?" Moses asked.

The mouth faltered, a tremble curling the pencil moustache into a clownish smile. "I do believe you have me confused with someone else, detectives."

"You're afraid."

Rock said, "We can help."

The man's clownish smile both thinned and stretched. The rivulet of sweat dripped, and another commenced. He removed his glasses again.

"No," Moses said, leaning slightly toward Rock. "I don't think we can. It's not fear. This guy, he struggles. He doesn't show emotion. He can't. He mimics what he sees in normal people. Right now, he's trying to show us he's… *amused*."

Like so many in this game, Moses thought. And in the business world. Tons of the most successful criminal lawyers were stone cold sociopaths, unable to feel empathy, finding sleep easy despite them winning the acquittal of murderers, rapists, and paedophiles. The man was trying to display *amusement*; a zombie learning to laugh.

Silas dropped the act, his attempts at a human face having failed. He didn't seem to care. "Quite, indeed, indeed. The inevitability was not that you would invade my domain with your shock-troops, or that you would come wielding that rather air-tight legal document and pluck out some financial trail that you believe will help you. It was inevitable that you would try *and fail*. There is no corruption here, Detective Inspector Glynn. That's the beauty of it; nothing we do here is illegal."

"DI Moses?" said Tahana, appearing in the doorway. "The guv's got what we need. It's all on-line. And there are plenty of questions to ask. He says to caution the suspect."

"Thanks." Moses folded the warrant and slipped it lengthways into his pocket. When Tahana retreated, he faced Silas. "You're confident this won't mean you sharing a cell with an apex inmate?"

"I am absolutely certain." Silas stood to his just-over-five-foot height and buttoned his tan suit jacket. "However, we will allow you to make certain arrests. If you play ball."

Rock snorted a sarcastic laugh. "If *we* play ball?"

Silas offered his wrists up for cuffing again. "Shall we get on with the caution? Then we can talk."

64

Above Kaspar Sevan's crappy strip club, in his loft-like office decorated with superhero and movie posters like a teenager's bedroom, Barney Gray kept coming back to the question: Was Kaspar faithful more to his own self-interest alone, or did that self-interest overlap too far with fealty to Malcolm Baines?

Kaspar had merely inhaled at Gray's request to access their liquid assets, reminding him they were only to be touched when Baines emerged from prison. Gray was the caretaker, after all, not some deputy or heir.

After a short period of further reflection, Kaspar parted from Travis and Carl, who wore their hand guns in shoulder holsters in plain sight. Although both bodyguards were hobbled—Travis through Mainey breaking his nose and one finger; Carl through losing a finger of his own to Burns' indulgence—their ability with firearms was not in doubt, even when utilising injured hands or their weaker side. The twins joined Gray as he paced, studying the pictures on Kaspar's wall as if in the art gallery he owned out by the Jewellery Quarter. Kaspar glanced once and fleetingly at Burns, who stood stock-still by the open staircase entrance; not hiding, barely even lurking, but she'd set herself back from the line of sight of anyone ascending into the office.

"It isn't personal," Kaspar said to Gray. "But Mr Baines has something of a long reach. If he learned I had helped you..."

Gray patted Kaspar's shoulder. "It's okay. I thought that would be your answer. You need to check with him first."

"Yes. And getting a private phone call in prison isn't an exact science. I will hold the bulk of the money until I hear back."

"There is an alternative." Gray moved on to the next picture, a huge Spider-Man in a gilded frame, swinging as he battled some green-skinned, pointy-eared villain on a flying skateboard. "We cut you in. Thirty percent more than you currently own."

Kaspar again fell in beside Gray. "That will mean stealing from Mr Baines' pot."

"Likewise, we want more than the share accumulated to date. You take a chunk, then we leave Malcolm enough to retire on. With that and the properties the Facilitator sorted for him, it should be plenty."

"You think he will not come after you? After me?"

"Take the money, Kaspar. Your share is six figures, at least. Liquidate your legit businesses, and you'll be out of here. Living a comfy life. Just… let us have access. Or clear out. Give us the safe combo." Gray sensed his speech pattern speeding up, gabbling like an excited job candidate before a board of interviewers. He steadied himself. "Say we robbed you. And you still keep that sizeable chunk of change."

Kaspar stared at the painting before them. Another glance to where Burns waited—lurked—in the shadows. Then to Carl and Travis, Carl's hand still bandaged from the injury inflicted by Burns. Finally, he returned to the picture. "These are valuable items. Mr Baines trusts me to invest wisely. After Stan Lee's death—the guy who created most of these—anything with his signature trebled in value. This piece has his autograph and that of the principal artist. I paid three thousand pounds for it five years ago. Three thousand pounds of Mr Baines' money. With inflation and the demise of Mr Lee, it is worth at least twelve thousand."

Gray whistled appreciatively, although why anyone would pay that for an inflated picture of a children's comic book cover, he couldn't grasp. He pulled out his phone and unlocked it, wondered if what he was about to do was too big a gamble, then figured *screw it* and hit send on a pre-prepared text, and returned the phone to his pocket. "That's a lot of cash."

Kaspar followed the motion of Gray's phone. "Urgent business?"

"Are all these pictures an investment?"

"Most. Who were you messaging?"

"Another partner. Another interested party."

A muted *thunk* from the door unsealing at the foot of the stairs resonated up and into the loft. Kaspar flicked a finger at Travis and Carl, who spread out and drew their guns.

"No need for that," Gray said.

Joshua's head came up the staircase first, then when his shoulders came into view, so too did two of his grim-faced sidekicks. Gray could name them as Markar Aviet, a cousin or something, and the sun-bed addict Sabazio Molinelli who liked to pretend to be Italian but had never been, nor (Gray suspected) could he point to the country on a map—low-rent thugs who hung on to Joshua and followed his every whim in the hope of a scrap or two thrown from the man's income and lifestyle. They'd been present when Kortenberg and Marsh concocted the plan with the dead hooker and Ratan Walar, so Gray had no doubt they'd be able to follow Joshua's simple instructions. No question of loyalty here; this trio, plus Ashley Mars, who was more than likely elsewhere cementing their alibis, represented self-interest at its most predictable.

Predictable that Carl and Travis would lower their guns but not holster them.

Predictable how Kaspar's face would crease as if a migraine were pressing behind his eyes.

And predictable that they wouldn't spot Burns from her position, ready to pounce if they didn't behave.

What wasn't predictable, though, was quite how high the three of them were. A little posse of arseholes, pumped up on steroids, coke, and from the near-empty bottle Joshua swigged from at the top of the staircase, more than a little champagne. He drained it, then hurled the bottle at the wall.

Carl and Travis jumped at the shattering glass, snapped their attention to Kaspar, seeking instruction.

"Joshua, what the hell?" Kaspar said.

"Silas cut me off, Dad." Joshua's voice slurred. His outstretched arms didn't help his balance as he turned a full circle, staggering at the end. "He said to take a plea, whatever that means."

Kaspar cast a dubious appraisal over Gray. "You know about this?"

"It's a power play," Barney Gray said. "He's spooked. We'll get him back on side. Time to clean house, though." Gray wandered, no sudden moves, closer to where Burns had secreted herself. "No stopping us once we erase the trail—and if it blows up, we're gone."

"And what do you need me to do?" Kaspar asked.

"You know what we need."

"I cannot give you that."

Joshua said, "Pussy. Guy in prison can't get to you. We run this. We could have him killed like that." He tried to snap his fingers, but they didn't work. He looked confused, then angry, as if about to break them for disobeying, then thought better of it. "He's nothing."

Kaspar ignored his son's response, keeping Gray in view. "What do you need me to do to keep Silas on board? No way is he part of your double-cross."

"It's not a double-cross," Gray said. "It's a change of direction. A new start."

"And you need Mr Baines' money to change your direction." Kaspar made his way over to his son. "Or Josh goes to jail?"

"We don't need all of it," Gray said. "But we will need some to help us stay free. And to keep your son out. You too, probably, if they come for us. And believe me, we will take whatever deals we can get."

Kaspar gave Joshua the kind of look only a father disappointed in his offspring can summon; equal parts shame, anger, and love. "What must I do, exactly?"

"Now?" Burns said, stepping from the shadows

to reveal she was holding a thick-bladed hunting knife. She aimed the point at the window behind Kaspar's desk. "All you need to do is look over there."

Kaspar looked. Plainly saw nothing. Stepped forward in front of Joshua.

As Kaspar blocked the range between Joshua and the two bodyguards, Joshua whipped out the small pistol Gray had given him and pushed the barrel into the back of Kaspar's skull.

Carl and Travis raised their large-calibre professional handguns.

Markar and Sabazio lifted their shirts to pull out theirs—replicas repurposed to fire live rounds.

Both Gray and Burns sidestepped as far from the line of fire as they could in under two seconds.

Kaspar said, "Joshy, what—"

Joshua pulled the trigger, blasting the bullet into the man's head. That part of Kaspar's skull caved in, popped like a melon, but no exit wound blew out. Gray knew the soft, hollow point bullet would ping repeatedly off the interior of the skull, ploughing through the brain, ripping it to shreds.

Kaspar's bodyguards squeezed their own triggers, instinctively avoiding Joshua, the man they'd been charged in the past with protecting, and the deafening volley of gunfire cut down Joshua's two friends. Six shots, maybe seven in each, their necks, chests, and arms pulverised by high-calibre slugs.

Joshua swung up the .22 issued to him earlier. "Bastards!"

But before Carl and Travis could turn on the lad, Burns was there with a kick to the back of Joshua's knee, lowering him into an arm lock to relieve him of the pistol.

"Easy, boys," she said to the twin eyes of Carl and Travis's weapons trained on her.

Joshua struggled and raged, struggled some more, crying out whenever Burns pushed him into the ground at a more acute angle. "*I'm gonna kill you fucks, all a' you fucks, each and every one.*"

Gray stood between Burns and the two out-of-work bodyguards. "Lower the guns, lads. Clara, shut him up, would you?"

Carl and Travis displayed identical expressions of shock, but obeyed Barney Gray's instruction, while Burns switched her weight to press her knee into the back of Joshua's neck, forcing his windpipe to stretch as his cheek flattened against the polished wooden floor—a sickening technique banned in many parts of the world for good reason. If she'd used it on someone other than Joshua, Gray might have urged her to back off a bit.

The thrashing prick squeaked, still trying to curse, but it was less annoying than before.

Gray nodded to the two guns. "They registered?"

Carl, still slack-jawed with worry, looked at the weapon in his hand as if it had appeared there by magic. "Yes, but not to us."

Like any number of illegal guns, they were once

owned by police-approved citizens, but had been removed from the owners, through fair means or foul.

"Give me the serial numbers and your national insurance numbers," Gray said. "We have a techie geek who can sort that out."

"Josh…" Travis took a big step to the side, his consternation a mirror of his brother's. "He killed his… his dad."

"Yes, Kaspar was not living up to his billing as an ambitious gangster who wants to control every aspect of the underworld around here." Gray stooped to meet Josh's gagging face. "But Joshy-boy will take things to the next level. Right?"

Burns eased up enough for him to answer. "Why are you doing this to me? Why's she on me?"

"Be grateful she's only keeping you immobile. That right, Carl?"

Carl, still dumbfounded, raised his mutilated hand, again as if shocked to find it there—or in this case to discover the still-bandaged limb. "What do we do?"

"At last, a good question," Gray said. "As of this morning, according to police records, Joshua Sevan—a wrongly accused murder suspect—had been missing for several days, reported by his dad. Turns out, his supposed friends, Markar and Sabazio, kidnapped him. They ransomed him to Kaspar, but when Kaspar refused to pay up, they killed him, tried to kill Joshua, and you shot them dead with guns that will shortly be licensed to Kaspar's official bodyguards. And backdated three months."

"This is…" Travis chopped his injured hand toward the bodies, blood pooling across the floor, a stream forming to trickle down the stairs. "Is not missing persons. Is murder."

"We'll get here first. Reports of one of our targets turning up. Someone will get pissed that the report didn't cross-reference to a suspect in a murder case, but ultimately, we'll make sure CID leaves it clean. We've made other arrangements for Division 43, but if anyone from there shows, you stick to the story. Clear?"

Both Carl and Travis nodded so fast their features were a blur.

"This is just the start." Gray knelt by Joshua, now red-eyed and slack, coming down from whatever he'd snorted to give him the courage to execute his own father; not that he'd expected his friends to die, but that was a risk Gray had been happy to take. It wasn't a perfect plan. No plan ever was. They'd rehearsed other contingencies, like if Carl and Travis got killed, they'd have been fingered as the kidnappers, bringing Barney and the team into the fray. He said, "One piece of business left, Joshua. Then you'll be the big boss."

Joshua strained again, grunting as Burns reapplied pressure. He teetered on the verge of losing it, as Gray hoped for; without his dad's calm but firm hand, and without Silas Bonaparte protecting the bone-headed sociopath, Gray had complete control over the new head of the Sevan family. Although that control wouldn't last, with Joshua as the figurehead who appeared to control Kaspar's empire, they were almost home free.

They still needed to keep Baines in the loop as if it was a clusterfuck of Joshua's making which Gray was handling, and treat is as more bit of business to take care of. One more action from Baines, and Gray could promise it would all be back to normal soon.

Gray patted Joshua's cheek. "Hey, Joshy, I have a treat for you. Important job. You've met our colleague Agnes Marsh, haven't you?"

Joshua croaked a, "Yeah." Even under pressure from Burns, he managed a leery grin.

"Here's the thing. I have something urgent to attend to, a last bit of mop-up before we leave you to run this place alone. You, though, can help me out with Agnes. I don't think she's been honest with us…"

65

Silas Bonaparte bore the manner of a man deep in the throes of a sweat-soaked bluff, a suspect in a lot of trouble but trying hard not to show it. There was no sweat, though. And the old-fashioned interview suite with the two-way mirror and featureless walls served only to amuse him as he warped his face into several different emotional masks.

"He's like an insect," Moses said, observing through the glass, Wearne and Xian alongside.

They'd commandeered another police station, this one to the north of Birmingham, selected for its convenient location near the M6 as much as its modern facilities. Ever-increasing budget cuts meant it was only manned part time, which struck Moses as a waste of investment in such a deprived area, but Division 43 were making up for it.

Rock had almost finished setting up the camera. "Yep, he's an oddball alright. Makes you wonder how he got to where he is."

"By not caring." Moses watched him some more, the stressful mien reverting to a blank slate. "At a guess, I'd say he's never had a normal emotion. He's struggling to convey what he wants us to see."

Wearne and Xian watched on.

Rock said, "Clinical psychopath?"

"There's no clinical definition of a psychopath," Moses replied, a redundant comment since all in the room should know this, but it may have been useful to remind Rock, at least. "Or sociopath, for that matter. Anti-social behaviour disorder, yes. Psychopath, no."

"Don't wanna label them," Xian scoffed.

"More that most psychopaths aren't chopping people up with axes. They're highly successful, ruthless, and put on a human face when they need it. Willing to use people, not giving a single crap about the consequences other folk suffer. Sometimes they go to extremes, like that financier in America who ran the sex smuggling ring. Others…" Moses left his hand palm-up, directed at Silas.

"Others only go as far as they're willing to risk," Rock said, finishing with the camera. It would feed through a laptop and transmit the footage to Division 43's servers. "Ready?"

Moses and Rock left to make their way into the room. They were to lead, with Wearne and Xian behind the glass. Rock had an earpiece so the senior detectives could check facts from here and throw additional questions to her as they arose. Moses stayed clean of electronics, favouring his own approach, needing to concentrate on the words, the facts; reading Silas Bonaparte's emotional responses was not an option.

As they sat across from the lawyer, he split his lips into a smile and cupped his hands before him.

Moses reminded him, "You are not under arrest, but you remain under caution. You do not have to say anything. But it may harm your defence if you do not mention when questioned something which you later rely on in court. Anything you say may be given in evidence. Do you understand?"

"I have been studying criminal law for many decades, Inspector." Silas tightened the cupped hands.

"Yes or no. Do you understand?"

"I understand my rights. And just to be clear, I also understand that I have waived right to legal counsel but reserve the option to change my mind at any stage in proceedings. Is that satisfactory?"

"For now." Moses needed to shuffle papers, to do something—anything—with his hands. It was like spiders were skittering over the desk. With no papers, no tablets, nothing to use as a prop, Moses made do with spreading his hands on the surface and boring his eyes into Silas's. "Darren Vaughn. Gurinder Singh-Bahia. Monica Argall. Tajinder

Hunjan. Thaamir el-Shareef. Newt Marsden. Johanna Carrington."

Silas attempted another human smile, but it faltered. "Quite the rogue's gallery."

"You would know. They're your clients."

"That isn't privileged. Hardly a revelation."

"All arrested in the past twelve months. All with compelling evidence against them. All saw their charges dismissed when officers from DI Barney Gray's Missing Persons Unit either provided an alibi directly or indirectly, or someone, somewhere, messed up the evidence."

"Sounds like a compelling case for better training procedures for the police. Would you like to retain my services as a freelance advisor?"

Moses treated that like an appetiser. He'd memorised several facts to push here. "You have more than one company."

"Not unusual in this day and age. Accomplished people like myself require certain securities. If one interest encounters difficulty, there's no reason it should impact on my others."

"Like your accountancy business based in London, your property development company in the Isle of Man—with their favourable tax laws—and the brokerage firm in Jersey. Again, nice tax breaks."

"Nothing illegal."

"But laundering money is. Shifting dark cash from legitimate businesses and funnelling it out of the country without first clearing it through HMRC can land you in a heap of trouble."

Silas tilted his head so his gaze shifted to DC Rock. "You, my dear, you haven't known DI Glynn Moses very long, have you?"

"No," Rock said. "Just over a week."

"Then you surely cannot trust him the way you might, say, a colleague who you've worked alongside, fought alongside, killed alongside."

Rock turned a shade of pale Moses hadn't seen before, a tinge of red on her cheeks. She said, "Answer the question, please."

"Which question?" He popped his eyebrows in a simulacrum of curiosity, then faded to a frown, as if *confusion* had computed as a better emotion. "I think we were chit-chatting about my business arrangements. Please remind me—if there was a question, I apologise for forgetting it."

Moses hadn't asked a question, but without getting riled at the snotty attitude, he did now. "You took Malcolm Baines' laundered money and invested it in a property. Which property, and what business name was used?"

Silas tapped his fingertips together and clucked his tongue. "I have a lot of clients, Inspector. Perhaps you could elaborate? Or provide me with access to my records? At which point, I will compare the information you requested to the warrant you so kindly drew up in such fine detail."

Rock sat stock still—too still, like a cat about to

pounce. Like Moses, she seemed at a loss with what to do with her hands when props were not present, so folded them into her lap.

Moses said, "The house the team uses. Their 'Safe House'."

A flicker of genuine feeling flashed across Silas.

"Okay," Rock said, evidently spotting the same as Moses. "You really thought you'd buried that, huh?"

Silas's head turned on his neck, the flabby skin tense. "You'd know about burying things, Detective Constable Rock."

"Tell us about the house," Moses said. "Baines, Gray, the works."

Silas's neck went slack as he twisted back to Moses. A fake, single note of laughter. "If she has revealed the location of the Safe House, I would say Agnes Marsh is a valuable informant. I have no doubt she will reveal many more half-facts and partial truths. All of which will prove unhelpful. And if, as you suspect, the people she is working with have nefarious intent, she may be in much danger. But not from me."

With Agnes Marsh back in the mix and Division 43 unable to get a wire on her due to the scanning tech she claimed they used in certain locations, they had to trust her. Trust that she'd come good when the time came. Moses had argued against that, preferring to get her into protective custody in a different region, not least due to the woman's lack of experience with undercover ops. Wearne overruled him.

Then, shortly before explaining Agnes's decision to pass information to the Unit—admitting no wrongdoing herself—she'd received a command by text to meet at the "SH", and said she'd give Rock the address as soon as she received written immunity in exchange for cooperation. Which would take time, as that power existed far above DCI Wearne's authority. Agnes insisted on no tails; besides her concern for being exposed, it had too much security. No way to sneak in or around it.

"So it's true," Silas said. "Barney's new girl has become *your* new girl."

Moses's throat tightened. He'd taken too long to deny it, and now it was out there. "Doesn't matter. We have their crimes documented, their links to Baines, to the Sevans. We'll find the Safe House, and we'll get that trail between the sale, at least one of your companies, and Baines. And that will lead to the dark money. But if you admit to brokering funds that went into their Safe House, you might come out of this without an audit."

"You lack the evidence for such a probe."

"At the moment, yes. But you're a different animal. I think you're so valuable to these guys that you have complete protection. Even if you grass them up entirely, as long as you control their finances, you keep the upper hand. No executions. And since you aren't capable of love or genuine friendship, despite your domestic bliss, they'll never have leverage over you."

Silas stared. "Again, my apologies, the question appears to have gotten lost somewhere between your mouth and my ears."

More silence followed.

Moses lowered himself, elbows out on the surface, fingers linked, his broad shoulders at Silas's level. "Because you have no personal commitment to anyone, you gotta have a tidy backup plan. Something that cuts you off from people like Malcolm Baines and Barney Gray and Kaspar Sevan. What is it? What are you going to do that sets you free but shafts the people who screwed up?"

Silas's smile spread, his smooth, dry head almost shining for the first time. "What a banal, obvious deduction, Inspector. The problem is, no matter what your warrants say, privilege cannot be broken."

"So, you go down with them?"

"Privilege, though, extends to past crimes. Alleged crimes, I should say. Client-lawyer privilege does not cover *future* crimes and other dangers of which I may suspect certain clients."

"Future crimes?" Rock said.

"What future crimes?" Moses said.

"Ah." Silas wagged a finger. "I may be willing to facilitate credible information that could, inadvertently, lead you to capturing certain elements in possession of false identification, including credit cards and passports. If I receive assurances that the confidentiality of my clients is not breached."

"We're closer to them than we thought," Moses said.

Rock snatched the same conclusion seconds later. "They're running."

"We've got them."

"Oh, not yet," Silas said. "I think you have much work to do still. I'll wait here, shall I?"

Moses and Rock filed out, then into the observation room, where Wearne waited alone.

"Bobby's gathering the team," Wearne said. "With Silas and Agnes Marsh on board, the only thing we need is Ratan Walar to testify. With Marsh's present involvement and Walar's experience of the past structure, it should be enough."

66

Having been accused of murdering Nadia Ako and seeing the evidence that had since appeared, and given his past accusations made by PSD, the magistrate's court had deemed Ratan Walar a risk to be freed on his own reconnaissance, so remanded him in custody until his lawyer could appeal the decision. Lacking more appropriate remand facilities, he had resided in HMP Dovedale for several days. In isolation. For his own protection.

The cell wasn't so bad, although he wished the newspapers' accounts of "cushy" prisons were true for a change. Prison was never cushy, no matter the security level. And Walar's granted him a decent space with a bunk to himself and a cold, steel lavatory which lacked a seat. The prison authorities had granted him a small selection of books, though, so that was something. The closest he'd get to *cushy* for a while.

Lying on the firm, plasticky mattress, Walar wondered what was going on outside.

His lawyer was not connected to the previous cases, nor to Gray or even the Facilitator Silas Bonaparte, so both knew nothing and could reveal nothing. It needed to be this way, or people may have added Walar into the mix with Gray.

Barney Gray.

Trusted to carry on what was deemed Baines' miniature empire, but expanded it too quickly, got too bold, too clumsy. With a puffed-out chest and an immortal sense of self-importance, it was hardly in doubt that he'd fall. And it was never in doubt Walar would need to be removed from the line of inquiry.

He knew too much.

He was too connected.

Without an accusation like this, Division 43 would uncover more than they needed to turn Walar into a target.

If he kept his head down, he'd be fine. No question.

The door's viewing slide clanked back and a pair of eyes peered in.

Walar sat up on his elbows. He didn't recognise the eyes, forehead and bridge of the nose as belonging to one of the regular prison officers, although they rotated the personnel often. With one of his other cushy luxuries being a small clock, though, Walar knew this wasn't a scheduled time for food or an exercise session.

A key in the lock.

Walar swung his legs off the bed and planted his feet on the floor.

The key turned, bolts *thunking* back in the housing.

Walar stood, watching the door, waiting. He wasn't a big man, or a particularly skilled fighter, and if this was a bunch of guards delivering a message or a warning or something worse, he'd have to be smart.

The door swung open.

It was something worse.

A massive bald white man stepped inside, the prison sweats too small for his bulk, and even the tattoos on his neck and forearms seemed to stretch. Although he looked fat, morbidly obese, Walar recognised him as Reginald Mullens, an enforcer he'd put away three years ago, and the fat only hid what were incredibly powerful muscles—muscles that had contracted and flared the day Ratan Walar tasered him. Mullens took up position to one side of Walar, watching him all the way.

The next man to enter was also known to Walar: Alexander Epworth, a lean black man wearing only a vest and sweatpants, his muscles having grown in the five years since Walar's investigation got him sent here for attempted murder. Epworth stood with his back to the wall perpendicular to the door.

Then the third man entered: Malcolm Baines.

"Hello, Ratan," said Walar's former boss. "Nice to see you again."

Walar let his gaze drop to Baines' hands. "Malc. What's all this?"

In one hand, Baines carried what appeared to be a five-litre can of sunflower oil, but in his other he held a box of matches. Palming the matches, Baines unscrewed the oil cap and the stench of petrol wafted out.

Walar held steady on Baines. "Malc…?"

"There's business to attend to." Baines handed the can to Epworth and tossed the matches to Mullens. "But let's have some fun while we're at it."

67

It felt like a result to Moses. A compromise, admittedly, but as close to the result DCI Wearne had demanded as they were likely to get. Access to the accounting records, taking out one corrupt unit, and more than likely solving the murder of Gabriella Childs. No additional time for Baines, no Kaspar Sevan, no Silas Bonaparte. But a result, nonetheless.

While Wearne worked on a deeper-sweep warrant with an actual judge over Skype, Moses ordered a selection of pizzas from the local Papa John's—they did a good vegan pie as well as the regular dishes. He and Rock found DS Tahana and DI Archer were more aloof and had a dig at them for needing the backup, but he hadn't experienced this brand of good-natured banter for many years. Even Xian and Ellingham slapped them on the back or shoulders each time they passed by in this small, commandeered station.

There was still plenty to do, though, and Moses and Rock landed the lion's share of the PAL updates while they awaited the food delivery. The others were tying off their own cases from before Moses and Rock landed, and Moses got the impression DI Bobby Xian was looking at a new one.

"What do you have there?" Moses asked him.

"Not sure." Xian was sat on the corner of the desk, a paper file in-hand rather than the usual tablet or phone. "Something we'll look into once our current case is in the ground. Weird group—hippies on the surface with cultish indicators. Might be sex trafficking involved."

"Why's it need us?"

"There's a minor royal implicated, like sixtieth in line, but he's pretty senior in the group. And three previous investigations haven't touched the leadership. No conspiracy proven."

"Protected from on high."

"Possibly, yeah." Xian closed the folder. "You want it?"

Moses took in the room, this police station in a small town north of Birmingham. Largely disused until Division 43 came along to press a corrupt lawyer and turn him against his clients. If they could penetrate those people, and groups like the sex cult Xian was looking at, perhaps Moses had a place here. Perhaps Division 43 could do the kind of good he'd always hoped to. He said, "I'll think about it."

The door to the outer section opened, the custody officer they'd roped in saying, "Pizza's here."

Moses stood, and the team made satisfying noises, anticipating the celebratory feast. The delivery guy entered with six flat boxes, three smaller ones containing sides, and two 1.5l bottles of Diet Coke. Except, it wasn't the usual youngster earning minimum wage.

"Hey there, Division 43," Barney Gray said, setting the pile of boxes on the first desk. "This is convenient."

Behind him, Clara Burns, Rudolph Kortenberg, and Cole Mainey spread from the doorway, like a rival gang assembling in some street musical, about to break into song. The custody officer sensed the immediate tension and retreated. Wearne looked up from her conversation through the open door to the sergeant's office but was still on the line with the judge.

Moses took point, Xian and Rock on either side, with Ellingham, Archer, and Tahana filling in behind.

"Sorry, folks," Mainey said. "Guess your secret squirrel confab isn't so secret."

Were they tailing Moses and Rock again, or was it something as simple as syncing Silas's *Find My Phone* or similar app service? Didn't matter. They were here for something more than pizza.

"Hope you tipped the delivery guy well," Moses said. "I know you can afford it. You joining us for lunch?"

"Thanks, don't mind if I do." Barney Gray shifted the smaller boxes and opened the top pizza, removed a slice, gooey cheese covering densely packed pepperoni; Rock's order. He bit into it and chewed deliberately slowly, his subordinates waiting. After he swallowed, he said, "You have a beef with us. Think we did something wrong. Let's make it official. Interview away."

DCI Wearne now emerged, her activities paused. "What the hell is this? Get out."

"You want us?" Mainey said. "We're here."

"Ma'am," Wearne said.

"Sorry?"

"I am a detective chief inspector. I expect to be addressed as ma'am, guv, boss, or some form of respectful nomenclature." Her eyes fired at Gray. "Is that too much to ask?"

"Well, *ma'am*," Gray said, "perhaps if you were to come to us more directly instead of sneaking around behind our backs—to our detective chief superintendent, for example—we might not be so wound up that we forget our manners. I hope you understand."

"DCS Cleland has spoken to you?"

"And we have checked the logs," Gray said with a half-smile at Moses. "No error. Joshua was with my officers at the time of the murder."

Moses bunched his shoulders, cricked his neck. "Don't tell me you have something on him too."

Burns put two fingers in her mouth and sucked them, in and out, like a lolly.

"DCS Cleland has been in a happy relationship with a gentleman called Alastair for almost ten years," Gray said. "But he wasn't always so comfortable with his sexuality. When a young lady several years his junior temped him a few nights ago… Well, let's chalk it up to nostalgia. He succumbed. And he takes a lovely photo. Not wanting to jeopardise his loving relationship, he has become rather pliable."

"You just slap some photos on his desk?" Rock said. "Like he'd fold on that alone."

"Not us," Mainey said. "We're the good guys, remember?"

"But," Gray added, "unstable young men who want to become the number one gangster in their territory, they're quite eager to approach coppers. And make additional threats. Threats that don't implicate us, of course."

"Christ," Xian said. "You guys used to operate from the shadows. Now you're moustache twirling arseholes with more surveillance than the Stasi."

"Because we've rattled them," DI Archer said. "They've had to break cover. Step things up."

Wearne headed back into her office, phone to her ear. Moses heard the name, Zachary, although it was unusual to involve the Police and Crime Commissioner in matters like this. He had no authority, after all. Ideas and policy. Maybe connections.

Gray offered the pizza to the three coppers with him. Only Mainey accepted, and Gray replaced the box, taking up his first slice. "DCS Cleland agrees there is nothing to the Joshua Sevan case. The DNA evidence is non-existent, witnesses are zero, and even the historical aspects of your witch-hunt are dead."

Moses sensed there was more. "We have your paper trail. We've got more than one witness."

Mainey was on his third bite and spoke with his mouth full. "I don't think so. But if you wanna go another round…" He bit a fourth time without swallowing the third.

Moses stepped forward, but DI Xian put a shoulder in the way.

"Not here," Xian said. "They're being more direct with us for a reason. You have to see that. This Bond villain bullshit is calculated."

Moses breathed hard through his nose. "Why are you in our faces, *Barney*? We'd have found out about Cleland laying down soon enough without you."

Gray shrugged. "Ego. Gloating. It makes me the smaller man, but I wanted to see your faces when you realised all your efforts were for nothing."

Wearne emerged again from her office. Ashen. Shock turning to anger as she eyed Barney Gray, chowing smugly on the pizza slice.

"You heard?" Gray said.

Moses couldn't help bunching his hands. "Heard what?"

"Oh yeah," Burns said. "She's heard what we heard."

"Tragic news." Kortenberg pulled a mock-sad face. "Nothing we did. Scout's honour."

Mainey said, "Any more of that pizza?"

Wearne focused on Moses, then Gray. "You animals."

Gray smiled.

"What is it?" Moses asked.

"Baines got to Ratan Walar." Wearne had clenched her own fists, her furious manner mirroring what Moses was feeling. "You animals burned him to death!"

Rock gasped, and the rest of Division 43 made similar shocked noises. Some turned away, but Moses bustled forward at Gray. Mainey shifted to intercept, but Xian and Ellingham pulled him back. Moses knew it would do no good, but still wanted to pound into Gray. He summoned the strength to comply. Unsure how long that would hold, he shook his guards off, then punched a chair which flew across the floor, landing on its back.

"Temper," Gray said.

"Get out." Wearne strode up to Gray, her eyes level with his, close enough to exchange breath. "Get out of here. Immediately. That's an order."

Gray nodded, satisfied. He and his team shuffled toward the door wearing shit-eating, self-satisfied grins. Yeah, it was the smaller thing to do, gloating, but it was clear they felt good about it.

"Wrap it up, folks," Gray said. "Wrap it all up and go away. If you keep coming, we have every base covered. Leave us clean, you stay clean."

"All of you?" Rock asked. "Aren't you missing someone?"

Gray looked around, confused, as if searching for keys he thought he'd given to someone else. "Ah, you mean Detective Constable Marsh? No, she transferred out. Wasn't right for this squad. And the pressure applied by your unjustifiable witch-hunt, well, it got too much for her. Or was it an alien hunt?"

Moses twigged on the reference. *Trembling Alien Entertainment.*

"We'll get you," he said, almost a growl.

"Nah," Burns replied. "This is all a misunderstanding."

Kortenberg opened his arms. "A bit of confusion got out of hand. No hard feelings, okay?"

"And let's not forget," Mainey said, crunching on the crust, "you can't protect what's important to you forever."

Gray opened the door to the reception area. "As fun as this was, we have missing persons to find. Let's hope you distracting us didn't result in a death or three."

Then they were gone. Walar was dead. Marsh…

No idea, but hopefully just chased away. That reference to *Alien* suggested a trap, something set to test a colleague.

And Moses reeled, counting backwards, counting down all the facets of the "win" that had crumbled before him.

68

While Rock lacked Moses's experience in reading dishonesty and obstruction, she had spent plenty of nights taking money off people over a hand of cards. She usually knew when someone was bluffing, even without all the facts to hand, so when she and Moses sat down again with Silas Bonaparte, it was clear Moses was grasping for one last handhold that might save him.

"We need more from you," Moses said.

"More?" Silas's plastic-action-figure face twitched, his tongue playing again at his thin lips. "You will get more when I get my legal assurances about the redaction of important clients."

"You'll get it." Moses kept his tone even, but his eyes were dead. Void of any fire, any authority. "Give me the names I'll need to conclude this. Confirm the address. Supply the chain of—"

"There's more to this visit." Silas shaped his hands into a dome on the tabletop. "Let's see. You want me to rush my official statement that will help you see off this future crime. This… minor matter. Minor in the bigger scope of things, of course. You need to connect this property to organised crime to raid it, and to arrest anyone within who may be in possession of elicit material such as fake passports. Ah, but…" The man's hands came together, palms flat, pointing at Moses. "But you lack the confidence you had before. The Trembling Alien warrant gave you nothing of use in your case and was never going to. Meaning, Inspector, the extenuating circumstances that precipitated your expectation of a *full* warrant have been superseded by new events."

Silas cocked his head.

"Give us the names," Moses said.

"Did something bad happen? While you were chasing my business, holding me here, questioning me, wasting time on warrants… did something happen to void your assertions of my guilt and that of my clients? Some error of judgment? Some of your evidence…" Silas parted his hands. "Up in smoke?"

Both Moses and Rock cottoned on to the reference to fire, and the pair tensed in unison. Rock was ready to fly over there and throttle the bald insect, so she could only imagine what was boiling inside Moses.

"We'll connect you through Kaspar and Joshua," Rock said.

"Will you?" Silas said. "Okay, then."

"How did you know about Walar?" Moses asked.

"A logical deduction. When you came in here looking so desperate." Silas glanced at them in turn. "If there's nothing else, I believe you reiterated I was under caution but not under arrest."

There was nothing they could do to stop him leaving. Both Rock and Moses stewed as the squat man passed them by and left the room.

"What happened?" Rock said.

"We were set up." Moses clearly struggled to keep from shouting, his arms and shoulders so stiff it looked like he was going to smash the place to smithereens.

"Set up? How?"

"You heard Silas. We spent all this time with him, focussed on him. Why were we focused on him?"

"To get to the others. To get the finances, then the warrant to raid the Safe House."

"But why? What put us onto him?" Moses sounded like he was testing her, that he'd already arrived at a conclusion.

Rock processed it, recalled the steps they'd taken to reach Silas. "Theo Goodman. We made a deal with him to—" She ceased talking, a second jolt of realisation hitting her. "He wanted his territory back."

"Who's more likely to grant that? Us? In the big bad incorruptible Division 43? Or Barney Gray and Malcolm Baines?"

"He sent us on a wild goose chase while Gray cleaned up behind himself."

"Theo *fucking* Goodman." Moses smacked the table. "I should've known. Slip in a sliver of truth to make the lie more believable. Yeah, he's played us so he can play alongside them."

But Rock wasn't concentrating on the betrayal, or that Theo Goodman had more invested than they realised. She put her hand over the one Moses used to hit the table, snatched his attention from his sense of anger. "Silas Bonaparte knows Trembling Alien was a plant. A trap to see whether Agnes Marsh would turn to us for help. If Barney Gray is cleaning house, where does that leave her?"

69

Agnes Marsh had gone dark, with no flashes of her number plate on traffic cams, her phone going straight to voicemail, and even the tech side couldn't ping her location. Since Moses had no idea what to expect next, he took a detour via a station with an armoury, spent thirty minutes with verifications and paperwork, and signed out a Glock 17 identical to the one Rock had been carrying. He'd never fired a gun at a human being, but if Theo was campaigning to reintegrate himself into the Midlands underworld, it would take willpower *and* firepower. Moses would not go in unprepared.

Besides firearms, they were primed with full electronic surveillance, able to listen in on calls and track Theo's movements, see his computers, and they possessed warrants to raid his properties. Through this, they discovered the first call Silas placed after walking free from the station was to Theo himself. With their metadata warrant following Silas too, they found him heading toward Theo's current location: the same warehouse Moses and Rock had met him and made their bogus deal.

With Rock driving, Moses listened in to an update on his PAL.

Theo, from several minutes before Silas arrived at his property: "Yeah, I'm ready. Bring the contract, I'm all yours."

"What is it?" Rock asked.

"What is what?" Moses answered, replaying the snippet a third time.

"This." She pointed between his face and the phone. "I might not have known you long, but I know when you're uneasy. Processing something. Hence… What is it?"

Moses lowered the phone, turned his attention to the road out front, to the armed response vehicle clearing the way through traffic with its siren and lights. "Something's missing. It's not as simple as Theo Goodman screwing us over." He hated this feeling, knowing the scenario wasn't making sense but the *why* eluding him—a kitten swiping at a length of string, understanding what he wanted, but unable to grasp it. "What are we saying? He suddenly got bored with his safe, affluent restaurant business and chose to dive back into drug dealing?"

"Maybe the business wasn't making as much as they said."

Moses flicked through files on the big-screened phone. "Nah, we pulled the financials. He's doing well, paying a small amount of tax, not zero, has a decent pension. He'll live a comfortable retirement, even if he takes three foreign holidays a year. It's not about money."

"Ego? He feels like a failure? Even his son sounded disappointed in him—didn't have the stomach for it."

Moses thought about that, about Lucas' dig at Theo in the café, but pushed it away. "He never used to be like that. Never wanted to be Scarface. Especially after Fiona came along. He… wanted to be better. For her. For Lucas too, but that girl." Moses recalled the first time he saw Theo with Fiona, the adoration as strong as for his son, only different. "She made him a different person. A better man. He was tempted, tried to go bigger with Malcolm Baines, but it didn't take. And not just because I grassed on Baines. I really don't think his heart was in it."

A light drizzle started, the windscreen wipers squeaking as they swiped once.

Moses pulled up the PAL again, specifically the historical facts section, looking for something, anything to scratch at the itch plaguing him. DS Tahana had come through.

"What do you have?" Rock asked.

Moses flicked through the preamble. "We logged every case, proven and otherwise. Going further back, though. Every case from Baines linked to Silas, to arrests where Silas was a brief. It's notarised here. The past ten years." He read the bullet points, tapping to bring up more detail. "The recruits… Barney Gray, Ratan Walar, Mainey, all came into the team together, people I never knew. Baines kept his cells separate alright. Looks like Gray pulled Burns and Kortenberg back together after Baines went down, then finally Marsh, who replaced Walar after they expelled him."

"They didn't exactly issue an open invite to their club," Rock said. "Bringing in Agnes Marsh was a risk."

"It was all going fine until we popped up. They didn't realise we were anything but regular plod when we arrested Joshua. We were the catalyst for them stepping into the open when they've always worked from the background. The pressure must've rattled Marsh. Nicola Dawson's death too. They'd have seen it."

"And now Walar."

Moses nodded along. "Marsh didn't come to you out of decency or guilt. She came to you out of self-preservation. To save her own arse."

"Have they done something to her?"

Moses chewed his response, irritated at a question that Rock would know he couldn't answer. "Shelve that for now. They'd still need an outlet. And the only lead we have is Theo Goodman." Without voicing the thread that his kitten paws couldn't snatch again, Moses recalled the only things they knew. "He lied. That's why we let up long enough for Barney Gray to get to Walar, sterilise Silas, regroup and do whatever he's done to neutralise Marsh. But what does Theo have to gain?"

"He's old school," Rock said, accelerating along a wider road, stepping up the speed to match their lead vehicle. "He has enough going on without reclaiming that territory. And I know him about as well as I know you, but he seemed… at peace."

"Yet here we are." The gun sat heavily in Moses's shoulder holster. "We can't ignore the evidence. If Theo is dabbling in that world again, I'm gonna burn his business to the ground. Legit or otherwise."

Moses thumbed the radio and told the lead car to lose the lights and let Rock head up the approach. Silent, dark, stealthy.

Rock moved into position. "There'll be another opportunity. Gray and his people will surface again."

"Just wait, Cap? Is that what you did in Afghanistan?"

"No. We use what we have. But we don't lose our heads."

The anonymous, featureless industrial estate blew by, Rock steadying her speed. And there, as Theo's warehouse came into view amid a Monopoly board of buildings differentiated only by small, removable signage, Moses's kitten claw snagged a stray thread on the dangling string.

He said, "It's not about who has the most to gain. Let's start with whoever has most to *lose*."

Rock pulled over, using a battened down burger caravan for cover. "Who has the most to lose?"

"Damn." Moses watched the rain. "Again, it's Theo Goodman."

"I don't understand."

"You will." Moses opened the door, and the rain sprayed inside. "We leave the backup as *backup*. If I'm right, it's going to be bumpy. But not the way we feared."

Moses issued the order to the ARV to cover the front, and Rock followed Moses with their guns drawn, dashing over the neighbouring land. They barrelled through the power shower to the rear door, arriving drenched. Neither needed to mention the car in the parking lot—Silas's—and neither needed much in the way of communication to access the building. Rock opened the unlocked door and Moses led the way.

Inside, Moses brought up the mental image he'd made of the layout earlier, sweeping left and right down the wall, checking each aisle as they went. His firearms training melded back into his muscles, commanding him to be cautious, more-so than if he'd been unarmed, stalking the territory. He wondered if this was how Army Captain Rock felt each time she ventured out in uniform, commanding her troops, armed to the teeth, surrounded by half a country of people whose only desire was to kill them all.

At the sound of voices, he raised a fist, a universal signal to *stop*.

Both listened.

Rock tapped his shoulder. He turned to her, waited for her to whisper or signal, but she aimed toward the voices. She frowned in irritation and chopped her hand forward, her Glock pointed that way.

Moses realised it was a military thing. Something he'd seen in documentaries and movies. Tap the lead infiltrator's shoulder to confirm they were covered by their teammates. Anti-terror officers drilled the same way, but Moses had never trained to that degree. He went with it, though, wafering himself to the wall approaching the loading dock.

Two voices. One animated, one calm.

At the corner, Moses let the previous movement flow, holding position as Rock peeled off ahead to a ready stance. He tapped her shoulder. She glided out, Moses dropping into a shooter's crouch.

He called, "Armed police. Hands where I can see them."

Only two people were present—Theo Goodman and Silas Bonaparte. They raised their hands and squared off to face the detectives.

"You don't understand," Theo said.

Silas smirked. "They really don't."

Then it was Rock's turn to cover Moses's approach. He rushed close to them and gave each a cursory pat-down for obvious weapons, of which there were none, and made them face the counter strewn with papers. A laptop was open, too.

"You're both in so much trouble," Silas said. "I'll be filing a complaint forthwith—"

"Yeah, yeah." Moses holstered his gun. "If I'm wrong, it's my arse."

Careful to give Rock a clear shot on both, Moses spun Theo to face him, the older man's face slack with fear, mouth working without speaking.

"You were going to be another figurehead," Moses said. "For this joker." He thumped Silas gently on the upper arm, rocking the lawyer more than the blow demanded. "He isn't simply an employee, is he? He's more involved in the decision making. Even Barney doesn't get that, does he?"

Silas held his pose, shaking his head with a short, whining laugh. "Another lazy, unfounded accusation. DI Moses, I'm going to enjoy eviscerating you in court. Your every misdemeanour, every threatening practice, every penny you took, will be out in the open. You'll be a poster boy for police corruption, and—"

Moses didn't bother to change the lawyer's position. Simply pistoned a straight punch from the side, dropping him with a single blow to his glass jaw.

Theo brightened slightly. "You could lose your job for that, man."

Moses watched Silas's slumped form shift with gravity, so he lay flat on his back. "That's okay. You can be the witness that says he attacked me, tripped, and fell."

"Why would I do that?" Theo gestured to the paperwork, a sad cant to his posture. "He is my new partner."

"Where are they holding Lucas and Fiona?"

Theo all-but stumbled, his knees holding him upright, but only just. "How did you know?"

"Because you have little to gain by screwing us over, and plenty to lose. They focused on what they can *take* from you, not what they can *give* you. When they offered you your old territory back, you said no." Moses allowed his dry mouth to open a crack before saying, "They took your kids, didn't they?"

Theo's head bowed, and he leaned on the counter. Moses glanced at Rock, who nodded to show she understood.

Moses clapped a hand on his old friend's shoulder. "I'm going to get them back, Theo. I promise."

70

The restaurant had been closed for refurbishment many times. Even back when Moses was riding with Malcolm Baines, it rarely lasted more than a year before it locked its doors due to dwindling profits and rising expenses. It was all a ploy. No matter how much the eatery made, it always lost money as far as HMRC was concerned. Lots of cash payments for food from non-existent customers, invoices from wholesalers that provided nothing but, well, invoices, and then the last of any profits got poured into the renovations. Renovations conducted by companies co-owned by Baines and Goodman, based in some tax haven, thus cleansing all the cash gleaned from the small-scale but not insubstantial—drugs business, with the legit money serving as gravy on top. Most recently, it had been a Lebanese-themed café but was undergoing what

Theo claimed was a genuine change of direction to another vegan venture—what he called a *Spice-led vegan eatery.*

"Not dodging the tax man again?" Moses said.

"You can see my returns," Theo replied. "All is legal."

He'd been quiet all the way here. Subdued. Sceptical that Moses could fulfil his promise, but with Silas unconscious on his floor, Moses was relieved to see the man's choices limited; cooperation had become mandatory.

They'd released the armed response vehicle and personnel with a thank you for their time, instructing them they could stand down as the threat proved less severe as first feared. In reality, Moses didn't want more witnesses if he had to go to another dark place. Rock did not object, so he assumed she understood the situation.

It may have been a repetitive phrase that grated after a while, but priority was always *the preservation of life*. No matter what arrests might slip by. And Moses was going to preserve as much life as possible, even if it meant taking a few himself.

"Park here," Theo said.

Rock reversed into a different space a hundred yards farther along the high street. It was an affluent suburb on the northern border of the Black Country region, a fast forty minutes from the warehouse. It linked with several blocks containing boutique shops, newsagents, even an independent bookstore. Moses had no compunction in hustling Theo out of the car with his hands cuffed behind him. Not taking any chances, but also enforcing the notion that Theo had nowhere else to go. He was completely within their power.

Theo kept his face directed at the pavement as they escorted him through sparse foot traffic as mostly white folk rubbernecked at the sight. None of the witnesses spoke up, eager to grab their bagel or sushi. The narrow one-way street beheld more coffee shops than seemed necessary for such a small area, plus one tea-room, which Moses made a mental note of since it looked nice and claimed on its A-frame blackboard to be carbon neutral. A microbrewery with its own little bar proclaimed real handmade ales brewed in the staff's own bathtubs.

"Yeah, your vegan spicy love-in will do well here," Moses said.

Theo positioned to reply but simply sighed. They'd arrived at his partially boarded building. He twitched his head to indicate a way around the side to a yard barred by more boards and a clunky combination lock, to which he recited the code. Moses punched it in, and they entered.

Theo first. Moses next, gun drawn, crouched behind the big Jamaican. Then Rock followed in a low crouch to limit her exposure.

The back yard was secure. Thick, heavy boards were bolted over the windows and rear door, but the one on the door had been jimmied off, leaving a regular barrier with a glass panel and peeling black paint. Comprising three stories plus an attic, it was built during the mining boom, its black stone and slender turrets presenting a grand facade—likely the former residence of a well-to-do pit owner, or someone appointed to oversee workers.

Theo told them which pocket his key was in. Moses retrieved it and, keeping Theo between him and the door, turned the key in the lock. Rock strode forward to breach as they'd been trained.

"No need for this," Theo said.

He was roundly ignored, and Moses offered Rock his human shield. Rock waved off his marginally chivalrous gesture as if somewhat offended by it. Moses tapped her shoulder.

She slipped in, barrel following her line of sight, which extended into the gloom and flattened herself against the wall to allow Moses through. He kept Theo in place, another huge breach in protocol, but figured the bad guys wanted the man as a front for a good reason so might hesitate to shoot through him. Depending on who had arrived since Theo departed to meet Silas.

The first room—a once and future kitchen—seemed clear. No electrics, but enough natural light streamed through the boards to see the interior. It was the same story with the rest of the place.

"The VIP room," Theo said.

He acted as relaxed as a handcuffed man could be whilst under the control of an armed police officer, not fearing the turn of a corner, the opening of a door. Within seconds, Moses was convinced this wouldn't be a firefight, but Rock wouldn't agree, so it was quicker to play the numbers.

Someone had ripped out the main lounge, only a dust-caked carpet remaining, with the VIP area toward the back—an alcove up three small steps with a bare curtain pole over the top frame. Moses could imagine a heavy drape pulled across, the inflated price of the menu affording diners an experience whereby they didn't need to sully their eyeballs with the sight of regular people eating regular food.

"I *am* sorry, you know, for real," Theo said as they cleared every nook and cranny of the lounge and bar. "You are a decent man, Moses. And I try to be decent."

"Shut up." Moses shoved him in the back to hurry him up. He figured Rock would only be marginally tamping at not following the drill to the letter, so pushed on to their destination.

Rock whipped around at his fast footfalls. "Moses?"

"It's fine," Moses said.

"You can't know that."

Theo stumbled up the steps, but Moses caught him and pushed him toward a bench attached to the wall, a perch that would once have provided a cushioned seat for the Very Important.

Through the gloom, in the light provided by the gap between two boards, a man lay on a camping bed, the sort with a slotted-together frame and a canvass stretched over. Naked. Only a strategically placed sheet for dignity. Bandaged and sutured, one eye swollen shut. His open one flickered at the movement but seemed to struggle to find focus.

"Dad?" came Lucas' croaking voice.

He was hooked up to an IV drip and there were three empty blood bags nearby.

"You got him treated," Moses said.

Rock came up behind and gave away no shock or surprise at the sight. "Room's clear, by the way. You're welcome."

Theo had fallen to one side, supporting himself on the wall by one shoulder, his forehead against the bare plaster. "I had no choice but to play along. To tell you what I told you. No matter you knocked the guy out. I am now not a successful restaurateur. I am a glorified administrator."

"Laundering Barney Gray's income," Rock said.

"Him. Or whichever of Mr Bonaparte's clients needed me."

It was too dark to see, but it sounded like Theo let go of a sob. "All my properties will undergo this treatment. Then reopen with highly successful cash flow."

"With Gray and Baines creaming off the profits in the shadow." Moses knelt by Lucas. There was nothing they could do for him that hadn't been done. "What happened?"

"Silas will keep them in line," Theo said. "With all the evidence he has on them."

Moses was no longer thinking about the bust, the case, or the win. "They cut him in front of you?"

Theo wobbled, then sat up straight. "I thought he was dead. But he groaned. I stemmed the worst of it, then called an underground doc I knew from the old days."

"What happened?" Rock asked. "Specifically?"

"They brought us all here late last night. Me, Lucas, Fiona. Joshua Sevan and some nutcase idiots I haven't seen before. They were not professional, but the snatch was well planned."

"Your daughter," Moses said. "She was a toddler when you were working with Baines."

Theo nodded.

Lucas croaked again. "Fiona…?"

"They did eenie meanie minie mo," Theo said. "Between Lucas and Fiona. They tied Lucas to a chair, then made me and Fiona watch as they cut him to pieces. Even when I agreed to do what they wanted, they wouldn't let up."

"Baines," Rock said. "Giving orders from behind bars. Get rid of the rat, cement their territory and power, and seize control of everything they need."

"Joshua Sevan did this?" Moses asked, eyes still on Lucas. On the blood. The bandages. The bruises.

"No, but he was watching," Theo said. "It was the woman. Gray's woman. From the police."

"Clara Burns." Rock said the name flatly, but a hint of anger bore through.

"No, it was the new girl. Agnes-something."

Now Rock sounded surprised. "Marsh? *Agnes Marsh* did this to your son?"

She was alive, then. Back on Gray's side? Was Trembling Alien Entertainment a plant to distract Moses and Rock, not to entrap the MisPer team's rat?

Theo said, "Joshua laughed a lot, high on somet'ing. Coke, I think. Maybe something else, too. His two nobody sidekicks stayed nervous. Couple of his other pals were dead, so maybe they thought he was bad luck or something."

"Which friends were killed?" Rock asked. "When?"

Theo shook his head. "I don't know. They didn't spill everything. But Josh was pissed, high. He ordered the woman around. She was calm. But, y'-know, not really. She did it, but didn't poke fun. Didn't laugh. Just did whatever Joshua said."

Moses rose, towering over Theo. "And they still have Fiona?"

"And they still have Fiona." Theo doubled over as if about to be sick. "You have to get her back. *Please.*"

Moses had promised. No matter how things panned out, no matter the bad things he'd done in the past, the lies he'd told, he always tried to keep his promises. And this one hung heavier than most.

He knelt before Theo and gently palmed the terrified man's face up so he could see the tears streaming. "Did they say anything we can use? Anything out of the ordinary?"

Theo shook his head. "No. They hardly spoke. Just instructions."

"Nothing?" Moses said. "Nothing at all?"

Theo exhaled, long and slow. Tired eyes, like he honestly wanted to help. Give them more. He said, "It was probably nothing, but… It ended with a threat as they left."

"After Agnes Marsh cut up your son?" Rock said. "They left with Fiona? Threatening you further?"

"Not a threat. I suppose I'd call it a parting shot. Gloating."

"Marsh or Joshua?" Moses asked.

"Marsh." Theo wet his lips. "She said, 'This is what happens when you break someone's trust.' No, wait, she said it strange. 'This is what happens when you break my trust.' Or 'break *a* trust.' Was a strange phrase, man. I didn't know what she meant. No one has trusted me in a long, long time. Certainly not the Sevans."

This is what happens when you break a trust…

Moses whirled to Rock, energy surging through him. "We missed something. And I think it was in Silas's papers all along."

71

They didn't have time to race back to North Staffordshire, so Rock set up a laptop in a tearoom Moses had spotted earlier and phoned through a request for data that would require a far higher threshold of proof to obtain. He hadn't told her why he wanted it, indicated he wasn't 100 percent sure himself, but promised it would make sense in a few minutes—once he'd wrapped his own head around it. While Rock made impatient sounds and tapped her fingers on a table secured using their warrant cards and curt, urgent language, Moses ordered a pot of Chai tea and Rock went for the closest thing to "regular," which was a Cornish organic brand that tasted like PG Tips. The £2.70 price tag meant she savoured it and forced herself to believe it was a higher quality than a supermarket brand. Perhaps the added cost came thanks to the colander-type basket in the miniature teapot, into which the beret-wearing anorexia sufferer scooped the leaves, before pouring in the boiling water. It was all presented on a tray with a cute cat figurine serving as a milk jug.

Moses remained grim, so Rock kept her observations private.

The place was narrow and decked out in pastel shades—lots of different ones—and Rock got the notion they were aiming for a seaside feel, with faux-driftwood planks on the wall painted eggshell blue and bearing motivational slogans alongside the odd random bit of rope. It only annoyed her for a few minutes, though, as the Wi-Fi proved fast and the police firewall accepted the security certificate.

In the farthest corner from the entrance, Rock accessed her PAL, which should've been identical to Moses's, with only the personal observations section differentiating them. Rock had written nothing in this facility, and Moses said he'd noted the exact same in his.

"It's all in the papers," Moses said. "And there's something in the timeline we've missed, but I can't see it. We need to go through it all, from Baines right up to a few hours ago."

Rock hadn't concerned herself with the timeline, but she was sure there was more to the trawl through Silas's papers. While they lacked the evidence to charge him, and Wearne hadn't called to inform them of a complaint regarding Moses's assault, Rock believed Silas Bonaparte held the key to taking the Shadow CPU down. Even if Trembling Alien was nothing more than a trap—or a distraction to derail them—it had opened up more avenues. Plus, the warrant covering Baines and his associates extended to Silas.

She pulled out the already-summarised files and dropped them into a separate document, hyperlinked to the original sources. "Where to start? Where we come in? Agnes getting recruited last year? The murder of DCI Flood's mother eighteen months ago? His son being taken for a ride six months before that? Walar's disciplinary getting him booted from the team shortly before the kid's half-abduction? Or the MisPer team cosying up with Kaspar Sevan? Maybe Silas repping one of the Sevan family's people for the first time—"

"Earlier," Moses said.

"Then the obvious place is when Baines goes to jail. Thanks to one brave junior detective constable."

"A detective constable covering his own arse. Who was worried about losing his missus."

"I stand corrected. But let's leave those details aside."

"Agreed." Moses poured his chai tea, the pot comically small in his massive hands. "Not the arrest itself. I think it might go back further. Any paths crossing between Baines and Silas?"

Rock whizzed through but found nothing relevant. Highlighted all the pre-arrest notes and a ctrl+F lookup connecting the pair gleaned nothing. "No link back then. They're not hiding that Baines' private pension and other accounting matters go through Silas's Isle of Man firm, though. Nothing illegal on the surface. Plus, Silas reps a ton of guys currently serving time."

"*Trust*. Odd phrase, odd threat. Joshua wouldn't pick up on it, but even terrified Theo thought it was out of place." Moses pinched the cup handle between thumb and forefinger. Lifted. Sipped.

Rock used her own teapot and poured a fresh sample, checked the colour was right, and filled the cup. Added milk from the cat jug. "Sounds like you agree with him."

Moses placed the cup daintily back on the saucer. "Back at the prison, Baines had to gloat. Couldn't help it."

"Yeah, taunting you. Crooks love it when they see a copper struggling. Love it more when the copper knows the truth but can't do a thing about it."

"I tried to steer him. Dunno if you picked up on that."

"I was busy digesting that it was all true about you." Rock tried her drink again. Still regular tea. "But you were up to more than that?"

"He compared my income to his," Moses said, eyes on his cup. "I made enough on the side, plus my legit savings and Frankie's, to scrape together a deposit on my house. Big house. Big garden. But we still have a mortgage. He, on the other hand, bragged about buying a house outright."

"And you think that's the same property as the Shadow CPU's off-book Safe House."

"*And* Baines' retirement plan. They can't have properties all over the place. It would be too much to hide. It'll be secure, and it'll contain ready cash, although the bulk of that will be off site. Maybe go-bags, IDs… it's where they feel *safe*. Hence the name."

"You sound certain about that."

Moses turned his cup on the saucer, an absent appraisal of the beverage before him. "I was supposed to get myself a place like that. Baines insisted we all did. The cheapest bedsit we could find. We weren't allowed to tell anyone about it, not even Baines. If we had to split, we split." His breath came out gloomy, sad. "I'd almost forgotten about that. It was the point I started to turn. To ask what the hell we were doing. Not enough to stop outright, but… a secret place to stash things in case I needed to run? Hide? Nah, that was too scary."

"But you had a place like that?"

"I started to set it up, sure, but never completed it. Never got as far as fake passports or driver's licences, so nothing connected me to any of it. I got out clean."

"Doesn't mean they did the same."

"They're playing all the same moves. All the same setup. Same structure. But bigger. Meaner."

Rock thought of Cole Mainey, the blows he inflicted upon Moses must still have hurt in places. She was about to ask about it when the PAL chimed to say the data Moses asked for had arrived. "Give me a few minutes."

Moses still didn't look up as he gave her a nod. Poured more tea.

Rock dug back into the relevant accounts and the profiles of Silas's other companies, Moses keeping his mouth shut except for the occasional slurp. This level of access bordered on illegal, the kind of mining performed by the NCA in pursuit of terrorism financing, of international smugglers and human traffickers. And performing the trawl on a lawyer was dicey, so much so that even Division 43 was limited to non-privileged interactions. Full access to Silas's commercial interests was a lot, though, including the sub-companies on Jersey and Isle of Man. Other than that, they still could not penetrate numbered accounts outside UK territory—the existence of which there was plenty of evidence.

She sipped her own tea several times, each colder than the last until it grew tepid, the concentration of sifting through Silas's company records easing her into a trancelike state.

Baines.

Walar.

Gray.

Burns.

Mainey.

Kortenberg.

No Marsh.

All were clients of Beancounter Incorporated, Silas's accounting firm. It also served the Trembling Alien Entertainment company that Moses had picked up on as a different front, volunteered by Marsh but essentially harmless; a front for a front, a Russian doll of a laundering operation. Besides their police pensions, each boasted small investments that had gleaned significant interest, start-ups and other companies based abroad—none of which were visible here—and paid a neat dividend. Again, nothing illegal, hence their real names. It was clearly laundering cash in a trickling stream which would add up to a healthy lake upon leaving the Force, but even MI5 or the NCA would struggle to make a case.

Gray's activities here were nothing that thousands of other coppers didn't do; only far more successfully and cloaked in darkness.

"Anything?" Moses asked.

Rock checked the time. It had been forty minutes since they last spoke to one another, and Moses had progressed to a mint infusion and a vegan scone. She said, "It all looks legit. It's not, but it looks that way."

"Other clients?"

"Hundreds."

Rock shoved the laptop away from her.

"Local clients?" Moses said.

"Dozens." Rock lifted the lid on her teapot. It had gone cold. "But." She pulled the laptop back into reach.

"But what?"

Rock rearranged her files, ignored the names, sifted out the shell companies and concentrated only on the properties. "Six within an hour's radius of West Brom—DI Gray's base."

"We looked at that, didn't we?"

"Yes, but only individuals. Aliases and known associates. Agnes said *a trust*."

"Trust?"

"No, '*a*' trust." Rock delved back in and pulled out a client based in Belize. Showed Moses.

"*The Haven Maker Trust*. Where's Belize?"

"South America. English speaking. Lots of poverty. Affluent upper class with a Pacific coastline. Sterling goes a long way. And guess what the extradition arrangements are with the UK?"

"Non-existent."

"Big time. So, what does a charitable trust trying to improve children's lives in South America want with a six-bedroom house in Tipton?"

72

Agnes had hidden her revulsion at cutting human flesh as well as she could have hoped. She didn't laugh or joke as Joshua Sevan had, but faked a laugh at some line concerning kebabs afterward. She didn't hear the joke, but the two jackals Joshua rustled up had found it hilarious.

Earlier that morning, while Gray had instructed her what had to be done to keep Silas off their scent —and as relayed from inside HMP Dovedale—he sold Joshua's inclusion in the exercise as her "backup." She was ostensibly in charge of intimidating Theo Goodman and making sure he cooperated, but from the moment she was alone with Joshua Sevan in the heavy Mercedes, she hated Gray for the assignment. And she had never felt less safe. Even approaching Juliette Rock had been more comfortable.

Joshua didn't so much stare as *leered.* He was

high but trying not to show it. Gray had fed him a downer to even him out a bit, and a hefty shot of vodka helped stabilise him enough to communicate, handle a gun without shooting himself in the face, and walk without falling over. But not sufficient to drive.

At least not that Marsh was willing to risk.

She was in jeans one size too big and a long-sleeved top, but that hadn't stopped Joshua's eyes from pawing her form as they drove toward the meeting point. He'd opened his mouth into a lop-sided scoff and pulled out a popper tube and sniffed a dose.

"You're no model. But I'd fuck you."

"Charmed." Agnes had practiced what Burns taught her when it came to what she called "rapey" guys—a childish term for someone who used sexual assault as a weapon and to salve his own ego.

Be firm with them, but do not take the piss.

Give them instructions but do not make them feel undermined.

Then, when you need to, slash them across the thigh, close to the cock.

The two women would never be besties. Burns was too remote, too far removed from humanity to bestow actual friendship. But as she'd chauffeured Joshua Sevan, Marsh warmed toward the detective sergeant, radiating from the stub-bladed combat knife which she kept in a concealed pocket on her thigh facing away from her passenger.

She said, "Who are we meeting?"

Joshua had sniffed again, roved his gaze over her left leg as she worked the clutch, licked his lips, and told her about the two men coming up from Bristol specially to help snatch the family. Even in his hyper state, Joshua had marshalled the operation well, pulling the Goodman trio off the street as they conducted a weekly check on their supplies, and moved them to the wreck of a restaurant to torture Lucas Goodman until Theo promised cooperation. Gray had ordered Marsh to perform the task, something she'd never experienced to this degree. Beatings, yes, a slap, a slash across the forearm to make a point, but never full-on butchery.

She didn't want to die. Didn't want to risk angering DI Gray or Joshua. The more she thought about it, the more it struck her as a lot of effort and risk simply to keep Silas and the boss man sweet. A lot of blood, too.

Better him than me, she thought as the straight razor parted Lucas' skin and blood spread over his chest.

Then, after a dozen or more cuts, and it seemed Lucas would bleed out on the floor, they'd taken Fiona from her father and sent the broken former gangster to do his duty as a double agent—working against both Division 43 and feigning allegiance to Silas Bonaparte, allowing the team the prep time they needed.

She hoped her barely coded message sent up the

smoke signal she intended. No way Joshua had picked up on it, and the other two spoke little English, so she remained hopeful. But if Rock and Moses didn't come through, if they didn't locate Fiona Goodman before it was too late, Marsh vowed to do whatever it took to survive this, to stay out of prison.

Survive.

Her motto for life.

Survive. Live.

Now, with the jackals on their way back down south, she was alone again with Joshua in the Mercedes, heading to Tipton to meet up with Barney Gray and the team, readying to blow town.

"Wanna stop for a bit?" Joshua asked her.

"A bit of what?"

He took a baggie of white powder from one pocket. Waggled it near her face. His little finger stroked her cheek. Eyebrows hopped. Which led Marsh to suspect something.

They know.

Why else would Gray pair her with Joshua? Why give her this job when Joshua was well enough equipped to do it without her? She'd worried Gray was losing trust in her and assumed this assignment with Lucas and Fiona Goodman was a soft test for her to prove herself. Now she saw other alternatives.

Joshua gets his way with her.

Or she has to kill him.

Either way, she's out. Become a plaything,

broken and ruined, or face the consequences of killing or severely wounding a gangland figure. Without assistance, there was no way she could cover up such a feat. If he lived, he'd betray her to the authorities, and Gray could be long gone.

Be firm with them, but do not take the piss.

"I'm good, thanks," Marsh said. "Just want to get back to the boss and crack on."

Joshua held the baggie in place. Marsh didn't dare take her eyes off the road.

Give them instructions but do not make them feel undermined.

"You might want to put that away," she said. "If the police see it, I don't know if I can badge my way out of a search."

Joshua gave a *humph.* His little finger stroked her cheek again, and he put the drugs away. His hand rested on the seat cushion, spidering close to the gap between them.

Then, when you need to, slash them across the thigh, close to the cock.

Not yet.

If he makes his move, do what you have to.

Survive this.

She was sure Gray knew she'd gone behind their backs, that they were just playing this out. If Joshua jumped her, that would cement things. That was why they'd switched phones, why they'd told her to watch Joshua when really…

He was watching *her.*

Was she his reward for a job well done? A goodbye gift before they cut their losses, robbed their king while he remained locked in a castle, and migrated to the high life?

She was still mulling this over, with Joshua edging his hand ever closer to her leg, when she realised they were at the Safe House. She suddenly wished she'd disclosed the location to Division 43.

Baines had hidden the property in plain sight amid the other big houses on Martin Grove, around half of which had fences and gates, enclosing neat cars and small perfectly formed front lawns; money on show in a town not known for money, therefore a minimal chance of the police happening by. The neighbours isolated themselves, took no interest in others, and most importantly they let DI Gray's team come and go without interaction.

Maybe I'm okay. Being paranoid. It was a test. And I passed.

The camera at the six-foot iron railing gate recognised the car's licence place and, pre-approved for admittance, it swung open, admitting her to the white block paved driveway that held two cars already blocking the double garage. She slotted her vehicle alongside, turned off the engine, and sat for a second, as if expecting a garrotte from the backseat or for Joshua to jump her.

It was Joshua who opened his door first. Moving stiffly, clearly annoyed, but leaving her be.

If they wanted her dead, surely they would have

done it much earlier. Used Joshua and his jackal duo. She'd be in the ground already or ablaze in a stolen car.

Marsh got out and approached the three-storey house, the gate swinging closed on an air hinge.

You're not blown. You proved yourself.

The door appeared to be a regular wood design, dark red, no windows, with two external locks, but under one of the panels was a palm reader. Applying her hand released the eight deadbolts and the steel slab opened, a quiet sloshing sound from within signalling the presence of water which completed the security feature; a breach team would struggle with the disguised steel, the deadbolts an added measure, water within the door absorbing kinetic energy from any battering ram, negating the element of surprise should any bad guys—or cops—come a-calling.

Joshua followed Marsh inside, so close his breath heated the back of her neck and his chest brushed her back. She kept going, unwilling to allow his groin to get close, even through his trousers and her jeans.

"Hello?"

"Down here," came Rudolph Kortenberg's response.

She followed the voice through the hall and into a well-appointed kitchen, only the fifteen-year-old furniture giving it an outdated feel. Baines, apparently, had said he wanted to keep it this way so he could decorate it himself upon release. At the end of the kitchen, a door to the basement was open, the light left on.

Marsh checked over her left shoulder. Joshua had kept up with her and there was only two feet between them. He had nothing in his hands. She used the moment to touch the pouch hidden on the right leg of her loose jeans, the weight of the Gerber 06 combat knife not as reassuring as she'd like. Then onward, into the cellar, its unpainted staircase a stark contrast to the rest of the place.

Spanning the footprint of the house, the basement was clean and had been decked out ready to become a wine cellar, but the baroque design of a French winery didn't suit it. The wall of empty racks hung open, the room beyond containing a safe and a hub of computer equipment not sanctioned by West Midlands Police.

Goosebumps peaked on Marsh's arms and neck. As she fingered the hidden door wider, she tried to get a read on Joshua's location, but she was too focused ahead.

"Agnes!" Gray said, his greeting that of seeing a friend who'd been travelling the world for a year. "Great to see you. Sounds like you did a fine job."

"Spot on." Joshua sidled past.

"What's all this?" Marsh asked.

The safe was open, Mainey pulling out stacks of cash—a shade under six-hundred-K as Marsh understood it—while Burns divided them into bags that already contained plenty of bills. Five bags on the workbench. One each. And it looked like more than a hundred grand apiece. Kortenberg arranged passports at the other end of the table, checking pouches the size of wallets containing what looked like credit cards.

"Joshua made a good decision," Gray said. "Plenty more to pick up later."

Raided the king's gold store, wherever that was.

"Cool. And that?" Marsh pointed at a digital SLR camera on a tripod facing a white wall.

"This one is for you." Kortenberg dropped the pouch he'd been checking into one of the full bags and proceeded to the DSLR. Beckoned Marsh over. "Come on."

Marsh again eyed everyone's position. Smiles from all except Burns. She never smiled unless hurting someone she deemed had wronged her.

Agnes marched over with the breeziest gait she could summon, painted on the happiest sardonic grin, and said, "Make sure you get my good side."

"They're all good sides," Joshua replied.

Marsh responded only with a flit of a smile at him. Then faced the camera. She couldn't sound *too* happy. "We should have done this weeks ago."

"Ah, that's on me, I'm afraid." Gray clasped his hands together. Pain in his face. A boss about to deliver redundancy notices. "Sorry, I have to admit… didn't fully trust you. Rudolph said I was being too cautious."

"I did trust you, actually." Kortenberg offered a little wave. "Okay, maybe ninety-five percent."

"Even Clara was sold."

Marsh glanced at Burns, who offered a half-salute. Back to the camera.

"Needed you to commit," Gray said. "Like these guys."

Marsh couldn't help eyeing them all in turn, receiving nods in response. Comrades.

"Face this way, please," Kortenberg said. "I'll get some snaps to our artist and have the documents back in a matter of hours."

Marsh frowned at the lens. "That fast?"

"Neutral expressions." Kortenberg used a placating tone, as if talking to an infant who didn't respond to raised voices.

"But you proved that you're one of us," Gray said. "How did it feel?"

Marsh knew what he meant but asked anyway. "How did what feel?"

"Describe it."

The last thing Marsh wanted was to relive that experience, but she dredged it from the corner in which she'd stashed those feelings. "It wasn't hard. The guys did most of the work. Bundled Lucas and Fiona up, kept Theo in line. I worked the guy with the razor for a while, until Theo spilled his guts and promised to cooperate."

Gray waited.

Joshua whirled his hand to say *continue*.

"Then I hurt Lucas some more," Marsh said.

"Using?" Burns asked, listening in, a rare smile twitching as she paused her task.

"The combat knife."

"Why the combat knife?" Gray asked.

"It looked scarier." Marsh sensed her stomach heat up as she recalled not believing Theo, telling Joshua they needed to make their point harder. It was another survival mechanism. Playing the role. "It got what we needed."

Kortenberg came out from behind the DSLR. "And I have all we need. Thank you."

Marsh sidestepped but halted with another frown. "I didn't hear any shutters on the camera. Are you sure you got the photos?"

"It was on video mode."

"Why? You need stills for a passport and—" Marsh stopped dead. Cut herself off. A cold spike of panic jolted through every muscle in her body.

"We needed a confession," Gray said.

"Confession?" Marsh dropped a hand to the rip-off pouch.

Too late.

The rope looped over her head. It tightened around her neck before she could hope to get a hand in the way.

"Specifically," Burns said, yanking her backward, "a deathbed confession."

73

Tipton is a town northwest of Birmingham, southwest of Wednesbury, in the borough of Sandwell. Its population dips under 40,000 and only dots of the area can be considered anything close to wealthy. The house owned by The Haven Maker Foundation was located in one such area, and it took Moses and Rock less than twenty minutes to blue-light it over, killing the sirens before they got too close. Moses drove for a change. Not because he thought Rock couldn't handle it, but because his hands and feet itched to get there. If the Shadow Unit was bolting, as he feared, it could mean they'd already disposed of Fiona Goodman. He could only hope his instinct was correct that they would not give up a hostage so quickly.

Then there was Agnes Marsh to consider.

She'd come to Rock not out of conscience but

out of fear, out of a desire to live, to stay out of prison. After what she'd done to Lucas, the best she could hope for was special consideration, minimum security, if she was going to be instrumental in convicting Gray.

If she wasn't another plant.

"We're gonna get them," Rock said, surprise shading her words.

"Only if Marsh turns." Moses checked the sat nav—three minutes out. No sirens. No lights. "If we can catch them on the premises and link them directly to it, we'll have them."

Rock unlocked her phone and called the dispatcher. Asked for an ETA. Listened. Said, "Are you serious?" Then bit her tongue, thanked the caller and hung up. "AFOs have been diverted. They're en route to a suspected armed robbery. They've allocated a second unit to us. Twenty minutes out."

Compartmentalising, driving down his annoyance, Moses kept focus on the priorities. "Try Marsh again."

She did. Pinched her lips and stabbed the hang-up icon. "No."

The phone had been out of range or switched off for hours, and Wearne's tech had been unable to track it. They could, by some trickery, force the device to switch on if it was simply not active, meaning someone had destroyed it or shielded it in something like a Faraday pouch.

A stone's throw from two stabbings over the past

year, Moses was impressed by the street. Houses in a uniform mansion-like style with differing gardens and front drives. He rolled past the property they believed belong to Malcolm Baines. Ostensibly a residential home, only the external cameras gave it away as a stronghold. Even the spike-topped fence wasn't designed to keep people out, just a deterrent.

Three cars.

He pulled in two properties down and asked Rock about surveillance.

"It's not up yet," she said. "Background info only. Utilities are all connected, but no phone line. Insurance in the charity's name. No mortgage."

"And it's occupied, but nothing on the voter register." He drew his Glock and ejected the magazine, popped the bullet out of the pipe, and checked the slide. Dry fired it.

Rock pulled her gun too. "Going to war?" She did the same as Moses, working the mechanism to be sure it was up to scratch.

"Something like that." Moses slapped the magazine back in and worked the slide to make the weapon ready, and slipped it back in his holster. "Preservation of life?"

Rock got her Glock in position. "Agreed. AFOs might be too late."

Moses pocketed an extending baton, got out and jogged with his partner up the block. They paused ten yards from the Safe House.

Moses pointed out a black dome the size of half a tennis ball. "Can't avoid the cameras."

"Then we do it fast," Rock said.

Without drawing the weapon, she sprinted for the property, jumped to grab the top of the six-foot fence, swung her legs up and caught the dull spike with her sole, then pushed herself over, landing deftly in a crouch. Moses ambled more than ran, used two hands on the flat bar beneath the staves, and heaved himself up. Foot on one point. Swung himself to the other side, landing more heavily than he planned. Rock arrowed for the front door, gun out, aimed at the floor in a two-hand grip.

Moses joined her without drawing but hammered on the door with the ball of his hand. "Police! Open up!"

The banging hurt more than his landing.

"Door's metal," he said.

Rock stroked it by the hinge side. "Probably deadbolted too. It's like a drug dealer's house."

Moses clocked the red light of a camera over the entrance. He slapped the two-foot-high window to the left of the door and shouted close to the glass. "Detective Inspector Gray. Anyone else in there. Come on out. You're surrounded."

No reply.

"Surrender any hostages immediately!"

Again, no reply. Nothing but the cold of an empty house.

"Maybe we were wrong," Rock said, firming her grip. "Maybe no one's home."

"Those cars are here for a reason." He pulled out the baton, flicked open the concertina metal with a heavy ball of iron on the end, and swung it at the window. The pane cracked when it should have shattered. "Laminate coating. Makes it tough to break."

"What next?"

"I said tough, not impossible." Moses swung three more times, shattering the glass under the treatment, but it held to the laminate sheets. He used the flat of his hand to slam it inward. One side of the pane caved, letting the air inside. He called through the gap. "This is DI Moses. Come on out. We have a warrant to search this house."

Nothing.

But there was an aura to an abandoned house. A stale odour. It was missing here, a lived-in musk hinting at human occupation. Not to mention the cars.

"Cover me." Moses made for the bay window through which he could make out a lounge behind net curtains. He tried to smash this window too, but succeeded only in jarring his shoulder, the iron baton thudding off the surface.

"Ballistic glass?" Rock said.

"They're getting ready for a breach. By the time we gain access, they'll have disposed of everything."

"I've seen this level of security before. Even with the best equipment, AFOs'll be too late."

"Preservation of life, Cap."

Rock kept one eye on the door, flitting her attention between windows and other approaches. "What are you thinking?"

"I'm thinking we ask for forgiveness instead of permission."

74

Gray wasn't one to panic, even when he lacked the upper hand. It was one thing Baines had taught him—being prepared was key. Okay, he resented Baines for treating him like an underling when he'd been keeping the man's business spinning for years. He could offer little input except to berate Gray occasionally via one of the phones dropped over the fence by high-altitude drones or through an intermediary who'd show up in Silas's office to relay the message. But for Baines' early mentorship, his guidance through the catacombs of prep, execution, and backdoor escape planning, Barney Gray was truly grateful.

For starters, he knew Moses was bullshitting them about their General Custer-like situation. They weren't surrounded at all. The IT setup here piggybacked Gray's own access to the police network, so although Moses and Rock operated off the main grid, he kept tabs on all authorised firearm officer deployments, warrants issued, and ops that flagged anything of note that might affect their affairs. Not to mention personnel records, data-protection breaching trojans—such as the deep dive on the Moses family churning out the hidden cottage—and total access to the DVLA and traffic cam data. Monitoring it via his unregistered phone meant it was often a few minutes behind, but when he was right there at the terminals, he kept tabs on deployments in real time. In addition to that sliver of an advantage, when working the terminals he could also use Detective Chief Superintendent Cleland's authorisation codes to call teams off. Which he did right now, redirecting AFOs to intercept suspects of a bank robbery fleeing north, allegedly shooting out of their car windows as they went.

Gray and the team would be heading south in about ten minutes. Once this last complication was taken care of. If they had to kill Moses and Rock in their escape, all the better.

Agnes Marsh should be dead. Dangling by the neck from a beam out in the main cellar, she had fought Burns hard enough to stutter her opponent's clinical technique and forced fingers between the rope and her skin, before being hauled into the air by Mainey. Kicking and thrashing around, her eyes bugged, flesh fat and red from her chin upwards. They couldn't interfere. It needed to look like a suicide. Plenty of people who hanged themselves changed their mind at the last moment, clawing desperately to attempt a second shot at the life they despised, but if anyone stepped in with Agnes—for example, pulling hard on her to hasten her demise—the additional pressure might show on the autopsy. As it stood, they gave the brass a suicide, accompanied by a confession recorded through the DSLR camera's directional mike, the file having edited out background noise as a precaution, a professional enough job to avoid arousing suspicion.

They all watched her death throes, listening to the commotion above. Only Joshua appeared agitated, pacing, scratching his head with the barrel of a .45 calibre handgun.

"You'll get your chance," Gray said.

"When?" Joshua's eyes were red. He needed a fix.

When we've wiped the cameras of our presence and let the detectives in. Then once we've gone and switched the cameras back on, you can kill them for us and take the fall.

"When Agnes is done," Gray said. "Then you take over your loser dad's empire and run it your own way."

"Yeah, yeah." Joshua examined the gun in his hand as if it was the first time he'd seen it. "He was a loser. I'm gonna get everyone in line. *Everyone*."

"Nearly there." Burns observed with cold detachment as Marsh's movements slowed.

"Get ready," Gray ordered.

They gathered the bags, IDs, handguns. Simple plan. Although he hadn't explained it to the halfwit, Gray was expecting Joshua to go nuts, then in the ensuing melee Gray and the team would flee to the south-east coast. He'd already set up a human trafficking gang to smuggle themselves in reverse to mainland Europe, where they were to travel overland and deposit the cash in Switzerland. The money would get washed while they travelled separately to Belmopan—the capital of Belize—where they'd be able to access the dollar accounts set up for them. Then they'd spend the rest of their days in comfort. Not *luxury* like Baines planned, but close to it.

Agnes fell still.

With the sleeve of his sweater over his finger, Gray checked her wrist. He couldn't feel a pulse. "Let's go."

They all hustled up the stairs. Rucksacks and holdalls, a ragtag convoy of travellers. They paused in the wide hall.

The only thing left was to pinpoint Moses and Rock, decide which door to open in order to ambush them, and send the tweaking psychopath out to blow them away.

All was quiet.

Gray checked the CCTV feed on his phone and couldn't see them. "Where are they?"

“Gave up and gone down the pub?” Mainey suggested.

Burns pulled her gun. “They wouldn’t give up.”

Kortenberg leaned toward the lounge, listening, as if expecting them to be hiding there. “Could they have got wind of you redirecting the AFOs? Backed off?”

“Possible.” Gray got his own gun ready. Maybe using Joshua would have to wait. “Be ready for anything.”

“What about me?” Joshua asked.

“Boss will be in touch when he gets out of clink. Blame your dad for everything.”

“You sure that’ll work? Cos I need to be sure. Can’t be fighting everyone. Need to be sure it’ll work.”

Gray was positive it wouldn’t. But the four detectives were gambling everything. No cavalry. No backup. All they needed was to get over this final hurdle—a clear run to the coast, and they were gone.

“It’ll work,” Gray assured him.

“So, what do we do?” Mainey asked, a rare trace of fear creeping from him.

“We go out mob handed. Shoot our way free if we have to.” He hadn’t yet revealed that he planned only for Josh to go out that way, but expected Mainey would understand the unspoken intent.

With three taps to the phone screen, Gray erased the digital CCTV files. Some techie might eventually recover the images, if they discovered the room where they were stored, but it was unlikely to happen before Gray was sunning himself in the up-market corner of a shithole country, living like a prince.

"Any objections?" he asked.

"Two V five," Burns said. "Easy maths."

All armed their guns, ready to fire.

Gray rehearsed in his head what to say to Joshua, what would encourage him to blast his way to an early grave, allowing the others to slip out in the confusion. But he never got the chance to voice it.

A roaring sounded. From outside. A massive *bang* followed by a clattering *clang*.

"What's…" Gray squinted to see through the gap smashed in the window next to the door and identified the source of the sound: a black Lexus having crashed through the electronic gates on the street hurtled toward them. "Ah, shit. RUN!"

75

Agnes Marsh could hear little except the chugging of blood, the pounding akin to a migraine. Her throat was closed. No air could squeeze through her windpipe. Without oxygen, her brain would shut down, and she—everything Agnes Marsh was, had ever been, ever could be—would fade to black, and she'd be remembered as a murderer, a traitor to her brothers and sisters in blue. She doubted anyone could even come close to understanding that she'd done all of this out of a desire to be a good copper and put away or otherwise punish people who deserved it, while, yes, earning a little extra on the side. That the worst acts she'd committed were out of nothing more than an instinct to live, to survive, would be forgotten.

She'd heard them talking, all antsy, desperate to

get the hell out, but waiting to be sure she was dead first. And she'd been weak, so weak. There was no escaping this through brute force. Even with her fingers in the rope, flexing her muscles and taking in tiny breaths at the merciful intervals she gouged out for herself, the rope kept on tightening. She had seconds, maybe minutes at most. And it seemed no eleventh-hour rescue was forthcoming.

So, she'd fallen slack. Choking back the gagging. Sensed a hand at the pulse point on her wrist. Not bare skin, nothing to leave a fingerprint or foreign DNA such as oils from the skin. Hoping, so desperately hoping, that the constriction of blood flow had sapped her pulse enough to go unregistered through the cloth between the person's finger and her wrist.

Through the dull, underwater strain of her hearing, she'd made out the command to leave, and—willing herself to keep still—counted to twenty. Purple and white stars burst inside her before she got to ten, but she couldn't risk revealing herself to them too soon. The stars had expanded into flowers of white, fluffy dandelions blooming and set free by a stormy wind, speckled at the ends by blue and red and more purple.

Twenty.

Agnes grabbed at the hidden pouch on her leg. Her fingers were numb. She foolishly attempted a breath, but with no passage for the air, her body panicked, spasmed. Hands clawed once again at the rope biting into her neck. Her nose felt swollen; eyes blind, ready to pop; ears full of sand—

No.

She had to live. She had to survive this. She would not die.

Her hand slapped to her thigh. Picked at the seam and tore open the pouch hiding the knife. Her fingers, unfeeling, guided by muscle memory alone, sent a weak signal to her brain to say they were touching something hard. She willed her thumb to work in tandem with her forefinger to grip it. Once in place, she levered her bicep into action, heaving the blade upward. Her eyes made out a ghostly shape as it passed by her face. Her other hand, as heavy as a sock stuffed with gravel, rose to the rope at the back of her head.

The knife met the rope. Now all she needed was the strength to cut.

Once across, but she detected no change. No slip, no twang, but then in her dying state, she might not sense such relief.

She sawed at the fibre again. Twice more. Her grip weakening.

Her left bicep obeyed her brain's command—a mighty tug to ease even a moment of pressure. Her vision didn't quite clear, but the room was visible, filtered through a static of shapes and colours. Her ears popped at the split-second release of pressure.

Then the boom resounded from above. A brief

but massive jolt. The beam holding her rocked but held steady.

And the knife fell from her almost-numb hand.

Falling, featherlike, horizontal in her vision. She had time to hear it strike the floor, the rumble and cries from above, and she knew there and then that she was not going to live after all.

76

Barney Gray dashed by everyone, but it was like running in mud, the ground sucking at his feet as he tried to flee the shock wave. The entire front wall blew in. The edges crumbled, bricks and mortar splitting and flying inwards like a Lego model hit with a hammer. Almost to the lounge door, the others turned tail the same way—Joshua right behind him, then Kortenberg and Burns, with Mainey the slowest to react.

But none of them would make it to cover.

The door itself held, but with nothing to secure it, the unit with deadbolts still engaged rose with the impact and seemed to hover momentarily like a red, rectangular ghost drifting through the explosion of dust and mortar, then drove onward at full speed. Its edge caught the floor. It pinwheeled twice and crashed down on Cole Mainey at the back of the fleeing pack, forcing a scream from the big man as he slapped face-down. The remaining four dived for the kitchen, rolling.

No one seemed to get away unscathed, with chunks of brick, cement, and wood raining forth.

Gray lay still for several seconds, checking himself for serious injury. Assessed the situation.

A dust cloud. Thick fog whirled amid piles of wrecked wall and window frames—sepia movie footage of a bombed-out World War II home. Mainey wailed for help, but the words were garbled amid strained terror. Joshua and Kortenberg sat upright, patting themselves, moving legs, arms, as Gray had done. Burns appeared to be missing. Had she run a different way, or was she dead, beneath the larger section of the collapsed house?

He gathered his wits, found his gun, and knelt up. Joshua beside him did likewise, but the idiot's head twitched, and his teeth had bared. Kortenberg pressed himself against the wall and used it to push upward, favouring his left leg. He had no gun in hand. Mainey cried out again and Gray zeroed in on him, his legs pinned up to the thigh, his top half visible, caked in dust and writhing, a zombie emerging from its grave.

Then more movement sounded from the front. The car's crumpled nose and smashed windscreen holding the maw open, allowing Moses Glynn to pick his way through, his redhead sidekick following. Both armed. Clambering over and around the smoking wreckage, sticking close to the edges, no clear shot at either.

Moses blinked, drawing down on the assembled crew. Grinned. “Afternoon, everyone,” he said. “You’re all nicked.”

77

Moses hadn't rehearsed anything cool sounding, but he liked the ring of it. "Afternoon, everyone. You're all nicked."

Rock slid along the car, using it as cover. She'd pegged the guns, as Moses had, although no one fired. But they had to treat all the guns as live, all suspects as dangers to life.

Rock called to them, "Maintenance of a firearm is important. Yours are filthy right now. We have top of the range, freshly cleaned Glocks. You look like you've got black market trash. Replicas, maybe, retrofitted to fire live rounds."

Moses had only glimpsed the fact they were armed and used the piles of rubble as cover, but joined in, expecting Rock was correct. "If it's bunged up in any way, that's a backfire waiting to happen."

The big man, Cole Mainey, was trapped, and unlike his previous bravado, he let nothing hamper his cries for help. He was keening, a wild animal in a bear trap. "Help me, you fucks. You gotta help me."

"AFOs are en route," Moses said. "They'll bring medical backup."

"They're not en-fuckin'-route." Mainey screamed again.

Moses hadn't heard from the squad they expected would at any moment, and Rock hadn't said anything about another recall or delay. Inserting himself into the mind of Malcolm Baines and, by proxy, that of Barney Gray, he guessed they had some facility to spoof a countermanded order.

"Your call, folks," Moses said, keeping his bead on the figures at the rear of the hallway. "Surrender now, give us Fiona Goodman and Agnes Marsh, and we get you medical help. Or you can take your chances with those shooters, hope they don't blow up in your face."

Three gunshots detonated in the cramped space, deafening reports grouped close together. The car pocked, bullets flying wide, but Rock wasn't about to wait.

She fired. Twice.

Someone hit a solid surface.

Barney shouted, "No, wait!"

Silence echoed through Moses's ringing ears.

Rock held her aim. Moses peeked out, gun

trained on the humanoid figures in the fog. Now clearing. Gray held his pistol by the barrel, Kortenberg slumped against the wall having slid down to his haunches, a red smear on the wall behind him. Cordite from Rock's discharged weapon tainted the air nearby, but that was all.

"There's someone else there," Moses said. "Is it Burns?"

"*Joshua, get out here*," Gray shouted. "It's over."

Joshua must have ducked back into the kitchen area.

Gray came into view, the gun dangling safely, his other hand extended in surrender. "I'm cooperating. I need to get to my friend."

Kortenberg, still alive, pressed his hands over two gushing wounds, a gun beside him—a repurposed twenty-year-old Browning.

Rock said, "He needs to give up his weapon first."

"He didn't fire," Gray answered. "It was Joshua."

"He's still a danger," Moses said. "Still threatened detectives on duty."

Gray lay the gun down—a Glock like Moses's, probably a police-issue that had mysteriously vanished from the database—and stepped slowly and deliberately toward Kortenberg. "I'm going to help him."

"Stay where you are," Rock ordered.

Gray's hands were up by his shoulders. "You people, you're so righteous. You think you're the good guys here, but guess what? None of us are angels."

Mainey strained to cry out, weaker. His gun on the floor, out of reach, one of the repurposed replicas. Still. Must be bleeding out under the door. "Boss… do what they want. Get an ambulance… Fire brigade… Anyone…" His face crinkled in pain, tears streaming.

"You're going to let the man die," Gray said. "In pain. And Rudolph, too. Call the damn backup. The ambulance."

Gray was right, but Moses had to consider their ruthlessness. The hidden dangers of Joshua and, presumably, Clara Burns. Perhaps even Agnes Marsh, hiding, ready to pounce from somewhere—if she'd re-joined their cause. Rock's eyes flicked to his, plainly considering Gray's words.

"Preservation of life." Hands on his head, Gray stretched his leg to toe at the gun by Kortenberg's side. He kicked the firearm out of reach toward the lounge. "I'm going to kneel. And try to help my friend."

"Friend?" Moses said, alert for any other movement, especially the kitchen where it seemed Joshua was hiding. "You have friends?"

Gray stripped off his own jacket, then his shirt and wadded it up, leaving him topless pale, lean, but loose skinned, like he'd lost weight in recent years. Pressed it to Kortenberg's chest. The wounded man gave a grateful, blood-soaked grimace. Gray put an arm around his head and hugged him. There was no saving Rudolph Kortenberg, even if there'd been a paramedic crew chilling out on the driveway when the bullets entered then exited his body. Everyone present knew this. Gray wasn't trying to save the man; he was saying goodbye.

"Time's up," Moses said.

They had to neutralise Gray, cuff him, then clear the house, flush out Burns and Joshua, and attempt to locate Marsh and Fiona.

"Now," Rock said, coming out from behind the car.

Moses did likewise, both stalking in a fast crouch-walk. Rock trained her weapon on the danger spot of the kitchen door, where they knew Joshua had stashed himself, while Moses covered the boss and his dying colleague. His friend.

Kortenberg's eyes glassed over. His head lolled lifelessly to one side. Gray positioned the man gently and released him. Closed his eyes with his thumb and forefinger, then stared. "If you're going to do it, do it."

"You have the right to remain silent," Moses said. "You—"

Gray looked up. "I wasn't talking to you, you unfeeling bastard. Now!"

Joshua bolted from the precise spot where they'd assumed he was. An actual battle cry hollered from him. Gun up. An action hero making a final play at his enemy.

Rock shot him—once in the chest before he could squeeze off a shot. When he didn't go down, just froze and looked annoyed at the bloody hole in his clothes, Rock fired another into his head. The back blew out in a spray of grey and red, dropping him without ceremony. Rock dashed over to kick the gun clear, habit rather than worrying about him rising with it.

Moses hadn't shifted an inch, kept his focus on Gray. "Well that worked out well."

A woman's voice caught them by surprise. "Gaffer wasn't talking to that prick either. He was talking to me."

Clara Burns emerged a fraction from the lounge, its doorframe buckled but not cut off. She held the repurposed replica gun, which Gray had kicked away from Kortenberg, trained on Rock, whose back was to her. A glance over her shoulder led to Rock raising her hands, Glock pointed at the ceiling.

78

Moses wanted to whip himself. *Stupid, stupid, stupid.*

Gray remained in place but twisted his mouth into a sad smile, eyes narrow. Mainey coughed a laugh, but his movements were languid, strength draining. Moses's only target on Burns was her arm, and about an inch of face, her eyes taking in both detectives; she'd shoot Rock before Moses even aimed.

"Tough call," Gray said. "Bit of a standoff."

"You go with the bags," Burns said. "I got this."

"We can still get an ambulance." Moses shifted to his right, positioning DI Gray between himself and Burns.

Gray blinked, a split-second examination of Mainey, then another bleak sigh. "He's not going to make it."

"Boss…" Mainey croaked.

"Sorry, mate." Gray sounded like he meant it. "Wasn't supposed to happen this way."

"Let us go," Burns said. "You might get to Marsh in time."

Rock's head turned so Moses viewed her in profile, bearing her gaze on Burns. "Where is she?"

"Hanging around." Burns firmed her grip. "Maybe this shitty gun blows up in my hand or maybe it blows your head off. I admit I like my hand the way it is, but if you don't put down that gun in three seconds, we're going to find out."

"Then what?" Rock asked.

"Then we leave. You see if your snitch is still alive."

"Fiona Goodman?" Moses said. "We need her too."

"Too late." Gray shrugged and gestured with both hands open toward Moses. "You did it, my friend. You killed her by coming here."

Moses struggled to resign himself to such guilt. "If you killed her, you killed her. No matter the reasons."

"Have it your own way." Gray shook his head, grave and regretful. "Time's up, Clara. Do it."

Moses pointed his Glock at the floor. "Wait, okay!"

"Guv?" Rock said.

"I don't have a choice," Moses answered. "Do the same."

"Fine. I'll drop it. In ten seconds."

"Why ten seconds?" Gray said.

Burns came out of the room a little, shoring up her stance to a two-handed grip, then resolving it into a single hand again, this time on her left. Exposing more of her. Presumably didn't trust the gun any more than Rock did. Wanted to hedge her bets, using her weaker hand.

But Moses still had the same question. *Why ten seconds?* Five now. It meant Rock knew something.

She had a plan. A chance. An avenue Moses couldn't see.

"You sure, Cap?" Moses asked.

"Positive," Rock said.

Moses returned his gun to DI Gray's centre mass. "No deal. You're still nicked."

Gray frowned, jerked his head to see what no one else but Juliette Rock had. At that second, Rock leapt sideways, a messy fall that she executed too fast to plan, landing hard on rubble. Her gun skittered away.

And a blur of movement erupted from the kitchen, a person propelled forward in a desperate lunge.

Agnes Marsh.

Stumbling low, wobbling drunkenly. A small knife in her hand. Angling for Burns, she swept the blade up into Burns' arm. A weak lash of an attack, too slow. At the impact, the gun fired and blood flew, and Marsh dropped.

But it was enough of a delay. Rock, without her gun, launched a more precise attack, her hand the closest she had to a blade, striking Burns' wrist, releasing the replica. Without a moment's pause, she went in harder, an elbow into Burns' neck. Moses enjoyed a moment of pleasure, impressed by her quick action, but it cost him.

Gray came in at him, a rugby tackle that caught him by surprise. It didn't knock him over, but Gray was tougher than he looked, despite the loose body. Stronger. And faster.

A flailing elbow caught Moses's gun and knocked it clear, but Moses rolled with the motion, braced his back leg, and hoofed Gray into the air. Twisted. And came down, using Gray as a cushion.

Snaps sounded—ribs most likely—and Gray's howl of pain shouldn't have given Moses such pleasure, but it did. He yanked the man up, swiped his cuffs out, pulled the yelling DI's hands behind, and slapped the bracelets on him.

"Ahh, get an ambulance," Gray pleaded. "You did my collarbone."

Moses pulled him aside, resulting in another yelp and wail. "Where's Fiona Goodman?"

"Fuck you."

Moses stood on his neck.

Gray screamed so hard that it was barely audible. Dogs must have been changing direction all over Tipton. Moses twisted his foot as if stamping out a cigarette. The man trembled, went stiff, and passed out.

"Damn."

Moses then rushed for the lounge. Agnes Marsh lay in the doorway, shaking, one weak hand over the bullet wound high on her chest—with luck it had missed a lung. But her face was pale, almost translucent, her eyes ringed with red. Unable to speak, she eased her head toward the interior. Twice. *Look that way.*

Moses followed her gaze and stepped in.

With a quarter of the bullet-resistant bay window collapsed in on itself, furniture strewn, he arrived at the end of the fight. The two women facing one another. Rock, though, was bleeding.

Her stomach.

Still standing, but unsteady.

Her hand over the gash. Blood oozing.

Burns faced her in a fighting stance, a straight razor in one hand, stained red. She glanced at Moses. "It's not too deep. Guts are all in place. But she needs treatment. And your pet rat, she's dying too." She turned briefly to the damaged wall, a hole formed of the caved-in quarter window. "I go, you can save them. Try to take me in? You'll lose precious time."

Rock dropped to one knee, folding her stomach over, staunching more of the wound. Her eyes implored Moses, the shake of her head saying, *Don't let her go.*

And every urge inside Moses agreed. The rage built deep down and he knew he could take Burns.

She seemed to read his mind. "I'm good with this. I'll slash at you. Your arms will need stitches, but you'll only need to land one solid blow. One big blow and I'm done."

He was already picturing it. Could feel the cartilage crunch beneath his fist.

"But how long would it take to do that?" Burns went on. "You're strong. I'm fast. You're brutal. I'm skilled. Can you calculate how much time Agnes has? How bad is Juliette's injury?"

Moses watched the razor sway. The single *I'm waiting* eyebrow arch on Burns' taunting face.

"Go," Moses said.

Burns snatched two of the bulky holdalls and scrambled toward the wrecked frontage. She rabbited through the hole in the quarter-window and was gone in seconds.

79

The gash was shallow, but Rock gritted her teeth hard and stifled a shriek as Moses examined her. A straight line, six inches, blood flowing. "I'm not an expert, but I've seen plenty of stabbings." He sat her up against a wall and she nodded hard as he removed his suit jacket.

"How bad?"

"Skin's cut but doesn't look to have got as far as the muscle. At least, not deep. But stay there, okay?" He left her pressing hard with his jacket.

Only about 90 percent certain of his diagnosis, he still had two other lives to preserve. He pulled out his phone and dialled 999 and gave his name and the location of the house, demanding a major response unit, including fire and rescue crews and every paramedic in a ten-mile radius not already dealing with a life-threatening situation.

Crawling beside Agnes, he lay her flat, tugged at the arm of his shirt to rip it at the seam, and screwed it up to jam over the bullet wound. She gasped at the air, jaw working.

"It's okay," Moses said. "Hold still. Can you speak? Do you know what happened to Fiona Goodman?"

The raw line around Marsh's throat almost glowed, the swelling surrounding it like a goitre. Her fingers bled, presumably from fighting a noose or garrotte. Her eyes seemed to plead with him. A whispered croak.

"Fell… Thought I was dead, but… Rope snapped… Must have…"

He bowed over her, his ear as close as he could.

"Sorry," she managed to say. "You…"

"Fiona," Moses said. "Is she alive?"

Urging her to speak was against regs. To do anything but order her to lay still and await help while he stemmed the bleeding and tried to keep her airway open was against regs. He needed to get some cold water into her throat. The swelling alone might kill her.

Again, Agnes said, "You…" But it petered out. She tried to swallow, but that made her cough, which made her inhale sharply. She calmed. "Overdose… You killed her…"

"No. No, I didn't. It was you lot. What did you give her? Is she dead already? You—"

Agnes Marsh's hand slackened, slipped from the

wound, and her bloated face ceased all movement. She was dead.

Moses closed his eyes, angry at himself for letting Burns go. For not anticipating the countermanded order to divert the AFOs.

"Moses…" Rock had pushed to her feet, shouldered herself along the wall to get out of the lounge, and stood over them.

"Sit down," Moses said. "Ambulance is coming."

"You killed her." Rock looked pale, exhausted. "Gray said that too."

Moses whirled back to the unconscious DI. Scrambled over and slapped him.

No reaction.

Mainey was still there.

Moses crawled that way, but the big man was unconscious too. He checked for a pulse. Weak, but still alive. He slapped the man's face. Jiggled his shoulders so his head bobbled to stimulate the brain.

Mainey's eyelids flickered.

"Mainey." Moses patted his cheek. Not torture, not threatening, just trying to wake him up. "You can still come out of this with a lick of cooperation. Where's Fiona? What did you do with her?"

"I…" Mainey's lip curled. A grunt. "I look… like a rat… to you?"

Moses held his gaze, and the lip curled into a tighter, more petulant pose.

"Fuck you and die," Mainey said.

"You first." Moses let the man's head drop and stood upright. He turned a full circle. "I killed her?"

Rock leaned on the hallway wall, more stable than the lounge doorway where Agnes Marsh's corpse lay. "Not your fault. Seriously, Moses. It's not. We did our best."

"Go sit," Moses said. "You still lost blood."

She gave a single laugh and grimaced against the obvious pain. "Under that frame?"

Moses assessed the crooked cant of the door frame and her words slapped him like a damp towel. *Under that frame.*

Why the hell did that make sense of something?

Of what Gray said.

What Agnes said.

You killed her.

"Oh, Jesus, no. Their favourite trick." Moses darted toward the wreckage at the front, scuffling up over the car bonnet and over the roof to the outside. He ignored Rock's shouts and made it into the sunlight.

He scanned around for Burns in case she'd been dumb enough to hang around, but one car was missing, so he guessed he was safe. She'd be in the wind, needing treatment for her arm, although she might wait until she was clear first. They'd reach out through Theo's people; he knew doctors.

Sirens sailed from a direction he couldn't determine. Several directions. Only now did he see dozens of householders peering from their homes, the racket from the Safe House having been too much for their cocooned lives. At his appearance, a buzz mushroomed from the witnesses, as if asking each other telepathically what they should do. Moses had no time to reassure them.

At the rear of the Lexus, he pulled at the boot, jammed his fingers in the release catch, but it didn't move.

He slapped the metal, then scurried back up the roof, over it in an army crawl, dislodging half a dozen loose bricks from the precarious wall above him. They crunched around, one grazing his arm.

Rock had struggled to the front of the vehicle but couldn't climb up. "Moses, what the hell!"

"Their favourite trick," he said, penduluming his legs down and dropping to the rubble. "How'd they get Ratan Walar in the clink?"

"The dead girl… Framed him…" The penny dropped for Rock. "You don't think…?"

Moses yanked at the door to get to the manual release inside. It opened only an inch, rammed up against the pile of shattered bricks and wood and cement.

"Damn it. Must have been watching us at the restaurant. Did it when we were inside with Theo and Lucas."

He felt for his gun, but he'd lost it in the scrap with Barney Gray. He balled a fist and drew it back.

"Moses?" Rock said.

"Yeah?"

"What are you stood on?"

Moses looked at his feet. At the pile of bricks. "Right. Thanks." Clearing his head, he scooped up a brick with three inches of mortar still attached and flung it through the Lexus' window. Oddly relieved that he'd had someone nearby to curb his stupid instinct, and that his hand wasn't broken and shredded, he leaned through the hole, diamond shards speckling around him, and hit the boot release.

He heard the clunk and raced back over the bodywork, under the crumbling frontage, and down to the ground. The hatch opened to a young black woman lying, unmoving, amongst a nest of blankets and rags. Her eyes were open, one arm twisted back on itself, nose bloodied. A cut to her head and an unnaturally bent arm. The tourniquet still in place above her elbow on the unbroken side.

Moses's mouth gaped. Breathless. "Fiona."

He resisted the urge to drag her out, instead sliding his arms under her. Supporting her head. Raising her up, out of the boot space. "I'm sorry, I'm so sorry."

He swept her steadily from the car, away from the house, and laid her down on the smooth driveway, just as the first ambulance pulled to a stop by the gates. Two paramedics darted from the vehicle and they had to insist Moses move away from her.

It was as if he was dreaming.

This little girl he'd held, the daughter of a man he'd considered a friend. This woman, with her desire to help, to do good deeds, who had inspired Moses to start his own family.

They'd wanted to frame him for her murder, although it seemed unlikely to stick. But finding her dead in his car… it'd have been enough to delay him. They'd have to arrest him, question him. Rock too. By the time the fit-up was clear, the Shadow CPU would have been gone, mission accomplished.

Now Moses's rash actions had killed her.

Killed this sweet girl. The girl he'd promised to recover alive. To protect.

"She's breathing," the female paramedic announced to her colleague.

Moses snapped back to the present. "She's okay?"

The male said, "Not okay, but… alive. Is she on drugs?" He was removing the tourniquet.

"Not her. Not intentional. Someone drugged her."

"What with?" the female asked impatiently.

"I don't know." Plodding now. The ground had turned to marshmallow. Moses wiped his face—sweat and grime came away. "Probably heroin. It's what Joshua Sevan was moving into."

They'd have no idea who he was, but they had a lead on heroin.

"What else?" the male paramedic asked. "What happened?"

Quick answers needed. No long explanations. "RTC. Road traffic collision."

"Arm's broken," said the female. "Head injuries."

"I'll get the gurney." The man hopped to his feet and jogged for the ambulance as another pulled up and a fire engine entered the street at the opposite end.

"She'll be okay?" Moses asked.

The female gave him the puppy dog eye treatment and a sympathetic head-tilt. "We'll give her something for the OD in the ambulance, then get her to a hospital to treat the rest. I can't promise anything. Except we'll do our best for her."

80

Hours passed. Long ones. The critical cases of Fiona, Cole Mainey, and Barney Gray were taken to the three closest hospitals, while Rock was declared merely "urgent." With her being at odds with two-thirds of the other casualties, Moses recommended she go to the Queen Elizabeth in Birmingham. It was here that they patched him up for the cuts sustained during the raid on the Safe House, and he had to explain his other injuries resulted from a fall some days earlier. They needed four stitches to suture Rock, then ordered her to rest. Given the nature and circumstances, they granted her a private room, in which Moses made himself comfortable.

There were two rounds of formal interview, which he provided willingly, explaining away his breaches of protocol—such as throwing a car through a residential stronghold—again reciting the all-encompassing get-out clause, *the preservation of life*. That Agnes Marsh's life had not been preserved was irrelevant; only his intent and judgment mattered.

Moses made calls to his family, and to Wearne and the prison in which Baines was incarcerated, demanding the most senior supervisor he could speak with pass on a message. "Moses came to visit in Tipton. It's all gone."

"Are you sure that's what you need us to pass on?" the confused telephonist asked.

"I'm sure."

DCI Wearne arrived in person at eight p.m. Stolid and tense, she remained standing on the opposite side of Rock. "Is she conscious?"

"I'm awake," Rock said, having drifted in and out of sleep. "Tired. Apparently, as the body heals razor cuts, it takes a bit of energy."

Moses offered Wearne the seat he was in, but she declined. She said, "Debriefing."

"I'm off duty," Moses said. "I'll report first thing."

"You could. Or you could tie things up here and take a day off."

Moses may have been mistaken, but he thought her features softened a fraction. He said, "Okay, deal."

"Loss of life?"

"Agnes," Rock said. "She saved us."

"After torturing a man half to death." Wearne's face returned to its permascowl. "And shooting a young woman up with a serious heroin overdose."

"She wasn't the most experienced copper," Moses pointed out. "But she'd know she didn't use enough to kill the girl. She was hoping we'd find her in time."

"Instead of chucking her through a wall," Rock said.

"She'll live," Wearne told them. "Should recover fully. Arm fractured in two places. Broken nose, some cuts, and the drugs don't appear to have done her lasting harm, but they'll monitor her organs to be sure."

"Mainey died, I assume?" Moses said.

Wearne gave a curt nod. "He'd lost too much blood. As soon as they pulled him free of the wreckage, they couldn't clamp him fast enough. He died at the scene. Barney Gray will live to see trial, though. Broken collar bone, two cracked ribs, a dislocated shoulder."

Moses was glad to hear it. "Fit him with a cell next to Baines. See how that goes down."

Wearne's response was a snort of derision. No need to verbalise that it would never happen. They wouldn't even be in the same prison. She took a breath and recommenced. "He hung on to Joshua's original clothing. To keep him in line, I assume. The bag has his prints on it, and the fake IDs with Gray's image would put him in jail on their own.

With the guns, your accounts, and assuming testimony from DCI Flood in Professional Standards now he's out of danger, we should get a conviction."

Rock raised the bed, sitting herself up at a shallow angle. "The Shadow Unit is finished?"

"Clara Burns is out there somewhere. Malcolm Baines' power base is pretty much done. The Sevan family line ended with Joshua, although he could have fathered any number of babies around the area. But yes, I think we put them out of business."

Moses sighed, fatigue starting to catch up. "And Gabriella Childs? Nadia Ako?"

"For Gabriella, we have Joshua's real clothing and his DNA will be on there. The pathologist is being questioned, but DI Xian thinks she'll break. Especially since the threat is neutralised. Ms Childs' family will get answers, if not the conviction of the man in court."

Moses nodded. "Nadia? The girl in Ratan Walar's car?"

Wearne again softened before tensing up again. "That's less certain. We have passed on our intelligence to the National Crime Agency and they'll be raiding the properties we identified through our data sweeps and historical location data of Joshua's phone. If they can find someone to testify that it was Joshua Sevan who took her out hours before she died, it's likely the inquiry will determine he was responsible for her murder. Ashley Mars has been arrested and appears ready to cooperate."

"Not Detective Sergeant Walar?"

"You're keen to exonerate him." Wearne wasn't asking; a flat statement.

"He got out from under Baines. Was doing good work."

Moses could not deny the parallels between Walar and himself. The bad egg. The change of direction. The conviction to his new path.

"He didn't 'get out'," Rock said. "They forced him out. Disciplinary proceedings."

Okay, so not parallel. But similar. He had been a decent detective once he'd been exorcised of Baines' influence—by choice or not.

Moses said, "He doesn't need exonerating for the past. But Baines murdered him. Are we going to let that go?"

"Not our area," Wearne replied. "DCI Chalmers from Force CID is taking it up. I know her personally. There will be movement on that soon, but it's too early to say who will get nicked for it. Someone will."

It was the most Moses could hope for. "And Silas?"

"You can guess," Wearne said.

Rock looked aside. "Can't be touched as he did nothing technically illegal?"

A tight nod from Wearne. "Got it in one. But he's curtailed for now. And we'll monitor him."

There didn't seem to be much more to say. Mainey dead. Marsh dead. The Sevan family destroyed. The Goodmans alive but scarred, and unlikely to step back into the nefarious trade with which Silas had tempted him. Baines stripped of power. Silas unable to expand or poke his head up for fear of being spotted. Rock down, but not out.

"Have we earned our day off?" Moses asked.

Wearne lingered on Rock and addressed them both. "Go home, rest, recuperate. Once we catch up with Burns—and we will—it's over."

SATURDAY

81

Moses was actually due more than a single day off, and he'd taken them. He'd slept in the next morning, then at lunchtime called Division 43 and said he'd be back the following Monday, not Thursday. No one objected.

On Wednesday evening, he learned Rock had gone home, armed guards still in place because Burns hadn't yet been detected. Not a hint so far. Judging by the other bags recovered at the scene, she'd escaped with over a hundred grand, although Moses had speculated there could be more stashed elsewhere.

It was Baines' way.

Having sent Frankie and Eko into hiding, also with the requisite armed support, Moses spent Saturday alone. Reading. Listening to music. Texting back and forth with his daughter, who was finding her new digs cramped, but the change of scenery interesting, although not particularly exciting. He assured her they'd be home soon, but not this weekend. Protective custody sucked, but it worked.

Moses didn't get many quiet evenings to himself, and he was secretly enjoying this. Sure, he missed the girls, but it was relaxing to just be himself. Little luxuries he couldn't enjoy around Frankie without prior planning.

Tonight, he opened a bottle of wine he'd been saving and cooked a paella, a lone treat since Frankie hated the tofu and animal-free flavours made to taste vaguely like shellfish, and geared up a Jordan Peele horror double bill. Again, he rarely got to watch horror movies, and he'd been putting these off for years. Never the right time, or there were other priorities, or he was in the doghouse with Frankie, or…

Or.

There was no *or* tonight. He was home alone and intended to make the most of it.

He plated up the paella and carried it through to his living room on a tray, sat the optimum distance from his 60-inch TV for both vision and the surround sound he'd installed long ago, and was thankful for the lowering light. Their patio doors in this room led to the strip of grass on the side of the garden, not the main stretch, but it still reflected too much during the day. For now, though, it was just right.

The Blu-ray hummed to life and the main menu faded into being. Moses selected the "play film" option, but a gentle breeze stopped him in his tracks. A faint clunk.

Moses regarded the room again. Took in the window, which was closed and locked. He followed the ripple of air, seeking the direction of the breeze.

Not the internal door.

Must be the patio.

Moses set his tray of paella aside and crossed to the double doors with the blinds half-drawn. They were open. A couple of inches, but they hadn't been open twenty minutes earlier, because he'd checked.

"Burns?" he called. "Clara? That you?"

As with the previous nights he'd called the woman's name upon hearing something strange, he got no reply. However, this was the first strange noise to be accompanied by a minutely open door.

He opened the blinds, pulled the cord so they expanded. Pushed open the door and stood in the frame. An easy target if she was hiding out here with a gun. He wasn't expecting a gun, though.

And he was correct.

Finally.

A pair of feet swung down at him, blocky tactical boots slamming into his face. She'd been on the sloping awning over the patio, and that surprised him. He assumed she'd have made her way into the house. But no matter.

About damn time.

Clara Burns landed as he regained his balance. All in black, the balaclava pulled up like a woolly hat so he could see her face. A straight razor in her hand. She went at him hard, slicing his forearm before he could dodge.

Blood slewed out, down his arm, and she aimed a kick at his groin. He half-blocked it, but she rang the bells enough to send a bolt of pain through his pelvis.

The razor came up again, but it was a feint; he tilted aside to evade it, which was when her thumb landed in his eye and he yelped in both surprise and pain. He jerked back, avoiding lasting damage to the eyeball.

The woman *was* fast.

A searing fire slashed across this thigh, the razor cutting deep, and Moses suddenly found himself in more danger than he had been in years. He could put no weight on the leg, dropping to one knee, and her boot to his face came too quickly to defend.

Against brawlers, MMA practitioners, even semi-pro boxers, he could tough it out, play with his opponent until he wore them down with his sheer size and strength. Here, though, his first swing at her came after she'd cut him twice and landed three hefty blows.

And she evaded that first punch.

Darted aside. Slashed his upper arm and landed a knee in his kidney.

He needed space, distance between them.

He rolled, crushing his dinner plate and daubing paella over his back. She was coming at him already, and he only had one decent leg.

With less than a second to mount a defence, he bent his standing knee and launched forward with a fist pulled back.

She wasn't the only one who could offer a feint.

Moses dropped the haymaker as Burns slashed her razor in that direction, then drew back his head. He landed his forehead in Burns' face. Her nose crunched, and his skull followed through, connected hard with her brow, cracking that part of her face too.

They landed two feet apart.

Moses again rolled away. Up on his good leg. Assessed his enemy.

She was up too. Fighting stance. Razor at the ready. Her nose bled freely, flattened to the left, while her right eye was swelling, almost closed already.

"Hi," Moses said, calculating how much damage was being caused by blood, wondering if his home insurance would even pay out. He'd manoeuvred close to the patio doors. "Think we could finish this outside?"

"I'm good, thanks." Burns charged.

She went in low. Moses backed up, hop-staggering in a lope to the wall, then surprised her by switching direction and coming directly at her. He grabbed the wrist on the razor's side and lifted her off the ground. His open wound cascaded down his arm, excruciating as he flexed his muscle to tighten his grip. Burns' face contorted. She dropped the razor.

Moses flung her like a doll through the open door where she skidded on the patio flagstones, coming to a halt in a heap. As Moses emerged, she righted herself.

"Hold it," Moses said. "I wanna ask you one thing."

"What's that?" Burns glanced around, her body positioned like an animal ready to either flee or pounce.

"Your real boss." Moses felt exposed here, despite the residential setting. It was an extensive property, with a lot of garden out back, which was accessible from this side.

"My real boss?"

"Is he here? Because it looks like you accepted my invitation."

"Your what?"

"Oh." Moses was sodden with his own blood. Nothing close to a major artery, but it would demand treatment. Preferably soon. "You didn't work this out for yourself? Let me fill you in. You were about to get out, flee the country. But then you were recalled. You're here under orders."

She said nothing, just firmed her jaw.

He was right. The plan had worked.

Two days earlier, on Thursday, Moses, Frankie, and Eko showed up uninvited at Rock's house and treated her to a takeaway. She was still on painkillers, moving around without a stick, although she wouldn't be doing crunches for a while. It was a quiet evening, and only when Frankie and Eko adjourned to wash up did Moses voice a concern.

"Ever get a feeling we missed something?" Moses asked her. "Something that might end it completely?"

Rock admitted she did. "Probably because Burns is still out there."

"Yeah." He powered up his work phone and showed her the highlighted sections of a document they drew up together some days earlier. "This is what's bothering me."

Rock evaluated the data, handed the phone back, and her eyes rolled up to observe the ceiling. "That's odd, yeah."

"We didn't spot it because we were looking for something else."

"And you think you can use it to draw her out?"

"Not this alone. Not how we're set up."

"What do you want to do?"

Moses craned to listen for Frankie and Eko returning, but they were still at the sink. "Can the girls stay here a few days?"

On Friday, Moses did the rounds. Tidied up, shaved, dressed in his best three-piece pinstripe, dark purple shirt, and black tie, he visited Silas Bonaparte's offices. He walked in, strolled up the main office to Silas's own domain at the end, and watched through the glass. Silas was meeting with clients—two women in their fifties—and he only glanced up at Moses once. But Moses stayed where he was. Even when a buff white kid in his twenties sidled up, set his shoulders, and asked if he could help, Moses presented his warrant card and said, "Police. Piss off." And the kid scurried away.

As the meeting broke up, Moses departed without saying a word to Silas.

Back on the street, Moses watched the office window, and the lawyer's stubby outline manifested in the glass, where it remained until he got in his car, and drove the hour and a half to HMP Dovedale.

Here, he came armed with a list of Baines' known associates, prison foot soldiers who kept the former DCI in the manner to which he'd become accustomed and demanded to see them one after the other. A litany of scum, of tattooed thugs, mostly bald for some reason, who entered the conference suite with the same swagger and defiance as every hardened can't-make-me-talk criminal Moses had ever faced.

He said nothing to them. Just sat face-to-face every time until they snapped and started shouting to be released. The record was eighteen minutes, a coke dealer named Oliver. When done with his non-interviews, Moses left the prison and went home.

"I needed it to look like we were pressing your guys inside," Moses now told Burns. "After, we isolated half of them from the others, so they'd think we'd cut a deal. Learned the truth about the boss."

"You know all about old Malc," Burns said.

"But I didn't know about Ratan Walar, did I?"

Burns' battered face withdrew, almost slinking into shadow without moving her head.

"Yeah, took me a day and a half of downtime to figure out what we'd overlooked. Is he gonna come out? I'm assuming he's here."

Seemingly paralysed on her feet, Burns gave only the slightest tell.

"To be honest," Moses continued, pacing slowly only two feet from the wall, the angle protecting him from the street and woodland at the rear, "I worried we went overboard withdrawing my protection detail from the house. But it'd have placed someone in more danger. Made you come at me elsewhere."

The softly spoken reply came from inside the house. "You think that means you're in control?"

Moses pivoted with the calmest body language he could muster, as Ratan Walar stepped out of the same door he and Burns had come from. He must have broken in during the fight, backup in case Burns' assault went wrong. The gun looked foreign, but not an adapted replica or cold war relic; something Russian, probably, and well maintained, expertly put together.

"You don't strike me as someone worried about gunshots," Moses said, conscious of the biting pain from his wounds, his clothes sodden. "Why the blade?"

Walar shrugged. "Lady's choice."

A glance at Burns earned Moses a faintly amused wink from her one good eye. Moses said, "She likes cutting."

"And she's good at it."

"Like she killed Nicola Dawson to get away from our holiday cottage?"

"Unfortunate." Walar appeared solemn, like he meant it.

Moses risked a glimpse at Burns, who hadn't shifted, who didn't appear moved by the fact of a murdered police officer. "And that's a lady?"

Burns said, "Never claimed to be."

"Not shooting straight away?" Moses kept his dripping arms to the side, away from his body. Took a step backwards, closer to his garden. "That's a bit James Bond baddie, isn't it?"

Walar's eyes narrowed. "What was it? That gave me away. We left enough of my DNA on the corpse to fool any pathologist."

"Getting yourself put away was a nice stroke. I mean, you probably didn't expect it'd be a dead hooker, and I doubt you planned it that way. But they had a murder victim to dispose of, and they needed to get you off the streets, so you didn't have to talk to me anymore. Always a danger we'd figure it out if we kept on probing your story, checking the facts. Then we proved you faked your death. We found one of the prison guards who phoned in sick hasn't been seen in a while. Guessing you switched places, chucked in enough blood and hair for a preliminary ID. And if the pathologist raised any questions, you'd do what you did with Davina Mishkin, the examiner in the Joshua Sevan case. Subtle."

Walar advanced. "In case you hadn't noticed, Glynn, subtle doesn't cut it anymore. Keeping hidden was my best defence, but the actions people take… No one cares. You deny something strongly enough and with enough power behind you, people accept what they want to accept. The brass looks the other way on corruption because it's too expensive to manage. And when some of us make a bit of cash on the side, tip over the boat all the way, it becomes too much of an embarrassment to admit it happened. Do you really believe there was no way out for Cleland? He could have confessed everything, but you know why he didn't?"

Moses backed all the way into his garden. It was dark. The motion activated lights failed to ignite their white blanket of illumination. Must have been deactivated. "You had dirt on him."

"If what we had came to light, it'd have been nothing compared to the embarrassment of Barney Gray's team being outed. A decorated officer, a decorated team of detectives, going unchecked for years? You know how much reform and pressure would drop on the police after that? How much red tape and new regulation?"

"I guess we're going to find out the answer soon, since it's all out in the open." Moses made a cheerful face, although he was beginning to worry about blood loss. His arms hung heavy in their submissive posture. "You want to know how I worked you out? So you can avoid that mistake in the future? I'm not gonna help you with that."

Walar aimed the gun lower, approximately at Moses's knee. "Hard way." He lifted it to Moses's head. "Easy way."

Burns was several feet to Walar's left. Moses's right. She said, "Die in pain, or die quick."

Moses shook his head. "Die quick, you stage a suicide. Well, with my cuts, it'll look suspicious, but hey. Plant enough shit in my house, it might wash. If you get the right SIO under your thumb. Nah, I want my murder to be investigated. Properly."

"Have it your way." Walar took a phone from his pocket and unlocked it. "I'm surprised you didn't anticipate this. I mean, you know how we do things. And I hate to be unoriginal, but these methods... they work." The screen opened on a photo of Frankie and Eko arriving at Juliette Rock's house, carrying Aldi shopping bags and flanked by close protection officers. "It's what makes a classic a classic. So, at the risk of sounding obvious..." He hushed his voice as if conveying a secret. "They can't be bodyguarded forever."

Moses mulled it over, considered rushing him. But the wiry detective hadn't shown a hint of tiring from holding a heavy metal weapon. He seemed alert. He'd planned this out, and the only reason Moses wasn't dead already was that he wanted information, wanted to know the mistake he made.

"Simple," Moses said. "How I found you."

Walar pocketed the phone and switched to a two-handed grip. "Oh, yes?"

"The timing. It niggled me. But I was looking at Gray and Baines, Theo Goodman and Kaspar Sevan. Not you." A stab of pain circled Moses's upper arm, the wound affecting him there more than the opposite forearm gash. His thigh throbbed. He didn't have much time left. "Can I sit?"

"No." Walar lowered the gun toward Moses's groin, still too far out of reach. "Carry on."

Moses made a show of his bleeding thigh aching, limped a little more to his right, the leg almost buckling, but he gritted his teeth against it. "You got kicked off Barney's team two years ago because you almost got caught. Getting cocky as Baines' heir apparent. But DCI Flood, the PSD guy who had you punished, he got threatened eighteen months ago."

"He went after Barney again."

"But Flood dropped his case thanks to his son getting taken for that ride. Your 'classic' way of controlling people. Thing is, then Flood's mother is murdered. *After* the case is dropped."

Walar's head made a quarter turn, his face partially away from Moses, but both eyes stayed on him. "So?"

"When we interviewed you, on the night we said assassins were coming for you, you were certain the mother's car accident was connected to the threats against Flood. More to the point, Flood was convinced. That meant someone had to tell him."

"You can't link that to me."

"It was a punishment. Not a threat. That meant someone who'd been wronged. Someone with a power complex, who'd had that power stripped back and wanted to reassert himself. Gray refused to kill Flood's child, and that rankled with you. Going after his elderly mother… that's a low move. But there wouldn't be the outrage of a dead kid." Moses fought a brief dizzy spell. His blood pounded through him, and he needed to control that better. "You knew too much about it for it to be historical information. You were there. You orchestrated it. Maybe even carried it out. Because from that moment on, your squad of gangsters posing as cops stepped things up big time. The alliance with the Sevan family, the direct, unambiguous links to Silas Bonaparte. All the brazen shit you thought you could get away with because you had the will and the means, and the tools…" Moses gestured to Burns. "To do it. Baines was subtle about his income, his property purchases, but you wanted more, and you wanted it fast, and you didn't care who got hurt. Even approved of Gray's plan to run to Belize. You didn't share with Baines the real reason you needed to fake your death."

Walar had remained in place throughout Moses's monologue. And as for controlling his temper and his blood flow, Moses had failed miserably.

Out of breath, his leg shaking with the effort of supporting the fraction of his weight that he'd put on it, he said, "Tell me I'm wrong."

"You're not wrong." Walar threw Burns a pitying laugh. "Why the hell didn't we recruit this guy instead of Barney Gray?"

Burns showed Walar her razor. "Because he's a sanctimonious prick."

"Oh, yeah, forgot about that." Walar firmed his stance. "Shame no one will prove he was right."

Moses said, "I think that's enough."

"Enough of what?" Walar asked.

"Enough of you."

Walar glanced around as if expecting a helicopter to descend or a cadre of AFOs to materialise. "Bullshit. You couldn't know we'd come here. For you."

"No, we couldn't. But the thing is, it isn't just me who wouldn't lie down. It was all of us."

"All…?"

"That was the trap. Every member of Division 43 was under threat. All our houses. All our cars. All our families. They're all protected the way I am."

Burns said, "You don't look so well protected."

"Yeah, well. That really is all about knowing when to lie down." Moses allowed his leg to give way, and he fell like a tree to the grass.

And, although Walar's handgun followed his descent, it was too late. His chest burst open a split second before a rifle shot split the air. A second shot landed close to the first, but the shredded impact knocked him backwards. He was wearing a ballistic vest. The shots may well have penetrated, though, Rock's position in the woodland having been far closer than most police snipers in similar situations, which she needed to be due to both the landscape and the radar mike aimed at the house.

Moses guessed what would happen next before it hit, and covered his face, peeking out between his fingers.

A red hole burst in Ratan Walar's head, the nose caving dead-centre, before exploding out the back like a smashed melon. He folded in place, neutralised.

Burns should have run. She should have moved behind the cover of the house the way Moses had, cautious of what secondary attack might come.

But she didn't.

Her instinct was to kill. To avenge. And her sprint toward Moses was fast, low. With Moses on his backside, not flat to the lawn, Rock couldn't be sure of a kill shot.

Didn't stop her from trying, though.

She was being too cautious, as the bullets raked beyond Burns' attack, a bit to the side, nothing close to Moses.

Then Burns was upon him. The razor arced. No time to pancake himself to the floor. He could block one more slash, but not a second. All he could manage was to swing his one good foot at Burns' shins. That brought her down faster.

He had her in terms of reach.

His blood-soaked forearm thrust out and his fist powered into her chest. Under the combined force of Moses's punch and her own momentum, blood leapt from her mouth and bones snapped—ribs, maybe the breastbone itself. He felt the hard part of her go soft. She froze in mid-air, the razor flying from her hand, then she snapped back and to the side. Propelled five feet.

She spun, bounced, and came to a halt as she crushed Moses's rose bush. There, she lay motionless but for a strangled gasping of breath, a fish tossed up on the shore by a storm.

Moses lay on his back, facing the sky. The stars.

He enjoyed watching the stars. Had to manually switch off the outdoor lights to do so. He and Frankie did it often, with Eko starting to take an interest.

He thought he could see Mars, a red hue to a bright dot, but had it in his mind that this was the wrong time of year.

Juliette Rock loomed over him, decked out in a combination of military camo and police vest. "You resting?"

Moses moved his head toward Burns. "Is she…"

Rock cast a glance that way. "Immobilised. Medics are on their way. This was a dumb move."

"Yeah, but it worked."

Rock crouched, getting up close to each wound. "They're going to hurt more than mine."

"Does it still hurt?"

"I've been lying on it, watching your house for two hours. Even with the gel cushion, yes. The six-inch gash in my abdomen hurts."

Sirens. Close.

"Ambulance," Rock said.

She was framed by stars. Going blurry.

"Thanks," he said.

"For what?"

"For doing this."

She bit her lip, glanced again at Burns, then

down at him. "Division 43 is supposed to be better than them. We got down and dirty. Dropped to their level."

Moses sighed. Wanted to sit up, but the effort was too great. "That's on me, Cap. You did great."

"If I did so great," she said, "you wouldn't be lying on your lawn, bleeding out."

"I'm happy with your performance."

"Thanks, guv. But I can't do things this way. We got them. And I'm glad we did. But this isn't police work."

Moses was about to reply, but Rock stood abruptly, and was gone from his vision, leaving nothing except a field of stars.

WEDNESDAY

82

Alone in her kitchen, Juliette Rock was able to move without the injury reminding her every few seconds. If she tried too much, it flared up, and she'd obey her body's instruction to calm things down a bit. Cooking seemed to be an activity that failed to aggravate the wound, and after the paramedics carted DI Moses off in an ambulance, it was the first thing she thought of.

Cooking.

Weird, that.

Now, for the first time since those early days outside the military when Rock planned to morph into a domestic goddess, she gravitated toward the unused cookbooks. Learning something new always helped when she found herself adrift, unable to make a firm decision.

Wearne had rejected her resignation on the

grounds that she'd been through a traumatic episode. Taking a life, apparently, suggested she wasn't thinking straight. That wouldn't hold water for long, though. She'd killed at least thirty people whilst in the Army, and now two civilians—Joshua Sevan and Ratan Walar.

Moses was technically responsible for Cole Mainey's death and could well have killed Burns had the paramedics not arrived so quickly and relieved the pressure on her lungs. She was being charged with the attempted murder of a police officer and the actual murder of Nicola Dawson, with more crimes pending.

Rock shook the past away. Decided on a tortellini recipe—pasta parcels containing asparagus and goats' cheese—in a mascarpone sauce.

"Huh, no meat," she said. And that brought her back to Moses.

She hadn't travelled with him to the hospital. She sent him a few text messages wishing him well, but also asked him not to talk her out of the transfer request. He hadn't.

The doorbell rang.

Rock placed the book down and headed to the front, checked the camera feed she'd had installed, and opened up. Frankie Moses gave her a tense smile.

"Is this okay?" she asked. "Me coming here?"

Rock stood aside. "Of course."

The two went through to the kitchen, where Rock offered a drink, but Frankie declined.

"I won't keep you long," she said. "And I need to be clear. Moses asked me not to come."

Rock accepted that. "Is he out of hospital?"

"This morning. Stitches, bandages, painkillers, lots of groaning. You know what men are like. But it was last night that made me want to come."

"Last night?"

Frankie appeared downcast, as if she wasn't sure she should go through with whatever she was here for.

"It's okay," Rock said. "Let's hear it."

Frankie nodded, a grateful expression as she appeared more at ease. "DCI Wearne came to see him. At his request."

Curious.

"He wanted reassurances," Frankie said.

"What of?"

"That they'll continue doing what they're doing. Rooting out corruption. Protecting the detectives if they have to bend the rules some."

"Bend the rules." Rock summoned a physical effort to prevent herself from scoffing. She may have rolled her eyes. "We did more than bend them. And we got away with it. Setting traps. Getting in fist-fights. Demolishing buildings. Not even a disciplinary. Comes a point when we have to ask, is Division 43 another form of corruption?"

Frankie tilted her head, her eyes soft, sympathetic. "Glynn asked himself the same question. DCI Wearne did point out they could only go so far. You got some leeway, being newbies, and she took her share of the blame for not giving you all the information she should have. Another mess like this, and people will start to question Division 43's oversight. Everything in future will be tighter."

"Still." Rock hugged herself as if cold but dropped her arms to shrug. "Secret searches, extra judicial surveillance, even looking the other way for over the top beatings. How long until we endorse torture?"

"It comes down to the people, Juliette. Wearne knows you won't let it get that far."

"And Moses?"

"That's why he needs you. Because of the questions."

Rock had already questioned it and found it wanting. She looked away from Frankie.

"But," Frankie said, "that's why I'm here. For so long, Moses has needed a place where he could utilise his skills in full. Not chasing down coppers—which was another guarantee he wanted—but going after the people who routinely get away with criminal behaviour. Politicians, the super-rich, religious institutions. Juliette, I've never seen him so enthused. He wants to dive in with both feet."

Rock had felt the same when they sold her on the new division. But the reality hadn't lived up to what she'd hoped for. "And why do you have to come here?"

"Glynn needs someone like you. Keep him going. Keep him from getting too jaded when it doesn't go right. He was trying. He kept going because his partner believed in the cause. And for a while… he was back. The real Glynn Moses. The guy who switched his name around to impress people when he introduced himself. *Moses Glynn.* That commitment, that spark… I might have been pissed at him, but that's who he is when he's at his best. And it was because of you."

Rock pulled a cookbook toward her, this one filled with Indian-inspired recipes. "He doesn't need me for that."

"It could easily slip away again. He needs someone who needs him too."

"I don't need him."

"You don't think he has plenty to teach?"

Rock couldn't deny she'd been in awe of some of the connections he'd made. "It wasn't all him."

"I know." Frankie rummaged in her bag and took out the large-screen phone, unlocked it with a code, and slid it to Rock. "This is what he wrote in his personal observations."

"Moses gave you this?"

"No."

Rock picked up the phone. "DCI Wearne, then? She asked you to come."

Frankie gave no answer.

Rock read the PAL app, Moses's "personal observations" file not empty as he'd said the previous week, but filled with daily notes. They were date-stamped, and Rock didn't see a way to fake those as Kortenberg had done with the alibi statements. Not every day had an entry, but those that did, he'd clearly jotted in a hurry—replete with spelling errors and sloppy grammar.

Indeed, a "personal" insight.

The first entry was after their second day together:

Division 43 sucks ass, but Julie Rock is a solid detective. She performed well under pressure.

Then, the day after, they were attacked in the car:

JR is a fighter. Quik thinking. No giving up. I did not have to spoon-feed her my play with DI Walar. I exxpect her to advance rapidly as a detective.

It wasn't all complimentary. There were minor criticisms, one suggesting she wasn't thinking "outside the box" and plenty of observations unconnected with Rock's performance. But what was there, as she read it, she found her cheeks aching by the end.

Smiling too much.

"He had some bad mentors and some good ones," Frankie said. "He's never been a mentor to anyone. I think… while you're there, taking instruction, and taking no crap from him… keeping him in line more…"

Rock looked up from the screen. "You think I'll cave because a few nice comments?"

"I think you'll cave because you know you complement each other. He'd thought you were here because someone decided to fast-track an army brat into a command position, but that wasn't what he found. He respects you, Juliette. He wants you to be his partner, but he won't plead with you. It's your choice."

Banishing any sense of a giggly schoolgirl who'd been chatted up by the popular boy, Rock gave herself distance. Flattery never worked on her. She simply wasn't like that. But she had thought Moses was coasting by. Throwing punches, losing his temper. This cast his behaviour in a new light. He'd done all that in a more calculated manner than she realised. And he'd taken responsibility for it, dropped none of it on her.

She said, "He took it seriously."

"And he wouldn't have done if you weren't a good detective."

Rock returned the phone without giving an answer. "Thank you for coming."

Frankie plainly sensed it was time to leave and made for the door. Rock walked her out, and on the doorstep they exchanged a brief hug.

"You have the discipline of the military," Frankie said as she parted. "He has the know-how of the streets and the fact he was once a part of the corruption you're trying to weed out. Think about it."

"I will," Rock said, and closed the door to think.

LATER THAT WEEK

EPILOGUE

At 7:30 a.m. on a Saturday, there was no one present in the Division 43 squad room. Other than a skeleton staff upstairs serving as security for the supercomputer on site, Rock was alone with the trio of boxes she'd requisitioned from three forces neighbouring Staffordshire.

Utrinque Paratus.

Ready for anything.

The motto of the Parachute Regiment, the elite airborne infantry within the British Army.

The Paras.

That motto had been described as a tattoo on one of the police officers under Barney Gray's thumb. Kyle Brennan. The guy who'd pulled Ratan Walar over to get him off the street. Same guy who searched Frankie Moses's car and found the marijuana. They'd questioned him, but there was nothing linking him with Gray or Walar, and certainly not Baines. They cross-referenced his affairs with the lawyer Silas Bonaparte, but again there was nothing.

Literally nothing he did was illegal, and even his taped calls since taking out Barney Gray's gang showed nothing. His language was so caked in vague phrases it was impossible to prosecute. But they'd curtailed him for now, at least in the organised crime gang field. MI5 and the NCA were alert to him, and he'd know that, so that was two agencies—not to mention the Division 43 people—who'd be on him like flies on a turd if any of his clients surfaced again. But if they could connect him with even one loose end, it would justify opening a new book on him.

Rock had pulled all this up from home, doing her research on the tail end of the inquiry before giving Wearne her final decision. Watching. Taking in their findings. Nothing that made them change course from pummelling Barney Gray through the courts along with Clara Burns, the only other surviving member of the team, and attempting to pin more of the criminal empire on Malcolm Baines, to extend his stay at Her Majesty's pleasure, already transferred from HMP Dovedale to somewhere he hadn't built a miniature empire; a facility where he was nothing more than a bent copper serving time.

However, one thing did flag itself with Rock, and it stuck in her gut as firmly as the slowly healing gash across her skin. A name from her own past. The man she blamed for the premature end to her Army career.

Lieutenant-Colonel Jefferson Thorebourne.

It wasn't only his sexist manners that had irked her, nor his ability to bend others to his will, to frighten them into toeing the line. He had cliques. Favourites. He wasn't Airborne, but he was mates with plenty of Paras. A few Paras had even called her "Foxy Rocksy" and Thorebourne had laughed along with them.

Thorebourne's laughter—after the failed complaint against him—carried more than humour, more than leering overtones; it luxuriated in the scent of victory. More than that, it was what had sapped her restraint, her discipline, and she wasn't entirely sure she regretted punching her superior officer in the face. She regretted the lapse in discipline, scolded herself for the failure. But the visual of blood running down the bastard's face? Not so much.

There were other rumours, too. Of Thorebourne and others holding secret meetings, of missing stocks of taxpayer funded equipment being hushed up. At the time, Rock had thought it was to avoid scandals hitting the newspapers, accusations of incompetence, and maybe even that all-consuming fear of major government institutions: Corruption.

With her own records trawl revealing that Kyle Brennan had served in three bases at which Lieutenant-Colonel Jefferson Thorebourne had also served, only washing out a year before Rock, she needed to go deeper. Because while Brennan had no link to any of the key players, Thorebourne had a big, flashing light.

Silas Bonaparte.

The Facilitator.

"Detective Constable Rock."

Rock looked up from the papers scattered over three desks, standing to greet Wearne with a, "Ma'am."

"Casual look."

Rock was in her cosy clothes, tracksuit bottoms, a tatty rugby shirt, trainers. "I didn't think anyone would be here."

"We have several ongoing cases. Plus, the computer sent me an alert when you scanned your ID. I was concerned I'd forgotten about some appointment."

"No, ma'am. I needed somewhere to think. Somewhere… secure."

"The dead tree approach." Wearne eyed the organised chaos of papers. "A little retro?"

"I didn't want to leave a computer trail." Rock selected a file marked *Donald Conroy*. "This is a murder in Derby three years ago. No one was caught." She picked up two more. "Shafiq Bishop and Raffiel el-Hafeez. Muslim preachers who were killed one night apart in different cities. Again, unsolved." One more file, which made Rock nervous to announce. "Marion McArthur, the one member of a child grooming gang who wasn't convicted with her associates but was widely believed to be the key secretary who kept them organised. Bullet to the head, four months after the others went down."

"I remember her," Wearne said.

"I know, ma'am. You were SIO before coming to Division 43."

Wearne stared her down. "What are you implying?"

"Nothing. Just that it's unsolved, ma'am."

"I hope you're not suggesting there was something amiss with my handling of—"

"No, ma'am. I think it's a bigger issue. It's an assassin. And I think someone in the Army is facilitating it."

"What makes you think it's ours? Shouldn't the military police handle it?"

"First, the majority of victims are civilians, which points to an OC angle."

"What's the second?"

"Second is that the MPs should have already picked up on the markers. Someone knows more than they're letting on, and they're not doing anything. I'd like to ask why."

Wearne turned side-on to Rock, as if suspicious about something. "So, you're coming back to work?"

"You said we can source our own cases, ma'am.

Be proactive. If this is mine and Moses's next investigation, I'm back on board."

Wearne considered it some more. "Sounds like your expertise will help. Moses is taking a few more days off. You do the same. When you get back, assuming nothing higher priority lands, it's yours."

Rock started gathering the papers back together, filing them correctly. "Thank you, ma'am. I'll see you Monday."

When the assassination of a politician goes wrong, and the prime suspect emerges as a former special forces operative, files from previous murders point to a cover up within the British Army.

As a former Army Captain, Detective Constable Juliette Rock is the natural choice to delve into deep corruption unit Division 43's latest case. But as elements of her past crawl into play and senior Army officers intentionally hamper the investigation, she and her supervisor, DI Moses Glynn, face dead ends and obstruction at every turn.

And the killing hasn't stopped yet.

Moses and Rock may have to step outside police regulations if they have any hope of seeing justice done.

The second novel in this British Crime series is out now.

NOTE FROM THE AUTHOR

I just wanted to say a huge thank you for buying this book. If you've made it this far, I hope I am not being too presumptuous in assuming you enjoyed it. I also hope it means you will be happy to leave me a review.

Reviews are the lifeblood of up-and-coming authors, and positive feedback wherever you bought it (or on your preferred blog/social media platform) can mean the difference between an undecided reader hitting 'buy' and moving on to the next writer. If you have time, I would be truly grateful for an endorsement, no matter how brief.

Once again, thank you for buying this book – it really does make me happy to think I've brought even a small amount of pleasure to a stranger through my words.

Note from the author

A.D. Davies
www.addavies.com

NOVELS BY A. D. DAVIES

Moses and Rock Novels:

Fractured Shadows

No New Purpose

Persecution of Lunacy

Adam Park Thrillers:

The Dead and the Missing

A Desperate Paradise

The Shadows of Empty men

Night at the George Washington Diner

Master the Flame

Under the Long White Cloud

Alicia Friend Investigations:

His First His Second

In Black In White

With Courage With Fear

A Friend in Spirit

To Hide To Seek

A Flood of Bones

To Begin The End

Standalone:

Three Years Dead

Rite to Justice

The Sublime Freedom

Shattered: Fear in the Mind

Co-Authored:

Project Return Fire – with Joe Dinicola

Lost Origins Novels (as Antony Davies):

Tomb of the First Priest

The Reaper Seal

The Eagle Plague

HIS FIRST HIS SECOND

AN ALICIA FRIEND INVESTIGATION

Meet Detective Sergeant Alicia Friend. She's nice. Too nice to be a police officer, if she's honest.

She is also one of the most respected criminal analysts in the country, now assigned to a cold northern town, investigating the kidnap-murders of two young women. Now a third has been taken.

But Richard—the father of the latest victim—launches a parallel investigation, utilising skills honed in a dark past that is about to catch up with him. As Richard's secret actions hinder the police, Alicia is forced into choices that will impact the rest of her life.

The 1st book in the Alicia Friend series is out now!

THE DEAD AND THE MISSING

AN ADAM PARK THRILLER

From the UK to Paris to Asia, and back again – a girl's life hangs in the balance.

Adam Park is an ex-private investigator, now too wealthy to need a job.

But when his old mentor's niece rips off a ruthless criminal and flees the UK, Adam tracks the young woman and her violent, manipulative boyfriend through the Parisian underground.

Here, and onward in Asia, he learns of a brutal enterprise for whom people are just a business commodity.

To return the girl safely and protect the ones he loves, Adam will need to burn down his concepts of right and wrong, at any cost to his soul.

The 1st book in the Adam Park series is out now!

Printed in Great Britain
by Amazon

70287986R00414